Forbidden & Taboo Explicit Sex Stories Collection

(4 in 1)

Filthy Erotica For Adults - Threesomes, First Time Anal, Lesbian, Sex Games, BDSM, Orgasmic Oral & 69, Hot Wives, Virgins & More

Written By:
G.G. Goode

Goode Publications

Table of Contents

Book 4

Taboo Explicit Short Sex Stories Collection:

Forced, Filthy & Rough Forbidden& Erotic BDSM Sex Stories Collection:

Adults Erotica- Submission, Femdom, CNC, Spanking, Domination, Role-Play, First Time Anal, Gangbangs& More

Written By:
G.G. Goode

Goode Publications

Marie's Master

Marie went through her day absent-mindedly. It was a Friday, the last day of the work week and she couldn't wait for the weekend. She loved her job, usually, but today was one of those days. All throughout the day, she had something completely different on her mind. But she just had a few hours left until she could do it. Marie was the legal secretary to one of the biggest lawyers in the city. Her job consisted of him demanding coffee almost every hour on the dot, proofreading legal documents, scheduling appointments, keeping his calendar up to date, and various other personal issues he needed fixed. Although her boss could be difficult, it was also fulfilling at times. There was just something about keeping his life in order and making sure everything was perfect, that made her feel like her own was just fine.

Outside of work, she was a mess. She dressed the part of a high-end person, an upper-class woman that had her fiery red hair neatly pinned up. A woman who wore form fitting dress suits that showed off her figure. A woman who could coordinate fifteen meetings over a five-day week as well as business dinners.

On the contrary, though, she was the complete opposite person of who she fronted as in the professional capacity. Marie was actually a simple girl in her personal life, and she had one deep, dark secret that she couldn't allow anyone in her workplace to know about. Every single Friday evening, at 9pm, she would go to a club that promoted sexuality and fun.

It was called Hot Red and she was introduced to it by a good friend almost exactly a year ago. Her friend, Angela, suggested this kink club to Marie because she was lonely and regular, ordinary one-night stands weren't doing it for her anymore. Marie wasn't really looking for anything serious. She was twenty-five years old and a career woman, she didn't see herself finding the time for finding a man. Just the thought of it made her feel anxious – who knew how many men would waste her time and end up breaking her heart? She preferred to rather be alone than deal with all the potential problems that came with trying to find the love of her life. She just *knew* that her dedication to her career and her independence would be an issue to most men if she tried dating. It was hopeless.

So, The Hot Red Club was the perfect thing for her. She stared at the time on her desktop until the time ticked over for the end of her workday. She immediately began packing her stuff up. It was the same every Friday. The Hot Red was seemingly the only thing she enjoyed anymore and when the day for it came, it was the only thing she could think about. She shut down her computer and got ready to leave. Marie made sure she had everything and got a fright when she looked up and saw Angela standing in front of her, next to her desk.

She was a tall woman with silky white blonde hair, cut in a bob. Angela and Marie went way back, they knew each other since they were in high school. They instantly connected and they worked together in the same office due to their close connection, although Angela was in a different department – she worked as an associate. She had just finished her law degree about a year ago and was working her way up in the field. They were inseparable. They even lived a five-minute walk away from each other. The sly smile on her face showed that she knew where Marie was going in a few hours. It made Marie blush. They were close but Marie was different to Angela, she didn't like people knowing the specifics of her sex life.

"Hey, babe. Where ya going? What are you in such a rush for?" Angela asked.

"You're being disingenuous. You know *exactly* where I'm going!" Marie said, "Now shush. I'll see you tomorrow."

"No, I don't know where you're going, what are you talking about?" Angela said with tongue in cheek.

"Shh. Stop it. You always tease me about it. I'm going to The Hot Red today. There, I said it. Are you happy?" Marie whispered. She looped her bag over her head so the strap lay diagonally across her chest.

"I just wanted you to say. I love seeing you all flustered," Angela said, "You think you're gonna be seein' that hunk again, hmm?"

Marie's boss walked past them and tipped his hat to say goodbye for the week. Angela said goodbye to him. When he was gone, Marie let out a sigh.

"The workplace is not the time for this, Angie. Mark literally just walked past, and he could have heard you," Marie said, flustered, "But yes. He's been there every Friday to see me since those first few weeks I started coming to the club. So, he will definitely be there today."

As frustrating as her best friend was, she loved her to bits at the end of the day.

"Hmm, I really wish I could meet this guy. He sounds like a real hunk," Angela said. Most of the people were out of the office by now, so they could talk freely.

"It's just sex, Angie. It's not like we're in a relationship," Marie said.

"Oh, really? You've never fucked anyone else at the club except for that one girl, that one time, other than that, you only fuck him. It sounds pretty exclusive to me, anyway. Besides, I love the whole mysterious, broody vibe he gives off. Maybe you two can become official someday."

Angela winked at Marie. Marie sighed.

"You're such a hopeless romantic, babe. I know you're just trying to make me uncomfortable because for some reason, you find that fun. Come on, I'll walk you home," Marie said.

They made their way out of the office and walked together. Angela looped her arm in Marie's as they walked. Their relationship was so close that they could be mistaken for being in a relationship. There is just something special about a best friend relationship between two girls, though, they cuddled and shared a bed without judgment. They told each other everything. But Marie especially loved her best friend because they were polar opposites. Angela was tall and blonde and bubbly, whereas Marie was shorter, a little more curvy and more introverted than her.

Marie stopped in front of Angela's apartment and they went inside. Marie sat down at the small kitchen island as Angela pulled out two glasses and a bottle of wine.

"I hope you have fun later today, babe. I'm so happy you found something that keeps you satisfied. I can't wait to hear about what you get up to today," Angela said.

"Sometimes I wonder if you just like hearing about the juicy details because it turns you on. Besides, I always have fun. How couldn't I, when in a BDSM club?" Marie giggled.

"Okay true. And so what if it does? I should really try it sometime. It's just so daunting to go alone, ya know?"

"What happened to my brave and strong best friend? Since when are you scared to do anything involving being around people?"

"Well, it's different when sex is involved. I'm a little more nervous about it," Angela said. She tucked a tuft of hair behind her ear.

"Well – if you ever want to, you know, try it, you could come with me some time?"

"What? Are you serious? I don't want to impose... and I mean, would you even be comfortable with a threesome? You're very...territorial over Alex," Angela said.

"Oh! I wasn't actually thinking of a threesome when I mentioned bringing you along, but if you want to... I wouldn't uh, be against it. As long as you're the submissive kind, you'd fit in perfectly."

"Well, babe, we've made out so many times when we were drunk that I'm not shy about being naked in front of you... I've always wanted to say this to you, but it was never the right time. But you're pretty fuckin' hot. I'd definitely do you. Problem is, though, I'm very much a dominant type."

"Oh! Uh, oh my god. Okay. Thank you, Angie. Maybe I'll speak to Alex and see what he thinks," Marie said.

Angela bit her lip. "What would you think about being dominated by two people? Alex and I could work together on our little submissive slut."

Marie shifted in her seat and felt an intense hotness in her panties. She was sure that she was wet just thinking about it.

"Angie – that actually sounds incredible. I will need to ask his permission first, though, since he's my dom and all, but I'll let you know. I would actually love that. Come to think of it, that's my ultimate fantasy."

"I'm so glad you're on board for it. If he says yes – oh man, I'll be so happy. Look, I know we're best friends and despite us kissing and all that, are you sure you'd be one hundred percent on board for it? Like, it won't affect our friendship or anything like that?"

"Not at all. I don't think it would change a thing. Honestly, I think it would bring us closer together. Was this your plan all along? You know, since introducing me to the club?"

"No, not really. I mean, I have thought about it but I was too scared to say it in case you said no. I wouldn't want to make things awkward."

Marie sipped on her wine and looked her best friend in the eye. Before Marie could react, she was pinned down on the kitchen island and Angela was sitting on her lap, holding Marie's hands above her head.

Marie was soaking wet now.

Angela was significantly bigger in overall size and stronger than Marie, so being pinned down by her meant she couldn't move an inch.

"I couldn't wait any more," Angela whispered in her ear, "You're just so fucking sexy."

Angela planted kisses up Marie's neck. Marie breathed heavily and let out a moan when Angela nibbled on her ear – her ultimate weak spot. The sensation of having her hands held so tightly and not being able to move sent Marie into a spiral.

"Think of this as a test for next time," Angela whispered.

She planted her lips on Marie's and she whimpered. Every single inch of Marie's body was ebbing with pleasure even though they hadn't even gone that far yet. Was she always attracted to her best friend all along? There was just something about kissing a woman that could never compare to kissing a man – Angela's lips were soft, and she tasted sweet. There was no stubble to scratch her face. She could smell her flowery perfume and felt like she could sniff that and only that for the rest of eternity.

Angela let go of one of Marie's hands and held both of her wrists in one. Angela slowly unbuttoned Marie's white shirt, her breasts bursting out once they were released from the pressure of the thin fabric.

"No bra, huh?" Angela said, "Such a naughty, naughty girl."

"Bras are uncomfortable," Marie said softly.

"You should go braless more often, your tits are glorious," Angela said.

Before Marie could reply, Angela dove her face into her breasts, planting kisses on her supple flesh and occasional nibbles as she came closer and closer to her nipples. Her bites were not as gentle as her kisses were, but Marie loved it anyway. Something about mixing pain and pleasure made it all the more enjoyable.

Angela's hands slowly trailed down Marie's body, she counted the inches as she came closer and closer to her wetness. Angela reached Marie's inner thighs, her long nails tickling her as she went. She lifted up Marie's knee length skirt and looked down in delight. She let go of Marie's wrists and fully lifted her skirt up to her waist. With great force, she ripped her pantyhose apart so she could touch her panties. Angela didn't hesitate to rub her clit through her panties. Marie wore a pair of plain white cotton panties, her wetness making them sheer and showing off her plump labia.

With two fingers, Angela stroked up and down the lips of Marie's tingling cunt, pressing down on her clit and making circular motions. Marie let out a soft moan each time Angela touched her hole and then her clit. Angela had a pleased smile on her face the entire time. With her other hand, she played with Marie's ample breasts, taking her nipple between two fingers and pinching softly. Angela looked Marie in the eyes and nodded, as if to ask if she could go any further. Marie nodded back enthusiastically. She couldn't wait any more.

"Would you be a good girl and tell me when you are close to cumming?" Angela said seductively.

"Mhm-mm. Yes," Marie whimpered.

"Yes what?"

"Yes, mistress," Marie said.

Angela bit her lip and smiled again.

"Good girl."

Angela slipped her fingers underneath the waistband of Marie's panties and slowly inched herself lower and lower. Again, it felt like an eternity before she touched her where she wanted it.

Expert fingers rubbed her clit then stopped each time she felt she was almost close, to her surprise, Angela shoved two fingers inside of her, slowly pumping in and out of her before increasing the pace. With her thumb, she rubbed her clit as she fingered Marie. She felt an intense pressure building up inside of her, knowing she couldn't take it anymore.

"I'm gonna cum," Marie moaned.

"Good girl," Angela whispered.

The touch stopped abruptly to Marie's disappointment. She pulled her fingers out of her and shoved them in her mouth. Like the *good girl* she was, Marie lapped up her own creamy juices off of Angela's fingers.

Angela pulled her own panties off then mounted Marie, scooting upwards to Marie's face. Angela pulled her skirt up and out of the way and gripped Marie's hair tightly, lifting up her head.

"You're only allowed to come once I am satisfied," Angela said.

"Yes, mistress," Marie said.

She admired Angela's neatly trimmed pussy. Her pink lips were inviting, and she dove into her cunt without hesitation. Angela's moans came in no time and it filled Marie with an intense determination to make her best friend cum. Marie's tongue flicked at Angela's clit, alternating between that and suckling on it lightly. She noticed that Angela especially liked it when she flicked at her clit with her tongue with great intensity, so she kept that up. She continued with that and Angela's back arched, her thighs tightening around Marie's face.

Angela rested her hands on Marie's breasts and her grip tightened more and more as she came closer and closer to climax. Marie felt Angela's thighs uncontrollably shaking so she kept up with what she was doing and didn't stop until she reached climax.

"Oh my god, I'm gonna cum," Angela said through her moans.

Marie lapped up her juices as she convulsed and tensed and had her final release.

"Angela," Marie said, catching her breath, "That was incredible."

"You're so good at this," Angela said. She was practically panting, trying to catch her breath again.

"What can I say?" Marie giggled, "I'm good at giving pleasure."

"Yes, you are," Angela said. She reached down and kissed Marie on the lips, tasting her own juices in the process.

Marie checked her watch and saw what time it was. "Ah, dammit. I have to get ready for the club. Can we continue this at a later date?" Marie said.

"Aw, now I feel bad that I couldn't finish you off," Angela sulked.

"You don't have to, I love being denied an orgasm. So, it's a win-win," Marie said with a wink.

"Okay. I'll see you for brunch tomorrow?"

"Of course, it's tradition at this point."

Marie made her way back home. She had already laid her outfit out in the morning before she went to work. Just how her dom liked it: white knee length socks, a short red plaid skirt and a thin white button up shirt. She pulled it all on and double checked how she looked in the mirror with a spin. As always, she looked amazing. She unpinned her red locks and tied them up into a high ponytail instead. Lastly, she pulled on a long black coat so that she didn't turn any heads as she walked to the club. She buttoned it up and did one last thing: a beautiful red lipstick the color of blood.

She didn't need to bring anything with her, so she set off on her walk to the club. It was a chilly, cool night. The moon hung high in the sky. The closer and closer she came to the club, the more she flowed with anticipation – not to mention intense arousal. She hadn't even had the time to process what had just happened with her best friend, but she knew that she loved every second of it. If Angela was okay, their friendship would still be the same and maybe even better.

The club was in a back alley of a nightclub and bar and neatly tucked away between those two buildings so that there would be no prying eyes. There was only one person stationed by the front door, one of the bouncers, Frank who made sure no vagrants would be able to enter without permission and cause any issues. Marie waved at him and said hi and he smiled at her. She came here every weekend, so they recognized her and always let her in without issues.

Marie entered the main door and into the pseudo reception area. It looked like any normal business from this side, with a receptionist stationed at the front desk. It was bright and sleek with thick wood furniture and tables. Marie said hello to the receptionist.

"The usual room, hun?" she said. She was an older woman but looked amazing for her age. She too wore a bright red lipstick.

"Yes, please. The same as last week and all the weeks before that," Marie said.

"Great, your complimentary drink and food will be stationed there in a few minutes. There's an extra little treat since you've been doing business with us for so long," the receptionist said.

"Oh, that's great! Thank you so much," Marie said. She paid the fee for the night.

"May I take your coat?" the receptionist said.

Marie handed it over to her and the receptionist put it in on a hanger in a small closet type room behind her. Many women, just like Marie, made their way over here in sexy clothes, covered up by a thick trench coat, so they installed this feature a few months before. Marie could finally breathe, it seemed. She'd been anticipating this all week and she couldn't wait to see Alex.

She walked into a hallway to the right of the receptionist. Although she was wearing such a skimpy outfit, she felt the most comfortable in this outfit and in this place. The Hot Red Club was her favorite place to be. The place in which she felt most like herself.

There were various closed doors on the left and right of the big hall before her. In the center of the room, were various couches and other types of sex furniture. There were other scantily clad women, both Marie's age and older than her. Some of them were kissing one another and others were fawning over men in their area, sitting on their laps or nibbling at their necks.

She sat down and waited for her room to be prepared before she headed inside. A few minutes later, a man came up to the door of her room pushing a big trolley. The contents of the trolley were hidden with a big white cloth draped over it. He entered the room and came out a few minutes later.

Marie took a right and entered the room marked number six. She closed the door behind her, and it was instantly silent. The good part about the Red hot club was that the private rooms one could hire were soundproof so they could make as much noise as they wanted without anyone hearing.

The room was big, decorated specifically to Marie and Alex's needs. On a small table next to the bed, various bondage implements were laid out neatly. Paddles, whips, ball gags and the like. There were two other levels to the table, and they were full of sex toys. Marie inspected a different small table on the other side of the room. Two bottles of expensive looking champagne sat in an ice bucket. Two plates covered by silver cloches were on the table too. She decided to wait for Alex to arrive before she took a peek.

Marie got comfortable and waited in participation for her master.

The door opened after what felt like an eternity of waiting and she quickly sat up straight and smiled when she saw Alex. He wore a dark suit. His raven black hair was slicked back. His facial structure was as if it were carved out of stone. He was a true god among men. He seemed slightly off today. She could feel it in the air but knew it wouldn't be appropriate to ask just yet.

"Alex, hi," Marie said. She felt a nervous lump in her throat. Although they had been seeing each other for nearly a year by now she couldn't help but feel nervous in those first few minutes together.

"Marie," he said. He sat down in front of her and loosened his tie. "I'm late. Sorry about that. Had some personal stuff to take care of. What's this?"

He looked down at the booze and food in front of them.

"It's been a year since I've been coming here so they left us a little treat," Marie said.

Alex lifted the cloche and so did Marie to reveal crepes, strawberries and a chocolate sauce beautifully presented.

"Well, isn't that sweet?" he said.

"It really is. Do you want some champagne?"

"Yes, I would like that very much, slut," he said.

Marie bit her lip and tried to hide a smile. She loved being Alex's little slut. She stood up and picked up the icy cold bottle of champagne. Applying pressure to the cork, she pushed it until it popped off.

Marie bent over the table, knowing that her master would be able to see her bare ass. Her skirt was so short that it would reveal all.

She poured some champagne into the glass. Alex grabbed her ass then lightly smacked it.

"Thanks, slut. I like the outfit today. It suits you very well," Alex said.

His voice was low and gruff, it never ceased to turn her on.

"I put it on just for you. And well, because it makes me feel sexy," Marie said.

She placed the glass in front of him then hers on her side of the table. She gave Alex a smirk.

"Would you like me to do a little spin in it?"

Alex nodded.

Marie spun around in place, the momentum lifting her skirt and revealing her bare, smooth crotch.

"No panties today?" he glared at her.

"No, I was just too wet, so they started becoming very uncomfortable," she said, looking down at the floor.

He gulped all of the champagne down in one go.

"What made you so wet, Marie?" he said.

He looked her straight in the eye causing her to look away.

"Look at me," he shouted. He stood up and had his hand around her jaw, forcing her to look at him.

"Promise you won't be mad? I know you said that I have to ask permission first before I do anything with anyone, but things happened so fast and – and..."

"What the fuck did you do, slut?" he reprimanded.

He pushed her towards the bed in the center of the room, causing her to drop backwards onto it. The weight of his body suffocated her, but she loved every second of it.

"I – I fucked Angela. Well, she fucked me. I never got the chance to orgasm because I had to get ready to come see you," she whispered.

"So, you fucked someone else without asking me first?"

"Yes. I did, but I can explain – I" She was cut off.

"I don't care what your excuses are. You know the rules, Marie. Now it's time for you to get punished. Besides, I'm done with talking. We have fun first, then we talk. Those are the *rules*, stupid," he lightly slapped her face, "How many of our rules have you broken in the last twenty-four hours?"

"I'm sorry, Alex," Marie said softly.

"That's not what you call me, whore. What do you call me?"

"Master. I'm sorry, master," she whispered.

"Good. But you understand that I still have to punish you, right?"

"Yes, Master. Please punish me for being bad."

"Good girl."

Alex got off of her and flipped her around onto her stomach. He put her hands on each side of her hips, pulling her upwards so that her head was flat on the bed and her ass was up in the air. Usually, Marie would come up with silly things just so that she could receive punishment from him, she was a masochist, after all, but this time she didn't even need to make anything up to get what she wanted tonight. With her face smothered in the sheets, she smiled to herself.

"Stay," he demanded.

"Yes sir," she mumbled through the blanket.

A few moments later, he came back with a spreader bar and started restraining her with it. The cold steel nearly burned her skin as he clipped them around each of her ankles. He pulled her arms beneath her, through her legs and clipped them in. She moved her head to the side so that she could breathe. As per usual, she tugged at the restraints to ensure she couldn't get free. They were as tight as they could be, and it made her especially wet. She loved the feeling of being so helpless and weak.

Alex returned once more with a rubber paddle in his hand. He moved her skirt out of the way, pushing it down her body. He looked at the sight before him before caressing and lightly smacking and grabbing her ass. Although he was her dom, he still made sure that they played safe which was something she loved most about him.

He laced his fingers through her auburn hair, shoving her face back down into the mattress so that she couldn't expect his strikes.

The first one came, causing her to wince in pain. Then the next and the next and the next. Twenty lashes later, Alex stopped. Her ass cheeks were almost as red as her hair and they stung like hell fire. Alex kissed some of the more bruised spots on her ass before getting up and disappearing again. Marie felt herself near-dripping wet despite the pain.

Suddenly, Alex put a high powered Hitachi wand against her clit, in exactly the right spot.

"Will you come for me, whore? You want to come so bad, don't you?" Alex purred.

Upon hearing his words, she almost felt herself come instantly. He held it there until her thighs were shaking uncontrollably and she couldn't hold it in anymore. Her moans echoed throughout the room.

"Oh god. I'm gonna cum," she moaned.

"Good, don't stop yourself. Let it happen," Alex grunted.

She climaxed upon his final word, but he didn't pull the Hitachi wand away. He kept it in place. If she was getting punished, why was she allowed to even cum?

She gasped as she came again seconds later. Her wetness dripped down the wand and onto the bed.

"Keep it coming, little one," he said.

With his other hand lubed up, he massaged her asshole. At the first touch, she came yet again. When he finally felt she was ready for him to enter and he slipped a finger in, she came once more.

"Oh god, I can't take it anymore," she moaned.

She could hardly think any more. She was reduced to a true come drunk slut.

"Oh, yes you can. You are a strong whore, aren't you?"

"Yes, daddy," she whispered.

Marie lost count of the number of times she orgasmed to that little wand when Alex finally pulled it away. Marie was panting by this point and her legs couldn't stop shaking. The bruises on her ass were the furthest from her worries by now. She realized what Alex had just did: orgasm torture as a form of punishment. He'd never done that before, so it had come as a surprise. As torturous as it was, she enjoyed it and hoped they could do it again soon.

With one swift motion, Alex flipped her around onto her back. She stared deep into his eyes, practically begging him to fuck her. Slowly and meticulously, so as to punish her even more, he took his time undoing the cuffs around her wrists and ankles.

"You've made quite the mess, little one," Alex said.

"Oopsie," Marie giggled.

Alex threw the spreader bar to the side, it dropped to the floor with a loud thud. Marie wriggled with anticipation as Alex climbed on top of her. He unzipped his suit pants and pulled out his thick, long cock. Marie's breath quickened once again. She had already orgasmed so many times that she would have thought she'd be done with sex, but she realized she wanted his cock now more than ever.

She nodded at him enthusiastically to let him know that it was okay. At first, he teased her, sliding the head of his dick up and down her slick lips, tapping it against her clit. She just couldn't take it much longer, though.

"Please, please fuck me. I want you inside of me," Marie said.

"Beg harder, slut. You'll only get my cock when you beg hard enough," Alex grunted.

Marie propped herself up with her elbows and frowned at him.

"But – but I want it right now, daddy. I'm running out of patience," Marie whined.

Alex responded by continuing to rub his cock up and down her wet pussy, adding slight pressure when near her entrance, but not enough to be inside of her.

"Please," Marie moaned, "Please, there's nothing like having your cock inside of me. I just want you inside of me so badly. It's all I think about day in and day out."

He shook his head. She could see that he was trying to stifle a smile. He was enjoying the hell out of this. She'd try harder.

"I'm sorry I fucked Angela, daddy. I won't do it again without your permission. I'd never want another man's cock inside of me, though. Please remember that."

She slid her hand down her body, stopping to spread her lips for him.

"Please, please fuck me."

In an instant, with the help of her being well lubed up from cumming so many times, he shoved his cock inside of her, filling her tight hole up instantly. Marie let out a moan and spread her legs wider for the hunk inside of her. At first, he slowly pumped in and out of her, knowing that it took her a bit of time to adjust to his size. Once he found himself at a steady rhythm, he leaned forward. She wrapped her arms around his neck, one hand lacing her fingers through his hair.

While he fucked her, they kept an intense, constant gaze, never breaking eye contact. It was a kind of intimacy that Marie had never experienced with any other man in her life. As enjoyable as all the bondage was, this was one of the things that kept her coming back for more and more. He increased the pace, then moved in for a kiss. They kissed, forgetting about just about everything else in the world, until he lifted his head, and grunted. He thrust hard, hitting her cervix in the process, he came inside of her.

Again, they kissed. He slowly thrust in and out of her a few more times while their lips touched, before pulling out of her, shoving his cock back in his boxers and laying down on the bed next to her. He got comfortable, then gestured for her to come over to him. She did as he wanted, then rested her head on his chest. He kissed the top of her head, then wrapped his arms around her, squeezing her tight against him.

"How are you feeling, baby?" Alex said sincerely. His voice was softer and calmer now, as it always was after one of their sessions, as if he had become a whole different person.

"I'm okay. Feeling a little worn out, thanks to you, but I feel good," Marie said.

She listened to his heartbeat, one of the most comforting things she loved doing.

"Good. How's the ass doing? I kind of got a little carried away. You're quite bruised and might not be able to sit comfortably for a long time," he chuckled nervously.

"Honestly, I don't know if it's like a slow burn until the pain starts happening or if I'm just so satisfied and full of endorphins that I can't feel it. Besides, you know I love bruises. I love looking at them days later, knowing that you gave them to me. It turns me on so much," Marie admitted.

"Oh, I understand, yeah. It's like the mark of being owned by me."

"Exactly."

They cuddled for a while, then ate the rest of their snacks and drank the rest of the champagne. Marie admired him as he spoke about some stupid philosophical thing. She hated to admit it, but she loved Alex, so she'd let him go on rants about things, even if she didn't know much about the subject. That was something she knew proved that she loved him. She listened to him drone on about things without interrupting or losing focus.

"Anyway, enough about that. I wanted to ask, how was it with Angela? Did you enjoy it?" he asked.

"Oh! Right, yes. Actually, it was amazing. She's also very dominant, she's very similar to you. With her being a taller, bigger woman than me and all, it made it even more erotic. I loved it so much," Marie admitted.

"Hmm, getting hard just thinking about you with another woman."

"Well, she actually asked me if she could join us some time. Like, as a threesome kind of thing, but with two doms and me, the one submissive."

"Holy. Shit. That sounds incredible. Of course I'd be down, baby. You know I just get super into the moment and I'm just cruel because it's a sexual thing. I hope you remember that," Alex said. He looked at her seriously.

"Of course I understand that, love. Of course. It's just sex. I don't take those things personally, because well, frankly, it turns me on immensely."

"Okay, good. You must let me know any time I take it too far, okay?"

"Of course. There's a safe word for a reason."

"When would you like to do the double domination thing?" Alex said after a moment of thinking.

"Uh, next weekend? But if that doesn't work with you, then we can do it any other time, too. I'm happy with anything, really. You just let me know."

"Well, I was actually thinking next weekend... I'd like – I'd like to have a date," Alex said.

"A – Date?" Marie asked.

Her mouth hung open. She wasn't expecting this whatsoever.

"Yes, a date. You mentioning that we have been seeing each other for almost a year made me realize that I should have asked you this a long, long time ago," Alex said.

"Yes! Date next weekend. Double domination the weekend after," Marie shouted.

She jumped onto his lap and straddled him.

"Mm, you're excited," Alex said.

Marie bit her lip and figured out what she wanted to say.

"I wasn't sure if it would be appropriate for me to ask, since, you know, our relationship is only for Fridays and we're based on purely just sex and I was scared I'd ruin things by asking," she admitted.

"I love you though, silly," he said.

The Stranger

Yasmin was away on a business trip, in a different city, far from home, far from her husband. She took in a deep breath before stepping inside of the high-end cocktail lounge, within one of the best hotels in the city. She had a plan for the evening, and she was rather nervous about it. She decided she would have a few drinks first before she went through with it. Perhaps some liquid courage would help guide her through this potentially eventful night.

She decided on an outfit that suited the venue she was in, a couture cocktail dress, one of the best she owned. She had to bring it all the way there in a black garment bag to make sure it didn't somehow get damaged in her luggage. It was an important night, after all, so she wanted to look the part.

Although the dress was long, it was still sexy. It had a slit that made its way up her thigh, stopping just before it showed off her delicate bits. The waist had a built-in corset to show off her curves and the neckline was low, showing off her cleavage. She felt like a femme fatale in this dress, hunting her prey. At least, now, she'd use this dress to its full potential rather than it just sitting in a closet somewhere collecting dust. It cost her over five hundred dollars, after all.

Although she wasn't poor whatsoever, she still didn't like wasting money. Yasmin was one of the top lawyers in her district, defending some of the most high-risk clients in the state. Needless to say, she made a lot of money. More than what she could do with. She had everything she wanted in life and more, but she was getting older. In her late thirties now, she realized that, well, she was bored.

That was one of the problems that came along with being rich. She had everything she needed and wanted at all times. She never struggled to pull the money together to pay the bills. Or had to save up a few months to buy a good pair of shoes that would last. She never had to worry about a single thing. How could any excitement come from that? There was no struggle. There were no problems.

She felt the same with her husband, Jason. He was so good to her, too good for her, even. They were college sweethearts. They were a healthy couple. Their communication was tip top. They had a few big fights over the years, but that was normal in a good, healthy relationship. Yasmin's mother often told her once she started growing up, that couples that brag about never fighting weren't truly happy. Without fights and conflict, things couldn't be truly healthy between a couple.

After their fights, they'd talk everything through and fix their bad behaviors and such. Jason was a kind, caring man that would do anything for her. Their sex life was – she could say great, but at the same time, she felt the same about their sex life as she did about money. Jason was not a selfish lover in any way. It was just… he was too gentle and caring. Things were too good, and she was bored. Just so bored. So, she decided this weekend, she would be treating herself to someone else.

Yasmin walked up to the bar, her hips swaying and blonde curls bouncing. As she stopped in front of the young bartender, she noticed his eyes linger down to her breasts. She smirked at him and he panicked once he realized she noticed him staring.

"Sorry, just a little distracted. What can I get you, miss?" he stammered.

"Uhm, what would you suggest?" Yasmin said. She was too nervous to decide on what to have, besides, she didn't know if this place even served her favorite drink. She wasn't in the mood to look at menus at the moment, either.

She bent over the bar counter, knowing he would stare.

He made quick glances at her breasts and it made her chuckle. The attention was welcomed.

"Well, miss, what kind of experience are you looking for in your drink? Rough and hard or the opposite?"

"Hmm," – she put her finger on her chin and thought about her answer – "I'll take rough and hard."

He saw the wedding ring on her finger, his demeanor changing immediately.

"Long island iced tea will do then," he said. She could feel him judging her.

Yasmin mentally cursed herself for forgetting to take the ring off. It reminded her of her husband, and it made her feel bad for even flirting with the bartender in the first place. She let out a sigh and waited for her cocktail to be made.

"Should I open a tab for you, ma'am?"

He didn't look at her this time, his eyes slightly diverted to the side.

"Yes please. Room thirty-three. Thanks," she said.

She awkwardly walked off to a booth and sat down on the cushioned seat. She drank three Long Island Iced Teas before she finally mustered up the courage. Upon fetching the forth, she sat back down and stared at her left hand. The moment she pulled off the ring, the ball would start rolling. It was about seven in the evening, so the cocktail bar would become busier and busier. Yasmin's hands were shaking violently as she slipped the diamond ring off of her finger. She slipped the ring into a small pocket inside of her small purse, zipping it up afterwards. She closed her bag and kept it close to her.

Her hand felt so bare, so naked without the ring on it. She stared at the pale line on her finger. Her nails were perfectly manicured. Yasmin looked after herself very well, honestly, because the closer she came to turning forty, the more terrified she was of *looking old*. It was a stupid insecurity of hers that she knew she needed to work on, but at least it meant that she looked her best in every single moment. She did her hair and make-up every day. She used all the best creams and serums to keep her skin looking good.

That was something she realized as soon as she started making good money, the only reason celebrities looked so good was first of all: they had no stress to take a toll on their bodies and second of all: with enough money, they could look however they wanted. When Yasmin was younger, she thought those near thousand-dollar face creams were a gimmick, but now, she realized they truly were worth the money.

Her thoughts were interrupted when she saw a man in a suit, sitting at the same bar she was at earlier. Shortly afterwards, a near scantily clad waitress came up to her table with a tray in her hand and a drink on top of that.

"Hey, uh, that gentlemen over there said I should give this to you," the young woman said. Her hair was dark, and Yasmin could tell she had definitely been drinking on shift.

"Oh my, that one over there?" Yasmin asked, then pointed.

"Yes, exactly. The one with the dark brown hair," she said, "Do you want it?"

"Oh, yeah. Of course I would," Yasmin said.

She picked the small whiskey tumbler up and inspected it. It was her favorite: whiskey, bitters, sugar, orange juice, with ice and mashed cherries on the bottom and an orange peel wedged into the edge of the glass. There was even an extra maraschino cherry atop the ice, stem attached. Once the waitress went back to the bar, she said a few words to the man. The waitress smiled and nodded her head at him before she receded into the back of the cocktail lounge, out of sight.

The man then spun around in his seat, the same cocktail as hers in his hand. He leaned his back against the bar, before raising his glass in her direction. Yasmin returned the gesture. It made her feel all warm and squishy inside. No man had ever done that for her before, Yasmin thought that random men flirting in the form of buying drinks was only reserved for the movies. Regardless, it sure made her feel special. He was around about her age, maybe a few years younger.

His hair was brown and neatly combed into a slick side part. He wore a gray suit perfectly tailored to his well-cared for body. His face was shaven, barring the five o'clock shadow peeking through. His features were strong and well chiseled. His smile was charming.

Needless to say, he was an attractive man and she wanted him. Thoughts of Yasmin's husband were in the far reaches of her mind. This handsome stranger was all she wanted, and she wanted him now. The heat between her legs was steadily growing, almost too much for her to handle any longer.

She called him over with a come-hither motion. He stood up, slicked a stray hair back into place and walked over to her with one hand in his pocket. She bit her lip when he came close enough for her to smell his cologne. It was musky and reeked of masculinity.

"Well, hello there, beautiful," was the first thing he said.

Yasmin hesitated, unsure of how to reply. Her cheeks glowed red and hot. She wasn't used to this and she didn't know what to do. She hadn't quite prepared for this.

"Hmm, not much of a talker, are ya?" he asked.

He sat down next to her, both their backs to the wall of the rest of the cocktail bar. They were semi-secluded where they were seated, with dividers between them and the other booth seats.

"Thank you for the drink," she said softly, "What made you choose an old fashioned?" Her voice was shaky and unsure.

"Of course, I could tell that a woman like you would enjoy a classy drink like that," he took a sip of his own drink while making eye contact with her, "I hope you like it."

"Oh, of course. It's absolutely delicious. Thank you."

"Besides, I couldn't stand to let you sit here all by yourself any longer. What's an alluring woman like you sitting alone in a place like this?"

"I could ask you the same thing," she teased, "I'm here for a week on business. They flew me over on Friday so I could be settled before I get thrown into a barrage of meetings and such."

"Hmm, so a career woman, then? That's sexy. What do you do?" he asked. He spoke in a low and gruff full-throated manner. He was sure and serious about every single word that came out of his mouth. His blue eyes were cold and filled with primal desire for the woman before him. This stranger was turning out to be exactly her type, strong, manly and most of all, mysterious.

"I'm a lawyer, allegedly," Yasmin joked.

The man laughed, "And a sense of humor? Damn."

"What do you do?"

"Oh, not as cool as a lawyer, I'm an accountant. But, I'm good at more than just numbers," he said, looking deep into her eyes.

He put his hand on her thigh, the one exposed by the slit in her dress. His hands were warm and rough. Yasmin bit her lip, she wasn't quite sure how to react to his advances, though, so she took another sip of her drink. Next, she fished out the stemmed maraschino cherry, putting it between her lips and sucking on it while making eye contact with the stranger. She batted her long, curled eyelashes at him. His hand slowly crept up her thigh. He stopped just before he reached her crotch. Hopefully inconspicuously, she slightly spread her legs.

"Are you staying at this hotel, too? Or are you just at this lounge for the hell of it?" he spoke, as he came closer and closer to her sopping wet cunt. His gaze never faltered from hers.

"Yeah, I'm in room thirty-three, actually," she said. Her breath quickened, his fingers softly traced over her outer labia, teasing her desperate bits.

"Oh, is that so? I'm on the same floor, close to your room. Maybe I could pay you a visit some time."

"Oh, yes," she moaned softly as he found her wet hole, slipping inside of her without hesitation, "Yes, I would like that very much."

Slowly, he slid his finger in and out of her, so as to not arouse suspicion to what they were doing. Fortunately, the bar was quite busy, so no one would pay them any attention. The sheer thought of doing something so scandalous in front of so many people excited her. He brought his face close to her ear and whispered.

"I'll warn you, though, I like to be rough. If you slipped me your room key, I'd come into your room and take you no matter what you are busy with, be it on a business call or you in the bath. I like to take what I want when I want it. And I want you."

He nibbled on her earlobe before pulling away. Yasmin's breath was taken away: all the words she would have liked to say in this moment, all the words she fantasized about saying were caught in the back of her throat.

"I don't know what to say," she said softly.

"Don't say anything, slut. Just enjoy it while you can," he said.

His harsh words sent hot flushes all throughout her body. As she bit her lip again, he slipped a second finger inside of her, stretching her out. She fantasized about his big cock inside of her, filling her up to the brim.

She downed her drink, he did too.

"Should we head up to my room?" she asked.

"Of course we should," he whispered, "I want to fuck you so hard. I love that you're not even wearing panties. You were hunting for your prey tonight weren't you, you filthy whore?"

"Yes, I was expecting to get laid. I mean, look at this dress. Look at me. Can't you see I'm practically begging for someone to bend me over and have their way with me?"

"Well, I'm one lucky man," he said.

Yasmin grabbed his hand and led him to the elevator. There was a moment of silence before the elevator door closed. In seconds, the stranger pinned her against the mirrored wall of the elevator, kissing all up her neck and breasts. He pushed his crotch up against hers, turning her on even more. She hadn't even touched him, yet he was hard for her. It made her feel sexy and desirable. She couldn't wait to see what was hidden in those expensive suit pants.

The elevator doors slid open with a loud *ding* and they separated from one another when they saw a family standing in front of them. Embarrassed, she grabbed his hand and pushed past them, leading him to her hotel room.

She inserted the card to her room, then let him in. He walked a few steps before turning to face her. Yasmin had her back to the hotel door. She looked at him seductively. She sauntered over to him. Her arms wrapped around her waist, before he placed his hands on her ass and squeezed. He lifted her up and she wrapped her legs around him as he picked her up and carried her over to the bed. She kissed the nape of his neck, occasionally sucking hard on his skin, leaving small bruises in his flesh. She softly chuckled. That'll be an embarrassing thing for him to deal with in the morning.

He turned around and dropped her onto the bed. She landed with a few bounces. He stood up and inspected the marvel before him.

He loosened his tie then pulled it off of his neck.

"Get higher on the bed. I'm going to tie you up," he said sternly.

She did as she was told and scooted upwards. The stranger looped the tie around the bed frame, before wrapping it around her wrists, crossing in between each one to be sure it was secure. He tugged at the makeshift cuffs.

"Nice and snug," he said.

"What are you going to do to me?" she said, concerned.

"Have my every which way with you, my dear," he whispered.

Yasmin bit her lip again, causing it to sting. She had bitten her lip so many times that night that it was going raw.

Slowly and carefully, he unbuckled then slipped off each of her high heels. He caressed her smooth legs, moving up between her thighs. From inside of his suit, he pulled out a small pocket knife. Yasmin blinked rapidly at the blade as he withdrew the blade, the shiny metal glistening in the bright white hotel lights.

"W-what are you going to do with that?" she inquired.

"Whatever I want to," he said. He shook his head. "Do you have any scarves? I'm tired of hearing your complaints."

"I – I'm sorry, I'll stop. I'm just nervous."

"Shut the fuck up. Where are the scarves? Preferably longer ones," he spat.

"There," she looked in the direction of where she would have pointed, if her hands weren't tied. Her heart was beating heavier in her chest by now, not out of arousal, but fear.

He rummaged through the nearby drawer before finding a red scarf. He mumbled a 'This'll do.' before coming back to her. He forced her mouth open by applying pressure on each side of her jaw, before placing the material in her open mouth, then tying it around the back of her head. Yasmin bit down on the soft silk scarf. He got on top of her again and stared at the bound-up goddess before him.

The blade tickled up her thigh, stopping at the seam of the slit of her dress. She lifted her head to see what he was doing. She shook her head violently, making a few muffled sounds but nothing worthwhile came through the saliva-soaked gag.

The stranger held the fabric taut, blade side up. Yasmin tensed up as the first bit of fabric started ripping. She tried pleading with the stranger to stop but the gag prevented her from saying any words. She felt helpless, hopeless, and weak.

The blade slowly ran diagonally up her chest. Her dress had been split in two. He held the knife in his hand and pulled the fabric to the side to reveal her bra. He smiled at her and made direct eye contact with her while he cut the bra off of her. She felt a relief at the loss of pressure on her breasts.

"Hmm, your tits are incredible," he moaned.

His rough hands touched her breasts, grabbing them hard. Despite the pain, Yasmin enjoyed the way he treated her. Despite the fear and anxiety, deep down, she enjoyed this. She had never had sex with anyone else but her husband. When they started dating in college, she had lost her virginity to him. Still, he was so soft and gentle with her.

The stranger, on the other hand, didn't care. He was going to take what he wanted, and he didn't care if she had anything to say about it. She could feel the wetness between her thighs, each time she moved them or rubbed them together they were slick and smooth.

The stranger didn't kiss her breasts like her husband usually would, instead, he left red bite marks behind that would likely form bruises. Yasmin decided to play along with this fantasy and tugged at the tight restraints, writhing in place as he steadily made his way between her legs.

Slowly but surely, he unbuckled his belt and took his pants off. This man was in no rush. He knew that she couldn't fight it so why would he hurry?

Yasmin looked on in awe of the sheer size of his cock. She could practically see the veins in his cock throbbing. He was enjoying this, a lot.

"Spread your legs," he demanded.

Yasmin refused. In response, she clamped her legs shut.

"I said spread your goddamned legs!" he shouted.

Yasmin whimpered, finally complying. Slowly she spread her legs apart. He lifted her knees. He stared at her sopping wet cunt, slowly stroking his big cock.

With his other hand, he rubbed her clit. She wriggled underneath the pressure of his fingers, but it just added to the pleasure. Somehow knowing that she was close to orgasm, he suddenly stopped to shove his cock inside of her. He pushed her legs back over her head and fucked her harder than she's ever been fucked before.

His cock slid in and out of her slick cunt with ease. His cock hit her G-spot with the angle he was fucking her. Her moans were muffled by the gag in her mouth. By now the scarf was soaked with her spit. She bit down on it hard as he rubbed her clit with his thumb.

Yasmin buckled under him, her back arching and her legs shaking as she reached orgasm. He grunted when her muscles tensed and relaxed around his cock. He pulled out of her, then shoved two fingers inside of her, furiously thrusting his fingers up against her G-spot. Yasmin's eyes rolled to the back of her head as all the tension within her released, to her surprise, she squirted. The clear, warm liquid sprayed onto the bed.

Gently, he pulled his fingers out of her. With one hand he yanked the gag from her mouth. His hand firmly took her by the chin, his thumb tracing the outline of her plump lips. He pulled down and shoved her mouth open, then his fingers that were inside of her plunged into her mouth. She lapped up her wetness off of him. She was hungry for it, lapping it up as if it were sweet honey.

"Good slut," the stranger said.

She moaned around his fingers.

"Absolutely exquisite," he groaned, "But I'm not done with you yet."

His strong hands gripped her thighs firmly, rotating her around so that she was on her knees and her ass was facing him. The tie around her wrists tightened as she flipped around, causing even more strain. Her arms were lifted above her head, her face forced into the mattress. With her knees together and her ass high up in the air, it formed a perfect heart shape. The stranger admired her figure.

As if thinking she were too perfect and wanting to taint her all too perfect physique, he picked up his belt and struck her suddenly. She inhaled sharply. It wasn't what she expected to happen, which made it hurt even more. Immediately, red began forming on the pale flesh of her plump ass. Again, he struck harder this time, testing the limits. She moaned, not out of pain, but pleasure. She'd never been handled this way – never been so man handled and treated so badly. It was thrilling and exciting for her to be treated like such a slut. She bit her lip, preparing for the next impact. This time, when she bit her lip, she drew blood. Her mouth tasted of copper. As she was distracted by that thought, he struck again, giving her two lashings on the opposite cheek. These stung harder than before and she inhaled sharply through her clenched teeth.

He ran a finger from her clit all the way up her slit.

"You're still so wet," he chuckled, "You're really enjoying this, aren't you?"

"Yes, sir," she whispered, "You felt so good inside of me. You're so big and I love how full you made me feel."

He grunted in response. He seemed to have really liked the way she responded to that.

"Good girl," he said.

She felt some movement on the bed.

She gasped as suddenly the tip of his cock breached her lips. He shoved his cock inside of her wet cunt and fucked her ferociously. He was done playing around with his toy – he was ready to have his own release. He fucked her in a primal, deviant manner. He gripped her hips tightly, guiding himself in and out of her.

He fucked her so well that she was succumbed to a groaning mess.

She could tell that he was nearing his own climax by the loud groans escaping the back of his throat.

"Oh, yes, fuck me harder," she moaned, "Come inside of me."

He increased the pace for the last few moments before his cock twitched inside of her and he came.

His breaths were just as heavy as hers. He collapsed next to her on the bed.

Yasmin went to the bathroom to clean herself up. She grabbed a comfortable shirt from her suitcase, then lay next to him. He put his arm out, gesturing for her to lay in his arms. She rested her head on his shoulder and looked up at his deep blue eyes. His face was plastered with a big smile.

"That was amazing, honey," she said.

"No, you were amazing," he said softly.

"I liked the extra touch of cutting my dress off. You'll have to buy me a new one, though. It was my fanciest dress," she giggled.

"Pfft. I already planned for that. I had it all planned out, Yasmin. Did you have a good time, though? I hope I didn't go too far."

"I loved every second of it, Jason. I was kind of hesitant to try this when you mentioned it first, but it ended up being everything I wanted and more. I like you being rough. I would love to do this again sometime," Yasmin said.

"Well, you mentioned that you wanted to try something different. I loved being someone else, you know? It was as if it were easier for me to be rough since it wasn't really *me,* if that makes sense. I always worry about hurting you or being too rough, but it just came so easily today," Jason, her husband said.

"Thank you for going out of your comfort zone just for me, honey," Yasmin said.

They had planned this for months and decided that her being away on a business trip was the perfect time for it. As she had told him, their little affair fantasy role play was everything she wanted and more. They had grown closer because of it.

Mason's Plaything

Mason was a twenty-seven-year-old man. Within the modern age of dating, he found himself struggling to find someone to settle down with. He was a six-foot three man, who looked after his body, had a lot of friends, a booming career and he even made time for hobbies. This and more, brought him a lot of dates.

The only problem was that only about two out of fifty women he's tried to be with ever went through with a second date. Those two, never went through with a third date. He was lonely and lacked true human connection. As things were in the modern times, sex would definitely happen on the first date. That was a given. After having sex with him, the women never came back. Those two women who had a second date with him, had decided to save themselves for the second date. They also never came back. They would enjoy his company at dinner, his jokes, his life stories. All would be well at first.

He wasn't unattractive. He was strong, he was charming, he had a sense of humor. He had green eyes and pitch-black hair. As some people would tell him, he had the whole *dark and mysterious* vibe about him. Women liked that. That's why he could land himself so many dates.

It hurt him to the core that he couldn't keep a romantic relationship with a woman going. He was getting older now, with each year that went by leaving him with a sense of doom at the thought of having to spend the rest of his life alone. The longer he waited, he felt, the less chance he had at finding the perfect woman to marry.

Although he was *nontraditional* in the bedroom, he still wanted to marry a wonderful woman he loved and spend the rest of his life with her. He scrolled through Tinder, swiping left and right, hoping to find someone who would maybe, just maybe stick around. A woman he'd been chatting to for a while, Sabrina, sent a message through. They'd been talking to one another for weeks over text but hadn't met yet. He didn't even know what her voice sounded like.

Most of his previous dates would instantly want to meet up on the next available date he had free, so this could have been a sign that she could be the one. Perhaps, they could have a third, fourth, fifth date.

Sabrina was taking things slowly.

That could have possibly been a good thing. He was growing to like her, or at least the words she put on the screen. She seemed like an interesting person, having just completed her law degree and starting her life as a lawyer. She was witty and intelligent. Strong.

Interesting.

That was too, what the other women he had tried dating had lacked. Sure, they were attractive, dare he say, out of his league, but they only cared about getting in his pants so they could subsequently get their grubby little paws on his money. He could see it from the look in their eyes the moment they set foot in his penthouse apartment – they wanted to run him dry if they could.

But then things would go wrong after they fucked, and he'd never see them again.

He texted her. They had a conversation about how work was going and how life was treating her. Since she had an actual career, she was quite busy, so she would sometimes go weeks without speaking to him. In a way, that could have been what made him so fond of her and him wanting so desperately for it to work out. The longer he waited, the more he thought about her and the more he fantasized about how good things could be.

After a few fun conversations about stupid clients and silly mishaps, she finally brought it up. She asked him if he wanted to meet up with her. He replied instantly, almost so fast that it could have seemed desperate. He couldn't wait.

"Alright, babe. This weekend, then. I will book everything and plan it all. We'll make a day of it on Saturday. How does that sound?" he asked.

"Sure, that sounds great! I would love to. I suppose having a whole day to spend together is great for a first meeting. We can *truly* get to know each other! What should I wear?" she said.

"Wear anything that makes you feel good! I'm not fussy. Comfortable. Sexy. Cute. Whatever your heart desires, sweetheart."

"Hmm. I'll think about it."

She was the same age as him and seemed quite mature too. Something in the back of his mind bugged him, though. Why was she also single, at the age of twenty-seven? Perhaps he was just being too pessimistic. Someone being single didn't necessarily need to mean that there was something wrong with them.

Just because he was single because there was something wrong with him – he stopped himself from thinking about it further. He would be good on the weekend. He would behave. He wouldn't scare her off. Mason promised that to himself. How hard could it really be just to control himself? He waited in anticipation for Saturday.

***

Mason, among many other facets of his being, was a hopeless romantic. He made sure to look good and dress well for his dates. He brought flowers every time. He made sure to smell good. Mason opened doors, pulled out chairs, complimented them. He would take his women out to the best places he could afford, which was *a lot*. Mason was the owner of a startup company that grew in popularity like hellfire over just a mere three years since its start. He was a millionaire. He could have lived in a mansion, but that life wasn't really for him. He liked living in a penthouse; he loved the view overlooking the city, especially at night. Mason loved that the entire section of wall that faced the city was purely made of windows. It stretched from his living room, all the way to the kitchen, to his bedroom. In every room of his house, except for his bedroom, he had a view. There was nothing quite like waking up to a glorious view like that.

It was Saturday and he woke up early to prepare for his date with Sabrina. He purchased flowers, made sure his apartment was spick and span in case she wanted to come home with him, and got ready for the date. He decided on a white shirt, with the sleeves rolled up, and a dark pair of pants. He patted on some cologne. Everything seemed so perfect so far. Their date would go well. Everything was going to be fine. He checked himself out in the mirror, took a deep breath, and left the apartment with the flowers in hand.

He got inside his 1969 Pontiac Firebird. Old school and expensive, but he loved it. He'd looked after it so well, that it even still had the all too familiar new car smell. There was nothing more attractive than some of the old school cars. Newer models were just so – uninspired in comparison.

Sabrina would be ready soon, so he drove to her apartment. She was just a little way out of town. As soon as he drove into her stomping ground, he was filled with a strange pit in his chest. She lived in a shit hole town. Every person he drove past seemingly stared him down until he was out of site, as if they were plotting how to steal it from him.

He pushed the uncomfortable feeling aside. He had a girl to romance. So, what if she lived in a bad part of town? She was soon to be a successful lawyer. Everyone had to start at a place like this as some point in time. He understood how tough it was to get a job straight out of college. He assured himself that everything was fine. Everything was going to be just okay.

He parked outside of the building that he had been guided to. It was tall and dilapidated. It didn't stand tall and proud like his did, it was slouched and sad.

He locked the door behind him before making his way inside the creaky front gate. She was on the fifth floor. There was no elevator, he had to climb the stairs there. Babies cried and old men coughed. Strange smells emitted from some apartments, he didn't even dare figure out what they could be.

He knocked on her door. She opened a minute later, wearing a nice, sleek dress that hugged her petite body. It was red and left nothing to the imagination. Her breasts were much bigger than he had imagined from her pictures. Her hair was soft and shiny, a silky, healthy light brown. Definitely a calm comfort against all he had to endure to come here.

"Hey," she said sweetly. Her voice was higher pitched and more feminine than he had imagined.

"Hi, Sabrina. I brought you flowers!" he said.

He handed them to her. She smiled in return, taking the large bouquet in her arms.

"Aww, these are beautiful. I'll put them in a vase, then we can head out. Is that alright?" she asked.

"Of course," he said.

"Come in then, come in," she said excitedly.

He stepped inside. Her apartment wasn't as bad as he had imagined it being considering what he had walked past on his way into it. He bit his tongue. He couldn't mention how much of a shit hole her town was. That would just be rude. Besides, he was just coming from a place of privilege. He had money. That's what money gave him. Comfort and security. If this was all that she could afford, it was fine. It didn't mean she was any less of a person than he was. His pre-date nerves were just setting in and he was overthinking things again.

"You're a lot more handsome than your pictures make you look," she said. She stood at her sink with her back to him. He could tell from the way that she said it, that she was smiling while she spoke.

"Thank you. And you're more gorgeous than I could have ever imagined," he said.

She placed the vase on the small dining table in her living room. Sabrina grabbed her purse, then fixed her hair in the mirror that was in the hallway, near the door.

"Right then, should we get going?" she said.

He nodded at her. She looped her arm in his as they walked down the five floors and towards the car. He wondered if it was a safety thing considering all the ruffians in the area, or a thing of just being physically affectionate.

They got in the car. He wasn't usually this awkward and silent. Things were already off to a bad start and he felt like a total dickhead for it. He drove her to one of his favorite places in the city. He knew she would love it.

"Right. You're quiet. It's because of where I live, right?" she said abruptly.

He inhaled sharply. He wasn't expecting her to be so upfront, but he kind of loved it. He loved a woman that would speak her mind, no matter how awkward things became as a result.

"Oh man, I feel like such a dick. I'm sorry. I just, I don't know if this makes sense or if you've ever experienced it before, but when I step foot inside of certain places, and it feels *off* it makes me feel kind of weird," he admitted.

"You mean, like that weird heaviness in your chest? Like, someone's got a heavy grip on your heart? Something like that?" she asked.

"Yes. Yes, exactly. So, you know what I mean, then? It's nothing against you, it's just, I felt that when I stepped foot inside your apartment block. Actually, this town."

"Nah, man. I get it. I feel the same things sometimes. They're called the Murder Flats for a reason," she chuckled.

"The what!?"

"The Murder Flats. People have been killed there," she said.

"Wow. Why do you stay there then?" he asked, genuinely curious.

"Honestly, my grandpa used to own it, and passed it down to me when he passed away. I'm kind of using it as a way to save extra cash before I move into an actual house. It's difficult to think about buying a house when you are busy paying rent, you know?"

"Yeah, I get that. But are you safe? I understand the need to save and all, but it really is a little rough around there," he asked.

"Well, it used to be a really nice area when my grandpa bought the apartment. Just went to shit over the years. Everyone in the area knows him – they won't mess with me. He was one of those cool, scary old men, ya know? Besides, I have training in defending myself if anything happens," she said.

"Oh, okay, that's pretty good. I'm happy about that. Quite an interesting grandpa. Wish mine was as interesting. I just remember that he was cruel," he paused for a moment, "And he smoked a lot. Still remember that smell."

"Oof. Yeah, chain smokers. Not good. Anyway, sorry about getting so heavy on ya there, honey. I just wanted to clear things up a little, so you didn't think I was crazy."

"No, Sabrina. I didn't think you were crazy. You seem great and I like you a lot so far," he admitted.

Mason found that over the years, the best talks he'd have with people were on long drives in his car. So, he would often take the long route, sometimes circling around the block a few times if he realized they needed more time to talk. The passengers wouldn't even notice since they were both just having such a good conversation.

He had done that just now, with Sabrina. Already, he counted too many things that he loved about her. Her honesty. The way she sat in the leather seat of his car. How she nervously twirled her brown locks when speaking about something uncomfortable.

Maybe he was just falling for her too hard, too quick.

They arrived at their destination. He opened the door for her, like a gentleman, and helped her out. He couldn't help but stare as her tight dress rode up her thighs as she swung her legs out. He noted that her panties were bright while. He was already pulling a semi-hard on in his pants.

He'd rip those off of her and shove them in her mouth later so she couldn't scream.

He shook his head, as if to physically shake the deviant thoughts in his head away.

Not now. Not today. Please, he begged himself, *just be normal, Mason. Be normal.*

"Hmm, such a gentleman, huh?" she chimed.

"Anything for a beautiful woman like you, Sabrina," he said. He did a jokey bow for her and it made her giggle.

"You're too kind," she said.

"No, I am not. Women deserve to be treated nicely at times," he said. He meant what he said. He was conflicted between his deviant, lustful side, and the hopeless romantic side that wanted to give a girl what she deserved, respect and love.

"Well, aren't you the charming one?"

He gave his key to a valet to park his car inside the building. The valet was a short, chubby man but seemed like he could be trusted. Mason instinctively slipped him a twenty dollar note for his trouble.

She looped her arm in his as he led her up the stairs. They walked a few flights up the side of the building until they reached the roof. He held her hand and helped her up the last step. Her face lit up once she saw where he had taken her. A high-end restaurant and bar on the top of a tall building, with a view of the city from where they would eat. The bar was separated off to the left of the seating area, and people would have to fetch their own drinks.

There was a cocktail bar as well as having an open plan kitchen, something he loved. It was great being able to watch the magic happen in the kitchen, trying to guess if they were busy with your meal or someone else's. A greeter told them a waiter would be with them shortly and that they could be seated where he had reserved a spot. The restaurant was awfully busy at the time, but that was good. Mason loved the hustle and bustle and the background noise that came along with it.

He had been in empty restaurants before and they were kind of eerie. When going out to eat, that all too familiar sound was expected.

"Woah, this is lovely," she said as he pulled the chair out for her to sit down.

As he pushed her chair in, he noticed that she was light and small. So easy and fun for him to have his way with her however he pleased.

She seemed happy and not nervous whatsoever. He liked that too. A woman with confidence. A woman who held her head high.

He let her have the seat that overlooked the view. He wanted to be able to see the twinkle in her eye as she watched on at the night.

"This is amazing, Mason. Thank you for bringing me here," she said sincerely, "What do they serve here?"

"Japanese food. I hope that's to your taste – I usually take girls out to a simpler place for the first date until I know what they like. I know that you like Japanese food, though, so I settled on this in the end," Mason said.

"Hmm. Take a lot of girls on dates, do you?" she raised an eyebrow at him.

"No! Not really. Shit, I didn't mean for it to come out like that. I'm not some douche bag," Mason scratched the back of his head nervously. He was really losing his skill in charming women. Doing the same thing over and over again was getting to him. Doing the same thing over and over expecting different results was one of the definitions of insanity, after all.

"I'm teasing you, stupid. You're a grown man. I don't care if you go on dates every weekend. What happened in the past doesn't matter, it's what happens between us that truly means something. Honestly,

I can't stand those kinds of people that demand to know every tiny detail of my life. Often, it's brought up in later arguments and it just makes things messy, you know?" she said.

How insightful.

"Yeah, you're right. Besides, the person you are a year ago isn't the same person you are now. Not to mention, when in a relationship, you become a whole other person entirely compared to when you're single. So why judge someone for who they were when they were single? If you're with them, it shouldn't matter."

"Exactly. Gosh, what do you think about ordering some drinks? I've actually had such a tough week and need some down time. I'll pay for the cab, so you don't have to drive drunk," Sabrina said.

"You don't need to worry about that, Sabrina. I'll sort it out. And of course, I'd love to have a few drinks. What's your drink of choice? I'll order it at the cocktail bar," he said.

"Bit strange having a cocktail bar inside of a Japanese restaurant. Anyway, uh, something sweet. Strawberry daiquiri? Or something like that, anyway," she said.

"I thought the same thing when I came here the first time. They try to stay true to tradition in their food though, at least. They still need to cater to the alcoholics, though," Mason said, "If the waiter comes, I'll have some golden parcels for a starter. Order yourself anything. Dinner's on me."

He walked off to the bar. A few people were seated on some bar stools, other at some tall circular tables, here just to get sloshed. He pushed through the crowd and stopped in front of the bar. The bartender was busy serving someone else, so he took a seat on the only available stool, next to a curvy, tall woman. He waited patiently, occasionally sneaking glances at the woman next to him. He couldn't help it. There was something that drew him to her.

Perhaps it was the overly feminine aura she emitted. Or the way she sat so up straight, a posture usually only seen in ballerinas. She was older though, perhaps in her mid-thirties to early forties, apparent from the smile lines on her face. It was beautiful, though. It showed that she had lived a good life and smiled a lot. A red lip accompanied it, along with a neatly pinned up, curled hair do.

She was alluring. Dare he say, a delectable MILF.

She looked over at him, but he didn't look away.

"What are ya looking at, handsome? Do ya need somethin'?" she asked. Many of her words had a distinct southern twinge to them.

"I need to rip your clothes off and fuck you till you can't think about anything but me," he said in his head.

He couldn't say that to a stranger, so he lied instead. "Oh, just looking. What are you doing here, sitting all alone?"

"I'm just getting pissed because I don't want to go home alone. At least I'm around some people now," she said honestly.

"Hmm, that's unfortunate, a woman like you doesn't deserve to be alone on a Saturday evening," Mason said.

"What's a woman like me?"

He eyed her up and down. Her cinched in waist, her abundant breasts. Her big smile, framed by deep red lips. Her near white-blonde hair.

"You're a seductress," he said.

The bartender made his way over to where Mason was, wiping his hands on a white cloth.

"What can I get you, sir?" he asked.

"Top shelf whiskey and a strong strawberry daiquiri, please," Mason said.

"You're on a date," the Seductress said, "Aren't you?"

Mason sighed. He was. He was on a date with a wonderful, smart woman, but he was flirting with a MILF. It was a cold, wake up call that he needed to get his shit together.

"Uh, yeah. I am," Mason admitted.

"First date, isn't it?" she smiled at him.

"How do you know that?"

"You're wearing your best shirt and your best cologne that you save for special occasions," she chuckled.

"Well, miss, you're a perceptive one," he said. His cock throbbed and he hoped it would go away soon.

"I'm known for it."

The drinks he ordered were set in front of him and he made his way back to Sabrina without saying goodbye to the MILF. Mostly out of embarrassment for flirting with her while he was on a date, secondly, because if he didn't leave, he'd take her home instead. He just *knew* she wore a matching set of lacy lingerie beneath her clothing, a garter belt to match. He knew from just seeing a little bit of the lace lining of the top of her thigh high stockings.

Sabrina smiled as she sat back down. She paled in comparison to the utter goddess he had seen at the bar. He forced himself to forget about her. She was a great person. He needed to stop being such a horny bastard.

"What took you so long, Mason? Everything okay?" Sabrina asked.

"Ah, sorry to keep you waiting. Long line at the bar. I got what you wanted, though!" he handed her drink to her. His hand hurt from touching the cold, icy glass for so long. He rubbed his hands together to get feeling back into it again.

"No worries," she said. She tucked an artificial curl behind her ear. "I ordered starters, by the way."

"Oh, great! I wanted to ask, what made your week so tough? Want to talk about it?"

"Ugh," she sighed, "You know those difficult people that won't work with you no matter how hard you try, constantly making unrealistic demands and getting mad when they can't be met?"

"Oh, yes. I know them all too well. Mostly men or women in their fifties or sixties. Miserable bastards," he said. It was true, he dealt with those people in his company at least twice a month. Entitled people that thought just because they were older, they could do and ask for whatever they wanted without consequence.

"Well, since I'm a newbie in the lawyer world, trying to make my way up, my boss is throwing all the evil clients my way, the ones that no one else wants to work with. This asshole is treating me like shit because legally, I cannot help him sue his neighbor for building a shed on his own property. Said neighbor had gotten all the permits for building beforehand. But mister Asshole doesn't want to stand for that," Sabrina said.

"What a moron. What are you going to do with him?" Mason asked.

"Dude, he basically stalks me, I swear. He just keeps coming back to me with new things, hoping some tiny detail will help him sue his sweet neighbor. I spoke to the neighbor and everything, and he's just a sweet old man that doesn't want any trouble. God, I hate this guy. He's called me so many derogatory things but there's nothing I can do about it because well, it's my job. My boss is just as much of a moron as him. But he's been in the industry for ten plus years, so his word is law," Sabrina said.

"Man, that's the reason I'm my own boss. I just couldn't bow down to someone else, I swear. If anyone treated me like shit just because they were my boss and an authority, I'd punch them in the face. I'd never last in that environment," Mason admitted.

"I get that, honestly, if I weren't so patient, I'd do the same. But it is what it is, you know? These are the first steps before eventually, I can start my own practice. It's all just progress. Going through the motions in life. Sometimes, you have to do shit you don't want to do just because you *have to.*"

"Yeah, makes sense. That is true."

Her dirty mouth was charming. He wondered what kind of verbiage she used in bed.

But would she even go home with him tonight? He couldn't expect it just because they were on a date. It wouldn't be fair to expect that of her.

But, God, was he hankering for some good pussy. He hadn't fucked anyone but his own hand in weeks. He needed that closeness. That intimacy. As good as masturbating was, it paled in comparison to actually being with a woman. He stared at The Seductress that still sat at the bar counter, drinking gin. Her posture stayed straight. She spoke to a young man, shortly leaving with him after. Deep down, it made Mason kind of sad. He'd never see her again. What an intriguing woman.

He reminded himself to focus on things right in front of him.

"Focus, Mason. Keep your fucking dick in your pants and enjoy her company," he demanded from himself. He chose to forget about the blonde-haired goddess from then on and focus on the woman in front of him.

They got to know each other better throughout dinner. The drinks flowed near endlessly as they forgot about all their responsibilities and troubles. He genuinely enjoyed her company. She was a lot more entertaining in person than over text. Her sense of humor shined through. While she spoke of something she was passionate about, he almost felt like he was falling for her.

Her eyes lit up when she spoke of her family that lived back in Brazil, although he could see the sadness of being apart from them mixed throughout.

She was a good, hard working person. She didn't know about his money or what he specifically did for a living and he wanted to keep it that way at least for a while. If money weren't in the mix, maybe she'd like him for who he was, instead of his fortune.

Would that be lying? He wondered. Lying by omission was a thing. Did he want their potential relationship to be based on lies? He was five and a half whiskeys down. He could already feel himself nearing the point of loss of inhibitions.

"Sabrina, I hope you enjoyed the food," Mason said. Although he was drunk, he didn't look it.

She patted at the corner of her mouth with a cloth napkin, hoping not to mess up her lipstick.

"Of course. This place is incredible, Mason. Thank you for introducing me to this. I don't really get out that much anymore. It's just work, work, work and no play."

Her brown eyes stared up at him. She gave him *that* look. She wanted him to fuck her. She kept shifting in her seat, as if her panties were so wet that she was uncomfortable. She bit her lip occasionally, played with her hair as they stared each other in the eyes.

She was ready.

"Pardon if this is too forward, but would you like to head back to my place for a few more drinks to end the night off?" Mason said. Even though he knew she would say yes with no hesitation, he would be a gentleman about it.

"I'm so happy you finally asked," she purred, "I would love that, Mason. Besides, you've seen *my* apartment. I would love to see yours."

"Hmm, sounds like a fair deal, sweetheart. I'll settle the bill and we can go on our merry way," Mason said.

She nodded quickly. She couldn't fucking wait to get in his pants, could she? What a filthy slut, throwing herself at a man she had just met today. He paid up, leaving their waiter a nice, fat tip. He hurried, impatient to get home and have his way with her.

With alcohol in his system, he could no longer suppress the deviant thoughts in his head. As they taxied to his apartment building, he reminded himself that even if he had those thoughts, he could still control those actions. It was easy. He could do this.

The taxi's brakes came to a screeching stop in front of the big building. It was tall, lit up by the people that lived inside. She craned her neck to look at the top of the building.

"Holy shit," she breathed, "You actually live here?"

"Yup. Follow me, Brina," he said.

"Sure. I'd get lost in there if I didn't. How many floors are there in it anyway?" she asked.

"Thirteen," he said as they stepped inside of the cozy elevator.

"Woah. Okay," she said. She leaned on his shoulder. From the corner of his eye, he could see her staring up at him admirably. Her entire world had changed, knowing that he lived in a place like this. Only the best of the best lived here. Millionaires, billionaires and celebrities. He could tell she was wondering how much money he actually made and how he made it.

"You're on the thirteenth floor?" she asked.

"Yes, I am," he said. He wasn't paying attention to the conversation. He was just thinking about fucking her. Thinking about what she was wearing underneath that tight, red dress. She stood on her tip toes and brought his face down to hers. For a moment, she just stared.

She pushed her body against his. Her crotch brushed up against his hard on and when she felt it, she pushed up against him even harder, knocking him against the back of the elevator. She ran her fingers through his hair, lust apparent in her eyes.

She kissed him. It was sloppy, but good. Her tongue brushed against his and he welcomed it. Mason grabbed at her ass, accidentally pulling her dress up in the process. He didn't hesitate to rub her over her panties. He found her clit, applying pressure and rubbing up against it. She'd pull away to take in a breath or to stop herself from moaning in between each kiss. Finally, she let out a moan as the elevator doors slid open with a *ding*.

They wasted no time to enter his apartment. As soon as the doors closed, he picked her up and they continued what they were doing. She wrapped her hands around his neck. He walked over to the big sofa in his living room, not even opening his eyes to get there.

He dropped her down and got on top of her. It was a big sofa, so they had ample space to mess around on it. While they made out, she slowly began the task of unbuttoning his shirt. Once the last one was done, only then did they stop to breathe again. She pulled it down his shoulders then off his arms.

She let out a soft 'mmm' when she saw how ripped his body was. Every woman loved a strong man, it just meant that he could protect them. It was one of those primal instincts within every person.

"You're so fucking sexy," he said between kisses down her body. He pulled her tight dress up from her thighs and she spread her legs in response. He nibbled on her soft flesh, making sure not to hurt her too much. When he was lower and he was face to face with her panties, he admired them. A white thong. Simple, yet elegant. She had a wet spot right where her hole was, revealing her pink lips beneath. He kissed her mound, working his way down. Her smell was sweet and musky.

He pulled the panties to the side and dug his face in. Sabrina was freshly shaven – she went into this knowing they would be fucking by the end of it. His cock was rock hard as soon as he licked her pussy – she was so soft, so wet. So slick.

She grabbed a pillow to her right and moaned loudly as he used the tip of his tongue to flick at her clit. He reached one hand up to fondle her breasts over her clothes, the other hand, preparing to slip inside of her.

He slid two fingers into her. Guided by how tight her walls became when he did something with his tongue, he found the perfect rhythm and intensity in which to work his magic. In no time, her walls pulsated around his fingers and she came with a high pitched, boisterous moan.

Satisfied with his work, he wiped the wetness from his face and started unbuckling his belt, ready to fuck her. She propped herself up on her elbows, then looked at him with a frown.

"Do you have a condom?" she asked.

Fuck.

He hoped she wouldn't ask and that she was on birth control instead.

Mason didn't typically like using them unless absolutely necessary. He was cut, so he lost a lot of sensation by wearing one. He felt himself going soft at the thought of having to wear a rubber. Nothing compared to fucking a woman raw. But he wouldn't be a dickhead and not do it. He still wanted to fuck her anyway. At least he'd last longer this time.

"Yeah! Sure, of course. Just caught up in the heat of the moment. Uh, I'll go grab it," he said.

"Thank you, Mason. Thanks for not being weird about it. I didn't want to ruin the moment or anything. I'm sorry," she said, likely noticing his facial expression had dropped.

Mason bent over her and kissed her on the lips. He wouldn't let this ruin the great night they had already had.

"Of course, sexy. It's just to be safe. Don't you worry your tight little ass," he whispered.

She giggled in response.

Mason rushed off to his bedroom to search for one. He hadn't used a rubber in so long that he had forgotten where he kept them. He checked the en-suite bathroom, thinking that was one of the places he was bound to have put it in. There was nothing there. He rummaged through the room, not finding it anywhere.

"Everything okay in there?" she shouted from the living room.

"Yes! All good. Be there now," he said back.

Finally, he found it in the drawer, the one that wasn't on the side of his bed. It was hidden underneath a book. Thank god, he thought.

He turned around, she stood in the door frame with one hand holding it. She was just in her bra and panties now. He just stared at her a moment, then grunted. Fuck, she was sexy.

"Hey, big boy. Sounded like you needed a little help in here," she said seductively. She looked around at the mess he had made in the room by rummaging through everything.

"Heh, got it in the end!" he said.

"Good. I want to fuck you, Mason. I want to fuck you so hard," she said.

He admired her body. She was small and thin, but looking much better without her clothes on. Although her breasts weren't massive, they were big enough to have perfect cleavage in the matching white bra she was wearing. She walked over to him and he sat down on the bed, the condom sitting next to him. He glared down at the condom. He really wasn't looking forward to wearing it. Made him feel like a dumb teenager all over again, it made him remember how he used to nervously fumble with it and forget to put it on. At least, as he got older, he learned how to find the right size and all.

She kneeled between his legs, finishing the job of taking his pants off. He lifted his ass to help her remove them. His massive cock sprung out from beneath the fabric of his boxers as she removed those too.

Her mouth fell open and her eyes widened at the sheer size of it. They always reacted that way. He nearly chuckled, but stopped himself.

"I – I," she took his cock in her small hands, hardly able to wrap her fist around it, "I don't know if I'll even be able to fit this in my mouth, let alone my pussy."

"We'll just have to try, right?" he said.

"Oh yeah," she moaned, "Yeah, we will definitely have to try."

She sat on her haunches to bring her face closer to his cock. Steadily, she stroked his cock while she prepared to take him in her mouth. She licked from the base, to the tip of his cock. He grunted as her wet tongue ran along his frenulum. Her tongue circled round the tip of his penis a few times, before she pursed her lips and slowly slid her lips over it.

He grunted.

"Fuck. It's been long," he said to himself.

She slid her lips lower and lower, her mouth being forced open wide. She gagged before she could reach half of the way down. It made him smile how much she struggled to fit him inside of her.

He laced his fingers in her hair, lifting and dipping her head down on his cock. He was slow and gentle – he didn't want to be as rough as he usually was. He stopped before she could gag each time before lifting her head up.

He wanted more though. It wasn't good enough.

It felt so good. So, fucking good.

As though possessed by something else, he began face fucking her with a ferocity she didn't seem used to. She gagged and groaned. He didn't stop when she started slapping his leg for him to slow down.

He carried on fucking her, staring down at her teary eyes and enjoying her suffering.

She had had enough, though, and pulled away from him even though his grip was so tight. She took a moment to catch her breath. She wiped the tears from her eyes. Seemingly deciding to let his force slide, she took the condom wrapper, tore it open. She pinched the tip of it, then slid it down his cock. She stroked his cock a few times, making sure it was secure. She crawled on top of him.

She firmly gripped his cock and guided him inside of her. She moaned loud, putting her hands on his chest to keep herself steady. She lifted and lowered herself down onto him repeatedly. She was having fun riding him, but he looked off to the side.

It wasn't really doing it for him. Not really. But he'd let her have her fun and be satisfied.

As she dropped down her small frame on him, she'd grind up against him, stimulating her clit against his pubic bone.

"Oh, god, oh god, yes," she screamed, "I'm gonna come."

Snapped back to reality, he looked back at her and thrust up into her as her walls tightened and relaxed around him. Finally, some sensation. This set him into a frenzy. He sat up, picked her off of him and pushed her onto her knees on the bed so her ass was facing him. She giggled at the sudden change of position. She was on her hands and knees, but that was not the way he preferred it.

So, he pushed her lower body down, so her face was against the bed. For a moment, he considered taking the condom off. But she'd notice. Besides, that would be kind of creepy.

"Mmmm, that was incredible," she said, "Your cock took some getting used to, but I'm hooked."

"Of course you got used to my cock, slut," he said softly.

"Sorry, what was that?" she asked. She looked back around at him and frowned.

"Oh, I just said of course you did, Sabrina," he lied.

"Oh," she said.

She put her head back down on the bed and waved her ass from left to right, anticipating his cock.

He got onto his knees on the bed, gripping her ass. His cock stood tall and hard, he didn't even need to hold it to guide it inside of her. She moaned as he slowly slid inside of her.

"Oh god, that hurts," she moaned, "Please go slow."

The few brief moments that he wasn't inside of her must have caused her tight walls to not be used to his sheer size anymore. It made him feel strong and incredible.

He did go slow, as she requested.
But he got bored again.
This was just plain old fucking.
It was boring.
If he wanted that he'd get married to someone who didn't love him.

She moaned and enjoyed herself. Slowly, sneakily, he increased the pace, hoping she'd just get used to it. He liked it rough. He liked it hard. She would too.

He increased the pace. She felt incredible. So tight and so small. His hands were so big against her small body. So easy for him to dominate.

He fucked her harder, each time his balls smacked against her thighs, she let out a loud grunt. He fucked her in a way every woman wanted to be fucked at some point.

He enjoyed this more, but he wanted more. He pushed all the promises he made to himself away. She was propped up onto her arms again, looking back at him as he fucked her. He lifted a leg, putting his foot on the back of her head, making her arms collapse beneath her, forcing her face into the sheets. With his foot on the back of her neck, she couldn't move. He pulled her ass higher into the air, shifting himself higher above her. He pumped down into her harder than before, her loud moans muffled in the blankets of his bed.

"Ah, fuck," she moaned, "Stop, stop, you're hitting my cervix."

"Shut up, slut," he barked.

He fucked her even harder, letting out loud grunts continuously.

"Please," she begged, "Please."

She tried to move her head but couldn't with how hard his foot was forcing her down.

She kicked her legs at him, slapping him with her hands, trying to get free. He enjoyed her fighting, and didn't stop. In the scuffle, she became free, but ended up underneath him, staring up at him with her hands pinned on either side of her head.

"just stop when I say stop, okay?" she asked.

"Yes, I'm sorry. I just – I just get carried away," he said, "I'm sorry, sweetheart."

"It's okay," she said, she smiled at him.

"Do you want to carry on?" he asked.

"Yes, please. I want you to cum too, Mason. I've already come like three times," she laughed, "I came when we were in the elevator."

"In the elevator? Damn, I'm really good."

"Shut up and fuck me," she said. She bit her lip.

He put both of her wrists on one hand, with the other, he lifted and spread her legs for him.

"What a beautiful cunt you have," he said. It was a perfect, puffy pink pussy.

He thrust into her without hesitation.

He didn't go slow this time. He was done accommodating to her. He wanted his release now – he'd been anticipating it for days, saving himself just for her.

His free hand fondled her perfectly small breasts, pinching and squeezing her small nipples. They grew red from all the touching. She had her head bent backwards, her eyes rolled to the back of her head.

Her beautiful, pale and bare neck practically begged to be choked. He put it against her neck, only holding it at first. He felt his cock throb once he did. This was exactly what he needed to reach climax soon enough, even despite the condom.

He squeezed either side of her small neck, making sure not to press down on her windpipe.

He grunted as heat spread all throughout him and he was *almost there.*

Mason squeezed harder, her chest becoming flushed and her face too.

She pulled at his wrist, trying to get him away.

But he squeezed even harder.

"Stop," she croaked, "Stop. That's too hard."

"No," he grunted, "I won't stop, whore."

"Please," she begged. Her begging made his cock twitch. "Just let go."

His legs shook, his balls spasmed. He came with three more hard and deep thrusts.

As soon as she let go, she scurried backwards, away from him. She looked scared.

"What the fuck is wrong with you!?" she screamed, "I told you to stop. I could let the first time slid because you know, I was fucking horny. But then you choked me and didn't let go?"

"Listen, I didn't mean to hurt you," Mason said, "I had a really good time with you today. I just, I just get carried away."

Mason approached her to touch her shoulder reassuringly. She recoiled at his touch, slapping his hand away.

"Don't fucking touch me! You don't do that, Mason! You're a nice guy. I had such a good time at the restaurant. But you don't understand what no or stop means. You understand how fucking fucked up that is, right?" she shouted.

She rushed around the room, gathering her things, pulled her panties and bra on.

"No, no. That's not who I am – I swear, I just, I just get -" he started.

"Don't fucking tell me that you get carried away. Have some self-control, you piece of shit!"

She left the room, grabbed her handbag and made her way to the door.

"Please, let's just talk about this. I'm sorry," Mason pleaded.

"No. Fuck you and don't ever contact me again."

She left the apartment in her bra and panties, storming off and out of the building.

"Fuck!" Mason screamed, knocking a small vase off of the table.

He had done it again. He had fucked up again.

He hated himself for it.

Mason and Sabrina could have had something so good and so sweet, but he fucked it up, just how he had fucked up every other relationship in his life.

Shamefully, he removed the condom, tied it off, and chucked it in the bin. He had a shower, all the while feeling empty.

He felt like giving up. No one liked the way he fucked them, and he went too far *every single time*.

***

Sabrina blocked him on everything, and he never heard from her since. He spent the next few weeks burying himself in his work, distracting himself from the negative feelings. Just like he did every time this happened.

But, as the cycle usually went, he went straight back to the dating app, hoping that someone would come to accept him. He wasn't actually a monster, right? He just didn't go about things the right way. Fear and hesitancy stopped him from bringing up his tendencies when he first started speaking to someone. How would he bring that up, anyway?

"Hey, I like to choke and fuck someone so hard that they beg me to stop."

He couldn't just do that. It wasn't right. They'd run for the hills and never speak to him again.

Straight back to the app he went, though, but something inside of him wanted to do things differently. He set the age range between his, and fifty. Usually, he'd have it between twenty-five and twenty-seven, but maybe someone a year older would work.

Who knows.

Maybe that was what he was missing all along. Maybe that one woman that was right for him was just behind the surface of that age range.

He set his phone down and went about his day. His phone buzzed and he checked it.

He had matched with an oddly familiar woman. He remembered her eyes, those bright blue eyes.

The Seductress from the cocktail lounge. He couldn't believe his eyes. Could it really be her?

Her name was Scarlett.

"How fitting," he thought.

The age on her profile said she was forty-five, which took his breath away. She looked incredible for her age. She was eighteen years his senior, but he wanted to fuck her anyway.

He'd never been with a woman older than him before…

She sent a message first.

"Hey, you," she said, "You're the one from the bar. Your name's Mason? I like it."

He replied: "And your name is Scarlett. I like it too."

"So, what's a young man on you doing on this side of the world?"

"Trying new things, I guess."

"I'm guessing things didn't work out with that date of yours?"

"Yeah… Things kind of fell flat with that. Long story."

"Well, not to be a bitch, but I'm glad she's not in the picture. You really piqued my interest that night, Mason, and I am glad I can have a chance to have you all to myself."

"Hmm. Not bitchy. That's flattering, Scarlett. Where abouts do you live?"

"Literally a fifteen-minute walking distance from the bar," she said.

"Oh. Well, isn't that convenient. How did it go with the guy you took home?"

"Meh. He came in like five minutes, so I kicked him outta the house. Not dealing with that bullshit."

"Haha! Nice. Sorry to hear about him not pleasing you though. That's very unfortunate to hear."

"He didn't even bother to make me come first. He just couldn't wait to stick his dick inside of my pussy," she said.

He was at work and he had a hard on from only speaking to this woman for a few minutes. He looked around to make sure no one was watching, proceeding to adjust it underneath his waistline, in case he needed to stand up. He hovered over the 'send' button.

"I'd make sure you're fully satisfied before I even get my cock out, babe."

He decided to send it, to test the waters.

She replied instantly.

"Fuck. Now I'm wet. Listen, when I saw your profile on here, I had one thing on my mind and only one thing. That I want you to fuck me and have your every which way with me. You're tall, you're handsome, and I *know* you have a big fat cock in those pants of yours. Would you be up for that?"

"Are you sure you want to rush into things? I don't want to pressure you into having sex so soon. You don't want to get to know each other first?"

"Oh, shut up. I know what I want, and it's you. I mean, don't you think it's fate that we found each other."

"Yeah, I suppose you're right," he replied.

"Oh, and I'm guessing this is also running through your head. No, I'm not married and I'm not cheating on my husband. I got divorced like ten years ago and my kids are already outta the house. So, we're all good on that front."

"I wasn't worried about that. I saw you didn't have a ring on. It was one of the first things I looked at when I saw you."

"So, you instantly thought about fucking me when you saw me for the first time, hmm?" she teased.

"Well, yes. Honestly, I did," he replied. A smile was slapped across his face the entire time they had the conversation.

"Well, I know it's a little early and all, but would you like to meet up today?" she asked.

He stared at her message for a while, wondering if it was a good idea. What if she didn't like him, just like everyone else? He knew how to control himself now. After Sabrina had left, he made a real, true vow to himself. He wouldn't do that ever again. No choking. No slapping. No shoving.

"I can take time off whenever, really," he replied.

"Right, then, meet me at my place," she sent a pin of her location, "In twenty minutes."

It was spontaneous, but he was into it. It excited him to the core.

He left the office, leaving the floor manager in charge for the day. He lied, saying there was a family emergency. They'd be able to handle a few hours alone.

His car purred loudly on the trip there. He stopped in front of her place. *Just* outside of the city, her neighborhood was more suburban than his. He stopped in front of her house. It was a Victorian era style house, the classic white-picket fence house wife styled house he'd expected.

She fit the part, honestly. With her hair, the way she dressed and all, she looked like a 1950's housewife, even though they were in the modern times. He found it charming.

Once he parked in the driveway, he made his way to the door. This was insane. His hands were sweating. He couldn't believe he just left work early for a forty-five-year-old woman he had only met *once*.

She opened the door instantly when he rang the doorbell.

"Well, hello there. I'm honestly surprised that you came," she said. Her southern drawl was charming, and it made his cock twitch. She had a smile on her face, her eyes scanning him up and down.

Her house was white and airy, full of light.

"Well, can't blame me, can you?" he chuckled.

"No, I cannot," she smiled.

She touched his tie, feeling the soft fabric between her fingers. She twirled the tie around her hand and pulled him into the house. He closed the door behind him as she led him through the house like a puppy on a leash.

The house was well decorated and clean as a whistle.

She led him to what he guessed was the master bedroom.

"Undress me," she demanded.

She wore a white dress with a zip on the back. He did as he was told, slowly touching her shoulder, kissing her neck.

He unzipped her dress and it fell to the floor with a *thud.*

She wore exactly the type of lingerie that he had pictured. High-waisted garter belt, leopard print panties and bra to match.

She turned around and he looked at her.

"Holy fuck," he breathed.

Her body was incredible.

As though it had been carved out of stone by the gods. She was fit, curvy, and her tits were huge, almost spilling out of her bra.

"You like it, dontcha?" she teased.

"You're so fucking sexy, Scarlett," he said.

"Well, then I want you to have your way with me."

Without thinking, he shoved her down onto the bed. He got on top of her. Keeping in mind her previous encounter, he fingered at her lips to find her clit, expertly rubbing at it. He didn't care that her red lipstick would get all over him, and went in for a kiss. He kissed her hard and rough. She had a bit of a bush, but her pussy lips were neatly trimmed.

He pleasured her until she reached climax at least three times, using his fingers and tongue in alternation.

"Hmmm, that was so good, big boy," she purred, "But now it's your turn to have your fun with me."

She pulled his suit jacket off and undressed him. She bit her lip when she saw his cock, then looked up at him. He was on his knees on the bed now.

"This is even bigger than I thought it would be," she whispered.

"Thank you."

She got on her hands and knees, having no hesitation in taking his entire length into her mouth and down her throat. When he was in her throat, she would occasionally pulsate the muscles of her throat around his girth, squeezing on his cock. Her ass bounced as she moved herself back and forth onto his cock. He didn't know what to focus on, her ass or her face, with make-up filled tears streaming down her face.

It felt incredible and unlike anything he had ever experienced before. He didn't even have to guide her in order for the face fucking to happen, she sucked him off ferociously, with determination.

"Fuck," he moaned. He couldn't take it anymore, if she carried on, he would come.

Somehow knowing this, she pulled away and got onto her back.

"Fuck me, big boy," she moaned, "I'm so very wet."

She spread her legs, subsequently her lips, to reveal her glistening wetness. This woman took his breath away.

He reminded himself not to ruin things by being too rough. He crawled between her smooth legs, slapping his cock against her clit. She giggled when he did that, but grabbed his cock and shoved it inside of her. Pangs of pleasure rushed all throughout him upon entering her. He had to focus intently on not coming instantly – he understood now why the guy she fucked weeks ago had come so quickly.

She was intense. Sexy. Seductive.

Mason would never be able to get enough of Scarlett, no matter how hard he tried.

He carefully slid his cock in and out of her, holding her legs for balance. She moaned softly, her big blue eyes staring up at him as he did. She pulled her bra down to reveal her bare breasts. With each soft and careful thrust, they bounced and moved. He couldn't keep his eyes off of them. He felt those instincts in him once more, his hand going for her throat. He stopped just before he reached it, hesitating.

He fondled her breasts instead.

She looked down at his hand, then up at him.

Gripping his wrist, she pulled his hand up to her throat, then secured it around it. She gave him a reassuring nod. He squeezed, prompting a moan from her. He squeezed harder and her eyes rolled to the back of her head.

He fucked her harder while he choked her. She came on his cock, and he put both hands around her neck for stability as he had his way with her body. He grunted with each thrust. She was so wet and so tight, her pussy squeezing onto him with all its might.

"Was she...was she actually enjoying this?" he asked himself.

He pulled his hands away and shook his head. He didn't want to go too far. She chuckled through her gasping breaths.

"Why'd you stop, Mason? Didn't you like that?" she asked.

"No. I'm sorry. I shouldn't do that. It's fine," he said. He pulled out of her.

"What's wrong?" she asked, genuinely concerned.

"I shouldn't do that. It's not right. It's not right."

"Well, you seemed to like it, Mason." She glared at him.

"No. I shouldn't hurt women like that. I'm a monster," he admitted.

"Slap me."

She nudged him. She stroked his cock, it was slick with her pussy juices.

"No. I can't do that. I can't hurt you like that."

"Slap me, you fucking pussy."

He moaned as her hand masterfully jerked him off.

"Come on, you fucking coward. Hit me. Slap me. Fuck me like I'm some toy. Or are you too scared?" she demeaned him.

He snapped. He'd had enough.

"Shut the fuck up, whore," he spat.

He swung his hand at her face. Her cheek glowed red instantly. She didn't cry or tell him to stop, but instead, she moaned. He entered her again, but this time, fucked her with vigor.

"That's more like it," she moaned, "Do it again. Hit me. Fuck me hard. Hit me."

He did it again and again, slapping her across the face, then back handing her in the other direction while he fucked her. He could tell she enjoyed it – the muscles of her cunt pulsed with pleasure each time he struck her.

His hands were around her neck again when he was close to climax, the primal side of him taking over. She moaned uncontrollably by this point, and arched her back as he was about to climax. His legs shook, his entire body filled with ecstasy, as he shot his load inside of her. He was so drained by all the pleasure, in a good way, that all he could do was collapse on top of her. Scarlett let out a satisfied laugh, and wrapped her arms around him. He did the same.

He rolled over and lit a cigarette, and so did she.

The first intense, truly satisfying orgasm he had ever had came from a MILF.

The Living Doll

A tall woman sat on a chair within a massive, lavish living room, as though she had been put on display as a living work of art. The rest of the house fit the part, too, with large rooms and a frivolous number of windows. Her arms were tied behind her with a thick hemp rope. It dug into her skin but not enough to cut circulation. She could hear her heartbeat, it was so loud that it was the only thing she could focus on. Her legs were spread, each ankle tied to the legs of the chair. She wore a sexy, form fitting dress in the color red. It matched the red lipstick on her lips. The dress rode up her thighs, almost showing what she wore underneath said dress.

Today was a very important day and she tingled with anticipation for what would unfold. She was already wet, a wet spot forming in the seat of her chair. She had been tied to this chair since the last few minutes of sunlight and it was already pitch black outside now. The house was empty and quiet.

Her thoughts were interrupted by her husband kissing the top of her blonde head. It sent shivers down her spine.

"Hey, Stacy," he said. He sat in front of her, her chair was facing the three-seater sofa. The coffee table was to her left, moved out of the way to make space for her chair. There was another couch to her right, too.

"Hi," she said softly. Although she was bound, she wanted to reach out and touch his face. She was overwhelmed with arousal and love for her husband. She couldn't, of course and just tugged at the ropes that bound her wrists.

"Are you ready for tonight?" he asked.

"As nervous as I am, I am teeming with anticipation. My hands can't shake if they're bound, right?" she giggled.

"Mmmm, seeing you all helpless like this is giving me such a hard on, but I will wait. I should be patient, considering what will happen for the rest of tonight," he said.

"I'm ready."

"Good."

Her husband left the room and came back in with a big box in his hands. Slowly, he began unpacking its contents onto the coffee table next to her. Various vibrators, especially of the wand kind, dildos, and butt plugs were put down onto a small towel on the table. Next, he put down various whips and paddles. Some with long leather strands, a horse whip and her least favorite: a rubber paddle.

Next, he put down a variety of ball gags. A red one with a ball, one shaped like a ball for her to bite on, and another with a small dick shape, that would go into her mouth and cause major discomfort. BDSM wax candles. A lighter. More rope. Permanent markers. Lube. Cuffs. Lastly, he put down a pair of sharp scissors.

Her husband had prepared for absolutely everything he could have possibly thought would be useful. An overwhelming heat was forming between her legs and she hoped it would start soon. She really, truly couldn't wait for it to start.

"Which gag would you like for this evening, Madame?" he asked, speaking in a knock-off hoity-toity accent.

She giggled like a little schoolgirl.

"Hmm, sir, I would like whichever one you'd like," she replied in the same accent.

A sly smile formed on his face. He picked up the dildo gag and she inhaled sharply. Of course, he was going to torture with this one…

First, he gave her some water to hydrate before she wore the gag for who knows how long.

"Open wide, sunshine," he commanded.

She did as she was told. Slowly, he slid it into her mouth, and it filled her up. Her mouth was forced wide open by the short but thick instrument. He pulled it tight before strapping it in and securing it. Already, she felt saliva forming in her mouth from being forced to such an awkward angle.

He left the room again. From behind her, she could hear a loud grunt as he placed what he called The Fuck Bench down on the ground. It was one of her favorite contraptions, with countless straps to hold her in place, forcing her into the doggy style position. He had spent months trying to build it and was very proud upon its completion. Her hands and legs would each have two straps, along with one that went around her waist, and another that would go around her neck, keeping her snug and in place. Most importantly, she would neither be able to move nor be able to stop anything that happened to her.

She couldn't wait to be put inside of it. Seeing all the toys and instruments before her made her all the more excited for what was to come. He kissed her on the head one last time, before he prepared some other things unrelated to her.

She stared at the clock on the wall across from her. As soon as it struck 09:00 p.m., people started arriving. One by one, her husband greeted them. Some of them, he hugged and others he shook the hands of.

Some were old friends and others were distant acquaintances. His best friend and that best friend's wife arrived last. No one seemed to notice her as he did the usual, showing them around the house and letting them know where they could get drinks and snacks if they needed.

Time went by and the drinks were flowing. It was a normal, everyday house party, barring the twenty-something year old sitting in the living room, tied to a chair. Some familiar faces played beer pong, occasionally cheering in excitement when they won the game. There were many different men and women from different backgrounds and walks of life.

Not once, throughout, had anyone acknowledged her presence. Saliva dripped down from her rose lips, causing a wet spot on her chest where it uncontrollably fell down. Although people hardly looked at her and she was so horribly ignored, she loved it. She felt so unimportant. So insignificant, while people had fun all around her. She would have smiled if it weren't for the gag in her mouth.

Finally, after an hour, Stacy received recognition. Her husband's best friend, Adam, came up to her with a drink in his hand. He inspected her, then chuckled.

"How are you liking this, slut?" he asked. His wife joined him, leaning on him. She had already had way too much to drink.

Stacy could only make a few dumb sounds in response.

"Good. Honey, would you like to do the honors?" Adam said. He looked over at his wife, Angie. Angie nodded excitedly.

"Yes! I'm so excited. Oh, my god," she beamed.

From the coffee table, she picked up the pair of scissors. The cold steel glistened in the well-lit room. She opened and closed it a few times, before sitting on her knees in front of Stacy. By now, a small crowd formed around Stacy. All eyes were on her. More and more people came as the blade came closer and closer to her.

Angie lined the scissor up between Stacy's legs, the stretchy fabric of her red dress nestled between the blades. She made the first snip, dragging the blade up her thighs, then her stomach. People watched intently as Stacy's body was slowly but surely revealed. The blades were cold against her skin as she came to her stomach. The fabric essentially sprung out of the way once it was freed of Stacy's plump breasts.

Once the large vertical cut was done, Angie cut it off of her shoulders, then pulled the fabric out from underneath her. She was in only her underwear now in front of some familiar and some strange faces. Her face glowed bright red, although the entire situation aroused her so greatly. Now, Stacy was only wearing a lacy set of bra and panties.

She wore a see-through bralette and her nipples were visible through the sheer fabric. Although so many eyes were on her she wasn't embarrassed about being nearly naked in front of all these people. The prying eyes from both the men and women made her feel sexy. She could see all of them mentally undressing her. She just couldn't wait for them to remove all the garments covering her skin.

Angie put the scissors down, when she sat back up, she started caressing Stacy's breasts. Through the fabric, she twisted Stacy's nipples.

"Take it off!" someone shouted from the back.

"Should I, baby?" Angie asked, looking up at her husband. With a smile on his face, he nodded at her.

Stacy snipped the bra off of her shoulders, then cut it in the center. It fell off to the side. Her clit throbbed when her bare breasts were on show for all to see. She couldn't wait anymore, she wanted someone to touch her. She wanted her release.

Next, her panties were pulled down. Angie stared down in delight at the wet spot in her panties.

"Look, everyone. The whore is wet," one of her old male friends said. They'd fucked once when she was about seventeen years old. She was surprised to see him here today. She grunted and moaned through the gag, begging for someone to touch her.

From a box to her left, her husband pulled out a pair of nipple clamps that were attached to a chain. He put them on both of her nipples, then stepped back and sat on the sofa in front of her. He watched as people played with her.

They tugged on the chain, pulling and twisting, bringing Stacy great pleasure. The added pressure of the clamps on her nipples as well as the pain brought her great pleasure. She let out a moan each time they were tugged at. They stimulated her sensitive nipples and once they were pulled off and the blood rushed back to them, she felt an intense pleasure wash over her once more.

A man she didn't recognize, one with dark raven hair, picked up a wand vibrator. He pressed a few buttons, testing out which one he'd prefer, before settling on the highest setting. He forced her legs closed, then shoved the vibrating toy between her legs. The vibrations brought her to climax almost instantly. All the teasing and the anticipation for the night had made her so excited that she couldn't hold on much longer to her next climax. Her knees were tied together so that she couldn't pull away to get relief from the intense stimulation between her legs.

While this happened, people wrote various derogatory remarks across her body.

Whore.
Slut.
Cum dumpster.

Sex doll.

Plaything.

She giggled when one of them wrote 'BIMBO' in big letters across her chest. By now, the chair she sat on was soaked from all the orgasms she had had.

Some men stroked their cocks through their pants as they watched her.

Other women had less shame about it and slipped their hands under their panties.

She was in pure, utter bliss.

It all became a blur at one point, her mind jumbled from all the pleasure she had felt. She didn't even notice when the restraints were cut from her knees and ankles, her legs forced wide open. A man with slicked back, blonde hair and strong, toned arms pulled her down so her ass was on the edge of the seat. He crouched down between her legs, putting each one over his shoulders. He buried his face in the wet sloppy mess that was her pussy.

The blonde man lapped up her juices, his tongue swirling around her soft lips. His tongue went as far as it could go inside of her and it felt incredible. His tongue fucked her for a while until he was satisfied, then he flicked his tongue against her clit. She dug the heels of her ankles into his back, hoping to get some relief for her uncontrollable shaking.

She arched her back as she came yet again.

The man stepped aside to let someone else have a turn. A short, curvy woman, picked up a long, girthy toy. She weighed it up in her hands before looking at Stacy with a sly smile. Stacy shook her head. She'd tried that toy before, and she could hardly fit an inch of it inside of her.

"You have no choice do you, whore?" the sultry woman said.

Stacy nodded. She really didn't have a choice in the matter.

Stacy put her feet up on the edge of the chair. The woman slicked the toy up with some lube, before rubbing it up against her lips. Slowly, she pushed the tip of the thick toy inside of her. There was a slight pain, but she adjusted to its size as soon its eight-inch length was inside of her. Slowly, the woman pulled it out of her, twisting and twirling it along the way. She looked up at Stacy to read her facial expression to make sure she was okay.

Stacy nodded at her and the woman smiled.

She fucked Stacy with the toy, slowly but surely increasing the pace of it.

What felt like hours went by, as people took turns having their way with her. They tested various toys on her, pushing her limits. Not once, though, did she want it to stop. She wanted all of it. Every inch of every toy, every vibration that came her way. She wanted it all and more. Although, she was missing something.

Not once, had anyone put their cocks inside of her. No one fucked her. No one *truly* had their way with her. To have her fantasy fulfilled, she needed people to fuck her. Every time she came, she starred her husband straight in the eye. She could tell that he was hard, and she wondered if he was uncomfortable at all, being hard for such a long time without release.

Her husband gave her a nod, before standing up and making his way over to Stacy. Her husband unbuckled the tight gag around her head. Slowly, he pulled it out of her mouth, a long strand of spit following behind. Her mouth felt almost numb from the gag being stuck in her mouth for so long. She moved her jaw left to right, hoping to get some relief.

He put his mouth to her ear.

"Are you ready, my baby?" he whispered.

"Yes," she whispered.

He made his way over to her, grabbing her chin firmly and forcing her to look him in the eye. He demanded a more respectful answer.

"Yes, I am ready, Master," she said proud and strong.

"Good slut," he said.

He stood before the crowd.

"Hello, everyone. I hope everyone has been having fun so far. Now, though, it's time for the real fun. Are you ready?" he said loudly.

In unison, everyone in the room toasted with their drinks in the air. All of them let out great, excited cheers for what was to come. The bounds around her wrists were released, giving her a sense of relief from the pressure. Although her gag was out now, she didn't say a thing. She wasn't allowed to speak yet.

She stood up. Instinctually, she covered her breasts with one hand and her crotch with the other. Her breasts spilled out from underneath her hand. Her legs weak and shaky as her husband led her over to The Fuck Bench.

Roughly, he shoved her down onto it. Diligently, she settled her knees on the padded rests that spread her thighs apart. He buckled both of her legs in, one around each calf and one around each ankle.

She settled her elbows on the padded armrests. Her lower arms laid flat. Again, they were tied down with two restraints. She tugged on them with her arms and legs, making sure that she was secure. They didn't budge.

Her face was shoved down into a hole in the bench, forcing her to stare down at the floor. He wrapped the strap around the back of her neck. She wouldn't be able to see who, or what they would be doing to her. Her ass was straight in the air, on display for the entire room to see. She smiled down at the floor. Finally, she would have what she wanted.

People demeaned her, throwing insults at her and spitting at her. They called her a filthy slut, making her feel an intense tingle between her legs. She loved being humiliated, especially in front of a crowd. She worked in such a high intensity field, having to be so serious and professional at all times. She had to take care of her business image at all costs, lest she lose her reputation.

This was why she loved being treated like utter filth – it provided relief to her. Due to all the hustle and bustle of life and the high intensity of it, she liked to be treated this way. It made her feel less stressed and most of all, most satisfied.

Abruptly, a whip cracked against her big ass. It didn't stop as the person doing it swung against her, lifting their arm left and right as they struck her. She didn't groan out in pain, though, she moaned in delight. Squealed in ecstasy. Even when the rubber paddle hit her already red flesh, she loved it. As much as it hurt, it just added on to her pleasure.

The lashings stopped, and suddenly, she felt a cock slapping against her pussy. She was still as sopping wet as before. The slick skin of his cock rubbed against her with ease. Her ass was grabbed firmly, helping him guide himself inside of her. She wasn't sure exactly how big he was, but he was definitely girthy and filled her right up. He slipped in and out of her soft, wet cunt. He took his time with her body, relishing in every aspect of it.

She loved that she didn't even know who was fucking her right now. He pulled out of her, finishing himself off on her ass. The hot, sloppy liquid messed all over her backside. She giggled in delight. He didn't last very long or fuck her very hard to reach climax but she loved that. It made her feel sexy, desirable. One of the highest compliments a man could give in the bedroom was ejaculating so quickly because he enjoyed her body so intensely.

Man after man had his way with her, spraying his hot liquid all over her. It dripped down her curvy body, falling down onto the floor. Even the women had their own fun with her, prying and prodding at her body with their fingers, even using various toys on her. The women were more skillful at rubbing their clits – they knew exactly how to pleasure her. That was something she especially enjoyed about being with a woman. Despite this, there was nothing quite like cock. Not even big dildos could compare to Stacy's love for cock.

She had forgotten how many people had fucked her. Each and every encounter blurred into the other. She couldn't look at the clock anymore to tell the time, so she had no idea how long it had been.

Despite being so used and abused, she couldn't get enough of it even if she tried. She couldn't think about anything else but cock and cum. She was truly consumed by her carnal desire.

A warm cloth wiped away the excess ejaculate on her body.

Familiar hands touched her thighs. She knew who it was instantly as he shoved his cock inside of her. She could tell by the length and girth, the slight curve of his cock to the left. Her husband was behind her. She relished in the relief of knowing it was him. As fun as the night was, she wanted her husband to fuck her too.

He slid himself in and out of her while the crowd watched. He didn't fuck her hard at all. Cold steel touched the delicate skin of her asshole – daring to breach inside of her. The lubricated, metal butt plug was plunged inside of her. She let out a shriek of delight. She felt so full now, having a cock inside of her pussy and a plug inside of her ass. His cock hardened up inside of her even more than before.

He was rock hard.

He took his time with her, experiencing her fully. He put a Hitachi wand into a slot in the contraption she was strapped to and secured it into place. As soon as the vibe was turned on, her walls tightened around his cock immediately, almost so much that it made it difficult to fuck her. He took this as a sign to fuck her even harder. Her husband pumped in and out of her doggedly. He stopped suddenly, before pulling out, then shoving back in the butt plug a few times. Stacy moaned out loud. She had no shame at this point. She moaned loudly without fear of sounding weird or lame. All throughout, she hadn't forgotten that people's eyes were on her.

Moans from various men and women came from the sofas. People had started fucking because they couldn't take the arousal without release anymore. Her moans mixed in with the others as he fucked her ass with the butt plug, loosening up her hole.

When he was satisfied, he tossed it aside.

She gasped when she felt the slick head of his cock rub against her asshole. He didn't wait to shove it inside of her, though. He didn't care to take it slow now. He wanted to fuck her ass and he wanted to fuck it now.

She could count every single inch of his cock sliding in and out of her. For the first time tonight, this was too much to handle. With the vibe on her clit and the people watching her and her husband fucking her ass so intensely, she couldn't feel her limbs anymore. She didn't tell him to stop, even though it was too much because she was in two worlds divided.

It was too much.

But she couldn't let it stop.

She wanted him to come inside of her. He was the only person in the world that was allowed to do it – because she was *his*.

Stacy's husband smacked her ass a few times, making it jiggle. She felt no more of that familiar pain that came with anal. Only pleasure. She came three times already by the time he was close. She could tell by his increasing pace and loud grunts – that was the only time he moaned that loud during sex: when he was near climax.

His pace slowed and he thrust into her hard.

His hot come filled her ass up. When he pulled out, it leaked out of her ass, flowing down her lips and dripping onto the floor.

Stacy was happier than she had ever been.

The room got quieter and quieter as her husband rounded everyone out.

"Alright, everyone, it's time to go. My beautiful wife needs some rest. I hope you enjoyed the show. We'll inform you when she is ready to do this again," he said.

Some disappointed groans came from the crowd, but they left anyway.

Angie came over to her.

"Hey, honey. I hope I wasn't too rough on ya. Brunch on Sunday as usual, alright?" Angie said.

Stacy couldn't reply. She couldn't speak or make a sound. She had lost her voice from all the moaning she had done through the night. Angie grabbed Stacy's hand and squeezed; Stacy squeezed back. She seemed to understand and walked off. A few minutes went by as her husband sent everyone off on their way. He cleaned up the mess their guests had made, making sure everything was spotless before unstrapping his wife.

She was glad her husband anally fucking her was the last event of the night. She couldn't feel her legs anymore. Now that she wasn't receiving any stimulation and no one was fucking her, she realized how fragile and sore she felt. She was raw. Her ass stung from all the spankings. Her pussy lips were swollen from all the friction. She was covered in permanent marker and her red lipstick was practically smudged all over her face.

She felt a sense of relief wash over her when all her restraints were untied. He had a silk gown in hand already and wrapped it around her. They walked off together to their massive en-suite bathroom. He sat her down on the edge of their large, hot tub style bathtub. He turned the tap on and started filling it up with water and bubbles.

He removed her gown as well as his own clothes, then hopped in with her. She sat in between his legs with her back to him. Since the bathtub was so big, it allowed for him to lay back with her in his arms. They laid together in the hot water for a while, before he began scrubbing her back, washing her hair and then her face. He gently scrubbed away at the hurtful words on her skin. Luckily, they disappeared with ease.

She was quiet, but not because she was upset. She loved that about him: he didn't care to fill up silence with meaningless small talk. He was okay with things being quiet when they needed to be. He nurtured and cared for her. He held her tight against her body.

When their fingers and toes became too wrinkly, they got out of the bath. He wrapped a towel around her. She felt better after the warm bath – it soothed all her raw and aching bits.

"I laid out some pajamas for you, baby," he said, "They're on the bed."

She pulled on the pajamas. It was her favorite pair. Pink, fluffy and decorated with cute little sheep. They got into bed and she sighed happily when she was under the sheets, in the love of her life's arms.

The first real words she uttered in hours were: "That was incredible, honey. Thank you so much."

No Means Yes

The shots were flowing, and Aubrey was having a good time. It was difficult to keep up with friends in her late twenties, considering that everyone had work and their own lives to take care of. So, they made a promise to one another that they would meet up at least once a month to have some drinks and catch up on how life was going. Aubrey was in charge of fetching drinks from the bar this evening, so she got her friend's orders and made her way to the bar. They had their backs to her and were distracted by each other's conversation.

"Hey, can I have four shots of tequila and four beers please," she asked. It had been a good night, she needed this night with her friends. Life had been particularly difficult as of late and she needed the down time. Life was demanding and it was good to let go of that sometimes and just pretend that everything was okay.

The bartender did his thing and started preparing her drinks, handing them to her, one after the other. Suddenly, she felt the presence of someone that was standing a little too close to her for comfort. A hand groped her ass and squeezed hard. She spun around to see who it was, and she slapped the hand away.

"Don't touch me!" she said loud and firm.

The man undressed her with his eyes before looking up at her face. His hand moved up to touch her breast. Unlike before, she didn't respond in anger. She just froze in place, unable to move. Her muscle and bone petrified her in place. He touched her breast, squeezing hard, so hard it hurt. All she could do was shake her head at him. Words wouldn't escape her lips and she couldn't scream.

The man looked down at her body, his hand slowly running down her waist. The bartender finally stepped in when the man was just about to slip his hand under her dress and fondle with her panties. Aubrey felt violated and she couldn't do anything about it. She felt pathetic for having frozen up and needing someone else to stop this from happening.

"Is everything okay over here, ma'am?" the young bartender said.

Aubrey shook her head again.

"Is he giving you problems?" he interrogated.

"I don't know who this man is," Aubrey finally said.

"Come on, baby. I'm just having a little fun. It's harmless," he said. He was handsome, with a sexy five o'clock shadow, so his actions didn't remotely suit his looks. She would have expected to be groped by a greasy old man, not a handsome man around her own age.

"Sir, you're making her uncomfortable. It would be best for you to leave before things get too messy," the bartender said.

"Come on, can you blame me? Look at what she's wearing," he said. He gestured to her little black dress that was short enough to reveal all if she bent over.

"Sir, I won't say it again. Leave, now. I won't be serving you tonight," the bartender said.

"Fuck, fine. I'll leave. I was just having a little fun, I wasn't trying to start any fights," the man said. He took his broody eyes and dark hair and left the bar.

"Sorry about that, I – I don't know what to do in those situations," Aubrey said. She smiled at the bartender that saved her.

"There's no reason to say sorry. That wasn't your fault at all. These drinks are on me. We try and keep the creeps out of here, but you know how it is," he said. The tall, young man proffered the drinks over to her.

"I can't do that, please, I really don't mind. Let me pay," Aubrey insisted.

"No, ma'am. It's the least I can do for your troubles," he said.

Aubrey huffed and took the drinks to the table. Her friends welcomed her with bright smiles as she put all the drinks down.

"What took you so long, Brie? Everything all right?" the red haired friend, Callista, asked.

"Oh, nothing. Just got held up at the bar," Aubrey lied.

"Well, drink up, ladies," the blonde-haired friend said. They all raised their tequilas into the air in toast and downed them quickly. Aubrey stifled a cough – she would never get used to the taste of tequila. It was just dreadful, and she didn't understand how people *liked* tequila.

They spoke of everything and nothing until their drinks were almost done. Their careers, their family, reminiscing on the past. It was a surprise they were all still friends after all this time. Aubrey had been friends with this group of girls since they were all in high school. They were coming up to ten years of friendship.

"So... I know that you don't like talking about this stuff, but you can't hold it in forever," Callista said, "How is it going with that guy, Aubrey? What's his name, Nicholas?"

"Oh, yeah. His name's Nick," Aubrey tucked a curl behind her ear, "It's going good, I guess. I don't really know what to say." Aubrey wasn't much of a fan of sharing her personal life details until she was sure things were right. It was a thing she lived by – she didn't share exciting news until she achieved said goal or aspiration. The same thing with relationships, she didn't like to share much about them until she was sure that the relationship would last.

"Come on, all of us shared our spicy lil details," Callista said, "Do you really not have any news at all?"

Aubrey rolled her eyes and huffed. "Fine. Okay, it's going well. We've only been together for a year but I kind of think he's the one, you know? Everything just feels right with him. He just gets me, you know?"

"Mmmm, well, a year's a long time when you consider our histories with dating," her friend pointed to all her other friends sitting around the table, "I mean, I feel like my longest relationship was four months."

"Heh, I suppose you're right. But yeah, he's good to me. But we're taking things slow and exploring each other as we go along," Aubrey said.

"Hmm, exploring each other? Is that a sex thing?" Callista asked.

"Shh, don't be obscene. I meant personality wise and stuff," Aubrey said. Her face flushed at the thought of their sexual escapades.

"Sure thing, sweetheart," Callista said with a sarcastic wink.

Aubrey felt dizzy and hot as she sipped on her last bit of beer for the night. She had had a good time with her friends at this dingy bar, but she knew it needed to come to an end soon. She had work in the morning so she couldn't let it go on for much longer. Usually, they'd stay until closing and be essentially kicked out of the pub, but she needed to be a responsible adult and get into bed early this evening. She paid her part of the tab and said goodbye to her friends. She was offered a lift, but decided to make the short walk home. She needed some fresh air. She hoped that by the time she reached her apartment building, she'd have sobered up at least a little bit.

She wasn't really much of a fan of drinking, she only really did it once a month when she saw her friends. She didn't really see the appeal in getting drunk at all. It would make her lose control of her inhibitions and she'd make a fool of herself. Besides, hangovers were terrible for her. They made her want to never drink again. Her least favorite, though, was when she got home after a long night of drinking and got into bed. That uncontrollable spinning feeling that washed over her made her feel sick. Aubrey loved her friends, but she hated that they couldn't have fun without having alcohol involved.

The night air was cold and crisp, just as she wanted it to be. Even through her thick coat, her nipples hardened against the soft fabric of her bra. The streets were quiet and empty, and she made the walk without looking up from the ground. She knew her neighborhood like the back of her hand because she liked taking walks so often. She could make the trip home with her eyes closed. She walked a few steps, the heels of her boots clicking with each step. She stopped in her tracks when she heard footsteps behind her. The footsteps stopped. She held her coat close to her chest, crossing her arms over it. Aubrey was sure she was just being paranoid, so she brushed it off.

She looked behind her and saw nothing but streetlamps and parked vehicles. There was no one in sight and no one behind her. Aubrey looked around one last time, just to be sure.

"Hello, is anyone there?" she said out loud.

There was no response. She hovered in place for a while before she turned back around to go home. She was only a few minutes away from the comfort of her bed. She increased the pace of her steps, but she still heard the same footsteps echoing her own. This time, though, she looked back, and saw a cloaked figure just a little bit behind her. She increased her pace into a run, hoping and praying that her feet didn't fail her. She tried to harness her skills learned in high school running competitions, steadying her breathing as she sprinted away.

She took a turn, hoping to throw off the person that was following her. She ran down the small alleyway, hoping to not slip. She had finally gained some hope in getting away from her potential attacker. She swore at herself for not taking the lift from her friend. She was terrified and scared for her life. She had already been harassed by a man earlier and now it was happening again. By sheer unluck, she had turned into a dead-end alleyway, forcing her to stop in her tracks. Her heart beat so heavy in her chest that she felt like she couldn't breathe, that she was going to die.

Just as she turned around to make a break for it back down the alleyway, she was met by a looming figure standing over her. Before she could react or defend herself, she was met with a white cloth to her mouth. An overwhelming sweet smell filled her nose. The tall, strong man wrapped himself behind her, keeping the cloth over her mouth. She tried pulling and tugging his hand away to no avail. She lost feeling in her arms and legs and couldn't fight back anymore. Everything went black from there, and she had a dreamless sleep. All was peaceful. All was black.

As she was knocked unconscious by chloroform, she collapsed in place. Her knees buckled and her eyes closed. The man caught her before she hit the ground. He put her over his shoulder and carried her quickly to his car which was nearby. He looked left and right, before walking into the street. Aubrey was half conscious by now, she could see what was going on, the ground appearing and disappearing before her eyes, but she couldn't move, and she couldn't speak. He opened the boot to his car, then gently placed her within. When the boot closed, she passed out.

***

Aubrey woke up when she hit her head on something. She woke up in a jolt, trying to look around and figure out where she was. She was in a confined space and instantly overwhelmed by claustrophobia. Her mind was still foggy, and she felt nauseous. She tried hitting at the walls surrounding her, but it didn't work. She was stuck.

Finally, she understood where she was and what was happening, when she hit her head again. She was in a moving vehicle and going over a bump had caused her to hit her head. She wanted to scream, but nothing came out. She tried with all her might, but she knew it was futile. No one would hear her and there was nothing she could do. She heard the brakes come to a screeching stop. The sound of footsteps came towards her, before the man spoke.

"If you scream, I'll fucking kill you," he said firmly, "When I open the trunk, you will stay silent. A single squeak and you're done. You got me?"

"Uh, huh," she whimpered.

"Say yes, I will stay silent," he barked.

"Yes, I will stay silent," she obeyed.

"Okay, I'm opening the trunk now. Be silent."

The trunk swung open. She tried to sit up and get out and try to make a run for it, but her muscles didn't obey. The masked man took a piece of cloth out of his pocket. He lifted her head and wrapped it around her head.

Applying pressure in a specific spot on her jaw, he forced her mouth open. He secured the cloth in her mouth, before tying it tightly on the back of her head. Aubrey dipped in and out of consciousness as he helped her out of the trunk, and picked her up once more. This time, he carried her like his bride. Like his very own prized possession. She wrapped her arms around his neck, and passed out again.

When she awoke, she was in a near dark room. Judging by the brick walls and the dampness of the air, she was in a basement. She felt like she had finally woken up properly by now and hoped that she had control of her limbs again. She scanned the room to try and see if there was a way out, but it was dimly lit, and her eyes hadn't adjusted yet. She tried to tug at her arms, but they were secured tightly behind her back. Her legs were spread and tied to the chair, too.

Aubrey had become accustomed to the heaviness of her beating heart by now, although it was the only thing she could hear. She tried making a noise and screaming at the top of her lungs, but the gag in her mouth stopped her. She let out a frustrated groan at how useless she felt. She would have loved to be able to be strong and kickass like the women in the movies, always with a plan B for every situation.

But Aubrey had nothing with no way out of her situation. She didn't have a knife. She couldn't move from the chair, it seemed to be secured to the floor. She was powerless. She hoped that this was all some sick, disgusting dream, and she was actually in her bed, comfortable, under her sheets.

She knew it wasn't a dream when the masked man made his way down the stairs, his heavy-booted steps echoing throughout the room. When he reached the bottom, he turned to face her. He had a black hoodie on, with matching black pants. When he stopped, he turned on a light, and it burned her eyes. It filled the room with a clinical, white light. She looked around, hoping to see something that would get her out of this, but the room was impeccable.

She was in the middle of the room, on a bolted down chair. On her left, there was a double bed with impeccable white sheets. In one corner, there was a bar fridge, and behind her, she saw a comfortable looking sofa.

The man made his way over to the bar fridge and fetched something from it. He walked over to her and crouched down.

"I'm going to remove the gag. You can scream if you want to, but no one will hear you. These walls are soundproof, and no one will ever hear you. Now, be a good girl and drink some water. The shit that knocked you out is going to give you a headache if you don't drink something," the man said. He spoke quickly, but with an assertive tone. Aubrey nodded at him enthusiastically. She stared at him, her eyes begging him to let her go.

He took his time untying her gag, as though to torture her even further. He chucked it into a laundry basket. He really had planned for everything, hadn't he?

As soon as the gag was free from her mouth, she finally mustered the strength to scream. She begged for help, she roared with determination to get out of her situation. The man watched her with his arms crossed over his chest, as though he was enjoying this. She screamed until her throat felt raw and she was out of breath.

Her kidnapper burst out laughing. A loud, thunderous, belly laugh filled the small room. It made her feel like utter shit. It was all for nothing. She thought that could have at least helped something, but he found it amusing! It made her angry, but her eyes filled with tears.

"Are you done?" he teased, "I told you no one can hear you. Scream until you lose your voice. No one's going to know and no one's going to care, bitch."

Aubrey nodded her head at him. "Yes."

He opened the bottle of water and brought it near her mouth. As much as she wanted to fight it, she lapped the entire bottle of water up like sweet honey. The cold liquid filled her up and made her realize how truly thirsty she was before.

He crushed the bottle until it was small and chucked it away.

"Thirsty, huh?" he asked.

Still crouched down in front of her, he looked up at her. He stroked her cheek, catching a stray tear along the way. Aubrey frowned at him as she saw his eyes admiring the rest of her body. She wasn't wearing the thick black coat anymore, only her small, tight black dress. The thought of the man touching her while she was knocked out made her feel sick.

The tips of his fingers trailed down from her cheek, to her neck, to her prominent collar bones. He touched the soft flesh near her cleavage, before moving to her shoulder. He slipped the strap off of each one of her shoulders. He was gentle and soft.

When he gripped the fabric that covered her breasts, she tried to pull away. The chair was firm and stable, and her protests were for nothing. Aubrey couldn't move away from him as he violently ripped down her dress, tearing it along the way. He let out a soft grunt when he saw her tits in her bra. She was wearing a matching set tonight, black and lace and leopard print.

She shouldn't have worn such nice lingerie tonight. It seemed to have sent him into a frenzy, and he ripped her bra down, revealing her small breasts.

"Fuck me," he said, "A lot smaller than I would have anticipated. So, you wear padded bras just to make your tits look bigger? That's pathetic."

Aubrey looked off to the side and didn't say anything. This angered him.

"I'm speaking to you, whore!" he demanded, "I asked you a question."

"No," she sobbed, "It's just comfortable. And it makes my boobs look good."

"Well, I don't see how the bra's practical."

"My tits aren't that small," she sobbed, "Why are you doing this? Please, just let me go. I haven't even seen your face and I don't know how I got here. If you just drop me off at my apartment and blindfold me, I won't be able to tell the cops anything to identify you."

He ignored her and started touching her breasts. His hands were cold to the touch and he squeezed her tits so hard it hurt. He took each nipple between his fingers and twisted and turned. She bit her lip and stifled a moan. Having smaller breasts meant that her nipples were more sensitive, so any kind of stimulation made her instantly wet. She hated her body's natural response to her nipples being played with, but she couldn't stop it. He crouched down between her legs, one hand playing with her breast.

He pulled the mask off of his face. His five o'clock shadow and broody eyes were familiar. She wanted to try and beg him to stop, but knowing who he was now, she knew he wouldn't. He wanted her and there was nothing she could do about it.

"There, you've seen my face. Now I can't let you go," he chuckled, "You're all mine now, bitch."

"Please stop," she begged, "There's no evidence of you doing anything. Even if I go to the cops, they wouldn't believe me because I don't have any bruises or anything and we haven't gone that far yet. Please, stop."

Again, he chuckled and ignored her pleas. He fondled one breast, and the other breast, he took into his mouth. His tongue flicked at and swirled around her nipple. Her breathing became heavier and heavier and she couldn't hold it in anymore. She let out a moan. A heat built up between her legs, along with an intense throbbing. He pinched and twisted her nipple while he sucked on the other. A wave of pleasure washed over her, sending an aching and pulsating feeling down into her crotch. As much as she wanted to fight it, her body felt great, so she couldn't. She was torn between wanting it to stop and wanting him to push her over the edge. The only thing she could use was her words to make it stop.

"S-stop," she whispered, "Please, stop. I'll d-do anything."

His blue eyes stared up at her and he smiled, the right side of his mouth tugging higher than the left.

"Beg harder, little one. And it's master, to you," he said.

"What?" she scoffed.

"You call me master when you refer to me or else you get punished."

"O-okay, Master," she whimpered, "Can you let me go now?"

"I'm going to untie you at some point but I'm not letting you go, stupid," he chuckled.

Aubrey whimpered as the pressure around her legs was relieved. He touched her leg, moving his hand up her inner thigh painfully slowly. She whimpered as the tips of his fingers touched up against her panties. He applied a bit of pressure before rubbing up and down her slit. He pulled his fingers away and showed them to her. His fingers glistened with her juices.

"You're wet," he scoffed, "You soaked my fingers, even through your panties. All I did was play with your nipples. Are you really that much of a sex starved slut that that made you feel so turned on?"

"I… My nipples are really sensitive, okay. I couldn't help it, I don't know what happened, I'm sorry."

He shook his head at her. "Tusk, tusk. I knew you were just a dumb slut. When's the last time you had sex?"

Aubrey paused for a moment to think of something to say. "I had sex on Wednesday," she paused for yet another moment, "I have a boyfriend and we have sex often."

"Hmm. So, I'm going to be taking the purity of a taken woman, then. Did you think that I'd be put off of this because you have a boyfriend?"

"No," she defended herself, "I was just being honest. We're here now, right? There's no way I can get out. Why should I lie to you?"

He grabbed her face, firmly holding her chin between his thumb and forefinger. It hurt and it dug into her skin, hurting her teeth through her gums. It was an unexpected move, and it made her whimper in fear.

"You're just trying to manipulate me into letting you go prematurely. A classic tactic you've probably seen in movies, right? Sweet talk your captor so they become weak and falter."

"No, no. I'm not doing that," she said, "I swear."

"Whatever you say, slut. You're mine now and I control you. You will do what I say, immediately. Do you understand that?"

"Yes, master."

He nodded at her before letting her go, throwing her face to the side. He removed his hoodie to reveal a white shirt tucked into his dark jeans. He rolled his sleeves up, all the while making eye contact with her. She caught glimpses of his ripped body. Through his shirt, she could see he was buff and looked after himself well. She was torn between being both disgusted by him and being attracted to him and it confused the hell out of her.

He stood in front of her and plunged his fingers inside of her without hesitation. She clenched her jaw as two of his fingers filled her up. She was especially tight today. She bit her lip to stifle her moans yet again, hoping to not make him think that she was enjoying this. What if he didn't like that? What if he beat her because he didn't like her enjoying it, since he could be getting kicks out of her for not being into what was happening?

He plunged his fingers deep into her pussy, applying pressure on her G-spot as he pulled his fingers out, repeating this action so many times that she felt she was close to orgasm. He looked into her brown eyes while he fingered her, and she didn't look away. She wasn't sure if it was out of fear or because she got lost in the deep pools of his irises.

He got especially invested in this act when she couldn't hold the moans in anymore, quickly moving his other hand over to rub her clit. She felt an intense pressure build up inside of her, and she screamed profanities out into the room. She was about to squirt. Clear liquid sprayed all over as she reached orgasm. Her head became foggy and she couldn't breathe.

That was the best orgasm of her life.

He pulled away from her, wiping his soaked hand on the back of his jeans. She sat there in a pool of her own juices, feeling defeated yet sexually satisfied. This man had won. She had come and that meant that she liked it.

He admired her for a moment. She was a mess. Bra tugged down to her waist, her tight dress pulled up there too. Her legs spread, panties pulled to the side, the seat soaked to the brim. He bent over her and fiddled with the rope behind her. Suddenly, he pulled her down and she slipped off the chair, landing firmly on the ground, her hands still tied behind her back. It was even more uncomfortable now that her hands were raised up slightly behind her.

She looked up at the tall man standing merely a few inches away from her. Master unzipped his jeans and pulled his cock out through the zipper. She gasped when she saw how monstrous his girth was.

She stared at his long cock a moment and looked up at him again with a frown.

"Suck my cock, slut. You're a cum crazed whore, but I know you're obsessed with dick just as much," he teased, "Come on, show me your skills."

Aubrey whined a little and opened her mouth. He inched his cock forward and grazed it against her lips. As the head came closer to her mouth, she realized that she needed to open her mouth even wider, almost so wide that it would hurt her jaw. She put her tongue out and licked at the sensitive, smooth skin of the tip of his member. She wrapped her lips around it, before sliding his length inside of her mouth.

She looked up at him as she did this and was surprised to find that she was only halfway there by the time he nudged at the back of her throat. She had no gag reflex, though, so he pushed down through her throat with ease. He let out a satisfied grunt when her lips touched the base of his cock and he was all the way inside of her mouth.

His eyes were full of lust for her. A deep, carnal lust that terrified her. How could one man want her so much?

He laced his fingers through her soft hair. Both of his hands gripped her head.

Just as she was about to pull away and continue giving him a blowjob, he held her firmly in place. At first, she accepted it, but she soon realized what he was doing. His cock was all the way down her throat, but he wasn't letting her free and she couldn't breathe. She tried pulling her head back as she tried gasping for air, but his cock blocked her air passage. She felt dizzy and her face started going red when he finally released her. She hyperventilated until she could finally feel normal again. Tears streamed down her face, but she persisted and took him into her mouth again.

He stretched her mouth wide open with his big cock, but she eventually got used to it as she started enjoying it. She let out a soft moan each time his cock reached the back of her throat, adding more sensation to it with the vibration of her moans. She noticed him gripping her hair tighter and tighter. He thrust into her mouth more vigorously and each time he thrust, he let out a grunt. He was close...

Despite being used by this man, her cunt was throbbing for more. She couldn't wait for him to shoot his load down her throat, but he pulled away. She whimpered unhappily. He tucked his cock back in his pants and walked behind her. Her makeup was messed up. Her mascara was messed up, making black lines that ran down from her eyes to her cheeks. Her lipstick was smeared and messy and she looked like a cheap whore.

He untied her wrists. She stayed still, not pulling her arms in front of her for a while. She was hesitant and careful in her actions, hoping to not set him off in anger now that she wasn't giving him pleasure, it meant he wasn't preoccupied, and could be angered easily. When she eventually did, she rubbed at her joints to get some relief. Her pale skin was red from being bound for so long and she wondered if there would be marks left on her skin from it.

Aubrey still sat on the ground. Her Master gripped her hair again. This time, he wasn't gentle and pulled her hair, guiding her to the bed on the other side of the room. She kicked and screamed as her legs dragged on the ground. She tried to gain some footing but was being dragged too fast. He pulled her up and threw her down onto the bed.

It was a nice fantasy, when she was sucking him off. But fucking him was different... Was she ready for it? He was so big, and it would definitely hurt...

He got on top of her and pulled his cock out again. He was harder than ever before. She tried closing her legs to stop him, but it didn't help, he was already between her legs and she was pinned.

"Stop fighting it," he barked, "Just let it happen. Your hands are pinned, and your legs are spread. You're already so wet… You want it so bad, don't you, bitch?"

"No. Please, I don't want to do this anymore. Please," Aubrey cried. Tears streamed down her face, they were real tears and weren't fun and games anymore. She was seriously crying.

For a moment, his expression changed. He softened up and he looked at her with concern. His grip on her wrists eased and he almost let go. She looked him in the eye and gave him a reassuring nod.

He cleared his throat softly, and he went back into his cruel, demeaning attitude. He gripped her wrists so hard that his fingernails dug into her skin. With his knees, he forced her legs to open wider. She tried wriggling away, but she was fully pinned by his body weight. With her dainty wrists pinned down with one of his hands, he stroked the tip of his cock over her slit and up to her clit.

Her Master did this so many times that she couldn't take it anymore. All he needed to do was apply some pressure and push himself inside of her and she would get what she wanted. By now, the tip of his cock was slick with her wetness. She tried lifting her hips when he brought his member close to her hole and teased it, hoping that it would slip inside.

And it did.

She arched her back and her eyes rolled to the back of her head. There was nothing more pleasurable in the world than when he slipped it inside of her for the first time, especially considering his monstrous side. She giggled in sheer glee and ecstasy. Her master buried his face in her neck while he fucked her, kissing her at first, but nibbling her eventually. She wasn't sure if he was biting hard or not because she was so filled with euphoria and pleasure. He could have drawn blood and she wouldn't know because his cock felt so good inside of her.

She could feel every thrust and every twitch so precisely, every movement in and out of her. It was almost overwhelming for her, that she couldn't take the pleasure anymore. He was so into fucking her that he eventually let go of her wrists and he pulled his face up to hers. He dove his head down and kissed her, while he touched her breasts. She moaned into his mouth occasionally while she kissed him back.

She was lost in the moment and forgot about every single worry in the world.

All she knew and all she wanted was this moment with him.

She felt so full and so warm and every fiber of her being was tingling with pleasure. The weight of his body on top of hers and the sheer helplessness she had felt just moments before was her favorite feeling in the whole world.

"I want you to cum inside of me," she whispered in his ear.

Upon her final word, he gripped her wrists again and fucked her violently. Her small tits bounced up and down and their moans and grunts were in unison. His cock twitched and he squirted his load inside of her. She moaned one last time and finally felt herself come back down to earth again.

He rolled over onto his back and she snuggled up into his arms. Aubrey let out a satisfied sigh and closed her eyes, getting a little bit of rest after the busy night.

"That was pretty fucking amazing for your first time, Nick. I love you. Oh my god, I love you so much and thank you for doing this for me," she said with the biggest smile on her face.

"No, thank you. That was definitely an interesting experience," he chuckled nervously, "I wasn't sure if I'd be into it when you brought it up, you know, it's kind of weird to put myself into the headspace of a kidnapper."

"Yeah, I understand, honey," she stroked his cheek, "But you did well, and I am happy, okay? You don't have to worry, we both know this is just a fantasy."

"Of course. Of course. I just want you to know I didn't mean any of the stuff I said, it was just an in the moment thing and I would never actually say any of that stuff to you. I love you, Aubrey."

"I will say though, what a brilliant idea to just bring it up unexpectedly on girls' night. It was so sexy. It's been my kink since I can remember, and no one's actually been willing to do this for me. So thank you, I am finally satisfied. Also, bolting the chair to the ground was such a smart move. Gave me real psycho vibes."

"That's why I haven't let you in the basement for a few weeks," he said.

He kissed her on the forehead and cuddled her for a while. They headed upstairs for a snack before having a shower and heading to bed, falling asleep in each other's arms. Aubrey, for what seemed like the first time in her life, was fully satisfied.

Mother's Boyfriend

Nicky, a timorous girl, just turned eighteen at the start of the year. She was in the last year of high school and couldn't wait to have it over with and move the hell away from it all. She was an adult now and she was so tired of dealing with studying, teachers, and especially the people in her school. She just didn't relate to them and she couldn't stand it anymore. She was planning to go through the year keeping her head down and doing what she needed to do in order to get through it. At least she had that to focus on, since her personal life was difficult.

Her father wasn't in the picture and hadn't been for years. He was an alcoholic and went too far with his drinking, so she had to move in with her mother who wasn't much better. Her mother was a junkie and couldn't hold a job for long, not to mention find a committed relationship that wasn't toxic. Nicky over the years, had to deal with so many of her mother's boyfriends who were crazy and controlling. Because of that, they never really stayed in one place for very long.

She was going through another one of these big life changes. Over the weekend, her mother and her packed all their things to leave an abusive household. Nicky and her mother, Elizabeth, had a place ready for them to move into. They left when he wasn't home, and they didn't look back. Nicky compartmentalized her feelings on the situation- or at least tried to.

Things were bad with Elizabeth and her partner for at least the past six months and as usual, it was time for them to run away from a bad situation. How was Nicky supposed to react? It had happened so many times that if she let herself feel anything, it would just end up hurting her. Her mother was emotionally unavailable, and her father wasn't in the picture. How cruel was the world to shove both mommy issues and daddy issues onto her? She sighed as they were on the last legs of their trip to their new "home". Their entire lives had been packed into a single car.

"This is going to be really good for us, baby," Elizabeth said, "We'll be safe here. There's a lot of good people around here, and we're only forty minutes away from your school. Everything's going to be okay."

"I hope so, mom. I hope so. I'm so tired of never settling down," Nicky admitted.

"I'm sorry that I put you through this," her mother sniffled, "I didn't want to get you involved but you know how it goes. I mean, he chased me around with a gun."

"It's okay. Just… I'm going to be honest with you. You need to be more careful with who you pick as a partner."

"I know. I do know that, but actually implementing that is a little more difficult, you know? It's easy to say that I'll do better but humans are messed up beings and just do whatever even if they know they're not doing the right thing," Elizabeth said.

"Yeah," Nicky said.

It was a nice gesture for her mother to say sorry, but apologies weren't enough anymore. She wouldn't treat her mother badly, though. She wouldn't act out in anger, she promised herself that. Elizabeth was the only person she had left. Despite her drug problem and her bad taste in men, she was still her mother and she wanted the best for her. Maybe this new place really would be for the best.

They pulled up at the main gate of the smallholdings and it opened a few minutes later. Their new home was on a plot of land that had about four other small houses on it, far enough for privacy, but close enough for a sense of community.

Each of the little houses were cute cottage style places, painted in a baby blue hue. They pulled up to a cottage near the far back. It had a porch with two chairs stationed on it and a glass door.

"Alright, baby. Let's get unpacking," Elizabeth said.

They carried some boxes inside and Nicky admired the small cottage. The ceiling was high, with wooden support beams going across. The house was already furnished, with antique wooden furniture and a large sofa. The living room and kitchen were open plan, with two bedrooms that both had ensuite bathrooms. The kitchen was quite big and even had a little breakfast nook. For a last minute find, it really wasn't that bad.

When they made their way back to the car to fetch some more boxes, Nicky saw a man leaning against it. His face lit up when he saw both Elizabeth and Nicky. He was oddly familiar, but she wasn't sure where she knew him from exactly. Elizabeth went up to him and hugged him. She gave him a kiss on the cheek.

He was an older man, maybe thirty or so. His hair was dark, but it was starting to gray, giving him the classic salt and pepper look. He was cleanly shaven, and his features were clean-cut. His eyes were a pale blue. He wasn't an overly tall or buff man, but he looked good. He was a little on the leaner side, but his arms were still well toned. He dressed well, even though it was a Sunday and he probably wasn't going anywhere.

Nicky stood in place, awkwardly admiring the man who had just been kissed on the cheek by her mother. Nicky, deep down, felt an instant attraction to him and she didn't know why. She didn't know him, and he was so much older than her. The taboo nature of it sort of turned her on, though, and she wondered if he lived here too.

When she stepped closer, she remembered him. He had occasionally visited Elizabeth when Nicky was sixteen years old. Nicky felt something for him back then, but she didn't quite understand it. It was a strange connection with him, but she dismissed it as a stupid schoolgirl crush. He was kind and good to both Elizabeth and Nicky. He always offered help, but Elizabeth never accepted it until now.

"Nicky, this is Grayson," Elizabeth said, "Grayson, this is Nicky."

"Well, hello there. It's nice to finally meet you. I've heard a lot about you. I hope you enjoy your stay here. I know you'll come to find it quite charming," he said. He threw a wink in her direction and it melted her from the inside out.

Nicky reached her hand out and shook his, noticing how soft his hands were. His cologne was strong and musky, but it wasn't overpowering.

"Grayson is the owner of this plot of land and has graciously let us move in here on such short notice. He lives right there," Elizabeth said. She pointed to a slightly bigger cottage with more modern finishes right next to theirs.

"Oh, thank you for helping us," Nicky said. She felt her knees weaken and nearly buckle beneath her weight. Nicky tried to distract herself from her deviant thoughts by going to grab another box from the car. She knew it wasn't appropriate for her to be feeling the things she was feeling but he was just so damn sexy. Nicky wasn't really sure what her type was because she hadn't quite explored that side of herself yet. Because of her mother's bad luck with men, she kind of steered clear of boys in school, since she was scared she would make the same mistakes as her mother.

But Grayson, with his tattooed forearms and toned arms, Grayson really piqued her interest. She had never felt this way about *anyone* before. She had never looked at someone for the first time and wanted to fuck them so badly, let alone at all. For a long time, she was worried that there was something wrong with her because she never really had crushes on anyone growing up. Maybe she was just going crazy, though.

Grayson helped them carry the rest of their stuff inside. Him and Elizabeth chatted and laughed, but kept their distance. Nicky wasn't really that good with people and wasn't even sure how to broach the prospect of even speaking to him. She wasn't sure what she would say. She kept to herself and unpacked her things. Was this going to be one of her mother's new boyfriends? She hoped not…

Nicky finally exited her room after unpacking most of her stuff. She was hungry now and needed something to drink. Grayson was standing at the breakfast nook, drinking a beer. She stopped in her tracks and stared at him for a while. She didn't know how to deal with the uncontrollable throbbing in her crotch and as she came closer and closer to him, it intensified.

"Your mom's just out… buying some stuff so she asked if I could stay behind and watch you and help you with any unpacking," he said.

"Oh," Nicky breathed, "That's – that's fine."

"Look, Nicky," he looked from left to right before looking at Nicky in the eyes, "I've known your mother for over a decade. I met her before she had you, in fact. I understand that this might be a lot for you right now, so I want you to know that I am here if you need to talk."

"Thank you, Grayson. That's really nice of you, but I am okay, really," she said.

He glared at her a moment before proffering her a sip of his beer. "I know what happened with her last boyfriend and all the boyfriends before him. And your father is even worse. You don't have to bottle everything inside anymore. I convinced your mother to come here so both of you could have a safe place to just be. She means well, despite her fuck ups and I hope that she can get her shit together, for your sake."

She took a long, deep gulp of beer, nearly finishing half of it in one go. "Okay, you got me there. I just put my walls up, you know? I don't have anyone but my mother. Sometimes we can have open honesty between us, but that's only when she's not high on those chemicals. But she's high on those chemicals ninety percent of the time, and the other ten percent, she's coming down and she's hell to be around. It's just an endless cycle of her being a shell of a person and it kills me."

"I'm sorry to hear that, sweetheart. It's good you're here," Grayson said. Nicky took a step over to him and stood close enough to feel his body heat. "I'm sorry you've been dealt this hand in life. It sucks hearing this, but everything's going to be okay and I am here for you. I live right there, you just give me a shout. I'll be around all day most of the time. I work from home."

"Thank you for the offer, and thanks for listening to me. I hope my mom is okay soon, too. I'm kind of banking on it. I don't want to lose her to that stuff," Nicky said. By now, the beer bottle was already empty. She decided to change the subject, she was over the self-pitying conversation. "What do you do?"

"I do remote IT work. Mostly contract work, not really bound to any said company for long, but I prefer it that way. Don't like to be a rat keeping the wheel running for a company that's going to suck out my soul," all the while he spoke, he didn't break eye contact with her, "My second job, really, is well, this plot of land. Managing it, keeping it clean and safe and keeping the riff raff out."

"Wow. That's quite impressive. How did you get this piece of land? Did you inherit it or something?" she said. Her nerves from earlier had dissipated, something she wasn't used to. Usually, every time she spoke to any person that wasn't her mother, she'd be nervous and out of things to talk about within the first minute. With Grayson, though, it flowed like a waterfall and she didn't want it to end. He handed her another beer because he could tell she needed it.

"No, most people just assume that or don't even ask. I actually saved up over five years to buy this plot of land. Then another five to build all these little houses. Designed most of them myself, but got other people to build them, though. I'm not a jack of all trades," he chuckled. He nervously scratched the back of his neck.

His hand was firmly placed on the table. Without realizing, Nicky's hand was near his, and she brushed her pinky finger against his. When he didn't pull away from her touch, she didn't either. It came so naturally for her to move her fingers over his, and lace them between each other. She could tell he was holding his breath by his face going slightly red.

He moved his hand away to take a sip of beer. The tension in the air was heavy and thick and she could have sworn she could touch it and grab it and feel it in between her fingertips.

"So, do you have any plans for after school? You're on your last year now, right?" he asked. His voice was slightly shaky, and she couldn't help but smile at him for it.

"How do you know so much about me?" she teased, "Are you stalking me, or something?"

"I only know what your mother has told me…"

"I'm just busting your balls, silly. Yeah, I'm eighteen and in my last year of school. Honestly, I'm probably going to get some shitty part time job and have a sort of gap year before I get to college," she said.

"Why the gap year, hun?" he said. The more she spoke to him the more things about him she found attractive. His voice was deep. His smile was big. He had a small dimple on the right side of his cheek when he smiled extra wide.

"I've been struggling and fighting and running my entire schooling career, thanks to mom. I've had to study and do homework and exams and everything all the while being in toxic situations. I'm...I'm tired. Also, how stupid is it that I have to do twelve years of schooling only to immediately go into a possible four to seven years, depending on what I choose," Nicky said. She'd never opened up to anyone like this before. It was unfamiliar to her, but it tasted so sweet.

"I completely agree, Nicky. It's twelve years of school, up to an additional seven or more, and then it's off to job hunting. You find a job, you start in the low ranks, and over decades, you build yourself up in that field, but you'll never get that promotion that you are truly hoping for. While you do that, you have to hope that you find love and settle down and have a lovely marriage with kids. You have no time for yourself anymore and you become a shell of a person," he said. His deeply insightful words caught her off guard but attracted her too.

"Oh, man. I feel ya on that one. It's honestly so depressing to me. School. Study. Work. Marriage. Kids. You know, the other reason I'm hesitant to start studying is because I don't actually know what I want to do with my life. How can I make such a major life choice at only eighteen, you know? What also scares me is that even if I get that new shiny degree, I'm not guaranteed a job in that field and it could all end up amounting to nothing and all be a waste of time."

"Yeah, I understand that. It's scary, that's for sure. But it's also exciting and you have so much to look forward to. You've already gotten through everything and came out strong, you can do the rest easily," he said. He smiled at her and she nearly fainted.

"Thank you for the words of encouragement, Gray," she said.

"Of course. Anything to help… You're a lovely young lady. I'm glad that we could meet again," he admitted.

"Me too," Nicky said softly, "I – I missed you."

They were interrupted by her mother loudly opening the front door and coming into the house. Grayson broke eye contact with Nicky for the first time in what felt like hours. Nicky quickly put the beer bottle down and went back to the fridge and pretended to be busy with something else. They hadn't even done anything inappropriate, but they separated from each other as if they had.

Their conversation was normal, but she felt that if her mother had listened in on it, it wouldn't have been good. Although she could sense a bit of tension between him and her, she wasn't sure if he felt the same or not. Maybe she was just going crazy. Maybe all the stress had gotten to her and she was grasping at something that didn't exist just because she needed a sense of comfort.

Elizabeth came into the house carrying a few grocery bags. Nicky looked at her face and knew instantly, that it wasn't just a shopping trip that she had gone out for. She had just bought and used drugs too.

Nicky kept quiet and prepared herself some food. She wasn't going to say anything. Each day that went by her and her mother were drifting apart, and she feared that if she said anything to her, it would further drive a wedge into their relationship.

Nicky went through the motions of life, got ready for school the next day, did homework and everything, while her mother went slightly off the rails. She did job hunting and within a month, somehow landed herself a job in marketing near their new home. More time went by and it seemed like Elizabeth had finally gotten a handle on herself. Nicky grew accustomed to their new environment, out of the city just enough for comfort.

Grayson hung around occasionally and had dinner with them. Elizabeth would flirt with him, and although he would reciprocate it, he would sneak glances at Nicky when her mother wasn't looking. The more and more time they spent together, the more she was attracted to him. He was an intelligent and most importantly kind man and she just wished that they could spend some time alone together to get to know each other better.

One day, she had gotten exactly what she wanted when her mother came to her.

"Hey, baby," Elizabeth said, "Can we talk for a minute?"

"Yeah, of course," Nicky said and put down what she was doing.

"Okay, so, since I've been working so hard at this new place, I've been kind of promoted, if you can call it that. They're going to be giving me my new office and everything and my position will no longer be part time," Elizabeth said. She smiled as she spoke with her hands.

"Wow! Mama, that's amazing!" Nicky said. She got up and hugged her mother, "That's so great. You've come such a long way and you're doing so well. I'm proud of you."

Nicky always felt that she had to be an adult for most of her teenage years. She would have to look after her parents because of their crippling addictions and make sure that they were fed and had enough sleep. She had to be responsible and manage the house. She had to make big decisions that neither her mother nor father could. For once, Nicky felt a sense of relief. Her mother had finally gotten her shit together. She wasn't using as much anymore. Although, some weekends she would snort a few lines, she wouldn't do it during the week. It was an improvement, nonetheless, and Nicky needed to be grateful for everything that came her way. Things were looking up for both of them.

"Thank you, baby. I couldn't have done it without your support," Elizabeth said, "Look, since my hours are going to be increasing from now on, I can't fetch you from school on time."

"Oh," Nicky said, "What are we going to do then? I don't want to sit around at school for hours and wait to be picked up."

"Of course. That's why I was thinking, would you mind if Grayson picked you up from school? Some mornings he will have to take you, too, when I'm especially busy and need to get to the office earlier. Would you be okay with that?"

"Uhm…" Nicky hesitated. She washed over with many confusing, conflicting feelings, "What time would you finish work?"

"I'll usually finish between six and seven but that's really late. If you're not comfortable with Grayson, I'll understand, since you don't know him that well. I can try to organize for a transport service to pick you up or something?" Elizabeth said.

"No, no. That won't be necessary. I'm sure it'll be fine. I guess it's time to get to know him. You've been friends with him for longer than I've been alive, I'm sure I can trust him, right?" Nicky said. She pretended to be hesitant to be alone with him, so her mother didn't suspect a thing. She knew that it was manipulative, but she didn't care. Grayson had been on her mind every single day since they arrived at the cottage for the first time.

"Great, baby! Thank you for understanding and working with me. I told you that we're going to be okay," Elizabeth said. She tucked a tuft of Nicky's hair behind her ear.

"You were right. Everything is going to be more than okay."

When her mother left, Nicky hugged her pillow and screamed into it with excitement. She was eager to spend more time with him and she couldn't wait for it. She was nervous, too. They hadn't been alone together before… What if she made a fool of herself? The next day, she got ready for school but put in extra effort to make herself look nice. She put on some expensive perfume that her mother had bought her years before. She put on her best dress that was still suitable for wearing at school. A white dress that was tight around the bust and flowed down freely from there. She went through the whole day anticipating his arrival.

At the end of the day, she heard the familiar rumbling of his muscle car. She walked up to his car, her heart racing out of her chest. He waved as she came near his car and she waved back. When she got in the car, he looked at her with a cute smile.

"You look nice today," he said, "What's the occasion?"

"Do you want my honest answer, or do you want the appropriate one, Gray?" she asked.

"Are you saying the honest answer is inappropriate? What about both?" he said. He gripped the steering wheel before bringing the engine to life. He pulled into the road and took a different route than she was used to.

"The honest answer isn't appropriate whatsoever, and if anyone else knew, they'd judge me," she played with the long hair of her ponytail as she spoke, "The appropriate answer is that I just dressed for myself today."

"But you didn't tell me the true answer, then," he said. He glanced over at her as they came to a stop. His eyes lingered on her body for far too long for her to think that he didn't feel the same way.

"I got dressed up for you, Gray."

He cleared his throat.

"Why?" he asked.

"Because. I just wanted to look nice for you, that's all," she said, "Where are we going, by the way?"

"took the long route home."

"Oh. Why is that now?" she said. She bit her lip. Being so close to him was making her feel hot and heavy.

"This is the first time we're alone together and I don't want it to end," he said.

Nicky fiddled with her hands nervously and stayed silent. She didn't know what to say to that. She had thought up so many fantasies with him and come up with so many conversations she could have with him, but she wasn't expecting him to say that so soon.

He looked over at her with concern in his eyes. "Look, I shouldn't have said that. I shouldn't speak to you like this. I shouldn't say these things to you. It's not right."

"Why is that, though? I'm eighteen, Gray. And I have been for nearly six months. I'm big now and I've been feeling something for you for a long time."

"Please, please don't say that. We can't do this, Nicky. We just can't. Let's not speak about this again, okay?"

"Okay," Nicky's heart sank. She had hoped this day would end differently.

They drove in silence. The quiet in the car with him nearly killed her. When he pulled up to their cottage, he looked over at her again.

"Look, I'm sorry if that hurt you, but you need to understand where I'm coming from, okay? Your mother and I have been friends for a long time. It wouldn't be right for me to act on my feelings. She's got feelings for me too, you know? It's put me into a very uncomfortable situation because I don't… I don't like her the same way I do you. How would she react if she found out how I felt? She'd fall off the rails again and I would be to blame for it," Grayson opened up.

"So, you do feel the same way, then? Why should you have to limit yourself because of her? Her feelings aren't your problem. Besides, my mother… she might be flirting with you because she wants to keep you around, you know? It might sound a little harsh, but excluding her bad taste in men, she has a penchant to use sex and attraction to get what she wants. Maybe she's just acting this way because you've helped us, and she doesn't know how else to thank you."

"Well, when you put it like that, it makes sense. I wouldn't put it past her. She's a strange woman. Thinking a little deeper, I can definitely see her doing that. You're right. I'm sorry, this is just all so much to process," Gray said.

"She won't ever know, if we don't tell her," Nicky said. They both looked ahead of them and not at each other as they spoke.

"Mmmm," he said.

His hands still tightly gripped the steering wheel, and she admired his arms. She noticed a small tattoo of a little mushroom on his arm. It looked older, as it had bled a little bit over time.

"What's that tattoo about?" She ran a finger over it, feeling the slight bulges of the fine ink lines in his flesh.

"Oh, wow. Had that since I was fifteen, actually," he said. He looked at her for the first time in an hour. "I was a dumb teenager, and I gave that to myself. Stick and poke, I think they call it these days."

"Why a mushroom?" she asked.

"Magic mushrooms were a big thing back in those days," he chuckled nervously, "I was just trying to pull the classic rebellious teenager move."

"That's really cute, actually," she said, "I like it. It's got history."

"You should go inside before I do anything I shouldn't do," he said. His jaw clenched and twitched.

Nicky looked at the time. It was only 4:00 p.m. and her mother wouldn't be home for a while.

"Well, I don't like being alone in that house. Would you at least have lunch with me?" Nicky pleaded.

"I…" he sighed, "Something makes it impossible for me to say no to you. You enchant me, Nicky."

"That's one of the best things I've ever heard anyone say to me," Nicky said, "Wow. Should we go inside then?"

He nodded and walked with her into the cottage. Nicky closed all the curtains of the cottage and went to the kitchen.

"I'll make lunch," he insisted, "I don't mind."

"If you insist."

He made lunch for them. He was quite the cook, and the food ended up being delicious. Nicky and Gray spoke of everything and nothing, except for their conversation in the car. It was as if it hadn't even happened at all. One thing led to another, and they sat on the sofa together and watched TV. He hadn't left immediately after lunch as he had initially planned to do.

They watched some bad drama television shows that were already on when they turned the TV on. She didn't pay attention to it at all as she sneaked him quick glances occasionally. Nicky wanted for him to be looking back at her each time she did, but he wasn't. He sat up pin straight and stared dead ahead, as though he were trying his best to ignore her.

She finally had enough and scooched closer to him. He cleared his throat when her thigh came close to his. Nicky took her eyes off of the television and put her full attention on him. They were finally alone together after all these months and it was about time she got what she wanted. He seemed hesitant, but she didn't care. He had confessed that he wanted her too, so she couldn't wait any longer. She just needed to take the first step because she knew he wasn't going to.

She first started with a touch of his knee. He froze in place as she ran her hand up his thigh, stopping just before his crotch. His jaw clenched again. She stopped herself from giggling. She carried on and touched his crotch, delicately running her fingers over his member. She could have sworn that he was already hard, or he was just so big…

She stroked his length through his pants. His chest rose and fell rapidly. She sat on her knees next to him and put her hand on his cheek. She pulled his face towards hers and touched his lips. They were soft and plump just like a rosebud. They exchanged deep gazes with one another. An intense throbbing in her crotch drove her to press her lips against his.

He didn't kiss back as she had anticipated. They didn't rub back against hers, so she stopped kissing him.

"What's wrong?" she asked.

"Nothing. I mean, we should stop. We shouldn't do this," he said.

He softly shoved her out of the way and stood up.

"But you want me," she said.

"Yes. That's exactly the problem, Nicky. I want you, Nicky. I think about you every fucking day, but I hate myself for it. It's wrong and I shouldn't be making you do this," he said. He rubbed his hands over his face and started walking off. Nicky followed him, but he stepped away from her. They went in sort of a loop, until his back was facing the sofa again.

"You shouldn't be so sure that it's wrong. We're both adults here, right?" she said.

"Yes. But it's different. It's the power dynamic between us that could be seen as wrong," he confessed, "I don't want this to go wrong because I didn't simply push you away and control myself."

"I'm the one that kissed you first. Just blame me for it all if anyone finds out. Just say I'm a nymphomaniac, okay?" she said. Nicky smiled at him and bit his lip.

"No, this is not happening, Nicky," Gray said.

Nicky shook her head. She could tell he wanted it by the way he looked at her. He was just holding himself back. She pressed against his chest with a flat hand, and gently shoved him backwards. He was dumbfounded as she pushed him backwards and he didn't react. She pushed him a few more times until he stumbled backwards onto the couch with a bounce.

Nicky swung a knee over him and got onto his lap. He blinked at her when she put her arms over his shoulders. She kissed his chin and down his jawline, to his neck. He let out a soft moan as his hands sauntered over to her ass. He rubbed her hips, then tugged at the dress until it fell down her chest. Nicky pulled away to show off her assets to him. His mouth hung open at her dainty bralette. Her nipples peaked through the thin, sheer fabric.

He ran his fingers over her breasts, albeit hesitantly. He touched her nipples, gently tickling them. Nicky let out a soft moan as he moved the fabric out of the way and took her nipple into her mouth, gently suckling on it. Nicky ground her crotch against his, the soft fabric of her panties rubbing against his hard, throbbing length.

All her dreams and fantasies of him were finally coming true and every touch and tug and nibble sent her over the edge. He treated her gently, as though she would break if he were too rough.

She couldn't take it anymore, she wanted him to be inside of her. She was already wet enough. She was ready for him, even if he was big. She wouldn't mind the pain because it would turn into pleasure.

Grayson was overcome with an insurmountable lust for her and his strong arms gripped her and flipped her over onto her back. She giggled when she made impact with the couch. Her panties were soaked, and Grayson noticed this when he fumbled with her crotch. He stroked her clit, seemingly expertly, as if they had already explored each other's body's a thousand times over and he knew exactly how to please her.

He fumbled his cock out of his pants. How big his fist was as he grabbed his cock surprised her. Would she even be able to fit him inside of her? She scooted downwards and spread her legs to allow for easier entry.

Just as he brought his cock close, he stopped in his tracks and looked at her with wide eyes.

"You're not a virgin, are you?" he asked.

"No, no, don't worry about that. I lost my virginity when I was like sixteen to some guy," Nicky admitted.

"Okay, good. Because if you were… I couldn't do that to you," Gray said.

"Shh, stop worrying so much. The concept of virginity is bullshit anyway. Don't let that keep you back," she swallowed, "Fuck me, Gray. I want you to fuck me."

He bent over her and whispered in her ear, "I've been waiting for this moment for a long time."

As he said his last word, he lined his cock up, and shoved it inside of her. At first, there was a sharp pain, but she was washed over with a wave of pleasure throughout all her body. He kissed her as he thrust in and out of her, their tongues dancing together in each other's mouths. Nicky could hardly breath from all the pleasure she was feeling. This was nothing like she had ever experienced before. No man had ever made her feel this way and it was turning out to be better than she expected.

He fiddled with her breasts. He was rougher now as he let his walls down and had his way with her. Nicky accidentally scratched his back in a pleasurable stupor, and it was likely to leave a mark. With each one of her moans and squeals of delight, he would increase intensity and thrust into her harder. He was big and he filled her up nicely, not so much that it would hurt, but enough for it to feel incredible. Nicky never wanted this to end.

She felt the familiar kind of thrusts that would signify that he was close. He grunted with each thrust while he looked deeply into her eyes.

She gasped when she realized what was about to happen. "Don't cum inside of me," she pleaded, "I'm not on birth control."

Out of place and out of character for him, he put her hand over her mouth and came inside of her anyway. Her eyes rolled to the back of her head as he gave her a cream pie. Although she didn't want it just a few seconds ago, it felt incredible. No one had ever come inside of her before. Gray was the first person she had fucked without a condom and she understood why most men and boys didn't want to wear one. It didn't feel remotely the same. There was *nothing* like skin on skin. Grayson was different compared to the boys she'd slept with. They never focused on her clit and they just jack hammered her until they came, without worrying about her pleasure.

Grayson also kissed her a lot, keeping a lot of eye contact, and just his overall thrusting even felt better. It was a level of intimacy that she had never experienced before with anyone else. She started laughing out of sheer ecstasy. She didn't know what to do with herself since she was so overwhelmed with how incredible the experience was.

She heard the sound of a car door closing and keys rattling near the porch. Grayson scrambled to get off of her and get his cock back in his pants, and Nicky ran off to her bedroom and closed the door. She slid down with her back against the door and pulled her dress up so that she wasn't naked anymore.

She heard her mother and Grayson chatting, but it was muffled so she didn't understand what they were saying. Nicky bit her lip as she thought back to what she was doing with Grayson just a few seconds ago. She memorized every single movement, kiss, and thrust. She cemented it in her memory so that she may have it forever.

She didn't wash up after. She let his cum leak out of her and into her panties. It was oddly erotic to be walking around the house knowing that that was their own little secret. He was gone by the time she came out of her room. It was probably for the best, since Nicky wasn't sure she could hide her lustful glances at him for much longer, considering that they had finally done the deed.

She hoped that he wouldn't leave and forget about her like all the other boys she fucked had done. Maybe he just left because he was just as overwhelmed as she was. Nicky realized then why she was so attracted to him. He was everything she had ever needed. He was strong and funny and witty. He enriched her soul and gave her a better reason to get up in the morning. He pushed her to do better and do well in life. He acknowledged her. He paid attention to her. Although she understood how messed up it was, she couldn't help but feel that he filled the black hole inside of her, caused by her lack of a fatherly figure.

She had trouble sleeping that night because she couldn't stop thinking about how they ended things. They didn't even have a moment to catch their breaths and talk about what had happened. She felt turned on every time she thought about it. It was so wrong, so hedonistic and terrible, sneaking around and fucking each other. Them almost getting caught made it even sexier. However, a niggling feeling was eating at her. He had come inside of her despite her protests. This was the first time she had ever been unsafe with sex, a lesson she learned from her own mother. Her mother had her at the young age of nineteen, and she never wanted to make that mistake. First thing, as soon as she could, she needed to speak to Grayson about taking her to get Plan B. The prospect of pregnancy terrified her. Especially since this was the first time they had fucked, and they weren't safe about it.

The next morning, her mother had already left the house by the time she had had a shower and finished getting ready for school. She left a note with some money for lunch. It read:

Hey, baby.

Long, busy day ahead of me. Grayson will take you to school today.
Will see you later. Have a good day!

Love, Mom.

Nicky bit her lip. They could be alone again so soon after yesterday. How much could fate be more on their side? It was still nice and early so she could speak to him about it. They met up in his car and it was silent at first before he turned the car keys. He got out of the car and came back with a gift bag and handed it to her without looking at her.

"What's this, Gray?" Nicky asked.

"A gift. To say sorry," he uttered.

She peaked inside of it. An item of clothing, chocolates, and what looked like jewelry were inside. "I can't accept this. You don't have to give me gifts."

"I feel bad, Nicky. I didn't know what else to do," Grayson said. He looked over at her with deep concern in her eyes.

"Wait, are you saying you regret what happened yesterday?" Her chest hurt at the idea of him regretting what they had done.

"No, no! That's not what I meant. Look, I'm not good at these things, but I am trying to make up for the whole… you know, cream pie thing. I feel bad for doing it even though you said I shouldn't. It wasn't right of me," he said. He frowned at her.

"Yeah, I actually wanted to talk to you about that. We're going to have to go grab some Plan B on the way today. I can't get pregnant, Grayson," Nicky said, "That's why I wanted you to pull out."

"Okay," he sighed deeply and ran his hand over his mouth, "About that. I wanted to explain that to you. I can't have kids anymore. I had a vasectomy after I had my first kid. Something washed over me when you begged me not to, something I've never felt before, in a way. I'm never that rough and I never take things just because I want them with no regard for anyone else. I knew that you were concerned about pregnancy, so I think, since I know that's not possible… I just did it anyway."

"Are you serious?" Nicky exclaimed with a smile, "Oh my god, that's so sexy."

"What?" He was taken aback.

"You just take what you want. I wasn't upset because of that, I was just upset because I was worried about pregnancy. Now that that's out of the way… I feel I'm more attracted to you because there are no consequences to fucking you but having a good time."

Nicky looked from left to right to make sure no one on the plot of land was outside of their cottages yet. It was still early, so she decided to take the gamble. Nicky got onto his lap. He knew what was coming, so he instantly unzipped his pants and pulled out his hard cock.

"Already so hard?" she whispered in his ear, "I haven't even done anything sexy yet."

"Well, Nicky, you're a temptress whether you try to be or not," he said back, "I can't control myself around you." He planted kisses along her neck as he spoke.

Nicky giggled out of sheer joy that she finally got what she wanted. She had Grayson now and she wouldn't let go of him.

Masked Mystery

Desiree was a single woman in her early twenties, and she was wild. She lived a sheltered life growing up and as soon as she had the freedom to be her own person, she went off the rails. Not in the sense of ruining her life and career though, but sexually. As soon as she had enough money for her own apartment, she decided it was time for her to start exploring herself in every way possible. She tried one-night stands and random hookups, but it didn't quite satiate her needs enough. There was something missing and she wasn't satisfied enough.

Desiree wanted to give it a chance, since hookup culture was a mainstream thing, and it was so accessible with the technology of the day. But she just couldn't do it anymore. She lacked connection with these people, so the sex wasn't that great. As well as that, the men she went out with were selfish lovers. They fucked her until they were satisfied. One of them, a particularly scrawny man that she decided to give a chance, didn't even touch her body. He didn't play with her breasts or her butt, he just fucked her and that was that. This was her breaking point, pushing her to find other options to find satisfaction.

There were only so many orgasms she could have on her own with the help of a toy before she became sick of it. Cumming was good and all, but nothing like actually having hot, passionate sex. Desiree couldn't remember the last time she had a good lay. She searched online for options, because all her friends lived in a different state and she didn't necessarily want to talk about something like this over text.

Desiree sat down with a bottle of wine for the task ahead of her. Her inhibitions needed to be a little lower for her to go through with this. She worded what she was looking for a million times over, not getting any results. Until she landed on an erotic forum that had a section for the city she lived in. She scrolled through it, forgetting why she was even there in the first place. She went through countless posts consisting of escorts advertising their services and men looking for quick hookups. She grunted in frustration after hours of searching, until she came upon a post titled Masked Mysteries.

Her interest piqued and she clicked on the post. An image of a woman wearing red lipstick and wearing a full face, black leather mask appeared before her. Masked Mysteries was a club just a few miles away from her. They had a vetting process in which to do a background check on people before allowing them in the club, which was promising to her. In the past, the idea of erotic clubs scared her since she'd be surrounded by sex crazed strangers that she didn't know a thing about. This provided her with a sense of comfort. Not only that, but they also required a recent STD test to be sent through before being allowed in the club.

She let out a curious, 'Mmmm,' and read on. It was a no judgment zone, set up inside an old mansion. It had many different sections for the different types of sexual interests that people could have. From BDSM, to orgies, to couples. The possibilities were endless. There was only one catch, though: everyone had to wear masks that concealed their identities at all times.

She sent her application through without even thinking it through and made a point to make an appointment with her doctor to get the test done. She went to the appointment the next morning and got it all done.

She was in a daze, as if she were possessed by someone else. She always wanted to be sexually explorative, but she never knew she would go to such great lengths for it. She thought sex clubs were only for old and bored people, but from the few snapshots she saw from inside the club, people from all walks of life went there. She waited two weeks for her results from the doctor and kept the papers safe for when her application was accepted to the club. She knew it would be, since she had a squeaky-clean record and had never gotten into any trouble in her life.

***

The day she finally received word back from the club, she practically dropped everything she was doing to take a look at it. Maybe this would be her final sexual awakening. Maybe Masked Mysteries would be good for her.

Dearest Desiree,

We received your application, and we are happy to announce that you have been accepted to be part of Masked Mysteries!

Please remember to send through your STD test results, just attach it back to this email. Find attached some rules and extra info!

We would like to formally invite you to an upcoming event this Saturday. Wear whatever makes you comfortable, but please, bring your mask. You will not be allowed past the gates without it on.

Privacy is of the utmost importance.

Kind regards,
Owner of Masked Mysteries,
Mark

Desiree read through everything and it was common sense things, like don't be violent and a long page on consent. She agreed to it all, scanned her test papers and sent it all through. She couldn't contain her excitement. She just needed to find an outfit as well as a mask to wear. By sheer luck, she had a mask from an old Halloween costume from years back. A matte black rubber mask that covered most of the face, barring the mouth. It had small kitten ears on it, and she was happy to be able to wear it again. It was really cute and sexy, but no other occasion had called for it again.

Saturday came and she slept in a little longer that day. Apparently, the parties could go on for long, so long that they could run on into the early hours of the morning, so she needed the extra sleep. She was used to waking up at 6:00 a.m. every single day.

Desiree dug out an old outfit that she was too scared to wear out. A high waisted, form fitting skirt with a deep slit on the side. She wore a black lace bodysuit underneath, with a plunging neckline that would act as her top. She pulled the skirt over it and found a long red trench coat to hide the outfit underneath. She paired the outfit with a chunky platform pump. She hoped that she would be comfortable as soon as she arrived at the mansion, but she knew she wouldn't be okay with walking out of her apartment block and to her car without covering up.

Lastly, she slipped the mask into her handbag and made the journey to the mansion. It was atop a hill and stood tall and proud. It was dark that night, with no moon in sight, but the property was well lit up and it was inviting.

Before she stopped at the main gate, she put on the mask. She took a deep breath and prepared herself for the night. She would be open to trying new things even if they scared her a little, that was all part of the fun, right? The unknown, the taboo, the unspoken dirty deeds.

"You got this, Desiree," she said to herself, "You are going to have a fun night. Don't let anything hold you back."

She entered the main gates and was met with a valet, who took her car to a parking space. She stood in awe and looked up at the monstrous building before her. It was the biggest home she would have ever entered in her life, which was comical to her, since it would be because of a kink club.

She was greeted at the door by both a man and a woman, wearing a tuxedo and a sexy version of one, respectively. They held trays that had glasses of champagne on them and she grabbed one. The main entrance was extravagant with its crystal chandelier and marble floors. She felt as though she had stepped into a completely different life.

"May I take your coat, miss?" a short but buff man asked. All the servants of the mansion wore leather masks with tall bunny ears protruding from them.

"Oh, right, yes, please," she said, "Thank you." Desiree took the coat off and felt slightly naked in the outfit she was wearing. No one stared at her or judged her though, so that was a good start.

"Of course! Just go straight through. There, you will find the buffet and the lounging area nearby, where people like to hang out and talk and find a match, to take to the respective wing of their choice. The back garden is also for those who want a little peace and quiet. I'm sure you've done all your research, but I like to remind people that all the respective wings of the house have different themes. Near the buffet area, there are a couple pamphlets out on display, just in case you get lost and need some guidance," he said.

"Why, thank you again. That's very helpful. I should be okay. Right? Yeah. I'm going to be just fine," she said aloud, but meant to say to herself.

"First timer, huh?" he asked.

"Heh, yeah. Am I really *that* easy to read?" she chuckled.

"You're nervous. Don't be. This is a safe place. If anyone falls into trouble, a helping hand is nearby. Don't you worry at all about that. Just remember: let go, let loose, and have fun!"

"That's exactly what I needed to hear." She smiled at him.

She walked down to the buffet section, which was fully stocked with all the kinds of food she could dream of. It was glorious. At first, she perused the food and snacked on a few things to help calm her nerves. When she felt she was ready, she headed into the lounging area. She felt she was hugely overdressed for the occasion when she saw what the other women were wearing.

There were various sofas scattered around the large living room, most of them filled with people. Most of the women hardly wore anything at all. Some were just in lingerie, while others wore nipple stickers and a pair of panties. Bodies of all shapes and sizes were scattered all over. Big breasts, small breasts, curvy girls and skinny girls. Desiree felt represented in this room and eased up a little. She knew then, that no one would judge her.

She found a semi empty sofa. It was the only one that wasn't overcrowded. She sat down on the sofa. A tall, burly man sat on the couch next to her. His mask was black with small slits for eyes, not enough to obstruct vision, since it sat firmly against his face. Desiree observed the happenings in the room for a while, watching in awe at people kissing and touching each other's bodies. Some left the room, usually the woman leading the man away. It turned her on to see so many people lusting for each other in one room. It made the air almost thick, she could feel everyone else's accumulated arousal in the air she breathed.

"You're awfully quiet," the man next to her said suddenly. It nearly made her jump out of her skin since she was so zoned out.

"Excuse me?" Desiree said.

"I said, you're awfully quiet. You haven't been mingling with anyone here like everyone else is," he said.

"Neither have you, mister. Just like me, you've been sitting here for about an hour and haven't paid any mind to anyone. I noticed a few girls came up to you, but you turned them away. I'd have fucked the hell out of at least three of them, they were drop dead gorgeous. Model material. Is it your first day?" she said. The added anonymity that the mask gave her, made her feel more confident than usual.

"Yes. I'm guessing it's yours too, then?" he asked.

"Correct," she said. She turned her body to face his. He wore suit pants and a white, clean dress shirt. She noticed a tattoo on his forearm, two ravens intertwined together in fine delicate black ink.

"Well, then. You're just as nervous as I am," he said.

"I'm not nervous. Pfft. You're the nervous one. I'm just taking my time and scoping the place out before, I uh," she paused, "Take some sexy hunk to one of the million bedrooms in this house."

"You haven't looked at any man tonight in a way that makes me think you want to fuck them," he said. His honesty made her smile.

"And you haven't looked at any other women in that way. Wait, does that mean you've just been watching me all this time?" she crossed her arms over her chest, "Ugh. Yeah, I just, honestly, none of them are my type."

"What's your type then, kitten?" he said. She throbbed when he called her kitten, something she never realized she'd find attractive.

"How tall are you?" she asked.

"What's that got to do with my question?" he said. He squinted his green eyes at her.

"Just answer my question, mister."

"Six foot three. And a half," he chuckled and scratched the back of his head. Was he getting flustered? She sensed a tension with him that she had never felt with a man before. Was he into her? Because she definitely was into him. The more she spoke to him, the more she wondered how sexy he looked underneath all those clothes.

"My type's six foot three – *and a half* men with green eyes and black hair. Especially when they have a tattoo of Huginn and Muninn on their arm, and they come to a kink party, wearing fancy clothes, a contrast to the rest of the men here, who quite frankly, are slobbish and not what I expected from the pictures."

He coughed into his hand, seemingly from choking on his spit from inhaling so fast. "Y-you… You want *me*?"

"Yes, mister. I've been watching you, too, and I want you. There's just something about you that draws me to you. Hell, we're both new here, so might as well have a little fun together, right? We can't sit on this sofa all night and watch in jealousy at all the other people having fun without us."

She bit her lip in anticipation for his response.

"Honestly, I'm just surprised you know what the tattoo is. Everyone always asks me why I have two black birds on my arm, and it annoys the shit out of me," he said.

"I went through a really embarrassing Norse mythology phase in high school. I don't really want to get too into it, but it was *bad*," she said.

He looked around the room to see that there were only a few people left. She nodded at him in approval and stood up, extending a hand for him to grab. He took her hand in his and she led him to one of the vanilla rooms. This was the first time they would be together, so she didn't want to shove him straight into say, the BDSM section of the mansion. She definitely didn't want to take him to the orgy wing. Desiree wanted him all to herself. She wasn't going to share him with *anybody*.

They found a vacant room and closed the door behind them. It was a little quieter in here now that the door was closed since the passionate moans and grunts were muted. She had her back to the door and looked at him as he looked around the room. He turned to face her, and he seemed hesitant at first.

"You look great, kitten. I really, really like the style. That's also something that draws me to you. That baby doll goth look makes me rock hard," he said. She played with her raven locks and smiled at me.

"I like everything about you," she said, "Will you kiss me, mister?"

He took a few steps forward. All hesitancy left the room as he rammed his body against hers. She could feel the hardness in his pants pressing against her crotch. His lips slammed against hers, shocking her with its intensity at first before she eased into it. He clasped her hips and ran his fingers underneath the fabric of her skirt. His fingertips touching her bare skin sent shivers down her spine in the best possible way.

He nibbled on her lip gently, before firmly grabbing her ass and lifting her up. She wrapped her legs around his waist and her arms around his neck. Now, her entire body was pressed against his and there was no more space between them. It was an intense closeness, coupled with the incredible kiss they shared, that made her forget about everything else in the world but this moment. Desiree purred in pleasure, like a kitten getting its first drop of milk. She *almost* felt that just by kissing him, she could reach orgasm. It was confusing and exhilarating for her and she never wanted it to end.

His tongue brushed against her bottom lip, daring her to open her mouth. She did, and parted her lips and ran her tongue along his. They swirled and danced together in each other's mouths, only stopping to breathe when they absolutely had to. The experience was most visceral and nearly ethereal to her. How could kissing a man possibly feel so fucking good?

He secured his grasp on her ass, and walked back a step, before turning over and gently laying her on the ground. He didn't spare a second to have his way with her, he didn't care to go to the bed or to the love seat on the side of the room. He wanted her now and she knew it. It intensified it all for her, for a man that she didn't know, to be lusting after her so much that he couldn't wait any more. The man she had only met a few hours before, made her feel more wanted and sexier than any of her past lovers combined. He kissed her some more, his lips gliding against hers.

Desiree took on the arduous task of unbuttoning his white shirt and once the final button was down, she tugged it down his shoulders. He sat up and helped her remove it, their kiss breaking for the first time in what felt like an eternity. Desiree panted heavily from the lack of breathing, but stopped breathing completely to admire his physique. His muscles were defined and clean cut, but not over the top in the body builder sense. He was perfect in every way.

He kissed her collarbones and down her breasts, down to her stomach and then her hips. When he reached her thighs, subsequently the hemline of her skirt, he lifted it up and out of the way. Her bodysuit clung tightly to her crotch and she felt release when he unbuttoned it. The fabric sprung out of the way upon release from said pressure and she let out a little giggle. He groaned when he admired the neatly trimmed bush on her pubic bone, her labia cleanly shaven.

"You have such a pretty pussy," he said. He left little kisses along her crotch.

He waited not a second before diving into her wanting cunt, licking her clit while he reached his hands up above him and explored her body. He touched her waist, her breasts, everything he could fondle while he pleasured her with his mouth.

Desiree moaned and shook and convulsed under his touch. She bit her lip hard before grabbing a fistful of his hair and guided his tongue up and down her slit. He sucked on her clit softly, a sensation she'd never felt before. She didn't even know this man's name and he hadn't even penetrated her yet, but this was the best lay of her life. Desiree's body twitched and convulsed, her back arched and she let out a loud squeaky moan.

"I'm gonna cum," she screamed, "Oh my god, I'm going to cum."

He chuckled and carried on what he was doing, until she had her release. There was a smile on his face as he emerged from her crotch and brought his face closer to hers. Desiree wanted to kiss him. She wanted to kiss him not only because she was attracted to him, but also because he was the first man that had ever made the effort to make her come with oral sex. She was overwhelmed with excitement that there really, truly were good sexual partners out there in the world. One just needed to look…

He kissed her and tasted herself in his mouth.

Against his lips, she whispered: "Will you fuck me, mister?"

"Can I do whatever I want with you, kitten?" he asked.

She nodded enthusiastically, anticipating what he would do. "Yes."

"If you don't like something, tell me. Don't stay silent," he said.

"Yes, Mister."

He kissed her neck again, making butterflies flutter in her stomach. While he did that, he took his cock out of his pants. He placed it firmly against her slit and slid himself inside of her. She gasped at the intensity of pleasure that this stranger's cock gave her. He spread her legs and pulled one up to his chest, her foot daintily dangling in the air. Desiree giggled when he planted kisses on her feet. The masked man was slow and careful while he thrust in and out of her. His slow, steady moves made it feel even better, since she could feel every inch of him inside of her.

Desiree let go of every worry and care in the world and succumbed to the pleasure. She didn't worry to hinder her moans. She was loud and sexy and didn't give a fuck if anyone heard her. She touched his body and he touched hers while they fucked each other. They were so in sync, so in unison that it almost scared her.

He pinned her down and the weight of his body on top of hers was sudden. He kissed her again while he fucked her. It was sloppy and messy and spitty, but neither of them cared. They allowed each other to be free and enjoy themselves.

He trailed his hand up her chest after he pulled away from the kiss, and lightly wrapped his hand around her throat. He nodded at her to ask for approval, and she nodded back. Desiree loved choking, when done right, of course.

He lightly squeezed, adding more and more pressure to get a feel for what she was comfortable with. He looked at her occasionally to gauge where she was at, but she enjoyed it, so he didn't stop. His thrusts grew more and more intense to her while he choked her. Her eyes rolled to the back of her head as her body convulsed again. With a free hand, he rubbed her clit with his thumb and grunted when she arched her back and reached climax.

She lost all feeling in her legs as they shivered uncontrollably. He noticed this, and flipped her over onto her stomach. Satisfied with her satisfaction, he was ready to have his every which way with her. She tried to get on her hands and knees, but he stopped her with a gentle hand shoving her back down flat against the ground. He pushed her legs together and hovered over her.

He licked his hand and rubbed the wet spot against the tip of his cock. Desiree sighed happily when he entered her, but was surprised when he pulled out of her.

Again, with just the tip, he entered her, then pulled out. Over and over. It nearly drove Desiree over the edge. One of the best feelings in the world was when a cock first entered her, and he was doing it *over and over* again. She let out a soft whimper, although it felt great, he was teasing her, and she couldn't take it anymore.

Suddenly, he shoved his entire length inside of her. This position felt great to her, it was oddly different to any other position she had felt before. It felt really, really good. He planted little kisses all over her back as he pumped in and out of her. Desiree felt incredibly tight and overwhelmed by his size, but she pushed through. The intensity and shocking intimacy of it all made her want to do this forever.

This masked stranger, whose name she didn't even know, who's full face she hadn't even seen, was the best lover she had ever had so far.

He bent over her and she twisted her face to his. They kissed again with eyes closed. He fucked Desiree a little more roughly now, and she loved it just as much as when he was gentle with her. He pulled away quickly, and pulled his cock out of her. He shot cum all over her ass and up her back, some getting in her hair. She turned her head to see the mess he had made and giggled.

"What a big fucking load," she said.

The man struggled to catch his breath, and put a finger up, letting her know that he needed a moment before he could speak. Desiree laid back down and rolled over when he got off of her. They both laid with their backs to the ground, staring up at the ceiling. Their chests took a while to get steady.

He touched the tips of her fingers and she didn't pull away, so he laced his fingers in hers. Still holding his hand, she turned to face him.

"That was incredible," she whispered, "That was the best experience I've had in my life and I don't even know your name."

He chuckled and turned to her. He smiled at her. "Well, that's flattering but I'm sure that's not so true."

"No, I'm being serious, Mister. I've never cum so hard in my life. You're...you're really good. Usually, I don't do this with complete strangers, I at least have a date with them first before I fuck them."

"Today's full of firsts, huh? Yeah. I have never done this before. We just click, I guess. It wasn't my fault it was so good, it was because of our chemistry."

"I'm happy you feel the same way, Mister. Uhm, I don't know how to go about this now. Do we go our separate ways, or? What now?" she asked.

"I have no damn clue, Kitten. Just lay with me," he said. She rested her head on his chest and listened to his heartbeat.

After a while, they prepared to go their separate ways. Before they did, they embraced and shared one last kiss.

"Okay, you don't have to say yes to this if you're not comfortable. Can we do this next week? And the week after? And forever?"

"That sounds good to me, Kitten. Next week. Same time."

The six foot three and a half man came the next week. It was a surprise to her, since she was sort of scared that she would never see him again. She still didn't have his name, nor did she know anything about him. If he never came back, she would never be able to find him again. They had just as much fun as the first night they met. Every week for three months, they saw each other and spent time together until the early hours of the morning. He was strong yet sweet, taking what he wanted but also treating her lovingly and complimenting her body.

Seeing the Masked Mystery every weekend was the only thing she looked forward to anymore. She was addicted to him as a person and addicted to his cock. Her want for the intimacy and passion she felt when she was with him was insatiable. She wouldn't *ever* get enough of him.

One weekend though, she was invited to a family get together. Her aunt, who lived just out of town, was throwing a get together for her daughter's birthday. Desiree was disappointed to see that it fell on a Saturday. She couldn't say no to her aunt. They had been incredibly close to one another since she was a child since Desiree's mother wasn't around much.

Desiree didn't even have his cellphone number so she didn't know how to let him know that she wouldn't be able to make it. It stressed her out to think that maybe another woman would potentially seduce him. She felt territorial over him and wouldn't want him to touch anyone else. She sent an email to the club and decided to ask them to give him a note from her when he arrived at the club, explaining why she couldn't make it.

Desiree got ready for the party. She would arrive a little earlier to help her aunt set up for the party. There would be a lot of people there, so her aunt, Ellen, needed her to help her. Besides, it would be nice to spend time with her again and socialize for the first time in a while. Desiree had been burying her head in her work during the week as well as being fully invested in being with her new sex partner.

Desiree put on a long, flowing summer dress with a flower pattern on it. She put her hair up in a messy bun and put on minimal makeup. She drove to the party and helped her aunt set up. They took tables out from the garage and got some tablecloths and decorations. She helped Ellen ice the birthday cake and set out various condiments for the barbecue. Lastly, they put out some drinks in a cooler. After two hours of set up, they were finished. Desiree greeted people when they arrived, her other aunts and uncles and some cousins.

They fired up the barbecue in the meantime, so everyone could eat as soon as possible. Her cousin, whose birthday it was, hadn't arrived yet. She said that they would be there soon, though. The cousin who was coming, Angelica, was turning thirty years old. Desiree wasn't that close to her, since she had left the house at eighteen and wasn't around much since she had a career of her own.

Desiree socialized and had an overall good time. Until her cousin arrived.

She was latched onto a tall man with dark hair. Desiree was busy filling up some of the snack bowls when she looked up and saw him. Her aunt called her over.

"Des, come 'ere!" Ellen said.

"Sure," she said. She walked over to Angelica and held her breath when she saw the man in front of her. She knew who he was straight away.

"Des, I know you're quite close with my mom, so I wanted to introduce you to my boyfriend, soon to be fiancé, I hope," Angelica giggled.

Desiree's mouth was filled with a sour taste and she felt the veins beating in her forehead.

"Yes, Des, this is Gabriel. Gabriel, this is Desiree," Ellen said.

Desiree meekly put her hand out to shake his. He had gone pale and looked just as sick as she felt. His eyes were wide and so were hers. He shook her hand firmly.

"Nice to meet you, *Gabriel,*" she said through gritted teeth.

He had a girlfriend?

And that girlfriend was Angelica!? Desiree felt like she was going to pass out. Angelica was a blonde haired, blue eyed bombshell, who didn't really have that much of a brain. She wasn't smart. She wasn't witty. Her personality was dry, and she was painful to be around. Every time there was a family gathering, she had a different boyfriend. This was due to her being toxic and overall being a terrible person. She would use men for their money, since she was a materialistic person. She would poke and prod at their partners until they broke and left her. Or she would cheat on them to get an easy way out of the relationship. Or that's what Ellen had told her, anyway.

Desiree's heart beat like a drum in her chest. She couldn't fucking believe that he would do this. She felt like a dirty whore for being the woman he cheated on his *almost* fiancé with.

"Nice to meet you, Desiree," he emphasized her name just as she did his. She wasn't expecting this to be how they revealed their identities to one another. She had hoped that it would be a grand thing, and not a stupid mishap like this.

"Oh, he's just great! We've been dating for almost a year now and we couldn't be happier," Angelica looked up at Gabriel, waiting for agreement from him, "Right, honey?"

"Uh, yeah, of course. Of course, everything is amazing on this side!" he said. She could tell he was faking it. From the moment he stepped in front of her, he didn't take his eyes off of her, not even when he was speaking to Ellen or Angelica. She was so conflicted between anger and arousal. Every time she looked at this man or was near him, she wanted to jump on his dick and fuck him.

"Yeah, he's been doing really well at his job too, working super hard! He works weekends a lot these days, though, a lot of late nights! We make it work, though. Hopefully the hard work will pay off," Angelica said. She could tell that Gabriel was miserable in his relationship just by the look in his eye when Angelica gloated about them.

"Oh, that's great! Yeah, I get that. I work weekends a lot these days too. Saturdays are especially hard on me," Desiree said with a smirk.

"Yeah! Exactly. He's home so late on Saturdays, it's like he doesn't want to spend time with me!" Angelica said. It was exactly that kind of passive aggressive behavior in front of other people that ruined every one of Angelica's past relationships.

Gabriel nervously laughed. "Honey, don't say that. I'm working hard for you. Besides, that expensive perfume and those expensive handbags I went into debt for won't pay for themselves."

"Pfft," Angelica scoffed. She seemed to hate him standing up for himself and Desiree found it amusing as hell.

They exchanged some more *pleasantries* before going about the rest of the birthday celebration. The entire time they spoke to people, ate food, and drank, Desiree and Gabriel stared at one another from across the back yard.

Desiree was confused and had no idea how to go about this situation, which was rather sticky. Did she stay quiet or say something? Did she confront him or just go home? It made her even more angry that she saw his face now and it tore her apart. Despite her anger, she was more attracted to him now that she knew who he was and what he looked like.

The party became rather rowdy. Angelica was so self-obsessed that she gathered a crowd around her to boast about her travels and her glamorous life. How could one boast about things they didn't earn for themselves? She fucked men just so they could take her on vacation, especially the Machu Picchu trip she was bragging about right now, she fucked at least three old men to get there.

Desiree seethed as she watched Angelica kiss Gabriel's cheek. He mouthed a 'sorry' in Desiree's direction, but jealousy had overcome her. Desiree had stormed off to keep herself busy with something else, lest she went crazy.

She stormed off to the kitchen and looked through the walk-in grocery closet to find some more crisps for the table outside. The house was quiet, and no one was in the house. Everyone was in the backyard making a noise and busy with their own thing. Desiree wiped away a stray tear. She didn't want to cry, because it was just some meaningless sex, right? What was the point in being upset about him being in a relationship? They didn't know each other, nor did he know her. She should have expected it. She let out a sigh as she stared at the food in the pantry.

"Hey," he said. She jumped in place and held her heart.

"Jesus Christ," Desiree said, "Don't sneak up on me like that."

"Look, please just let me explain myself."

"No. You don't have to. It's fine, I'm not going to judge you. But I'm done. I won't be going to that club again so don't expect me there. I was excited to spend time with you, but I can't do this knowing that you're in a relationship."

"Desiree," he rubbed his hands over his face, "Wow, it's nice saying your name. It suits you by the way. In any case, I don't know if you know anything about Angelica but she's the devil. I've been thinking about leaving her for over six months. That's why I went to Masked Mysteries, Desiree. Because I thought, if I fucked someone else, that would give me a definite reason to leave."

"That doesn't even make sense," Desiree scoffed.

"Let me finish, please. I've tried to end things with her, but she always manipulates me into staying. I'm stuck, Desiree. I don't love her, and she treats me like shit. I didn't mean for things to happen this way. I have been having a really good time with you, and I was going to leave her for you in the end. But I wanted to wait for after her birthday before I did it, okay? I was planning on doing it next weekend. I already have most of my shit packed up. She hasn't even noticed."

"This is too much, Gabriel. I don't know what to say…" Desiree whispered.

"I want you, Desiree. You're drop dead gorgeous and you're a good person. You're smart and you're witty and you're a dork and I love that."

"I…" she started but trailed off.

He approached her and she walked backwards with each step that he took towards her. Before she could utter the rest of her words, he had her pinned against a shelf in the pantry. He closed the door behind them. A string of light streamed through the door, slightly lighting up the small space they were in. She looked up at his green eyes and his chiseled face. His body heat emanated through her dress.

"I'm going to prove that I want you and only you," he purred. He kissed her neck while she fumbled with his pants. She unleashed his cock, and it was already hard. He caressed and squeezed her breasts as she stroked his cock with her delicate, dainty hands. His cock stood tall and proud. He lifted Desiree onto a low overhanging shelf, pushing various food boxes and bags out of the way. She bit her lip, so she didn't make any noise. Knowing that they could be caught at any moment made it all the more tantalizing.

She lined him up and he thrust inside of her. He put his hand over her mouth because he could tell that she was going to moan. She bit onto his hand to stop herself from making any noise. He fucked her roughly and could feel herself getting close from the friction against her pelvic bone. Desiree's eyes rolled to the back of her head, her hands scrambling to find something to grab onto. In the process, she knocked a few things over. As a result, she knocked over an open bag of flour. It landed on the ground and a plume of white smoke exploded into the small space. It messed all over their bodies and clothing.

They chuckled for a few seconds, but were so consumed by lust that they carried on fucking each other. Desiree knocked her head on a shelf behind her head but didn't care about the pain because the pleasure overshadowed it. He closed his eyes and his mouth hung open, he moved in to kiss her one last time before he climaxed inside of her.

With three more deep, hard thrusts, he came inside of her. His cock pulsed and twitched inside of her and she was filled with his hotness.

"Oh my god," Gabriel said, "You're such a temptress, Desiree."

"Well, my name *does* mean desire in French," she purred.

When they exited to the pantry, they looked at each other's clothes. They were covered in white from the bag of flour that spilled. They burst out laughing at one another, frantically trying to wipe it off. It didn't come off of their black clothing and would likely be suspicious if they walked back into the party in the backyard.

"What have we done? We can't go back looking like this," Desiree said.

"Christ. They'll know. Despite this," he gestured to his white stained clothes, "We've also been gone for so long that they'll know anyway."

"Let's get the hell outta here then."

"Are you serious?" he asked.

"Did you come in her car or yours?" Desiree asked.

"Hers," he said with a frown on his face.

"Well, come home with me. They won't even see us leaving," Desiree said.

She grabbed his hand and he nodded.

Desiree and Gabriel ran away together, not caring about the consequences of what was to come. They'd deal with the issues that would arise the next day. The rest of the night would be for them and just them.

For once, they didn't fuck when they were alone together. They went out for drinks and chatted. They got to know each other better and Desiree was happy that this was how things turned out.

Drug Me

He was her age, they had been friends since they were in high school and had been inseparable since. They had sex a few times in the past when they both went through a dry spell consecutively. They were good friends despite their occasional sexual relationships, because they had laid out some rules after the first time they fucked. They promised to not pursue a romantic relationship, out of fear that that would ruin the friendship they had with one another.

Emily sipped on her sangria. They were on one of their weekly "friend dates" at his house, where they caught up, watched movies and talked about their struggles. Hunter was a big support system for her, and she appreciated him as a person.

"Did you have a fun weekend, Em? Get up too much?" Hunter asked. He was a handsome man with blonde beach waves and blue eyes. He almost didn't look *real* to her, that's how attractive he was.

"Made a girl cum with two fingers and my tongue," Emily winked at him. She knew he liked hearing about her girl-on-girl experiences, so she made sure to tell him about it as soon as it happened, "Other than that, got drunk and cried a little."

"Were you drinking tequila again? Tequila always makes you cry. Every. Damn. Time," Hunter said. He threw a skewed, cute smile her way.

Emily rolled her eyes sarcastically, "Well, yeah. Fuck, sometimes I hate you for knowing every tiny detail about me."

"Shut up, you love the shit out of me," he winked.

She bit her lip. "I do," she paused to think of a witty comeback to ease the sexual tension in the room, "But you're like a brother to me."

"Eugh, Christ, Emily! You remember that I've fucked you before right? And in the ass, too? Don't ever say you see me like a brother, or else I'll have to throw up on you." He shook his head profusely.

"Shut up! It's just a joke. Fuck," Emily said.

"Speaking of which, how have the sexcapades been going lately?" he asked.

"Don't remind me. God, it's just so boring lately, Hunter. I'm doing shit most people can only fantasize about, but it's never enough," Emily said. She swiped away her bangs that hung into her eyes. Her red hair was soft and shiny, one of Hunter's favorite physical traits about her. Although kids used to make fun of her for it, she grew to love her ginger hair over time as she grew into an adult.

"What do you mean, Em?" Hunter asked. He took a swig of beer. "I've tried everything, but nothing has quite satiated my needs, ya know? I don't know what else to do."

"Have you *really* tried everything?" Hunter asked.

"I guess not."

Emily bit her lip, and thought of her past experiences as they watched a movie together.

Emily tried playing with strangers in public:

Emily went up to a man in public one day, a filthy little secret under her white summer dress. She had a pair of panties with an attached vibrator. A small toy penetrated her, while a separate piece stimulated her clit. It wasn't on unless a button was turned on, though. A small, matte black remote that had a dial to set intensity. She went up to a man that looked about ten years her senior.

"Hello, mister, are you interested in having a little fun?" she asked.

He looked at her, wide eyed before clearing his throat. "I don't have money for that kind of stuff, sorry."

"Oh, god. No! No, that's not what I was doing. I gave you the wrong impression there. Here, take this remote. Turn it on, see what happens," Emily said. She touched his shoulder and felt his muscles.

He took the small remote and felt it in his hand. Slowly, he turned the dial up until it was all the way up. Emily inhaled sharply at the sudden stimulation of her delicate bits. With the toys inside and out of her both vibrating, it was a little overwhelming. He eyed her up and down, and he smirked when he realized what was going on.

He turned it up and down over and over again, trying to fully understand what was happening. He noticed her tense up when he turned it on high, her chest getting flushed from the pressure. In public, he helped her reach orgasm, while they had a conversation about meaningless things to make it seem like nothing raunchy was happening there.

She stroked his cock over his pants, feeling his hardness, and giving him a sly smile. Emily took the remote from his hand, gave him a kiss on the cheek, and turned on her heels to walk away.

"Wait! Miss! Where are you going?" he pleaded.

"I'm done with you, big guy," she turned around to face him but continued walking backwards, "Thanks for the fun."

"Can I get your number, at least!? You can't leave me hanging like that. I've never had anything like this happen to me and I can't just let that go," the man said.

Emily giggled like a schoolgirl, covering her mouth, and ending it by blowing him a kiss.

This one was a little risky, and although it was fun, it still wasn't enough.

So, she tried dominating others:

She bought a full latex dominatrix outfit. She dominated a woman in her thirties once, which was quite the experience. Women were wonderful creatures and deserved to be worshiped, she realized after making the MILF have multiple orgasms. She'd never forget that one. As fun as it was, Emily wanted more. She enjoyed the sense of power over people, but she wanted more. She went to kink clubs and BDSM conventions.

She got fully invested in it. She dominated some of her lovers who were willing to give it a try. She especially loved dominating, bigger and taller men. It was interesting for her, a five-foot three woman with a small, yet curvy frame, to have full control over a "manly man" that drank beer and fixed cars.

It was fun, but it lasted a few months before she gave up on it.

Emily tried pegging men. She cuckolded men, women, and even the husbands of bisexual men. She had threesomes, foursomes and orgies. She dabbled in public sex. She even tried being dominated herself.

They were all great, yet still not good enough.

So, she would be off to try and chase down the next best thrilling thing to do.

Every time she tried something new, she crossed it out of her notebook, adding onto the failures. Emily had never felt any true orgasm in her whole life. She had come, of course, but she never experienced the satisfying release that other women had when experiencing climax. Every time she finished having fun with someone in a new and exciting way, a little voice in the back of her head would tell her: "Not good enough. Something's missing." The spark just wasn't *there*. She never felt fully satisfied, so now, at the age of twenty-seven, she wasn't sure if she would ever have what she wanted. She was just about ready to give up. She kept this to herself and it was her own personal struggle.

Emily looked over at him after the movie had ended and wondered if it was time to confess her problem to him. Would he even understand?

"Hunter," Emily said, "Can I talk to you?"

"What's up, firecrotch?" he winked.

She playfully smacked his shoulder for that jab. That was her nickname in high school. "This is serious, Hunter. Come on."

"Okay, okay. Fine, I will put my serious hat on." He put an invisible hat on his head and tipped it towards her. She rolled her eyes at him.

"I've never truly felt a full, satisfying climax in my life and I'm kind of stuck with that burden, because I just want to know what it feels like to be completely, truly happy with a sexual experience."

"So you're saying, Em, that all the times we fucked… you were never genuinely satisfied with it? Oof, that hurts," he said.

"No, no. I loved the times we got sexy together, I promise you that. Ugh, I didn't want to make you uncomfortable with this, but I think since we fucked each other before, it's a bit too much of a sensitive subject," Emily said. She nervously twiddled her thumbs as she spoke.

"Sorry. Sorry, Em. I didn't mean to make this about me. Please, speak freely. I'll listen this time," he said.

"Earlier, when I said I've tried everything, I mean it," she listed off the things she had done in the past. His eyes widened, sometimes he would respond with a gasp at especially fucked up or risky things she had partaken in.

"Holy fuck, Emily," Hunter said, "And you just didn't have a good time in the end? Even the foursome with three other girls?"

"Yup. Oh, boy, I can make everyone cum, sure. But I don't know how to explain it, it's like, I'm about to reach orgasm, I feel what it's almost like, like my muscles contracting and stuff, but it just never… goes all the way? I never get the toe curling, eye rolling, Big-O that all women talk about. It's like getting blue balled, I swear. I've spoken to doctors about it and there's nothing *actually* wrong with me," Emily confessed.

He put his hand on her shoulder and rubbed it with his thumb. "I'm so sorry, hun. I really didn't know."

"No, it's fine. I just needed to get it off my chest. There's nothing I can do about it, anyway, right? Might as well just come to accept it and become a catholic nun," Emily joked.

"Well, there is this one thing that you didn't list off. So, I might have an idea for you," Hunter said. He bit his lip and his eyes shifted around the room, as if sifting through his brain.

"At this point, I'll accept anything and everything," Emily said.

"No. Actually, it's not a good idea. Let's drop it," he said. He scratched his head and pursed his lips. He fidgeted with the couch pillow and stopped making eye contact with her.

"Why? How bad could it be?" Emily prodded.

"It just might be a little too fucked up for you and I don't know if you'd be into it. *I am* into it, so if I tell you and you judge me, I'm not sure if things between us would change," he admitted.

"You know I would never judge you. I have probably done much, much worse. We've been through it all, babe. Fuck, I was even there for you when you went through that embarrassing Lord of the Rings phase and it was all you talked about. I'm still here, babe. Tell me. Firstly, I don't want you to feel ashamed and secondly, I'm really, really curious now."

He let out a deep sigh and closed his eyes. "Okay, Emily. Just, hear me out and don't interrupt. I have this kink, right. I've had it for a long time, and I don't know where it came from. I don't necessarily *need* it to get off, I just derive great pleasure from it. I've spoken to ex-girlfriends about it in the past but most of them packed their shit the next day and never looked back when I tried talking about the prospect of trying it out."

"It's not...coprophilia, is it?" she contorted her face in disgust.

"Fuck no, that's disgusting," he said, "I don't know if there's a name for what I specifically like. I've done tons of research online, though, so I know that both men and women love playing into this fantasy and I'm not crazy. I know how to do it safely and I know what to do if anything goes wrong. Girls don't like it because of the risk it involves," he said.

"How bad could it be, Hunter?" she asked. She was concerned, now. What could he be into that would involve so many risks and require so much research?

"I have a fetish called Free Use," he said.

"That's not so bad, hun. Why were you so scared of telling me that? I've heard of it before, but I've never tried it because the opportunity never really came around for it. It's the kind where the guy fucks a girl while she doesn't really react or pay attention to him, right? I'd be into it if you want to," Emily said. She gave him an encouraging smile.

"No, I'm not done yet," he took a deep breath.

She motioned for him to go on.

"I have a kink specifically for drugging a girl and having my way with her," he looked away in shame, "And no, I would never do this to anyone without their consent. I guarantee you that, Emily. I'm not a rapist and you know I would never do something like that. I couldn't do it unless I had a definite yes from someone beforehand, with a lot of planning and preparation. I don't know why I like it, I only ever had one girl give it a shot, but we never really spoke again after a few months of dating."

"I believe you, Hunter. You don't have to justify yourself like that. I know you're not some creep," Emily said. She gave him a comforting squeeze of the hand. "Please, don't be ashamed of your interests."

"The girl I did it with just wanted to do it at the house which was kind of awkward while I waited for her to fall asleep so I could you know, fuck her," he said, "What I haven't tried, which is my ultimate fantasy, is drugging a girl at a bar or club and taking her home with me. If you're not comfortable with it starting out in public, we can figure something else out. Like have it be a house party or something. That's also part of the fantasy, having other people around first until I can be alone with you and have my way."

"Oh, my," Emily purred. She felt an intense heat all through her skin and body. It was taboo, sure, but it intrigued her. The idea was fun to play around with in her head. She pictured him fucking her while she was unconscious. Her limp body receiving pleasure without him even knowing it.

"You hate me now, don't you?" he said.

"No, Hunter. This sounds pretty amazing, if I'm honest. I'd be down for this," she said enthusiastically.

"Phew," he breathed a sigh of relief, "Good to know you don't think I'm a psychopath."

"Nah, not at all. The thought of it turns me on, actually. You know, I'm pretty turned on just thinking about it."

"I'm already rock-hard thinking about having my way with you, Emily," he said.

"There's only one condition, though. Since I might not be conscious for a lot of it, I want you to record it so I can look back at it later. Is that fair?" she said.

"Fuck yes! I have that really good camera just collecting dust. It'll be good to take it out and actually use it again. Okay, deal."

They discussed the ins and outs of it and laid out some rules and no-nos. He told her he would be careful, but he would have everything prepared in case anything went wrong. Emily wasn't worried, though, because she trusted him. He had told her that he couldn't do it with someone he didn't have a deep connection with, which she understood. It wouldn't be the same with a woman he'd only known for a few weeks or months.

Hunter and Emily went to a dingy pub out of town that no one would recognize them in. They arrived separately, a few minutes apart. Emily had thought about what they would do today, and she preferred to make a big spectacle of it. She wanted to turn it into a fantasy situation of them pretending to not know each other at first to make it extra fun. She got more and more into the fantasy when they spoke about it. Deep down, it sounded sexy to her, most importantly, it sounded exciting.

She wore an extra skimpy outfit for the night, a short wrap around skirt and a tight tank top, with some tall heels. As she entered the bar, she noticed nearly every man that was alone lay their eyes on her. They followed her all throughout the pub as she made her way to the bar and sat on the bar stool. Emily smiled down at herself. She loved the attention. She loved being looked at like a piece of meat.

It made Emily feel desired and sexy. Emily had a bit of a sexual awakening as soon as she turned twenty-one years old. She stopped wearing baggy clothing to hide her body. She went to the gym, not to lose weight, but to feel good *and* look good. Emily got her shit together and started looking after herself, so her confidence went through the roof. She wore whatever made her feel sexy and secure in herself. It just sucked that she didn't receive the sexual satisfaction she was anticipating.

She hoped that this would be it. That maybe, this was just the thing she needed.

Hunter arrived. He wore a white shirt and a black leather jacket, paired with blue jeans. He looked alluring. If he was really a stranger, she would have tried to get his number by now. They exchanged cheeky glances every now and then. When she finished her first warm, bitter bear, he called her over. He had two drinks in his hand, one for him and one for her.

She bit her lip and smiled at him. Emily sauntered over to him and sat on the stool right next to his. They sat facing each other, so their knees would touch. Emily moved a little closer, so that her knee was between his legs and she could touch his crotch subtly.

"What's a sexy girl like you doing in a place like this?" he asked, looking around the dimly lit room filled with middle aged men that smelled of cigarettes.

"I could ask you the same thing, big boy," she said. Emily batted her eyelashes at him.

"I guess I'm just here looking for a little fun, and I got really lucky finding you," he said. She was slightly tipsy by now and she was horny. Somehow, she was more attracted to him now than she had ever been. Perhaps it had something to do with the night ahead of them.

They ordered their third drink. When the bartender brought their third drink, he looked at her.

"Are you ready, Em?" he asked. His face was serious. "I just want to be sure that you really want to do this."

"Yes, Hunter. I am ready. I want to do this with you," she said. She took his hand and placed it under her skirt, so he could feel her sopping cunt, "Just feel how wet I am. If that's not an answer enough then I don't know what is."

He smiled another big, skewed smile, a sharp canine peeking out from beneath his pink mouth. "Alright then. I'll take good care of you. Thank you for trusting me."

He looked left and right, before dropping a white pill into her beer. He made sure that no one saw it so that they wouldn't get in trouble.

They continued the role-play of having just met each other. Within half an hour, she started feeling dizzy and a little weak in the limbs. He noticed her clumsiness when she put down her beer so hard that liquid jumped out and spilled over the counter.

He kissed her on the lips. It was soft but rough, she loved every millisecond of his lips colliding with hers and that was the last thing she remembered.

Hunter guided the clumsy and loopy Emily out of the bar and put her in the back of his car. It was too difficult to get her to fit in the front seat with her acting so out of it. His cock throbbed, so hard that it hurt underneath the tightness of his jeans while he drove her home. He checked on her occasionally through the rear-view mirror, to be sure that she was okay. She was still awake, but had succumbed to being a bumbling fool by this point.

When he stopped at his apartment, he had to put her arm over her shoulder. She was dipping in and out of consciousness while he guided her into the elevator and took her to his apartment. He set her down gently on the bed and set up the camera. He had two for each angle. He had her Hitachi wand within reach as well as some lube. When everything was prepared, he admired her at first. Her skirt was slightly lifted, revealing her innocent white panties. The straps of her shirt were down and with just a simple tug downwards, her breasts would be revealed.

He took his shirt off and walked towards her, adjusting the boner in his pants. The throbbing was unbearable, so if he didn't get some kind of stimulation, he feared he would explode, and not in the good way. He decided to remove his pants and strip completely naked.

He got onto the bed and crouched down next to her. She seemed like she was asleep by now. He gently fondled her breasts. They were soft and supple. Next, he tugged her shirt down, her breasts bouncing out from the fabric. They fell slightly down opposite sides. He took both of them in his hands and caressed them, rotating and squeezing. He pinched both of her nipples softly at first. There was no response from her though, and he squeezed harder, twisting softly.

She let out a sleepy groan. *Good,* he thought, it was good that she could still feel what was happening to her. His dream of making a girl cum when unconscious would come true. He threw a knee over her and got on his haunches, his cock perfectly between her breasts. He pulled a pillow under her head and propped her head up so that it was at a better angle for him. He opened her mouth and shoved the tip of his cock inside.

He put his hands on her left and right breast, squeezing them together, so they engulfed his cock. He fucked both her tits and her mouth. He grunted and groaned, the pleasure becoming too much for him, so he had to stop. If he didn't, he would come too soon, and the night would be ruined.

He took a few steadying breaths before carrying on. He spread her legs wide and they stayed in place. He lifted her skirt out of the way. The white panties, however, he took between two hands and ripped them apart aggressively, before throwing them aside. He got on his haunches between her legs and entered her. She was so tight that it nearly hurt him, but he pushed on.

His mind raced. He couldn't believe that his fantasy was finally coming to life, not only that, but he would also have video proof of it. He fucked her limp body in various positions, only stopping to change when he felt that he was close. Occasionally, a soft, pleasured moan would escape her plump lips, but she was still asleep. It would catch him off guard, but it turned him on even more.

He took the Hitachi wand to her clit when he felt that he was ready to reach climax. Instantly as the vibe was pressed firmly against her clit, she tightened around him. He moaned as his body was filled with warmth all over. He wanted to see if he could make her cum first though, so he controlled himself.

When he felt her walls pulsating, relaxing, and repeating that action, he held it even tighter against her clit and he thrust into her with a great ferocity. Hunter grunted with each thrust. She arched her back, and let out another soft, purring moan. He couldn't believe that he had actually done it. It was so fucking sexy…

He couldn't take it any longer, and unleashed his load inside of her pulsing cunt.

Hunter cleaned up, put her in some comfortable clothes to sleep in, and tucked her into bed. He edited the video for her viewing the next day, before he got into bed and held her. He fell asleep with the hot redhead in his arms, clinging onto her for dear life.

She slept a total of twelve hours before finally waking up, feeling groggy. He had coffee and a nutritious breakfast ready for her. At first, they were silent, but Hunter's big, dorky smile broke it.

"I didn't know I'd have a sort of hangover," Emily said.

"You'll feel better after some coffee and food, I promise," Hunter said.

"Okay," she said.

"Emily. I think I love you. Thank you for doing this for me," he said.

"I... I love you too, Hunter," she said.

When she felt better, he showed her the video of their fun night together. They watched it together on his forty-nine-inch wall mounted television. At first, Emily didn't know how she felt about it, but as it went on, she couldn't help but notice the intense rush of arousal washing over her. It was glorious.

She started touching herself as she watched her very own porno, and Hunter joined in, stroking his cock too. They spent the entire day fucking each other, watching parts of the video, then pausing to fuck each other. She had finally had one of the best climaxes of her life. She felt like she could finally breathe when she got that final release.

Filthy Forbidden Erotic Sex Stories:

Adults Erotica Collection- BDSM, Daddy Domination, Gangbangs, Hot Wives, Anal, Bi-Sexual Threesomes, Foot Fetish, Role-Play, MILFs & More

Written By:
G.G. Goode

Goode Publications

The Cuffed Prisoner

Chained Up BDSM

I didn't really know how I got here.

The last thing I remembered were all of the people coming into the bar, asking for me. I said I was her, and then, with just one touch, I was knocked the fuck out.

But here I was, a prisoner in a strange place. I looked around, shackled, realizing the state that I was in.

"What's going on here?" I asked out loud.

I noticed that I was alone. The dark, dreary place had no signs of others. I almost wondered if this was some sort of dungeon. But then, I heard the door open up ahead, and the sound of footsteps.

I tried to gauge if there was someone else here, but it didn't seem like there was. I was all alone.

I also noticed my clothes were torn asunder. What did these people do to me? I knew I was wearing a sweater and some pants at the bar, but they were…gone.

So what was I here for?

The footsteps grew closer. I paused, bracing myself as I looked forward. That's when I saw it.

A man. He had blonde hair, piercing green eyes, and a smile that seemed to send shivers down my spine. I don't know if I should be thankful that he's here, or worried shitless about this.

"There you are. You're finally awake," he said to me.

"What are you talking about?" I said.

"Come now, quit playing stupid with me honey. I just wanted to see what you were up to cutie. If there were of course…any big changes in your face, and what was going on," he said.

Was this guy for real? I paused, trying to figure out if I was making the right choice, or the wrong one. Probably the wrong one.

I tried to move, but the chains were pretty strong, and as I sat there, he looked at me.

"So it's you. The conspirator trying to start a revolution in the kingdom," he said.

Oh, it was definitely that. I realized that he wanted me for treason.

See, I was a revolutionary in the shadows, someone who made sure that I worked for the people, but was never seen. I even went by a different name and made sure to hide everything. That is, until now.

And I realized at this point this man was one of the few royal guardsmen that could royally fuck me up if I'm not careful.

Fuck.

I tried to move, but I was unable to do so. He simply laughed.

"Look at you, pathetic. Man, I told them to disrobe you, but I guess that's not happening. Oh well, I'll work with what I've got," he said.

Work with what he's got? What did he have planned?

I looked at him, unsure as to what he wanted to do at this point, but then he grabbed my chin, looking into my eyes.

"I see. You don't show fear, do you?"

"Why would I?"

"Because you should know by now that little mouth you've got is going to get you into trouble," he said to me.

"So what if it does. It's not like you're going to kill me. You know better than that," I told him.

He looked at me, and then nodded.

"Very true. You are one of the richest people in town, hiding your wealth and pretending to be part of our side. I always despised people like you," he said.

"Well, I wasn't a big fan of you either. So what's it going to be? You going to torture me? Ask me to give that information up? Because I'm sure as shit not doing that," I said.

"No. I have a better use for you," he said.

I paused, trying to figure out what he had in mind. I didn't know what he would do, but then, his face curled into a smile.

"I'm going to make you pay for what you've done. With your body of course," he said.

Hold on…did he just say….

"My…body?" I asked him.

"Did I stutter?" the man said.

I looked up at him, eying his body. I noticed his eyes were glazing over me, and I took a deep breath, enjoying the nature of things. I felt really curious about this, and I was a little bit worried, but there was something pulling me to him, whatever it may be.

"No…you didn't," I said.

"There we go…good girl," he said.

I tried to hold back from moaning as he looked into my eyes. I was supposed to be a revolutionary, someone who didn't take shit from anyone! And yet here I was, my eyes glued to him, enjoying the way his eyes seemed to just look at me completely.

I took a deep breath, enjoying the way things were, and the way his hands reached out, touching the very tip of my shirt. I was a mess, and I knew that if I didn't stop, things would definitely get much more interesting.

His hands moved up towards my neck, holding my head up, looking deep into my eyes. I let out a gasp as he leaned forward, his lips mere inches from me.

"Well, how about we make a little deal?" he asked.

"A…deal?" I asked him.

"Yes. You didn't hear me fucking stutter. If you let me…have my fun with you, I'll let you go. Simple as that you know," he said to me.

I looked at him, seeing the way his eyes met mine. I had a weird feeling about all of this. And yet, I couldn't help but wonder just what else this man had in store for me.

"So you'll let me go?"

"When I'm done, sure," he told me.

I paused, thinking about this.

"Sure, let's do it," I said.

Before I knew it, he moved his hands towards my shirt, grabbing it and pulling it off. My breasts were exposed, causing me to let out a small gasp of surprise.

"Good girl. You know exactly what to do then," he said.

"I'm only giving you this because I know that you'll let me go," I spat.

He then smacked me, causing me to let out a small gasp.

"Don't speak unless you're told to. Got it. If you make too much noise, I won't hesitate to kill you and make it an accident," he muttered.

Shit, I really did need to be careful. I looked at him for a moment, and then nodded.

"Good girl. Now let's see what happens next," he purred.

Soon, he leaned his hands downward, touching my breasts. I struggled to hold back. I wasn't going to lie, this guard, even though he was a bit of an asshole, was kind of hot if I do say so myself.

"You have such a nice body," he purred, touching the tips of my nipples. I struggled to move about, stopped by the feeling of the chains. I let out a small cry, and then he smiled.

"Damn look at you. Already a slut for my touches and I've barely done anything. That's adorable," he purred.

I flushed, looking at him, struggling to say anything to him. I didn't want him to think that I enjoyed this or anything. But his hands felt good, and the little touch against my nipples was enough to make me shiver with delight, and moan slightly. Every single touch was enough to turn me the fuck on, and there was something fun about all of this. He continued to touch my nipples, teasing them with his fingers, rubbing them, and I let out a small cry.

"You're such a needy little slut, already wet as hell. I can see it between your legs. You want my cock, don't you? You can answer," he said to me, teasing my nipple.

I let out another sound, pushing my hips forward, letting out a gasp.

"I'm not…going to give you that satisfaction," I said.

"I see. Well, I guess that means I'm going to have to tease you even more. And I'll make sure that you enjoy it. You're lying right now, and you should be a little bit more open about your feelings. You're open about your feelings regarding the country, and being a traitorous bitch, I'm sure you can be open about how good it feels, right?" he teased.

I flushed, moaning in pleasure. Every single touch, every single motion, it was all…driving me fucking crazy. He then moved his hands downwards, resting against my pussy. He rubbed the edges, making me shiver, but I tried my best to hold back the moans that came with this.

"There we go. Good girl," he said, rubbing me there.

I shivered, letting out a small cry as his hands continued to touch me, moving towards my thighs, cupping them slightly. I let out a small, garbled sound, aching for more from him as I started to feel him move his hand around. Every little touch, even though it wasn't what I was expecting, continued to turn me on. I shivered, crying out loud as he did this.

"You're already losing control, aren't you? Such a good little slut," he said.

He then moved towards my legs, cupping and teasing them and watching me shiver with delight. The little ghosts of touches, the little caresses, it was all just…so fucking good. I ached for it, I needed more, and I knew for a fact that this was definitely getting to the point where even though I'd try not to show my feelings, it was only getting harder and harder to do.

"What's the matter? Struggling to hold back?" he teased.

He moved his hands towards my inner thigh again, touching and caressing them. He was right up against the very entrance of my pussy, and I suddenly felt that need, that desire, and that ache for him.

He then moved his hands towards my pussy, teasing the very tip of it, making me let out a small, choked sound.

"There we go…good girl," he said.

He then rubbed against me, making me shiver with enjoyment as he continued to press into me more and more. Everything was just…so nice. So damn perfect, and I ached for the feeling. I wanted more, and I wanted his touch.

I then noticed his hands move towards me, grabbing my pants. Was he going to pull them off? But no, he simply grabbed the sides, ripping them off my body. He slid them off, pulling them to the chains, and then he ripped them.

I realized he would probably do the same with my panties too. I didn't know what his plans were. But then, he grabbed my panties, throwing them off my body.

"There, now you look perfect," he said.

I shivered, realizing that I both liked this, and didn't like this. Would I get my clothes back? And if I didn't…what did he have planned.

He let his hands rest downward, touching the very tip of my pussy, rubbing the tip of it, and causing me to let out a yelp but I liked the way that it felt.

"You like that?" he said.

"M-maybe I do," I said.

"Come on, we can make this easy, or much harder honey," he said.

His hand dipped inside and started massaging the tender area and I closed my eyes. I was at this man's mercy. Even though it wasn't right, I wanted it, and soon, before I knew it, I tensed up, letting out a small cry, enjoying the feeling.

"Fuck," I breathed out.

"There you go. Good girl," he said.

There was only one thing that I could do. And that of course was to indulge in the pleasure, and the fun that came with this. His hands moved towards me, rubbing the tip of my clit, and I let out a breathy sound.

"Fuck," I said.

"Well, you going to finally let go? Going to finally make those delicious sounds as I tease you?" he said to me.

I shivered. Was I going to let him get the best of me? Maybe, but I didn't want to let that happen.

"Maybe," I said.

"Well, how does a little bit of teasing sound then? Fun huh?" he said.

Fuck I knew I probably should've kept my damn mouth shut. His hands moved outwards, touching the tip of my clit, rubbing it in small circles. I started to close my eyes, moaning in pleasure as I started to hold my body there, enjoying the sensation of this. He wanted me to respond, to react, and I knew he was doing this damn teasing to get the best of me.

He then moved his hands towards my entrance, just barely touching it. I looked into his eyes, seeing the smirk that he had, and I shivered.

He was enjoying this. The motherfucker was teasing me on purpose! I felt like he was getting a thrill from seeing me in an agony of want, clinging to every part of him, letting out a small moan of surprise and need.

"Fuck," I said to him.

"What's the matter dear?" he asked me.

"I'm just.... I'm just trying to hold back," I muttered.

"Why do that? You are clearly enjoying this," he said.

His hands were right there, creating the phantom pain that I enjoyed. I knew that letting go would probably be for the best.

Maybe I needed to do that. I started to close my eyes, realizing that I was already a mess, and that I wanted to just embrace it, and experience more.

That's when I let go. I started closing my eyes, letting out a small hum, feeling good about this. For a moment, I felt his fingers press deep within, making me shiver with delight, crying out loud. I started to hold the area there, pushing my hips up, feeling everything just slowly unwind.

He then started moving within me, pressing his fingers in. The feeling was making me lose my mind, every touch sending me to a whole new plane of existence. And yet, I loved it. I wanted him to do this, and I ached for him, wanting more.

"Fuck," I said, feeling the fingers moving within me become shallower. He was doing this on purpose.

To make me beg. He started dipping them slowly deeper in, and I bit my lip.

"Fuck,' I muttered.

"What's the matter there?" he asked me.

"I'm not...going to give in," I said.

"Whatever you say there dear," he said.

He then continued the torment, the tease.

"I'm…fuck," I said.

"You're what? Go ahead, spit it out. I'm sure you've got something very interesting to say to all of us," he said with a snide smile.

God this bastard! I felt like wanting to scream, but I couldn't do that. I needed to keep things chill, let him continue this. And see how long I can last.

But then he pushed his fingers upward slightly, pressing up inside of me, and as he did that, I felt that surge of pleasure, that affection, everything just hit all at once. I let out a garbled sound, and then, as I did it, I cried out.

"What's the matter? Trying to hold back?" he said.

I was, but I could feel the whole thing slowly tearing me apart. He was getting a kick out of this, like it was a game for him. And I hated it.

"Care to give in?" he told me.

I gritted my teeth. There was no way in hell I was going to. I paused, looking into his eyes.

"I'm…not going to," I told him.

He then dipped his fingers in deeper. I was so close. I could feel the release just begging to come out as he moved himself, teasing, dipping his fingers deep into my pussy. I grasped the chains, holding them. I'm not going to let it get to me though.

But then he hit that area again, causing me to let out a small cry, holding my body, tensing up.

"You can back out at any time hun. Just say the word," he said.

Fuck. I was losing my goddamn mind. I gritted my teeth, trying to figure out what to do. Finally, I sighed.

"Alright, I'll…I'll do this," I told him.

He laughed, moving his hand away.

"Do what? I want to hear what you have to say," he said.

This rat bastard. I don't know why he has done this to me. I don't understand what his reason for this even is.

"I want you to…to take me," I told him.

"Alright, whatever you say," he said.

I looked at him, and then, he moved the chains away from the wall. He wasn't taking me out of them, was he? But then he flipped me over, so that my ass was hanging out in the air, and as I looked forward, I felt a hand on my ass.

"You have such a nice butt. I figured part of your punishment before I even gave you what you wanted would be this. Wouldn't it be fun?" he asked me.

His hands gripped me there, and I gasped.

"So, what are you going to do?" I asked him.

"Simple. I want to see you squirm of course, so I plan to spank you until you finally give me what I want. I want to hear the moans that you make, the delicious sounds that are uttered," he told me.

This man. He was trying so hard to get me to give in.

"Well you'll have to do more than that," I said.

"I guess if you give me enough incentive I will stop," he said.

This guy was enjoying this far more than I expected him to. He grabbed my ass, squeezing it once more, and then, he let out a low groan.

"Oh, this will be fun," he said.

I couldn't move, my hands and feet were in the chains, and there was something so annoying and yet…so damn thrilling about all of this that turned me on, that made me excited for him.

He then raised his hand, slowly slapping my ass with a hard hit.

When it made contact, I let out a garbled sound, shocked at how good this felt. He then smacked me again and again, hitting every single part of me, penetrating deep into the fibers of my being. There was a thrill there, a need for something more, and when he hit me with his hand, I knew that he was enjoying this far more than he cared to admit. He started to smack me once again, this time hitting me with all his might, causing me to let out a small gasp of surprise and pleasure, enjoying the touch this man bestowed upon me.

It was perfect, simply perfect, and I enjoyed the hell out of it.

He continued to hit me hard with his hands, each smack making me lose all semblance of control, enjoying the feeling of this, loving the touch of his hands.

But the sting was becoming more and more obvious.

He would make sure to hit right up against my pussy, causing me to let out a small moan of surprise, enjoying the touch of it. He then would hit it again, this time with much more force, causing me to let out a small, garbled sound.

"Fuck," I said.

"You want more slut?" he said.

"Do your worst," I said.

Then, I heard something bigger get grabbed. I paused, wondering just what this man would bring out. then, I felt it right up against my ass, causing me to let out a howl of both pain and pleasure.

It was a pole. He was using it to hit me hard, and the caning started to make me grit my teeth. And yet, I found pleasure in it. Every touch made me shiver and cry out. He would purposefully move it right up against my glistening pussy, as if to tease me completely. I felt completely lost in the pleasure this man gave to me, and it was then when, after a few more moments he pulled this away, looking me in the eyes.

"There you go," he said.

I whimpered, turned on and ready for whatever he would give to me next. He would continue this, but I was losing it. I felt sore, but mostly I just wanted him to…to just take me completely and make me feel good.

He hit me one last time, causing a howl to come out of me. Then, he rubbed the cane against my folds.

"What was that?" he said with a tease.

I gritted my teeth, feeling frustrated by the way that he was teasing me. I wanted him to just outright take me and fuck me mercilessly, but I couldn't just say that. The last thing I wanted was to give him the goddamn satisfaction.

But maybe that's what he wanted. Maybe he just…wanted to see how far he could take it. I wondered this, but then he pushed the cane deeper against me, his hand touching my pucker and also rubbing the red there.

"Well, what do you say? Ready to give in yet?" he asked me with a purr.

Did I want to give in? Well, the horny part of me wanted him to just take me and turn me into the quivering little slut that he wanted, but there was that other part of me that was just begging to hold on a little while longer.

I took a deep breath, steeling myself for the next part, when I spoke.

"Take me," I whimpered.

"What was that?"

Fuck he was trying to completely tease me, making me his little bitch, and then, I sighed.

"Please take me," I said.

"I can't hear you. You're a little quiet there," he said.

Ugh, this bastard! I then sighed, looking over at him and then speaking.

"Fuck me! Please! I fucking need it," I said.

He then gave me one loud smack, causing me to let out a small moan of pleasure, and then I saw him smile.

"You want it so badly huh?"

"Yes," I breathed out, barely able to get my shit together.

"Then go on ahead. Let's really make this fun now," he said to me.

I watched as he spread me apart, looking me in the eyes, and then, shortly thereafter, he soon pushed all the way in, hitting that spot deep within me.

I let out a small cry, holding onto him, watching as he slid his cock deep within, and then back out again. He then looked me in the eyes, smiling.

"You good?" he asked me.

"Amazing," I breathed out.

But the truth was, I felt like I was about to lose my mind, and I couldn't help but wonder if there was more to this as well. He then grabbed my legs, spreading me apart, pushing in deep and making me shiver and cry out.

I grabbed onto him, holding him as he rammed his cock into me, but he made sure not to hit that one spot. He was trying to get me to beg to cum.

He was driving a hard bargain.

"Please," I whimpered as he continued to thrust.

"Please what? I'm getting close you know," he said.

Of course he fucking was. I started gritting my teeth once again, planning to scream out the feelings that I had, and what I wanted.

"Please just let me cum already!" I cried out.

He looked at me, seeing how needy I was, and then, he laughed.

"Well since you asked so nicely…here we go then," he said.

He then pushed his hands upward toward my breasts, pinching and teasing my nipples as he angled his cock, hitting my g-spot. I held the chains, feeling the limited movement change the way things were.

I wanted nothing more than to be taken completely, to enjoy the touch and the feeling of this, and as he held me, thrusting himself deep within me, I could feel my whole body practically tense up, losing control, and then, I held him, cumming hard against him.

I felt the orgasm shatter every fiber of my being. I screamed out, loving everything about this, and it was then when, after a few more thrusts he then groaned and held me, filling me up completely.

I didn't expect his seed to be pumped all the way into me, but I was completely at the mercy of this man. I loved every moment of this though. And as he finished, he pulled out of me, the cum dripping from my pussy. I was completely enthralled by the way that this felt, and for a second, I simply sat there, looking at him. He then gave me a small smile.

"There we go," he said to me.

"But…what now?" I asked him.

"What do you mean? You're free to go," he said.

He undid the chains, pulling them off of my body. I could feel my hands again, which was pretty nice. But as I looked at him, I had many more questions than answers.

"Why though?" I asked him.

"Why what?"

"Did you…let me go. After all this time," I told him.

He paused, and then, he shrugged.

"Maybe I just felt like being nice. I wanted to…make sure that you were taken care of," he told me.

I flushed, but then I nodded.

"Thank you," I said to him.

"Not a problem. I just want to see you do well, and I'm happy I can be there for you," he said to me.

I looked into his eyes, and then I nodded.

"Thank you," I said to him.

"You're most welcome. I'm sure this is something that you will definitely remember me for," he told me.

I smiled, happy and amazed at how good this was. I then looked around, wondering just what in the world would happen next. I was a bit shocked that he was doing all of this to be nice to me, and I was definitely thankful for this.

He finished getting the chains off of me, but then, he looked me in the eyes.

"Don't tell anyone about this. Got it?" he said.

"But why not?"

"Because I want this to be kept as our little secret. If the guards find out...I'll be in deep shit. So don't let anyone else know what happened here," he said.

The way his voice cut as he said those words made me realize just the significance of this. I then nodded.

"Alright, I'll do that," I told him.

"Good. I think that settles it. Now, don't tell anyone about this. I let you go because I pitied you. The truth is...I don't agree with the kingdom, and I don't like it, and I'm not that happy about it. But it's not like there is much I can do. So, I'm telling you right now, if you want things to go well, you should just let things go, and go from there," he said to me.

I paused, realizing he was doing this because he wanted to help me. Maybe he was on my side. There were many parts of the revolution who didn't have the guts to admit it.

And maybe he was one of those that did admit it deep down. I beamed, and then I spoke.

"Alright, keep this between us then," I said.

"Fair," he told me.

I got ready to leave, and then, as I got myself together, he was then gone. A part of me wishes that he stuck around. That he could...possibly work something out with me. Maybe he could assist me in the revolution, as a spy of sorts.

But I should be glad he didn't kill me, that he was letting me go. And as I looked around, I realized that getting out of this cell would be easier said than done.

"Shit, where to now?" I said.

It didn't help that I was naked too. He ripped all of my clothes. But to the right of me were some linens. I grabbed them, putting them on. Then, I saw some armor, left there in the corner.

Did he leave this on purpose? Or was it from someone else? Either way, I was thankful for the armor. I put it on my body, checking to see how I looked, smiling excitedly as I looked forward.

"There we go. We should be ready to go now," I told myself.

I was excited for this, ready to face the future. I saw that nobody was looking around, so I made my way up to the foyer, and then made a break for the entrance.

I didn't stick around to see what the guards would say about me, good or bad. But I was just relieved to know that I had my freedom once again. But a part of me wondered if there was a reason for this, or even what else I could do.

But I would miss him... even though I knew getting involved with a guy like that wasn't good for me, I wanted to. I wanted to find him again, and possibly...continue where we left off.

But I wasn't sure if it was possible. But I hoped that one day, he'd possibly continue to be the revolutionary that he wanted to be, and he'd come work with me, no matter what happened next.

Seeing Daddy

Daddy Domination, Roleplay

I sat there, waiting on the bed for him to call me. I knew for a fact that he was waiting for me, ready to see me put on a little show for him.

Daddy.

I felt a bit of excitement as I looked forward. Sometimes I didn't totally get into the little space aspects of this, but right now…I just wanted daddy to come in and have his way with me.

But alas, daddy, my boyfriend Quinn, was busy until 11. He told me to get into something nice and ready for him, so that's what I did. I wore a pink negligee, a little set of black stockings, and put my hair in cute pigtails. It let me be the "Princess" that I knew I could be. And it was a kink that I often loved to explore.

I wanted him to just take me and have his way with me, but I knew that may be too much to ask of him. However, maybe I could at least goad him a little bit.

I prepared the text message, and the video call, my body and mind excited to hear his voice. I sent it out, my fingers a little bit nervous as I pulled the trigger.

The truth is, I was always kind of a vanilla person until I met Quinn. Then, he showed me daddy domination. At first, I was a little bit nervous about doing this, but after he showed me a few things, there was a thrill, and excitement that came from this whole thing.

And I wanted to see just what would happen.

I simply sent it out.

Video call me daddy!

And then I waited. Moments later he sent over a text, asking why. And I smiled.

I had something to show him.

And that's what I said. Personally, I was a little bit nervous about doing this. It would be the first time we did this sort of thing while he was at work.

Quinn worked in a prominent law office as one of the main lawyers. Which meant he had to keep a very low profile with this sort of thing. But I felt the thrill. The excitement and the desire washed over me as this continued to happen.

I waited a little bit until of course, I heard his voice.

"What are you doing Patty?"

"I just had a surprise for you," I told him.

"Like what…."

"Turn on the video and you'll see it," I said with a smile.

There was hesitation, and then, moments later he did so, fumbling with the camera before turning it on.

I watched as he sat there, in his perfectly pressed lawyer suit, looking at me with an annoyed face.

"Patty please, you know I'm trying to finish up."

"But daddy, I'm ready for you now," I said, biting my lip.

"Come on Patty, you know I can't—"

"Can't I at least show you how much I want you?" I asked him.

There was a long pause, and then, moments later, he sighed.

"Fine. You can do that," he said.

But the tone of his voice didn't fit the rest of it. I smiled, excited for what this may mean for us. I spread myself on the bed, looking at him as I bit my lip.

"Like…this," I said.

I rubbed my entrance, watching his face contort into an obvious poker face.

"Daddy, I want you to come home. You promised you would," I told him.

"I know but I need to finish and—"

I let out a small moan, touching myself as I moved my hand against my folds as I looked at him.

"Come on daddy, you should know by now that this is what you're looking for," I said to him. He looked at me, biting his lip slightly as he spoke.

"I can't do this yet Patty."

"But I can't hold back daddy. I want you nowwww," I told him.

I started to rub myself, moving my fingers, watching as his eyes widened and his mouth dropped. I started to rub my finger against my clit, letting out a small sigh of need as I touched myself. I was horny and needy, aching for him as I continued to feel my body tense up, the desire, need, and lust growing within.

"Come on daddy, can't you take a little bit of time off?" I said.

"You know I can't and—"

I started rubbing myself more, my hands against my nipple. I let out a small gasp, needing something inside me. I wanted him to just quit, to come home and take care of me. I began to slide my fingers in, biting my lip as I looked up.

"I'm thinking of you, daddy," I told him.

"Really now?" he said.

"Yes, I want you to come home, to pound me, and to make me quiver and shiver. I can only take care of myself for so long," I purred.

"I see," he said.

I began to rub myself a little bit harder, watching his body start to struggle. He was hard. That's the face he made when he was turned on, and I smiled, excited to see more.

"Come onnnn daddy," I told him.

He sighed, realizing he wasn't going to get anywhere with this. He then took a deep breath, looking into my eyes.

"Fine. You win," he replied.

I beamed, looking at him, excitedly.

"There you go. I can't wait for you," I said.

"I'll be back when it's time," he told me.

I knew that's what he did. There was something fun, thrilling, and exciting about all of this. I smiled a devilish grin, enjoying the way he looked at me awkwardly.

Without another word, he turned off the video call. I pouted.

"He could've at least waited for me to say bye. But oh well," I muttered to myself.

I sat there, frustrated at the lack of his presence. I just wanted daddy here now. I started to sit there, spreading my legs, touching myself as I thought about him.

"Daddy…."

I continued to stroke myself against my panties. I'm sure this would be one hell of a sight. I was excited to say the least, and I was definitely ready for whatever would happen next.

I then continued to move my hands, daintily touching myself, enjoying the touch, moaning his name, when suddenly, I heard the car pull up.

Damn Quinn got home fast. I guess he couldn't take it. That's what he gets for ignoring me when I needed him the most.

"Come on daddy…give me some fun," I told myself.

I started pulling my panties downward, grabbing my favorite toy. It was a vibrator, about the size of daddy's cock, and as I started to turn it on, feeling the vibrations within me, I sat there, holding myself against the bed.

"Oh, daddy, please. Please fill me up," I said.

I started moving the toy against my body, imagining it was him. His rough hands holding me, grabbing my arms, and dominating me as he fucked me senseless. Feeling his hands against my throat, and I started to feel my whole body tense up, feeling the excitement wash over me.

I continued to hold the toy, pushing it deeper within. Every part of this was making me lose my mind, filling me up even more, and I knew that from everything that was going on that it was only a matter of time.

Each and every single touch sent me shivering, making me ache for more and wanting him completely. I felt my hands move slightly, pressing the toy right up against my clit.

I was so damn close. I knew that I needed to last, but maybe if I just had a little orgasm…

"What are you doing?" he said.

I turned to him, flushing crimson as he looked at me, seeing the toy in my hands, and a wry smile on my face.

"Sorry, daddy. I've been a very naughty girl," I said out loud.

"I can see that. You were getting off without me. That's something that I told you that you shouldn't do, remember? We had that agreement. And I saw that you were very close to orgasm there," he said to me.

I flushed but then nodded.

"Sorry daddy," I told him.

It was a struggle. I couldn't just sit there and wait for him, right.

But then, instead of responding, he went over, grabbed the paddle, and looked at me.

"Remember what we agreed upon. If you're a bad girl for daddy, you will get punished," he said.

Damn. He was already trying to make me feel more frustrated. I knew that this punishment was coming, but then, I smiled, curling my lips into a Cheshire cat grin.

"Make me."

Those were the two words that would make him respond. He quickly pushed me down on the bed, thrusting me on all fours. I shivered, enjoying the touch, and the way that he simply took over. He then grabbed my ass, massaging the cheeks.

"What was that? I thought we talked about that little mouth of yours princess?" he said.

"I said make me! I wanted to get off, what are you going to do about it and—"

Then he smacked me with the paddle, making me cry out. it felt good because I could get off to spankings, but also, I didn't really enjoy it.

"Well, princess? I'm waiting," he said.

He then smacked me again and again, causing me to let out a small gasp, enjoying the sensation and pleasure. Every single touch, every single motion, they were all driving me to the point of need, of desire, and making me want even more. He then hit me harder once more.

"Ahh, daddy!" I cried out.

"You get three more spankings for being such a naughty girl," he said.

I wiggled my butt, excited for it. He grabbed the paddle, hitting that one part of my body that made me shiver and cry out, sending me soaring, making me ache for him, and wanting him, to just take me and use me like the naughty girl that I was.

He continued to do this, every little touch sending me to the edge, making me want more, crave more, excited for the rest of it. After the third spanking, my ass felt raw, and then, he put me on my back, looking at me.

"So princess, what did you need that was so important you had to interrupt me from work?" he said.

"I just wanted your cock daddy," I told him, smiling as I spread my legs, my pussy wet with desire.

He cupped my chin and looked me in the eyes. His eyes said he was bothered and lusting for me, but the way his face looked, he pretended to be annoyed with me.

"Daddy said you shouldn't disobey the rules. You couldn't stop thinking about me though, could you?" he said.

"No daddy, I wanted to feel your cock inside of me," I told him.

He let out a small chuckle, moving his hand away from my chin, taking a moment to drink up the sight of me. I knew that this was what daddy wanted.

He seemed to be curious about this too. His hands moved towards my breasts, touching and teasing them, looking me in the eyes.

"Look at you, so turned on like the little slut that you are. I can't believe you, princess," he said.

"Daddy, I can't get enough of you. I want you," I told him. And I meant that as well. This wasn't me just bullshitting either, and it was obvious that he enjoyed this too.

"Well, daddy is going to give you a hard dicking, and he's getting out the restraints too since you of course decided to disobey him," he said with an admonished tone.

There was something so fucking hot about being told no like this. Maybe it was the fact that he was saying it to me like this, but I was so fucking hot and bothered that I couldn't get enough of it, and I ached for it.

"Well maybe I want that then daddy," I said.

He grabbed my hands, holding them above my head hard, but not so hard that it hurt me. He looked me in my eyes and then smiled before crushing his lips to my own.

The domineering, amazing kiss was enough to drive me crazy, and I thrust my hips upward.

He then grabbed something with his free hand, putting one of them through the bars of the headboard, and the other one binding my tiny hands together.

"There we go, you won't be going anywhere for now," he said to me.

"But I don't want to go anywhere, daddy. I want you," I said.

He looked me in the eyes, laughing.

"I can see. You've become such a needy slut for me that I can see it in your eyes. So tell me, what do you want daddy to do to you? Do you want him to tease you like this," he said to me.

His hands moved downward, touching my sides, making me cry out slightly. His hands moved down, touching the wet part of my panties, looking up at me.

"So wet already. You really are a slut, over here thinking about daddy like this," he said.

"Ahh yes," I told him.

I meant those words too. There was something so damn thrilling about this. I don't know why, but I wanted him to take me, to use me like the little princess that I was, and to be taken advantage of like this.

He then moved down to my feet. Fuck not there. He moved his hands downward, touching the bottom of my feet, my toes curling in response.

"Look at you. Already so damn turned on, completely at the mercy of my hands and my touches," he said to me.

I whimpered, completely turned on by the little touch. See...daddy knew that I liked the sensitive parts of my body touched. It didn't even need to be my pussy or tits, it could just be my feet, or even my armpits and sides, and I would become a panting, whimpering mess in front of him. And this of course was no exception.

He continued to smile, touching and teasing every single part of me, enjoying the way that this felt, and I couldn't help but enjoy it. I started to feel him press his hands to the bottom of my feet, touching and teasing me there, and I started to enjoy the feeling even more.

But as soon as I started to feel pleasure, he stopped, moving his hands upward, touching the inner parts of my thighs, letting his hands graze against the tip of my pussy, moving along the sides. That's when I let out a cry, and he of course, laughed at the sounds that I made.

"Just look at you. Such a mess already. Turned on and a little slut as well. My, you must be enjoying this," he told me.

"I…I am," I told him, completely in a rapturous moment, enjoying everything that came from him.

His hands then skirted upward, moving toward the tip of my breasts, touching them slightly. He looked me in the eyes, seeing the lustful look, and then he spoke.

"I didn't expect you to wear something so cute. Were you waiting to wear this for daddy? To take it off of you?" he said.

"Yes daddy," I told him.

I picked this out for him since I knew it was his favorite color, and he smiled.

"What a good princess. Always so sweet and supportive of me too. I love that," he said.

He reached upward, letting his fingers touch against the very tips of my nipples, rubbing his hands there, watching me moving the tip, letting his fingers rub slightly. But I knew that I was losing my mind.

I started to feel his hands move under my top, moving against my nipples, pinching and teasing them. He also let one of his fingers rest against my armpits, touching there slightly.

That's when I let out a sigh, completely and utterly lost in the feeling of this, enjoying his touch. I knew that he was enjoying this as much as I was, and that every single touch was enough to drive me crazy. He continued these touches, listening to the sounds that came out of me.

"So what's going on princess? Enjoying this?" he asked me.

"Yes," I said out loud.

"Yes, what?"

"Yes, daddy. I love this," I told him.

It was what I had waited for. There was something about the way that Quinn touched me that made me become putty in his hands.

Usually, I wouldn't let him have all the fun, and I would try to take a little bit of control as well, but then, he continued to press his fingers there, causing me to let out a small series of gasps and sighs, enjoying the touch.

He did this for a bit, watching me slowly come undone, when he pulled away, looking me in the eyes, seeing the need, the whole feeling, and the pleasure that came out of this.

"Well? What do you think? Are you going to be a good girl?" he said to me.

"Yes," I told him.

"Yes, what? I won't continue until I hear it from your lips," he teased.

That motherfucker.

"Yes, daddy. I will be a good girl.

He soon smiled, pressing right up against the very tip of my pussy. He rubbed there, making me enjoy every single moment of this. It was so enjoyable, that I couldn't help but love everything that came from this as well. I soon moved my body towards his touches, realizing that he was still teasing me, forcing me orgasm denial as well.

"Please, give me more," I told him.

"You're going to have to beg a little bit harder than that," he said to me.

Fuck, I couldn't help but ache for him, and I needed him. I started to push my legs forward, moving my body so that it was right there, waiting for him. I soon started to feel his hands move towards the inner part of my panties, going underneath, and then moments later stroking my folds. Every touch was making me whimper, and when he pushed two fingers inside, I let out a small gasp of surprise, enjoying everything that came from this. For a moment, I simply just laid there, basking in everything, enjoying the touches.

He then stopped, right as I was about to cum, causing me to let out a small groan of annoyance. I wanted him to just take me right then and there. He smiled.

"Well, do you want more? Because I can leave you like this," he teased.

"No daddy, I want this. Please…I need it," I told him, moaning out loud at the notion of this. I didn't expect this to just completely destroy me in the ways that it was. And yet, I loved it. I loved being taken like this by him, completely at the mercy of his touches, and then, after a brief second, he laughed.

"Alright. Good girl then," he said.

He soon pushed his hands towards my panties, rubbing down there, pushing in and out first with one finger, and then with multiple fingers, making me suddenly lurch and moan in response to this. I was already losing control, enjoying everything that came out of this, and it was then when, moments later, he pulled my panties down and off.

I was so close already that I groaned in mild annoyance at the feeling of this. But then, moments later, he moved towards me, looking me in the eyes as he smiled.

"Well, do you plan on begging for it?"

"Yes daddy, give me your cock, please," I said.

He laughed, and then undid his pants. I expected him to thrust it into me, making me feel the effects of it all, but then moments later, he moved his cock towards my mouth, pushing it in and watching his eyes start to widen. He choked me with his cock, and I felt the large member hit the back of my mouth, causing me to let out a garbled sound of pure pleasure, the enjoyment of such making me feel turned on and happy about it.

He continued to gag me on his cock, and I enjoyed everything that came from this. Every single touch, it was all just…so damn perfect, and he didn't seem to want to stop it.

He got his cock to the back of my mouth, holding it there as I gagged on it. He then pulled back out, making me catch my breath. He grabbed my chin, pulling it upwards.

"Does my little princess want my cock," he asked me.

"Yes, daddy. I would love that," I told him.

And I meant it. He then smiled, pulling my face back, and it was only moments later when I felt him spread me apart, causing my breath to hitch.

Would he be hard and make me lose it? Or would he be gentle? Something told me that he had planned to be hard and ruthless with me. And yet, I loved everything about that. He slowly pressed himself deep into me, making me suddenly gasp with surprise, amazed at how good this was. He soon pressed in and out, enjoying everything that came out of my mouth. And I of course, enjoyed the feeling too.

Every touch, every caress, every single press inside was enough to drive me to the brink. He held me there, but then, as soon as he was about to hit that spot, the one location that would make me orgasm, he stopped.

"What's the matter, princess? You want something?"

Fuck, I knew what he wanted. Me to beg of course. I flushed crimson, and then moments later I said it.

"Choke me…daddy. I want to feel your cock," I said to him.

I loved it when he choked me out. He wrapped his fingers around the spot on my neck, causing my eyes to widen and the pleasure to surge through me.

"Then my little princess will have that," he said.

He then thrust inside, causing me to let out little gasps and sounds of pleasure. He hit right up against my G-spot, causing me to howl in pleasure as I felt the throes of my orgasm hit me. I thought that he would join me, but he didn't.

No, after I came, he stopped for a moment, touching my hair for a second, and then smiling.

"Don't worry, I'll take good care of you," he said to me.

He then started to move his cock in and out of me, pressing right up against that spot, and it was only then when I cried out, feeling my whole body start to lose control, and it was only then when I felt him hit right up against there.

Moments later, I felt my whole body just tense up. He pressed his lips to my own, holding me there, and it was then when I let out a small, garbled sound, cumming hard against him as he filled me up with his cum.

He then finished up, pulling away, and looking at me. I was spent, my vision blurred, my whole body completely wasted and amazed at how I was able to stay conscious throughout all of this. He then touched my head, smiling.

"You good there, princess?" he asked me.

I nodded.

"Yeah…I think I am," I told him.

In truth, I didn't know how to register any of this. But then he reached for the restraints, undoing them and putting them off to the side. I looked into his eyes, and for a long time, we didn't say a word. Then, he grabbed my favorite stuffed animal, giving that to me.

"Here you go. Cuddle that while I get you some water," he said.

"Thanks, daddy," I told him.

Quinn beamed, and then left for a moment. Moments later, he came back with some cookies, and of course some water for me. I drank it, eating a couple of the cookies that he brought me. He simply touched my hair, looking me in the eyes as he spoke.

"How are you feeling?" he asked.

How was I feeling? I felt like I'd been hit by a train, but also, I really enjoyed everything that he gave to me. Even though he was rough, there was something thrilling about the rough nature of this, and then, I spoke.

"I'm pretty good. That was just pretty amazing," I told him.

"You liked it?"

"Of course, daddy. I loved every second of it," I told him.

He breathed out a sigh of relief as he heard me say that.

"Okay good. I wanted to make sure that I wasn't too rough on you or anything. Just when I saw you there, teasing me like that, it was turning me on and I felt like I needed to be there right then and there," he told me.

"Yeah true," I told him.

"Anyways, I think we're good. Do you want me to go and make you some food?"

"Sure daddy. Or I can try to move in a bit and—"

"Don't worry about it. I've got it," he insisted.

I looked into his eyes, seeing the serious expression there. Damn, he really meant it.

"Okay, daddy. Thanks," I said.

"Not a problem. Everything is in place for my little princess to have a good time," he said.

I smiled, leaning in and giving him a long, passionate kiss. I really did like him, and he was a big part of my life. I just had no clue what else to do at this point, other than to stay with him and to be with him.

For a long time, I simply relished in it. But then he went down to make me some food. And I sat there, thinking about what I did, and the fun that I had just had.

I would do it again. I would totally tease him again, and I knew from the way that he was talking that he enjoyed this as much as I did. I thought about it, and about what he felt.

In a strange way, I personally felt good about all of this. I looked over at my phone, seeing the video call that I had with Quinn. Even though he was frustrated, it seemed like he channeled that frustration of course, into something a whole lot more fun. And when I touched to view the video, I smiled to myself.

"I can't wait to have fun like this again," I said.

I moved downwards, touching myself, rubbing off quickly to the idea of Quinn teasing me like that again. He was a good dom. Someone who knew when to stay in his lane, and he never overstepped the boundaries that he had. There was something good about that, which made me realize that I could trust him.

I quickly finished myself off, taking my hands and rubbing quickly. Moments, later, I let out a small groan, finishing up. When he came back, he saw me there, and he simply smiled.

"You good there princess?" he asked me.

"Amazing daddy. I was just sitting here, waiting for you to come," I said.

He leaned in, giving me a strong kiss, and one that was quick too.

"Well, I sure as shit hope you didn't have to wait long. I made your favorite food. I figured you'd need this after the adventures that we shared together," he told me with a smile.

I quickly saw the food, taking it and beaming towards him as I dug in. It tasted amazing, just the way that daddy liked to do it, and I enjoyed every passing moment of it. He laughed as he saw me wolf it all down, touching my shoulders slightly, looking me in the eyes.

"I can only hope to give you something that you will enjoy, and something that you will remember from here on out," he said.

He was my daddy, someone that I could trust, and someone who took care of me. I knew that this was a different type of dynamic, but I could tell from the way that Quinn interacted with me that he enjoyed this. He then rubbed my back as he ate, whispering little sweet nothings into my ear. I quickly let out a small moan, pushing myself down next to him, and he simply smiled.

"I just want to give you what's best for you, what my little girl deserves, and something to remember me by," he said.

I smiled, thankful for that.

"Oh, don't worry daddy, I don't think I could ever forget you, you know," I told him.

He laughed, giving me another kiss, and I leaned in against him, feeling safe and secure near him. I knew that I could trust Quinn, no matter what the odds may be. He was someone that I adored, someone that I could rely on no matter what, and someone I was falling for every single day.

The Business Trip

MILFs, Gangbang

It was time.

One of the first business trips I would have with my department. We were going to Vegas, and the company was paying for the whole trip, plus I got a small little allowance every single day.

Not only that, but I also definitely needed a break. They told me I'd be going with my group, so I'd have to work with the people in my department.

The thing is, I haven't seen them at all.

I wondered what it was that they were up to. We did most of the work online, so most of the time it didn't really apply to us to all meet up. This would be the first time we'd all meet for something like this.

And yet, there was something exciting about that.

I looked around, seeing where the group was. When I got there, I stopped, my eyes wide.

There was a group of attractive men in business suits that were all sitting there. They looked over at me, waving slightly.

"You're Beatrice, right?" one of them said.

"Yeah. And I'm assuming you guys are a part of the division?" I asked them.

They nodded.

"Yeah, I'm Henry, that's Caleb, that's Cody, and Dan is here too. We're just waiting on one more person. Maria," Henry explained.

I listened, but I was kind of lost in Henry's eyes. He was attractive as all hell, and he looked at me with a small smile, excitement in his eyes.

Fuck was I already lost in the feeling of this? Was this…. right though?

I couldn't help but already notice my head was in the clouds.

"You okay there?" the guy who I noticed as Caleb said. He had really attractive green eyes, a smile on his face, and when he looked at me, I couldn't help but feel the rush of excitement.

"Yeah, I'm okay," I told him.

"Alright. Well, if there's anything you want, please let me know," he said.

Besides his cock. But also, I didn't want it to be that type of trip. We all met, and each of the guys had something utterly unique about them, and yet…. I couldn't help but feel like I was enthralled, completely lost in the way that they spoke, enjoying the feeling of this too.

That's why I didn't want to let them know anything. Could I stop this? I didn't think so.

Then, the guys looked over at me, eying me up and down, causing me to flush crimson. There was something thrilling, exciting about this. Sure, it was probably going to be your average business trip, but a girl could dream, right?

That's when I saw her. Maria. She walked down towards all of us, and I flushed, realizing how pretty she was.

It was rare for women to get me to feel this way, and when I saw Maria there, she looked at me, giving me a wry little smile.

"Hey there everyone," she said.

"Hey yourself," I heard Henry say.

She gave them a wink, and then her eyes immediately focused on me. the way she stared into my eyes made my heart skip a beat and made me ache for her.

That's when it made me realize—holy shit this could become something real.

I started to flush, thinking about what could happen. But then she looked at me, giving me a small wink.

"I didn't know we'd have some female company on this trip. That's exciting," Maria said.

I knew Maria was one of the superior advisors in the company, but I didn't expect her here. I looked over at the guys, who were salivating over her, not that I blamed them though. She was gorgeous, and I felt both jealous, yet also kind of aroused.

"Yeah, nice to finally meet you," I told her.

"Same to you too. I've heard about you from the team. One of our star moms on the team," she said.

That's right. I did have a daughter named Clarisse. She's eight, and she's with her grandparents while I'm gone. Sadly, that's the last real big action I've gotten besides some disastrous hookups.

"Thank you," I told her.

"Course. I get it because I've got three kids myself. All a little older though," she told me.

So she was a mom too? That kind of made sense. The guys couldn't stop staring at both of us.

But it was best if we got started with settling in. I followed her out of there, making our way over to the hotel.

The first night was a simple dinner, but the bedroom eyes she kept giving me, and the way the guys looked at both of us was definitely exciting. I mean, it was something that was on the forefront of my mind, but I also kind of wondered what they thought about all of this too.

For a long time, we all just sat around, all of us talking and enjoying one another, the excitement in our bones. I could sense that there was tension though.

The next day was business meetings. Again, the tension was so thick you could cut through it with a knife. And yet, there was something about the way that she continued to look at me which made me shiver, and I wanted to just ask her what she had planned.

But I feared what may come about from that.

Oh well, no sense in getting worked up over it.

That evening though, I got a text from Maria, saying that she got us all a place to party. I asked her what she meant, and she said that we should celebrate, simply because it's been one hell of a journey.

I decided to tag along. After all, it's not like I didn't like the idea of it. I wore a simple black dress, walked into the building and headed to where Maria had this all set up.

When I got there, she was dressed in a suit that hugged her curves, just barely hiding anything. I flushed looking over at her, realizing that she did something to me.

"What's up?" she asked.

"Well…I was thinking we could have a little bit of fun here. You know, something to truly remember what we're doing here," she said.

"What do you…mean by that?" I said.

I looked around the place. It was a meager room, a space with of course, a bed for the most part. The sheets were red, and I noticed a long couch somewhere around here. Why did I get a feeling that this was something that she had planned for a while? Maybe I was overthinking this, but she looked at me, smiling.

"Tell you what, why don't you have a seat, Henry, David, Caleb, and Dan will be here in a minute," she said.

I nodded, listening to Maria's words. I sat down, but I couldn't shake the fact that her eyes were looking at my body as if assessing something. I flushed thinking about it.

Stay calm. You don't want to get too excited.

As they all came in, they sat at each of the different seats, and of course, Marie was at the helm. The strong, confident demeanor that she had was such a turn-on, and when she looked at me, she gave me a small smile.

"So how are you feeling?"

"Good. But what is this?" I asked her.

"Simple. We were thinking of celebrating. We're all away from the office, and there isn't anyone to stop us or to bother us," she said.

"What do you mean by that?" I asked her.

She leaned forward, grabbing my chin, holding it there, and looking me in the eyes.

"I know you've been staring at me for quite a while sweetie. It's quite obvious. And Henry and the others told me the same too. That you would steal looks. And I don't blame you, perhaps you have a little crush on them? But isn't it hard for you to truly experience stuff like this, since you're taking care of a kid the whole time," she said.

Fuck, was she trying to tease me? I felt a bit embarrassed by this, but then nodded.

"Yeah, I mean…you are attractive and all and—"

I noticed all of the guys staring at me, and I noticed as well that Caleb was moving his legs back and forth, putting his hands through his blonde hair. Dan kept a very placid look on his face, as if analyzing something. David and Henry both had chill smiles, looking at me with a curious glance, as if wondering just what in the world we'd plan next.

"So, what do you say? Wouldn't it be…kind of fun to experience something different? With one another? Perhaps this could be something that you enjoy," she said.

"You mean like…all of us together?" I asked.

"Bingo. But that depends. Are you ready for it?" she asked.

I flushed. I had a feeling she would try to solicit something like this out of me. I began to feel my face redden, and I knew that she was enjoying this as much as I was.

"Well, that depends. If you want this too. I wouldn't mind it," I said.

Deep down, I did crave the idea of being treated like a little slut.

"Well tell you what, why don't the guys show you around a little bit. I want to watch, to see how far you go. And don't worry, this is between all of us, so if you end up enjoying this, it will be kept a secret," she said.

I sighed in relief, enjoying the fact that she wanted to keep this a secret. That was relieving to say the least. But then, I felt Henry step forward, taking my hand and giving me a wink with his soft blue eyes.

"Get on the bed," he insisted.

I flushed, but then did so, laying down on the bed. Henry, David, Caleb, and Dan all got up, following me to the bed. Before I knew it, Henry's hands were on my sides, moving towards my head, cupping my chin, and looking me in the eyes.

Fuck he was attractive, but my thoughts were soon silenced by the kiss that he gave me. it was soft and sweet, but also something succulent and fun, and I certainly was a bit surprised by this. I kissed him passionately, lost in the touch. Then moments later, Dan grabbed my chin, pulling me over to him. He still had the placid face that he had before, but his lips were strong, domineering, and I could barely keep up. I let out a small cry, enjoying the touch of this, craving more from this guy.

Then, there was David, who gave me a small little smile. He gave me a kiss, which was wetter than I thought, and I quickly enjoyed it, kissing him back, loving everything about this, wanting more from him as he did this. He stayed like this, his tongue greedily touching and teasing mine.

Then of course, there was Caleb, who after I felt David pull away, grabbed my chin and then kissed me. He was the youngest, so he felt the most inexperienced. But the kiss still was nice, and it helped me explore him. As we stayed like this, his tongue came forward, enjoying my own, and I quickly realized that I liked this as much as he did.

We all enjoyed the kiss for a bit, and I could see Maria sitting there, crossing her legs and giving me a smile that said it all.

"Come on, I know all of you guys wanted her. Give her something to remember you all by," she said.

Then, that's when I felt it. A hand move toward my shirt, undoing the buttons, pulling it off my body. I gasped, feeling my whole body slowly get exposed. I shivered, enjoying the touch of this as I noticed their bodies move closer.

That's when I noticed Henry's hands move downward, along with his lips. I noticed David and Dan's hands touch me too, exploring my body with the littlest of touches. Caleb also was curious, but he moved back, studying the scene in front of me. Henry moved towards my bra, touching my nipples with his hands, looking me in the eyes as he spoke.

"You do have the nicest tits you know. I have thought about it before," Henry said.

The confession alone was a turn-on. I'd be lying if I said I didn't want this, especially with the way his hands seemed to skillfully touch me, moving his hands around my body, and then, moments later, he pushed his hands to the back of my bra, touching my back. He looked at me for a moment to see if I wanted that, and then, he undid the clasp, holding it as he looked into my eyes, seeing if I wanted it.

And I sure as fuck did. He pulled off the cups, tossing it to the side with the rest of my clothes, his hands reaching forward to touch my breasts, moving his hands there. As she did so, I let out the smallest of moans, feeling completely lost in the touch of this man.

"What's the matter? You enjoying this?" he said, letting his fingers dance and graze around.

I was. I was very much enjoying this, and I knew that he was smiling as he did this, the subtle touch enough to make me lose my mind. His hands continued to dance for a bit, until both Dan and David moved him away.

"No fair quit hogging her to yourself," David said.

"Yes, this isn't just you Henry," I heard Dan say coldly.

"Sheesh, sorry guys. Fine, you can have a turn," he said.

I looked at them, and David moved his hands against one of my nipples and pinched it slowly. I gasped and held the edge of the bed, completely lost in the pleasure of this experience, and as he did this, he looked me in the eyes.

"You're so docile already. How cute," he said.

Then there was Dan, who seemed disinterested at the onset, but as he continued this, he gave me that glowering look, the one that screamed he wanted this too. There was clearly something more there, a desire, that was both raw and passionate, and as he continued to move his hands there, he pinched my nipple hard, making me shiver and moan with delight, enjoying this too.

I watched them both smile, and there was clearly a need for more, a desire to experience all of this, and then, moments later, I felt the hand pull on my nipple hard, pinching it, making me suddenly feel the pleasure from this. David pressed his lips to my nipple, touching it, and I rolled my eyes to the back of my head, completely in awe.

As he did this, I felt a pair of hands against my thighs, touching me, and when I managed to finally look down, I saw Caleb there, giving me a cheeky look.

"Want more princess?" he said.

"Yes," I panted, feeling my body relax. His hands moved towards me, moving up my legs, tugging at my skirt, and looking forward.

"Then allow me to show you something that you will enjoy then," he purred.

I looked at him, unsure of what he meant by that, but then, moments later, he pulled my skirt off, and then moved his hands to my panties, pulling them off too. I looked at him, and shortly after, he lifted my legs up, letting his tongue dart inside of me.

I grabbed the sheets, but moments later, before I could make a sound, I felt Henry right over me. Caleb's tongue was so skillful, touching and teasing me slowly, that I felt like I was at a loss on how to feel. Henry looked at me, licking his lips as he spoke.

"You look so delicious right now," he said.

"Ahh," I said.

He undid his pants, pulling out his cock, looking me in the eyes as he stroked it. He was sizable, and as I saw the underside of it throb for me, I licked my lips.

This was indeed what the fuck I wanted.

I opened my mouth, pressing my lips to his cock, sucking on it passionately, enjoying the touch of his cock against my lips. I began with kissing it at first, and moments later, I started sucking on the tip of it. The sounds that he made were delightful, and I felt like I could listen to those sounds again and again for as long as I could remember.

As he did this, I noticed Caleb's tongue move forward against my clit, holding onto it with his lips for a second, sucking on it. As he did that, I let out a small gasp, suddenly feeling completely mesmerized by the feeling of this. Moments later I felt my orgasm hit me, causing me to cry out, amazed by how good this was, and then, Henry pulled his cock out of my mouth with a pop. He touched my hair, looking at me.

As he did that, I noticed Dan and David both pulled away too, chucking off their pants, their cocks hard and throbbing. Dan was fucking huge, and I flushed thinking about that inside of me.

"Well, you ready for this? I want to feel inside of you," Henry said.

"You…do?" I said.

"Of course. You seem delightful, and I'm going to be the first one to pound you," he said.

I blushed as I heard those words, but then, Henry pulled away, and Caleb replaced him. He looked at me, nervous as all hell.

"I'm sorry this is the first time that I've done something like this," he said.

"It's alright. I'm just…nervous too. That's all," I told him.

He pulled his cock out slowly, and while it was smaller than Henry's, it still was quite girthy. I flushed thinking about how it would feel to have that inside my mouth.

As I felt his cock slowly enter me, I felt two of the cocks in my hand start to move, and I grabbed them, jerking them as I sucked on the cock there.

Then, I looked down and there was Henry. He had my legs spread, his cock right up inside of me. He touched me there, smiling.

"Not bad for someone who popped out a kid," he said.

I mean, it was years ago, but the thought was nice. I flushed.

"Thanks," I mumbled.

He smiled and chuckled, but not before pushing into me, filling me up with his cock. He slowly began to move, looking at me with a smile on his face as he began to move. I flushed, lightly gasping and groaning against the cock that was in my mouth.

This was so good, every touch of him sending shivers down my spine, making me lose every semblance of control as I did this. He continued to pound deep into me, and I was lost in the touch. Everything was so good.

He grabbed my hips, hiking my legs behind me, fucking me hard and raw, and after a few more thrusts, he looked up at me, groaning.

That's when I heard it, the sound of his last thrust, and then, the feeling of his seed spilling into me. I let out a gasp.

But as I did that, Caleb grabbed my face, holding me there, and shortly afterward, he thrust hard. I sat there, gobbling down his entire cock, completely lost in the touch, and then, when he got it deep into my mouth, let out a sigh of relief, filling deep within me.

His seed touched the back of my throat, making me gasp out in surprise and pleasure. For a long time, I simply just took it in, enjoying it, and then, moments later, he pushed his cock out of me, smiling as he looked me in the eyes.

"You good?" he asked.

I nodded, shocked at how…good it tasted, and how I felt.

But it wasn't over yet. Both David and Dan pulled away, and David looked at him.

"You thinking front or back?" Dan asked.

What were they talking about? Front and back? But then, I saw David smile.

"You can have front. I don't think she'd be able to take you from behind," he said.

What were they—

As soon as I was about to ask, I felt Dan pull me up, and shortly after, he plunged himself into me, making me scream out in pleasure as he moved himself in and out of me slowly.

But as he did that, I felt something behind me, and when it hit, I started to gasp.

It was a finger, but it didn't necessarily hurt. I figured that it was covered in lube, and as he plunged on in, I gripped the sheets, enjoying the rocking of fingers back and forth, moaning slightly as I felt the fingers plunge in a bit and as he hit there, I started to scream out, holding onto him, feeling good about everything as it continued to eat me fully.

The two fingers, followed by the third, moved against me, and then, as he plunged in further and further, I tensed up, moaning out loud. Dan continued to move in and out of me too, and I loved everything about this.

I let out a shiver, turning to David and looking him in the eyes.

"Give it…to me," I told him.

He looked me in the eyes, and then nodded.

"You sure?"

"Yes," I breathed out.

He nodded, pushing himself deep into me, and then, as he did so slowly, I shivered, moaning out loud, crying out softly, feeling good about everything. I started to let out a moan as he did this, pushing in his cock fully.

As I did that, I felt Dan plunge deep into me too. As I felt them both take me like this, I started to tense up, feeling like I was about to go insane with every single motion. I wanted them, and I wanted them to continue this.

After a few more thrusts, David grabbed my butt, thrusting it forward. As he did that, Dan started to move against me, thrusting upward too, hitting me in each spot. They continued this, and I was lost in the pleasure of this, enjoying it all. For a long time, I was loving everything about this, and then, after a few more moments, I noticed Maria get up, move toward me, and then, start to smile.

"There we go. Look at you, being used by all of your coworkers. You like this don't you?" she said.

"Yes," I cried out, feeling the throes of the pleasure that came from this.

"Well, maybe you could help me out too. Since I gave you this good little privilege," she said.

She slowly moved herself towards me, her pussy pushed in my face. I eagerly took it, and then, she pushed her face forward. I was buried in a bunch of muff, and then, she smiled. I used my tongue to tease her, and she pet my head.

"That's a good girl. You like this don't you?" she said.

I let out a small moan of surprise, and she soon pushed my face deeper. I pushed my tongue out, moaning against her crotch, and she smiled, rubbing her face there.

"That's a good girl. A very good girl," she said.

I let out a moan as a hand moved between my legs, touching me there, and then, moments later, I started to feel my whole body tense up. Dan then plunged into me, letting out a groan, spilling himself deep inside me, filling me up completely.

I loved this, being used by anyone and everyone. As he finished up, Dan looked me in the eyes, smiling.

"Damn you felt great," he said.

As he said that, he moved away, and then David started to move up and down, and then, moments later, I felt him let out a small groan. He let out a gasp as he filled me up completely.

Finally, there was Maria. Maria shoved my face into her pussy, rubbing against my mouth, and then, she let out a small moan, and seconds later, she let out a small gasp, cumming hard, holding me there. For a long time, she held my face there, smearing it completely with her juices.

I took a moment to experience all of this, completely amazed and feeling good about everything that she did. She moved away, looking me in the eyes.

I was spent. I felt like taking a nap or maybe ten as I started to look at them, moving away as I started to sigh. I felt good, completely spent, and she looked over at me, holding me there as she smiled. She then gave me a long, passionate kiss, and for a second, we stayed like this. I did love this, and when she pulled away, she grinned.

"That was fun," she said.

"Yeah, sure was," I finally breathed out.

"Good. I'm glad I could help you then," she said to me.

She gave me another kiss, and I smiled, excited to be there with her, and for a long moment, we stayed like this. She then moved back, smiling towards me.

"We could arrange this again you know," she said.

"But how?"

"I was thinking maybe…we could have another work meeting, and maybe we could bring them along. That would be good, right?" she said.

I turned to the guys, all of them sitting there and looking at me. I smiled, feeling good about everything.

"Sure, I'd like that," I said to them. They all smiled.

"Yes, but we should probably be heading back you know. We're supposed to be at a meeting in the morning" Henry said.

"True," Dan said.

"Well, maybe we can meet up once more before the end of the trip. I thought about this, and I knew that this was something that would be fun for all of us.

I wondered just what may happen next. Or if things would be good. But as they left, I saw Maria there, looking at me with a small smile.

"Well, how did you like that? I arranged it at the last minute, and I figured it would be good for you," she said to me.

"I really enjoyed it. Honestly. It was so different though from what I thought. I never expected all of them to well…want this sort of thing," I told her.

"What happens in Vegas dear," Maria told me.

She was right. This was something that we wouldn't talk about with anyone else, but it would be something that I would remember forever. I looked at her, and I then nodded.

"That is true. But what now?"

"Well, I would suggest that you definitely figure out what you want to do next. Maybe we can have a meetup at the end of next month or something. And you know, I always found you pretty cute," she said.

I flushed, thinking about that.

"You were the first…girl I've ever done that with," I told her.

"Well, you were quite fun to deal with as well," she said.

I flushed, and then nodded.

"Yes, it was. But I guess we should be going. I don't know…how long you have this place for," I told her.

"I'm not sure myself. But I can keep it around for a little bit, what do you think?" she said.

I nodded.

"That's true. I wouldn't mind…possibly exploring more of you too," I said.

She let out a low giggle, moving towards me and then cupping my chin and looking me dead in the eyes. "Well, I'm sure we can continue to arrange that," she told me.

She pulled me toward the bed, giving me another long, passionate kiss. She tasted like strawberries, and I let out a small gasp of surprise and pleasure, enjoying myself. Everything felt fucking good, and that night, we made love on the bed, enjoying one another.

The next day, it was back to business. We went to the meetings we were supposed to, and I looked around at the rest of them, and they gave me a small smile.

I felt ready for this, and ready to do this again with them. But we had to keep it a secret. I was definitely excited to see where things would go, and how they would pan out.

We spent the rest of the trip like it was normal. Like we all didn't just have a whole massive gangbang in a random room that Maria put together.

But at the end of the trip, I noticed Maria give me a small wink as she boarded the plane.

My supervisor, someone who I never thought to be the type to do this sort of thing, did it, and I loved it. And as she left, she gave me a small note.

It just had some dates and a location on it, which probably indicated where the next one of these would be. Would she get involved in the next one? Or would it just be me?

Regardless, I felt excited about it. Sure, I did need to go back to my normal life, and Clarisse of course, but this was a trip that I would always remember, and it was obvious that what happens in Vegas will stay in Vegas, but it also will give me memories to remember it by, and I'll always remember the fun that I had here, and also the new experiences that I had with them, especially with the ones from my department.

And I would definitely do this again if given the chance.

The Mom at the PTO Meeting

MILFs

"Alright, I guess it's time to make my way over there.

I readied myself, leaving the office and heading to the PTO meeting. It was the first one I was invited to. Apparently, we were planning a huge fundraiser and bake sale for the school, and they wanted everyone's support. Normally I didn't give a rat's ass about this kind of thing, but it was for my daughter Alicia, so I guess I could see what this is.

I've never been the type to go to this kind of shit. Usually, it was kind of an obligation rather than of course, an actual decision on my own. But there was something thrilling, exciting, and fun about the idea of heading to this PTO meeting to meet some of the other parents.

It couldn't be too bad, right?

When I got there, I walked in, pushed my glasses up, and looked around. All of them seemed like your average parent, older, together with someone, and seemed to not want to be there even if someone paid them.

But there was one woman in the corner. She wore a sleek business suit, had her brown hair combed back in a tight bun, and seemed just as ready to leave as the rest of us.

There was also an empty seat there.

"Can I sit down?" I asked.

"Oh, sure! I guess I'm not the only single parent here," she said.

"Yeah, true," I told her.

I flushed, seeing her eyes linger over me. She then extended her hand.

"Alyssa," she said.

"Arnold," I replied.

She was probably the prettiest woman I've spoken to besides well... my late wife. Alyssa looked gorgeous, and when she looked into my eyes, she smiled.

"So, I guess you got roped into this too huh?"

"Yeah, cookies and fundraisers and such. I don't really have time to do this," I told her.

"Me neither. I can support, but I don't really want to waste my time doing these fundraisers," she said.

"Indeed. I run my own company, so this is not up my alley," I explained.

"You do? Oh, wow, that's so cool. I'm kind of climbing the ladder, so I'm definitely trying to get to that point," she told me.

"For sure."

We began talking, but I couldn't help but wonder if maybe, just maybe, this may turn into…something more. Something deeper. I couldn't help but marvel and think about that, especially given the instances that were happening.

For a long time, we stayed silent. The head of the PTO began blathering about how they were trying to make sales and such, but I couldn't help but feel my heart skip a beat as I looked over at Alyssa. She was gorgeous, and she seemed to have a wonderful head on her shoulders.

And I couldn't help but find that really attractive if I do say so myself.

The meeting was soon over, but then, Alyssa got up, looking at me.

"Well, that sucked," she said.

"Ugh, yeah. I could've just had this all emailed to me. but nooo," I told her.

"Right. Same here. Ugh, I just wanted a night off for once, and I had to go to this," she told me.

"Yeah, I feel that. My daughter is with her grandparents, so I finally had a little bit of freedom," I explained.

"I see. Well, if you want…you can come over to mine," she said.

She was older, but god she was attractive. I really was only here for my daughter, but honestly…I liked the idea of this.

"Sure, I wouldn't mind that," I said.

I could see the look in her eyes. A rampaging desire. Something she refused to admit until now. I wanted her to tell me a little bit more, and some of the other interesting aspects of herself, and as she got up, I saw a hint of her thighs against her skirt.

I licked my lips, realizing just how utterly beautiful she was.

I didn't want to get my hopes up though. The truth is, I felt like…if I did that, things would get a bit harder for me, but I kind of liked the idea behind it. Maybe I wanted to just take her and have my way with her right then and there.

But I also knew that I should take this slow.

We left the PTO building, and Alyssa turned to her car.

"Want to possibly meet at my place?"

"Sure, if that's okay with you," I told her.

She gave me something, flushing.

"My address. Let's link up," she said.

I pocketed it, nodding.

"Of course," I told her.

She winked, heading to the car, and as I looked downwards, seeing the address, I realized she wanted this as much as I did. And that's something that excited the fuck out of me.

Maybe it was the lack of action I've been getting, but I was more than ready to explore her body, to see what she had hidden underneath that business suit.

I then got to the car and drove to the location she gave me. it was a nice little place, and when I got to her one-story house, I pulled up. There was a tiny garden with little potters there. I saw that Alyssa made it home earlier.

I didn't know she was so sudden and forceful, inviting me home like this. I felt like…this was only going to get more and more interesting.

Not that I minded.

When I got to the door I knocked, and moments later she opened up.

"There you are Arnold," she said.

"Hey! I told you I'd be over," I teased.

"Course. I'm excited that you came," she said.

And as she said that, I don't know, something about that seemed very genuine to me.

"Well, I'm glad to be here," I told her.

She opened the door, letting me inside, and when I got in, I noticed how pretty the place was. It was beautiful if I did say so myself, and when she showed me in, I couldn't help but feel a little bit excited about this.

"Wow, you keep the place nice," I told her.

"Thanks. I try my best, what with all the hours that I do," she replied.

"Well, you certainly know how to not only work it, but also balance out your life. That's pretty admirable," I told her.

She laughed.

"It's not as cool as you think it is. Anyways, have a seat," she said.

She patted the area next to her, and I sat down. Alyssa then sighed.

"I'm just really glad that you're here you know. It's been a long time since I've actually…gone out with someone you know," she said.

"Really? I'm surprised. You're quite beautiful," I told her.

"Oh, thanks. It's just hard. Being a single mom, trying to keep everything together. I also haven't really found the right man for the job, especially with my little girl involved and all," she said.

I smirked, looking at her and smiling.

"Well, maybe you just need the right man for the job," I told her, reaching out and touching her thigh.

She turned to me, smirking.

"Really? And you think you're the perfect one for this?" she asked.

"I could very well be. I definitely have…a lot of interesting points if I do say so myself," I told her.

She looked me in the eyes, and then she nodded.

"Well thank you. I'm glad that I can interest you, even if only a little bit," she said.

"But of course. Anyways, I do want to say that you're quite the looker. And we're alone…right?" I asked her.

I didn't want a kid to come in while I was plowing their mom, that's for sure.

She then laughed.

"Yeah, don't worry, she's at her grandma's. I got a bit of a reprieve tonight," she said.

"Well, perhaps I can help you take care of that tension you've got. Looks like you have a lot," I told her.

"Oh, if you even knew," she teased.

I leaned forward, grabbing her chin, seeing that look in her eyes. She was gorgeous, and easily my type. Before I knew it, my lips were on hers, enjoying the soft, subtle touch of her. She had softer lips than I expected, and there was something really nice about all of that. I looked at her as I did this, seeing her close her eyes, relishing in the touch of the kiss. I stayed like this with her, taking a moment to explore every part of her lips and beautiful body, before I moved back.

"You good?" I asked her.

"Amazing really. I didn't expect you to be so forward. I kind of like having a man in charge," she purred.

I liked being the man in charge of her. I quickly kissed her again, enjoying the touch of her body, and the little sounds that she made as I kissed her. There was something almost tantalizing, addicting, and needy about this, and as I kissed her, I felt that need for so much more, and I ached for it.

I grabbed her, pulling her smaller body into my arms, kissing her with a dire passion. Our tongues moved forward, enjoying the taste and feel of one another. And in truth, I couldn't help but enjoy everything that she gave to me, and the feelings that were brought forward.

She then pulled me closer, moving her body so that our hips ground against one another. I let out a small groan, feeling excited and needy. I wanted her, and as she pulled away, she smiled.

"Want to take this upstairs?" she asked.

"Sure.," I told her.

She smiled, grabbing my hand and bringing me upstairs. When we got in there, I moved her towards the bed, pushing her down, kissing her passionately.

It was a dream come true. Being able to savor and taste this woman, this different type of experience, it was all so damn perfect, that I didn't know how to even move away from it, but when she pulled away, she looked me in the eyes, giving me a teasing smile.

"I have something even more special for you tonight," she said.

"What do you mean?" I asked.

She gave me a small kiss, beaming.

"You'll see," she replied.

I started to flush, moving my hands against her body, touching her curves, feeling up every part of her. She let out a small gasp as I moved my hands upward, touching her breasts, and then she smirked.

"You have such a good touch, maybe we can…take this a little bit further," she purred.

That's exactly what I wanted. I wanted to feel her, to experience her, to touch her in every single way. I started to look into her eyes, and for a long time, I saw her look at me, a look of pure hunger growing between us.

Did she…want me as much as I wanted her? Perhaps that was the case. And even if she didn't say it outright, she definitely had a whole feeling that made me lose my mind.

Her hands reached up, touching me softly, looking at me in the eyes.

"Go on ahead," she said.

And that's what I did. Her body was still supple, even for being an older woman. There was a thrill that came with being with someone who was around my age, who had a similar history to me. Maybe that's why I was so gravitated toward her, and everything that she did.

I started to move my lips downward, kissing and teasing the flesh on her neck, and then, I saw her tense up, and for a long time, I started to feel her body just relax, taking in every part of me. I started to feel her body relax more and more, and as I reached up, touching her from under her jacket, feeling her breasts there, she let out a sigh.

"You have quite the hands there," she said.

"Thank you. I could say the same to you," I purred.

She smiled.

"You flatter me," she said.

I then slowly pulled off her jacket and shirt, watching as her eyes widen, and for a long time, I simply just basked in the feeling of this, enjoying her body, relishing her touch. I started to move my hands downward, cupping her breasts, touching them there, watching her slowly start to let out a small gasp, pushing her hands upwards, letting out the delicious sounds.

Fuck, I couldn't get enough of this. I began to pull off her bra, tossing it to the side. She laid there topless and beautiful, and I started to realize I was hungry for her.

It'd been so long since I had sex, and the fact that she laid there, looking at me with a small wink and smile, it was enough to drive me crazy, and it made me ache for her.

I moved my hands downwards, starting to touch the tips of her breasts. She let out a small moan, tensing up, and then, I began to move my tongue towards her nipple, taking it between my lips, suckling on it while I flicked my tongue over her. She let out a low groan, holding me there as I started to move and explore her, enjoying the sounds that she made as I continued to experience her.

The fact that she was here, relishing the taste of me, it was all just…so damn perfect and so good, that I couldn't help but wonder just what else she had planned for me next.

I continued to move my hands, teasing her other nipple against my fingers, pressing my fingers slightly, watching as her eyes widened, and the sounds that she made driving me to the point of madness.

But as I finished, she looked up at me, and I noticed something different in her eyes.

A hunger.

Before I knew it, she flipped me over, leaving me down on the bed. I looked at her, and she had a smirk on her face.

"Told you I had something special planned," she said.

"What do you—"

Before I knew it, her lips were on mine, a domineering kiss driving me to the point of madness. She continued to kiss me, and for a long time, I eagerly accepted it. Then, she pulled back, touching my face.

"You look so cute when you sit there, practically begging for more. I take it you didn't realize that I like to be in control, and sometimes…I just like to have a little bit of fun taking over, seeing you lose your mind like this," she said.

I gulped. I realized I was in bed with a woman who was secretly a dom. She pretended to be all innocent, and just your average horny MILF.

But she wasn't.

She quickly pulled off my shirt, moving her hands, teasing my pecs, moving towards the tip of my nipples. She then grazed her fingers, causing a sudden rush of excitement to shift through my body.

"Holy shit," I told her.

"What's the matter? You struggling to hold back? Trying not to lose control?" she teased.

"Yeah," I said.

"Well don't worry, I want you to lose control. I like seeing men come undone like this," she said.

She teased my nipples once again, making me suddenly relish the pleasure, enjoying the feel of this as she did this. She continued to tease every part of me, and as I realized the fact that I was with a secret femdom, I kind of liked it.

I thought she would just be your average little innocent woman, but this hit different, not necessarily in a bad way. In fact, it…it felt good.

I felt her hands tease my nipples, making me suddenly shiver and push forward, moaning in pleasure at the feeling of this. I started to look at her, seeing the excitement in her eyes as she did this.

"There you go. Good boy. Look at you, all coming undone like this. This is my favorite type of guy. The kind that lets me have pure control, that lets me touch and tease them fully and lets me watch them slowly come undone with every little touch," she said.

"Ahh yes," I told her. I thrust upward, watching her smile as she slowly moved her hands downward. She teased the very tip of my cock from within my pants.

That's when I jolted forward. I couldn't take it. I felt like she was just going to completely tease me for the rest of the session, till I came.

"Ahh please," I said.

"Please what?" she teased.

I looked at Alyssa, who tried to play stupid, but I knew that she knew exactly what I needed.

"Please…tease me. Let me breathe," I told her. I knew that my cock was practically begging for me to be let loose. She looked at me, smiling.

"There we go. All I wanted to hear from you. You're very easy to tease and work with, that's something that I very much enjoy from you," she said.

"Yes," I purred.

She then smiled, moving downward, teasing me. I shivered, moaning slightly.

"What was that? I didn't hear you?" she said.

Fuck, she really did play hard to get. I sat there, holding the edge of the bed, feeling her hands continue to move with each and every single touch.

"Please, just…let me out," I told her.

"Alright then," she said.

She undid the button on my pants, and then the fly, pulling them and my boxers off. My cock sprang out, and she barely touched it, causing me to let out a small gasp, holding the bed.

"Wow, you're really hard already. How cute. But I kind of want to tease a little bit more," she said.

"What do you plan on—"

As I said that, she got up, pulling off her skirt and panties, moving herself so that she straddled my head. She rested there, making me suddenly shiver with delight, enjoying the feeling of this as I continued to gasp, tasting all of her. She shoved her pussy into my face, and I eagerly tasted it all.

"There we go. Good boy. Now that you've satisfied me, maybe I'll do more than touch you. Or maybe I'll wait till you can make me cum," she said.

Hearing those words was such a turn-on to me. I was already losing my damn mind, and I couldn't help but feel it start to make me feel like I was at my wit's end. I started to thrust my body upward, feeling every part of this drive me to the brink.

"Fuck," I said under her.

She smiled, shoving her pussy further towards my face. I explored, savoring the taste, sticking my tongue against her entrance, fucking her restlessly with my tongue. As I did that, she held the bed, crying out loud, enjoying the feeling of this.

She continued to shove her pussy into my face, forcing me to eat her out. I enjoyed every moment of this, savoring the taste, the feeling, and everything that came from it. The sounds that she made, including the way that she tried to hold back her own moans, was enough to drive me crazy too. I looked at her, and she simply smiled.

"There we go," she said to me. I looked at her, knowing that this was indeed what she wanted, and it was something that I desired too.

I continued to satisfy her, enjoying the little sounds. When I moved my tongue upward, hitting that one part of her, I suddenly felt her body shiver, holding herself down. I struggled to breathe, but at the same time, I savored it, hearing the delicious sounds that came out of her.

"Fuck!" she said.

She then let out a series of cries, cumming, and smearing my face with her juices. She was filthy, and I loved it. She then finished, and she looked over at me, smiling.

"There we go," she said to me.

"Ahh," I said out loud as she moved away from me. I would kill to have her smother my face completely once again, but she stopped herself, looking me in the eyes.

"Well, what did I tell you? Pretty good huh?" she said.

"Yes. I want more," I told her.

She then laughed.

"Well, why don't I give you a little treat then," she said.

She then moved herself so that she was right over my cock. She touched it, barely letting her fingers drape there, and suddenly, I let out a small groan, completely enamored in the feeling that this gave me. She then laughed, seeing me slowly come apart.

"Look at you. So turned on that you can't even think straight. How pathetic," she said.

"Yes, I'm pathetic. I just want you," I told her.

That probably sounded so lame, but I couldn't stop thinking about this, and how amazing this felt. I looked into her eyes, seeing the look of pure desire there. She soon moved herself so that she was right up against my cock, letting her hands touch the tip of it, and then grabbing the shaft, jerking it slightly.

I looked at her, feeling completely lost in the touch that I felt. She smiled, jerking me right then and there, watching me with widened, expectant eyes.

"You're not allowed to cum yet," she said to me.

"Okay," I told her, cringing as I felt her hand grab my hard dick, keeping me right then and there. She continued to jerk me slightly, watching my eyes practically roll to the back of my head.

Then, I felt her lips. I suddenly realized that she knew exactly how to drive me to the edge. She soon moved her lips so that she was right against the tip of my body, and then, before I knew it, she pushed her lips to the tip, sucking on it before taking me downward. She let her tongue move forwards, getting from the underside over to the tip of my dick. I watched with a rapturous look, seeing her there, holding me there. I felt like I was at the mercy of her touches, and there was something shocking, but such a turn-on surrounding it.

"Yes," I said.

"What's that?"

"Please…more," I told her.

She then giggled, touching me right then and there, looking me in the eyes as she did it.

"Really now. What is it that you want then?" she said.

She then took her mouth and pushed downwards, getting about halfway. She stuck her tongue out, pushing against the underside. I let out a small groan, holding there. She continued bobbing her head up and down, leaving me a fucking mess right there in front of her.

I was completely enamored in the touch of this, aching for more, but also knowing damn well that she could just stop this at any time, and just make me lose it all right then and there.

I was so close already, and when her fingers moved towards my balls, touching there slightly, I felt my eyes practically loll to the back of my head. I was about to lose it, shivering there as I let out a small groan.

"Fuck," I told her.

"What's the matter?" she said.

I was about to cum. But I didn't want to cum.

"I can stop right now, and you can cum inside me. You want that, don't you?" she said.

"Yes," I whispered.

"What was that?" I can't hear you," she said.

This fucking tease. She was doing this to make me lose it. Then I spoke, realizing that I was at her mercy.

"Please. Let me cum," I said right then and there.

She giggled.

"Fine, I'll let you cum. But I'm on top," she said.

Before I could say anything else, she slowly slid herself down against me, holding me there. Her pussy felt so warm and tight that I relished the feel of it. I looked at her, seeing her smile there.

"There you go. Now just relax. I'll take great care of you," she purred.

And I knew that she would. She began to move up and down, letting her pussy completely smother all of my senses, making me lose my mind right then and there. I grabbed her, and I held onto her as she started to move her hips up and down into that one sort of style, making me lose all semblance of reality, completely mesmerized by the feeling of this.

"Holy shit," I told her.

"Yes? What is it?" she said.

"I can't…I can't hold back. Please let me c um," I said.

I felt a little pathetic for begging, but her pussy was so good. I reached up, touching her tits, feeling her let out a small moan of surprise as she started to move against me.

"There we go. Good boy. I want to hear you beg for it though," she said.

"Please, let me cum," I said, realizing how pathetic I probably sounded. But in truth, I didn't care anymore. I ached for her, I needed her, and then, after a few more thrusts, she pushed in, making me lose my mind.

I then came hard, feeling myself just lose it there. I reached out, rubbed her clit, and then, she let out a small gasp, cumming as well as I finished off with her. I was a mess, completely lost in the touch of her pussy, and I knew that she liked this too.

She finished, finally moving off of me, looking me in the eyes as she smiled.

"Damn," she said to me.

"What's up?" I said.

"It's been a while since a man kept up with me like that. I'm going to be honest, most of them can't handle a woman who…likes to be in charge," she said to me.

I flushed, realizing that she saw me as something more, something different. I mean, it wasn't what I was used to, but I tried my best to kind of accept it.

"I mean, I like to make things fun, whatever they may end up being," I told her.

"True. Anyways, you were a fun lay, and I'm glad I went to that PTO meeting," Alyssa teased.

I reached out, touched her hair, and looked her in the eyes. I never thought that I would nab a girl who preferred to be dominant. In a strange way, that was so fucking hot to me.

"You know, I kind of like that you're dominant. It's a bit different if I do say so myself," I told her.

"Course it is. That's why I struggle to meet new guys. A lot of them just see me as someone that they can top and take control of. But honestly…I like it when I can have my own little fun you know," she said.

"It's different, that's for sure, but I kind of like it," I told her.

"I figured you would. Thank you for that though Arnold. You really are the first guy I've met who just gets it, and I like that," she said.

I blushed. I'm glad that I could be an interesting person to her, and someone that she could trust as well. I reached out and looked her in the eyes as I touched her slightly, holding my hand there.

"I'm really glad that I can make you feel good," I told her.

"I feel the same way too," she replied.

I leaned in, giving her a long, passionate kiss as we stayed like this, enjoying the touch of one another. There was something exciting about this, and for a long time, I simply stayed like this, enjoying the soft touch of her lips. Then, she pulled back, looking me in the eyes slightly.

"So, do you want to…maybe go out on a date or something?" she asked me.

I was surprised that she wanted to do that. I mean, I couldn't really say no, but I also was shocked that this was something that she wanted as well.

"Sure, if that's what you desire?" I asked her.

"Yes, it sure as shit is. I really want that," she told me.

I beamed, reaching out and touching her cheek, looking into her eyes and smiling.

"Well, I'm glad that I can enjoy this with you then. I'm sure it'll be good for both of us," I told her.

She beamed.

"It sure will be. And I'm glad that you get it. I like being a dominant woman in the bedroom, even though usually…I tend to be more submissive outside of the bedroom," she said.

"Well it's different, but not something that I can't get used to," I told her.

She smiled.

"Thanks, Arnold. It's weird, you're like the first guy I've fucked who gets it. Most of them don't understand, and I like that a lot about you," she said.

"Well I try to, and I'm glad that I'm someone who you can rely on," I told her.

She beamed, giving me one last kiss.

And that's how I ended up hooking up with a MILF who was similar to me, and someone at the PTO meeting. This was fun, and something I would do again in a heartbeat. I felt good, happy, and ready for action next time. I knew that Alyssa was fun, and she was different, and I knew for a fact that she was someone that would be remembered in my head, and someone that I could never forget, no matter what happened between us next, and how things went from here.

Her Strange Fetish

Feet, BDSM, Tickle

"What was it that you wanted to talk about?" my dom boyfriend Glen asked.

I flushed. I wanted to try it, especially since it was something that I saw.

"Say glen, have you ever thought about well…. Feet stuff?" I asked him.

He looked at me, slightly surprised by my words.

"Can't say I have," he said.

"Well, it's just…it's something that I wanted to try during our next play session. I saw it and figured it…it might be kind of fun," I told him.

I figured that this may be something weird to talk about, but maybe Glen would get it. We have talked about what we want to try and like before. Feet was never something on the table though.

But it was because I found a video a couple of days ago. It was a woman, fully clothed, but the fetish was tickling. She ended up orgasming after that happened. When I saw it, I thought that it was the hottest shit, but I had no idea how to convince Glenn that it was okay to try it.

"Are you sure that you want to try it?" Glen asked.

"Yeah, I do. I figured it would be kind of weird. Plus, I mean, you're always commenting how nice my feet look. Maybe it might be something you could enjoy too," I told him.

He looked at me, slightly surprised by this, but then, he nodded.

"Are you sure about this?" he asked me.

"Yeah, positive Glen. Let's…try something new," I told him.

I figured this would be a little bit weird for us, but Glen took a moment to process it. He took a deep breath and then nodded.

"Yeah, we can try that next time," he said.

I beamed, excited to experience this.

"I'm sure we'll both love it," I told him.

"I think so too," he said to me.

So that's what we agreed on. In our next play session, we would try the feet and the tickling stuff. I felt excited to explore this. Because maybe it would be something new that I could enjoy.

It wasn't the first time I'd been into weird fetishes of course. I loved being degraded, and I loved being put into embarrassing positions. Maybe this foot thing was just the right step forward.

That night, I sat on the bed, waiting for him to come home. He told me to get on the bed and get ready. I braced myself, wearing a sheer pair of panties and a sheer bra that showed the outline of my rosy pink nipples. I flushed thinking about this.

Would he enjoy it? Or would this be another fetish that we'd toss to the side because we both ended up hating it? Honestly, I didn't know for sure, but I wanted to believe that there may be a chance for both of us to explore this, enjoy one another, and have a good time.

Then, I heard the sound of the door unlock. I moved towards the doorway, seeing Glenn there. He was dressed in a pair of tight leather pants, and he looked me over, smiling.

"There you are. Been waiting a while?"

"No Master. I was just…getting ready," I said.

"I see. Say my pet, there's something I've been curious about," he said.

"What do you mean?" I asked. I didn't know how he would respond to this, but I figured it would be a fun little thing.

He looked at me, and then down at my feet. I had painted them a pretty color to add to the experience.
"Your feet look really nice," he said.
"Thank you, Master," I said.
He then reached up, touching them, caressing them. It sent a jolt through my body, causing me to flush, letting out a small gasp and moan of pleasure.
"What's the matter? You like it when I touch your feet?" he asked.
"Yes," I said.
"Well tell you what, why don't you get comfortable, and Master can service these feet as much as you'd like," he said to me.
I looked at Glenn, nodding.
"Alright," I said.
I laid down on the bed, noticing that his hands moved to my arms, putting them in the restraints that we had. What did he have planned next? He looked over at my feet, letting his hands barely touch against the tips of them, caressing downward, watching as I let out a small moan of pleasure at the touch.
"Damn, turned on already?" he teased.
"It feels…nice," I told him.
"Well…Master can give you a nice little foot massage. And then a little bit of a punishment too after we're done," he purred right up in my ear, licking against the edge.
The way his voice came off right then and there made me shiver with delight, moaning in response as I started to feel my whole body react to his touch. I was completely lost in this, amazed at how nice this felt, and how this just…made me want more.
"Yes. I'd really like that."
"Yes, what?"
"Yes, Master," I breathed out, feeling my breath hitch as he started licking and caressing down my neck, touching and teasing every part of me, making me lose control, moaning in response, enjoying the touch of his hands as he continued touching me.
Even just the littlest of touches was enough to turn me the fuck on, and as he moved his hands down, just barely touching my body, I felt like I was on the very edge. I loved everything about this, feeling the enjoyment of it as I continued to feel his hands move further downward, past my pussy and thighs, going for what he had his attention on first.
My feet.
I knew that deep down glen also had a foot fetish, but he was quiet about it. At least, until now that is. He continued to touch the edges of my feet, tickling them slightly.
I suddenly tensed up, curling them, feeling my whole body jolt forward. I stayed against the bindings, but I let out a small gasp of pleasure, feeling him tickle my feet.
"Holy shit," I said.
"What's the matter there? You liking it?" Glenn said, touching my feet once more.
I quickly laid there, experiencing the pleasure that came from this. It was like a surge of energy, and of need.
"Ahh yes!" I told him, curling my toes as he continued to let his hands crawl against the tips of my feet, resting on the soles. He got to the back of my foot, and with just one little touch, I practically jolted forward, crying out in pleasure as he did this.
There was something about the way this man just touched my feet, making me lose my goddamn mind, experiencing the fun and loss of control as he did this. I loved it, and as he continued to touch me there, holding me, I suddenly started to tense up, moaning out loud.
"You good?" he said to me.
"Amazing," I finally breathed out. but that was an understatement.

I didn't expect to get off to the feeling of my feet being tickled. But then he got in between the toes, moving against the underside of my big toe, letting his tongue roll out, touching the very edges.

I cried out, moaning out loud, enjoying his hands and lips as he continued to suckle and tease every part of my toes. It was like I was experiencing a whole new world, a world of feet that of course was something that I enjoyed far more than I expected. I started to feel his hands move upward, tickling the underside of the front of my feet as he sucked on my toes, and I cried out, holding myself there as I felt the pleasure from being tickled just completely destroy me.

It was a weird fetish, and it wasn't something that most people were into, but seeing his hands there, touching and teasing every part of me, it was just…enough to drive me insane. I continued to hold onto the edge, tensing up as I cried out, moaning out loud as I felt like I was on the very edge.

It was then when, moments later, he then moved to the sides of my feet, teasing there with his tongue. When he did that, I suddenly held onto him, moaning out loud as I struggled to hold back. But it wasn't like there was much I could do, and not much to say. I simply just felt the feeling of losing control hit me, making me shiver with delight, crying in pleasure, and loving everything about this.

He continued to service my feet, no matter how dirty and gross they got. There was something so nice about it, especially since Glenn seemed to develop this fetish as he went along too.

Then, he pulled away, looking at my dainty, soft feet there. He touched the middle part of them, massaging my feet, and it was enough to make me scream out once again, holding onto it, and then, feeling my body get so close to orgasm. As soon as he touched it though, he stopped, looking me in the eyes as he smiled.

"You good?" he asked me.

"Amazing," I told him.

"Good. I like seeing you turned on," he told me.

"I love…I love what you keep doing to my feet, Master," I cried out.

"Of course you do. You're a little degenerate who gets off to feet. How nasty," he said.

He then moved toward the nightstand, grabbing something. As he did that, he came back over, resting the item against my feet. It was a small little feather tickler, and when I felt it there, I grimaced, biting my lip as I felt it.

"Holy shit," I told myself.

"You okay?"

"Yes," I said.

He let the tickler touch the very tip of my feet, making my toes curl, and my body suddenly lost all semblance of control. I began to feel my body suddenly relax, emerging deep into the bowels of pleasure as I felt it all take over me. His hands moved downwards, getting to the middle of my feet, moving there. I cried out, grabbing the chains once again, completely lost in the touch. I felt my body tense up, the pleasure driving me crazy. I didn't expect just mere tickling to drive me crazy, but the more he did it, even the smallest of touches, was enough to make me hold my tongue, cry out, and lose my mind.

He then pressed there once again, and suddenly, I felt the overwhelming sensation of pleasure as I felt my orgasm hit me hard, causing me to tense up, cry out loud, and then cum hard against him.

He then moved his hands away, looking at me as I laid there, completely immersed in the pleasure.

"Looks like you really do get off to tickling and your feet. I never expected this from you," he said.

"Ahh, yes," I told him.

He then moved his hands upward, touching the sides of my body. He began to tickle me there, making me hold my tongue, cry out, and tense up once again.

I was very ticklish. I didn't expect to get off to mere tickling like this, but it was hot to say the least, and I ached for more. His hands moved against me, tickling my sides, making me laugh out loud.

"Yes, yes"! I screamed, holding myself there, completely immersed in it all, the pleasure driving me mad. He continued to tease me, watching my eyes widen with pleasure and desire, the excitement growing within me. I began to feel my insides tense up, and I was turned on by tickling.

I didn't know this was a legitimate fetish until he did this just now. It was like I discovered something new and raw, utterly amazing, and with every single tickling touch, I felt my body jerk forward, the lurking feeling of being tickled and at this man's mercy just becoming an arousing moment for me.

For a few moments, I felt his hands skirt up and down, causing me to lose my mind. I loved being a sub to this type of feeling. Being a little bitch to my Master as he tickled me. but then, just as I was about to cum again, he stopped, looking at me.

"I have a little proposition for you," he said.

"What is it?" I asked.

"If you can last being tickled while I fuck you to the point where I cum, I'll let you get off with a tickle orgasm," he said.

I flushed. He was having a blast with this.

"So, I have to last as long as I can?"

"Correct. A test of endurance. For both of us," he purred.

I liked the sound of this. But it would be a challenge, considering how good he was at holding back to the point where I doubted that he would just get overtaken.

"Please. Please fuck me," I said.

I didn't mean to sound so needy, but my whole body craved it. I saw him smile, and then, I expected him to just plunge into my pussy.

"Not just yet. I didn't tell you where I was going to fuck you yet," he said.

What did he mean by—"

As soon as I thought that he then moved a lubed finger towards my pucker, which stood there, open for the taking. I flushed, tensing up, crying out as I felt the finger move in, teasing me right then and there. He began to press the fingers deep within me, making me suddenly lose my mind, holding me there as I tensed up, feeling the need for more.

More…please," I said.

I was so turned on, but I knew that he wouldn't let me get off with just that. He soon added a second finger, pushing all the way into me, causing me to tense up, suddenly crying out loud, completely lost in the pleasure of it. He pushed the two fingers in, and then grabbed my foot, teasing it against his tongue. I howled, begging for him to just fuck me right then and there. I didn't know how long I could last with all of this, and he seemed to get a thrill from this. Maybe that's what he was trying to go for. To watch me completely lose myself, and beg for more.

"What, you want my cock already?"

"Yes, please," I said.

He then tickled my feet, which caused me to scream out, holding onto the bindings, looking at him. I was at the mercy of this man's touch, and I loved every goddamn minute of it.

"Well since you asked so nicely, perhaps I could satisfy those desires. But I don't know, you seem to be almost too much fun to be with," he said to me.

"Ahh, please," I told him.

"Please, what?"

"Please give me your cock. I beg you," I said.

I normally wasn't the begging type, but I was already at my fucking limit. He smiled, pushing me back even further so that my feet were near my head. He then lubed up his cock, spreading my cheeks apart, and then slid himself all the way inside of me. I shivered, feeling it all hit me at once, making me suddenly lose control, completely aching for him, knowing that he enjoyed this as much as I did.

After a brief moment, he stayed there, looking me in the eyes, and for a long time, we simply stayed like this. Then, he began to move, and I suddenly felt that urge, that need, and that desire. But I was so close already. However, I didn't want to cum yet.

I knew that I wouldn't get off fully if I came right then and there. I started to look at him, seeing the smile on his face as he started to move his cock in and out, completely breaching me. I laid there, taking all of this, when suddenly, he grabbed my foot, rubbing it.

That bastard! He was trying to tease me on purpose! To make sure that I'd lose it right then and there. He was totally trying to see me lose my mind, and it was then when, after a few more thrusts, he then pushed all the way in.

"Fuck, you're so tight. I can't wait to get you off with your favorite move," he said.

I laid there, engulfed in pleasure, enjoying the touch of this, completely losing every part of my mind as he continued.

He pushed in deep, holding me there as he groaned, spilling himself all the way inside of me, watching my eyes widen as he filled up my hole. He finished up, pushing out, looking at me there. I was in a compromising position, my whole body just completely lost in the pleasure of this, and when he looked at me, he smiled.

"There we go," he said.

"What do you…mean," I asked him.

"I see you right there. You seem to be a good girl. But maybe I just…want to fill you up completely. And then tickle you, making you spill out all of the cum that you have inside. How about that," he said.

He touched me, teasing me there, making me suddenly gasp with pleasure. Was he really going to put it inside me again? Or was he just messing with me? His touches moved downward, getting to that area between my legs where my legs met my crotch. He pressed against there, making me suddenly huff with surprise, completely enraptured in the feeling of this.

"What do you say? You want to be filled up by me first in both your holes, and then tickled to orgasm?" he asked, touching me slightly with his fingers.

I liked the idea of it, but was he ready to do that again? I looked at him, and after he wiped himself down, he smiled.

"I'm waiting," he said.

"Yes," I finally said, completely lost in the feeling of this.

"Yes, what? I can't hear you," he teased.

That bastard! But then I sighed.

"Yes. Please fill up my holes, Master. I need it," I told him.

I didn't expect to sound like such a needy bitch, but I was already lost in the pleasure, in the fun, and lost in the feelings that this gave to me. He looked at me, resting his fingers against my pussy.

"Maybe I should tease you further too. Tickle you to the point of orgasm, but not let you have it. How does that sound?"

I wanted to refuse, but then, before I knew it, his hands moved upward, teasing the very edge of my armpits. As he did this, his hand moved downward, touching and exploring me. He looked me dead in the eyes as I laid there, completely lost in the pleasure that Glenn gave to me. the little touches set me on fire, and I knew that when I did finally orgasm again, I would completely lose it, and that's something that excited me too.

He pumped his fingers in and out, holding me there, watching as my eyes started to widen, completely lost in the feeling of this. He then moved his fingers upward, moving right up against my G-spot. He teased there, watching as I widened my eyes, holding him there as I continued to shiver, cry out with pleasure, and lose my mind and body.

Every part of me wanted more of this, and everything craved the touch of him. He continued this tease, these amazing feelings of pleasure, driving me mad, and it was then when, after a few more moments, he pulled away, and I looked at him with annoyance. But then, he tickled me while he tickled my armpits. He moved his hands to my clit, tapping and teasing there, watching as my eyes practically rolled to the back of my head, holding everything still there as I continued to experience him. I knew that he was doing all of this on purpose, to get me so close that I would lose my mind, but it was then when, after a few more moments, a few more thrusts, I was right at my limit.

But like he said, he pulled away, his fingers sopping wet from my aching need.

"Damn girl, you really want this don't you?" he said.

"Yes. Please. Give it to me," I said. I didn't expect begging to cum would be the one thing that I desired, but I knew for a fact that he had me in the palm of his hand, watching me, seeing the way that I reacted to everything. He then moved back, spreading me apart, looking at me there.

"You're so cute, hun. I can't wait to watch you squirm in response to what I have in store for you," he said.

Before I could say anything more, he spread my legs far apart, sliding all the way in. He held me there, but I already let out a garbled series of sounds, completely lost in the feeling of this, and I knew that he enjoyed this too. He started to push himself in deep, watching my eyes widen, and my whole body completely lose it. I started to feel like I was so close to my limit that I didn't know what would happen next. After a few more moments, and a few more thrusts, I started tensing up. I knew that I was at the end, at the limit, but he stopped me.

He pushed upward, narrowly avoiding that spot, and then, he let out a groan. A series of small spurts of cum filled me up completely, making me slowly lose my mind. Everything about this just felt so damn good, that I couldn't get enough of it. I looked at him as he made his last couple of thrusts, pushing away from me, seeing the cum that was there as it spurted out of my holes.

"Beautiful," he said.

I was so horny still. I needed a release. I looked at him, a look of pure need on my face.

"Right, you want this, don't you?"

"Yes. I need to cum. Please. I'm so close," I said, moving my hands there.

"Well, in that case, I'm going to make it an orgasm that you won't forget," he told me.

What else could he possibly do here? What else could he...do to make me lose my mind? But then, he grabbed a couple of ticklers, moving toward where my armpits were.

Oh, so this was what he had planned for me. He rested the feather tickler gently against me, looking at me, seeing the way that I seemed so passive because I was so needy. I begged for a release because I didn't know how much more of this I could take, or even what I could do anymore.

He smiled, watching me squirm. He then moved his hands upward, with the feather tickler. He got behind my head, resting them on my armpits.

"Then cum," he said.

He began dragging them there, and I let out a small moan. I started to feel my whole body begin to lose control, squirming about, and moaning. I pushed my legs together, the cum spilling out of me a little bit as I did so. I let out a small moan, suddenly feeling like I was at my limit. After a few more moments, he made his hands move a little bit faster, watching me tense up and cry out loud.

"Fuck," I said.

I knew that I couldn't hold back. But then he dug it deep into the crevice of my armpit, and then, as he did this, I suddenly moaned, holding myself there, tensing up as I felt the force of my orgasm hit me slightly. I looked at him, crying out loud, feeling my body tense up, my head spin, and my body move forward.

But what I didn't expect, was what else came out. there was something that came out of my pussy, spreading all around and creating a wet spot on the bed.

Holy shit. I squirted. I started to moan once again, feeling the high of my orgasm hit me hard, and he continued, watching me shiver, cry out with delight, and it was then after a few more moments, I suddenly started to tense up, feeling my whole body shiver, and then, I came hard once again, feeling the effects of this as he continued to tickle me.

It was like relentless feelings of pleasure, of orgasm, and of a feeling that was only going to drive me more and more to the limit. He pressed it there, and then, I screamed out, cumming hard, feeling like I was going insane.

After my fourth orgasm, he then stopped, pulling away to finally give me a moment of reprieve. I sat there, feeling filthy, but also completely satisfied in ways I didn't expect to feel. He looked at me as I smiled at him, happy and satisfied.

"Thank you," I told him.

"For what?"

"For…that. It's not every day I can admit my feelings about fetishes and not be seen as fucking weird," I told him.

He giggled.

"Well, you are weird, but you're my weirdo," he said.

"Thank you," I told him.

He leaned in, giving me a passionate kiss. We stayed like that, making out. he then undid the bindings, and I wrapped my arms around Glenn, my Master, and someone who seemed to understand my feelings and kinds. It's not every day that I got to experience something like this, and I felt really good about it.

After we kissed for a bit, he pulled back, looking at me.

"So how did you like it? Was I good enough?" he asked me.

"Yeah, it was amazing," I told him.

"Good. I'm glad that I can make you feel good," he told me.

I was glad about that too. I flushed though, and he looked at me with a bit of concern.

"Something the matter?" he asked.

"No, I'm just really happy that you gave me this chance. I feel a lot better," I told him.

"Yeah, I'm glad that you could trust me with this. Honestly, I think you helped unlock a foot fetish in me as well. I'm really just…glad that you're here with me," he said to me.

"I'm very glad too," I told him.

He gave me a long, passionate kiss, and I kissed him back, enjoying the touch of our lips. We stayed like this, kissing fervently for a little bit before he pulled away, smelling me.

"I think it's time for you and me to have a shower," he said.

"Yeah, I definitely feel that," I told him.

He reached out, taking my hand and squeezing it.

"And don't worry, you don't have to tell anyone about this. It'll be our little secret," he said.

I smiled.

"Yeah, it sure as shit will be our little secret," I told him.

"I'm sure that once we have everything sorted out, you'll be able to really experience the fun and kink of life, and I know that you will enjoy this more and more too," he said.

I beamed.

"Yeah, I do feel like it opened the door to something inside of me, something that I didn't expect to feel," I told him.

"Well, I'm glad that you're able to really express yourself, and feel good about it too," he replied.

"I'm really glad too. I'm just glad that…I could try this out in a place with someone who gets it. So, thanks babe," I told him.

"No problem," he replied.

He gave me a long, passionate kiss, and we stayed like this for a long period of time, just kissing and touching one another. I relished in this, and for a long time, I simply just experienced the moment, completely in awe at how good I felt. Everything just…really felt amazing. I was glad to have this, and then, as he looked at me, he smiled.

"And don't worry, I won't expose your secret to anyone. We can keep the feet and tickling between us," he said with a smirk.

I blushed but nodded.

"Thanks, babe. I do appreciate it. It's weird to really feel this way, but I'm glad that you're here with me," I told him.

"I'm glad too. And I'm glad that we can experience this together," he told me.

I smiled too.

We went to go take a shower, and I felt really good. Exhausted, but fucking good. I realized as I showered that I experienced something different, something completely fun, and I enjoyed every second of it. I wanted to feel more, and I knew that he did too.

But it was good to finally learn what I was into kind of, to really experience everything that I wanted to with it. I knew that it was different from what I was used to, and it probably was a bit of a weird kink for some people. But the fact that I had a partner who at least kind of understood this was…nice to say the least. And I felt like I was definitely happier too. There was a feeling of happiness, of settlement, and I knew that no matter what, we were in this together; and he would understand me, no matter what kinds of weird kinks I'd bring to the table next.

And that made me happy, made me feel good, and made me realize just how much he mattered to me.

The Cop's Newfound Fun

BDSM Roleplay

I didn't think that I'd take the demotion so terribly.

But I ended up feeling like a loser the moment I saw the email. They were making the department smaller, so the rookie cops that had been mostly on the sidelines were now demoted to grunt work at HQ.

It sucked. I missed driving around looking for people who needed help and arresting bad people.

Which was why I quit the force shortly after. It was totally my decision, unlike what my boss said to me. The truth was, I wanted to explore new horizons, and see what other kinds of lives there were out there. But I did miss the idea of roleplaying the scenarios, which was what made me seek out roleplay. I wanted to roleplay the high of being a cop once more, but I also…I also just wanted the sexual release from it. And that's when I met Tyra.

Tyra was a former dominatrix, but now did mostly house calls as both a dom and a sub. When we met u, at first, I was a little bit nervous, but she ended up showing me the fun that came with my fetishes and fantasies. Of course, it was strictly casual, but Tyra really did help me with release.

That's when I prompted the question to her.

"Anything you want?" she asked, her darker skin a perfect contrast to the perfectly white sheets. Her lips curled into that of a wry smile as her dark brown eyes looked into my bluish-grey ones.

"Yeah, I was thinking…oh fuck I don't want to make it weird for either of us," I told her.

"If you have something that you want, you shouldn't be afraid to ask you know," she said.

"No, it's just…I'm sorry," I said.

She leaned forward, touching my face and looking into my eyes.

"You pay for this, if there is something that you want, now is the time to tell me," she pointed out.

She was right, even if I didn't want to admit it.

"It's more just like…I want to try out roleplay. I used to be a cop before I went into investing," I explained.

"Oh, that explains that feeling I got from you. I got the vibe that you were a cop or a nonpracticing one," she said.

"Well, I don't practice anymore for uh…reasons. But yeah, I kind of want to try new things," I told her.

"So, what you thinking? Anything in particular you want to try?" she asked me.

I flushed. I then nodded.

"Yeah, I want to roleplay being a cop, and punishing the criminal," I said.

"That sounds like fun," she said.

"Okay, so it's not weird then. Thank fuck," I told her.

She reached forward, touching my arm and looking at me.

"Honey, I will tell you if something is weird. And you're not weird," she said.

"Thanks," I replied with a smile.

I then grabbed her arms, pushing her down onto the ground.

"So, I heard that you were a naughty girl," I said.

I pushed my hands behind her back, and she moaned.

"Yes, I've been a VERY naughty girl," she said.

The way she said that had me going. There was a thrill of being in control, of being in charge, but also keeping this to a strictly bedroom setting. It was nice knowing that no matter what, we could explore one another, and enjoy each other's touch.

I trusted her, and I'm sure that she trusted me too.

I then pulled her upward, my lips right near her ear.

"So, you willing to be my little pet? I can make those naughty problems go away if you choose?" I offered.

"Ahh, yes," she said.

The way the words came out of her mouth was enough to drive me insane. I was so fucking hot and bothered by the words she uttered that I couldn't get enough.

"There we go. Now get to the wall," I said.

Tyra had a small wall for play, with two rings there. When she got there, I grabbed her arms, attaching them to the cuffs that were there. She then turned to me, a beaming grin on her face.

"So, Officer, what is my punishment?" she asked.

"Your punishment is quite deep, and I'm going to make sure you'll be feeling it…well into tomorrow," I told her. I reached forward, grabbing her butt, squeezing it, watching as she let out a small cry, pressing forward.

This was a whole lot of fun. I started to touch her, lightly patting the side.

"So, I caught you trying to escape my clutches. You think I, an Officer would let you go that easily?" I asked.

"N-no Officer, but I've been very bad," she said.

"Really now, show me how bad you've been. Tell me what you've been doing," I said.

She let out a small groan, and then, she spoke.

"I've been…touching myself without your permission, and I've been hiding that from you," she said.

I reached down, rubbing her there, causing her to let out a small moan of surprise, thrusting her hips up.

"What a naughty girl, getting off without permission. What should I do with you then…. I said to her.

"Everything," she said.

"You're so horny and desperate. Perhaps I'll make your juicy butt a little more marked up. I do have some toys that I'd love to use on you," I said to her.

"Yes, Officer, use all the toys that you want to on me. I'm your little slut, the one that you can count on, no matter what," she said.

I laughed, touching her backside and feeling her flinch slightly at the touch of my hands.

"You're so on edge already though…perhaps you've been…savoring this moment, waiting for me to take this seriously?" I said.

"Ahh yes. I want this. I'm…slowly losing my mind," I heard her say.

And that was a mutual feeling, that's for sure. I loved being in control, the power this bred. I moved my hand against her soft skin, watching her slowly gasp, leaning forward for me to continue to tease her.

Seeing her like this was a thrill. I loved seeing her just obey my commands. I draped my hands over, looking at her.

"Well, it seems I found out that you were being naughty," I said to her.

"I'm sorry…Officer," she said.

I smirked. I let my hand move against there, gripping her backside, watching Tyra shudder with pleasure.

"Please, Officer, I need this," she said.

"Really now. So, you're telling me that you'll pay with your body, instead of the normal protocol? How lewd," I told her. I grabbed her butt once again, moaning.

"I don't need a ticket Officer. I can…pay in other ways to give you what you want," she said.

"Really. And how much do you want it?" I asked her. I brushed my hands there, and she moaned.

"Officer, you know I'm willing to lay it all down, and risk it all here for you," she said.

"I see. Well, if my little slut wants that, perhaps I can give you exactly what you want then. But if you don't perform well…this Officer will take you in, and the punishment will be a whole lot more," I said.

"I understand Officer," Tyra said. She looked at me, moaning in response to my touches. I simply smiled, enjoying the way that she responded to my words. I then leaned back, grabbing a pair of handcuffs from the counter.

"Follow me. A naughty girl like you deserves a proper place for punishment," I said.

I heard her moan in response, so it certainly worked out for me doing this. She followed me over to the dungeon that I crafted. This was something that I put together recently, and she'd be the first one to try it.

There were a series of bars here, and I grabbed the handcuffs, putting them between the bars. I then put her hands in there, cuffing them.

"This is good, right Officer?" she asked.

"Of course, you're doing very well so far, so easy to tease and make mine. I love seeing a beautiful woman like you become so obedient. It's quite fun to behold," I told her.

"Yes," she breathed. I moved my hands to the skirt that she wore, pulling it upward to reveal her thick ass. I touched it, watching it jiggle once more, and the delicious sounds that came out of her.

This was a thrill, and I wouldn't be convinced otherwise. I shook her butt, watching it jiggle and move slightly as she let out a small moan of surprise and pleasure.

"Well, what do you say? Do you plan to receive your punishment?" I asked her.

"Yes Officer. I've been naughty, and I'll do anything to get out of a ticket. I'd do whatever you ask of me Officer," she said.

I smiled, letting my hands graze and touch against the very tip of her backside. Then, I raised my hand, smacking her hard with it.

She let out a moan, and I shivered with delight, enjoying the way that she responded to my touch. I let my hand graze over the edge of her backside once again, touching it softly and then spanking her again. She let out another delicious moan in response to my touches, making me smile with delight.

"I see you're already giving in. You like this," I told her.

"Yes…I do," she said.

"Tell me how much you like it," I said, raising my hand once more, hearing her moan in response.

"Ahh very much!" she cried out.

"Good. I'm glad that you do. Perhaps that'll make the next part of this even more fun for you," I said.

I spanked her a couple more times watching her whimper and moan. There was a thrill that came from this

Tyra and I discussed the hard and soft limits that she had. She really didn't care as long as blood wasn't drawn. I watched her body respond to me, slowly moving as I started to let my hands move there. Then, I grabbed something else, watching her body respond to me. I started to watch her tense up, seeing what I had in my hands.

"Officer, what's that?" she said.

"Oh, this is your next punishment. You were very naughty back there, and you resisted arrest. Maybe I should add a bit more to the punishment too," I said.

I watched her tense up, seeing the delicious sounds that came out of her in response. She didn't know what would come about with this, and I was excited for it. I began to move my hands slightly, grabbing the nightstick, holding it against her ass.

I teased the flesh there, lightly pressing it and watching as she let out a small moan. She pushed her body outward and then stuck her ass out.

"Look at you, all ready to go with this," I told her.

I slowly pulled the nightstick towards her butt, lightly touching it. Then, I raised it. The smacking sound reverberated through the room, and she let out a scream. Usually, this was used for forceful reasons, but I wanted to make her feel pleasure, so I'd only keep it along the areas that felt good. That didn't mean though that I wouldn't smack her butt once or twice, touching and watching her respond to the actions that I made.

"Ahh yes," she said to me.

"What's the matter? Already so turned on you can't think straight?" I teased.

"Yes," she finally admitted.

"Well then, let's see if you can handle this then," I told her.

I grabbed the stick again, raising it by her thighs, touching them, and then smacking those areas. The area around there jiggled, and I simply smiled, enjoying the sounds that she made.

She was helpless, and I was in control. And yet, I knew for a fact that she trusted me, and wanted me to make her feel good. Feeling good was what I knew how to do best. I let my fingers drape against her backside, smacking the flesh there again, making her cry out in pleasure.

"What's the matter? You have nothing more to say?" I teased.

"I don't…this is so good. Officer, I know that I've been bad but…I love this," she said.

"Of course you do. You're a naughty little slut who likes to be teased and ordered around. There's something nice about this," I told her.

"Thank you, Officer. I'm all yours," she said to me.

"Good. As you should be," I said to her. I moved the stick right over the middle of her butt, raising it, and then hitting her hard. She howled in pleasure, and I smirked, enjoying the sounds that she made. I watched her quickly respond to every single touch of this, and there was an enjoyment that came from this. Seeing her just lose control on me like this was…quite fun to say the least, and I knew that this was a thrill that she enjoyed too.

I then hit her a few more times with this, enjoying the delicious sounds. But I wanted to see how far I could take it. How I could get her to respond to my actions and be at the mercy of my touches.

That's when I saw it.

The wand kit. This was something that I had wanted to try out. the violet wand was something that I knew some people could take, but others not so much. I knew that in the right scenarios, it would be quite a fun little experience. I soon moved my hands towards her, touching her skin on the sides. She whimpered, and I smiled.

"Now, I think you're handling your punishment very well," I told her.

"Thank you, Officer. I'll give you my body if you let me get out of this mess," she said.

I laughed.

"Of course. But it won't be right away. I want to see how much of this you can handle," I responded.

She flushed, and then, she nodded.

"Yes, give me more," she said.

I laughed, seeing her become turned on and a total mess here. There was something exciting about hearing those words.

"Good girl. And if you're satisfactory, I'm sure I can give you a little reward that you will enjoy too," I told her.

She moaned in response, and I let out a small groan of desire. I wanted to see her lose all semblance of control here, to see her just…completely dissolve into the needy slut that I knew she was.

There was something exciting about all of this, that made me ready to give everything that I wanted to towards her, and to make her squeal in response.

I prepared the wand, plugging it in and putting one of the bigger heads on there. I then moved towards her sides, seeing her whimper and shiver, and I smiled.

"Alright sweetie, this may hurt for a second. But who knows, maybe you're into that," she said.

I then put the wand gently over her, and she let out a gasp of pleasure and surprise. I started moving the wand around, hearing the sounds, the little crackling sensation of this. She let out a series of small moans, the little touches more than enough for me to enjoy. I watched her quickly respond towards me, and then, moments later, I started to run the wand against her sides, digging it in deeper, watching her cry out, the sounds lovely and delicious to me. I loved hearing her like this, and there was something about this that just turned me the fuck on.

I wanted to hear her lose control, hear her cry out in pleasure, and I knew that she was very easy to work with, to tease, and to make her lose her mind.

I started to run the wand a little further, right up against where her hipbones were, and then, I started to see her cry out, holding onto the handcuffs, the little bit of shock and surprise, along with the arousal, hitting hard.

And I loved everything about it. I continued to see her lose herself in the touches, the pleasure, and as I got right against her pubic area, I knew that she was struggling to hold back, completely immersed in the pleasure, enjoying all of the touches.

And this was something that I loved.

I enjoyed seeing her become so easy to tease.

I put the metal on there, watching her eyes widen with surprise. I wanted to see just how far I could take this before it was too much for her of course. I slowly moved the wand against her skin there, touching slightly, and she let out a small cry. There was a small redness that was there, and I couldn't help but love it. I loved seeing her become placid and easy to tease. It was a thrill, a feeling of excitement, and a desire for something else that made me just ache for her.

I moved the wand further downwards, the jolt of this making her cry out, wiggled her butt there, and made me just want to give in, to fuck her senseless. But I wanted to see her scream, to cry out, and to watch her lose all sense of herself.

I turned it up slightly, moving it there. She cried out, holding onto the bar, both moaning and staying like this.

"Officer…this is quite strong," she said.

"Of course it is. Did you think I would put this on the baby settings? You were a naughty girl, so you deserve what's coming to you," I told her.

She moaned in response to me, turned on by the words that I uttered, and I enjoyed seeing her responses. There was something exciting about seeing her just lose herself there, crying out, and enjoying the little touches and pleasure that came out of this too. I continued to run the wand there, watching her respond with the best and most delicious sounds. After a brief moment, I then stopped it, putting it off to the side, and then looking at her.

"Have you had enough?"

"No, Officer. I want more of you. I want all of you," she said.

"I see," I told her.

She looked at me, the ache, the excitement, and the obvious desire right then and there. I reached forward, grabbing her backside, touching it slightly, listening to the little moans that came out of her.

"Well, let's see what happens to you then. I want to see how you respond to me as well. Maybe you can…get away with just a pat on the butt then," I said.

I leaned forward, touching her butt, moving right behind her, and grinding against there. She let out a small cry, and I wanted nothing more than to just completely take her right then and there. I grabbed her waist, holding it there as I ground softly.

"So, tell me what you want then?" I purred into her ear.

"To…let you have me, Officer. I'm so naughty that I think I'll only learn my lesson if you give it to me," she said.

"Oh, really now? Has someone else tried to teach you a lesson before?" I asked, grabbing her butt and touching it.

"Ahh! Yes. I have been very bad. And I haven't fully learned. I may do the same bad thing again. You don't want that…right?" she said.

"Not at all. I want you to learn your lesson, once and for all of course," I told her.

She let out a small cry as I patted her butt. I thought about fucking her pussy, but I couldn't help but wonder what she would feel like if I just…took her ass tonight.

That's what I would do. But I wanted to tease her a little bit more before I did that.

And I knew the perfect way to do this.

I walked over to where I had some of the toys, getting a series of small anal beads that vibrated when turned on. I grabbed the lube, lubing it completely before slowly inserting them into her ass.

"Ahh," she said, crying out slightly.

"What's the matter"

"I wasn't…expecting this," she said.

"Well, you should always expect the unexpected. You never know what you're going to get," I told her.

I slowly slid the beads in, causing her to let out a small, garbled sound of pleasure, enjoying the little sounds that she made. Shortly afterward, I pushed it in all the way, amazed at how easy it was to tease her ass.

I knew that she was turned on, but damn this was hot. I quickly moved back, turning on the vibrations, and soon, she cried out.

As she did that, moving her body slightly, I grabbed the flogger, moving it against her legs.

"So, a naughty girl like you is already turned on by this. How cute," I said.

She let out a small moan, as I moved the flogger against her body, hitting her with the leather strings. She let out a small cry of desire, and I enjoyed seeing her like this. Seeing her just completely take it like it was nothing was a thrill that I couldn't get enough of. I started to move the flogger against her again, watching her cry out as I smacked her once more with it, watching her eyes widen with surprise.

This was a thrill. This was something that I loved, and I wanted to see her just totally lose it again and again. Every single time I moved my hands there, touching her softly, she cried out, seeing her body move forward. I reached for the vibrator, turning it up a little bit higher, seeing her respond to the actions with a little cry.

There was something just so nice about seeing her like this, seeing her just cry out with a lofty desire, a need that clearly seemed to only grow even more so. I loved hearing it, if I was going to be honest, I wanted to see her lose control.

But my cock was hard. I knew that I could continue this teasing, this tormenting, and I knew that she may want it too. But also…I ached for release, and I knew that her ass was hungry for me, hungry for the punishment that I had in mind, and I loved it.

I quickly moved myself so that I was right up against her. I started to rub her backside, watching her tense up, cry out, and enjoy this. Shortly afterward, I pulled out the beads, and each one made her utter the most delicious of sounds.

"What's the matter? Enjoying it?" I asked her.

"Yes. Very much…so," she told me.

"Well, I can give you something even more amazing to enjoy too," I said to her.

When I pulled out the beads, I put them to the side, seeing her look back at me. Her dark, beautiful skin, the eyes of pleasure that she had, this was all just so damn perfect, and I loved everything about this.

I then got myself ready, lubing myself up, spreading her cheeks, seeing her suddenly tense up, crying out as I began to slide all the way into her.

She let out a shiver, the feeling of the cock deep within her making her cry out.

"Oh, Officer. I didn't expect you to want that hole," she said.

"It was inviting, and I knew that it would be the best punishment for you," I told her.

But she seemed to enjoy it. Shortly afterward, I started to slowly move, and she let out a small cry, holding onto me there I began to press my cock deep within her, enjoying the sounds that came out of her as I did this. There was something exciting about all of this, and I had a feeling that she enjoyed this as much as I did. I then started to move myself, my cock slowly sliding in and out of her.

She let out the best sounds, making me hungry for more. I grabbed her hips, moving faster and faster, my cock fitting perfectly in her tight little ass. The heat between our bodies, the passion and desire that was there, I knew that it was only a matter of time. And she seemed to enjoy this as much as I did too.

I continued to thrust my cock into her, enjoying how tight she was, and how amazing it felt. Every single thrust, every single touch, it was all just tantalizing, and I ached for more of her. I pulled her against me, the chains rattling from the cuffs, and I moved my hands downwards. I massaged her between the legs, and she began to let out a small series of cries. She moved back, and I held onto her tightly, thrusting in deeply, enjoying the sounds that she uttered.

Every single touch, every single sound, it was all driving me completely mad, and I loved it. I soon held her close, pushing in, ramming my cock deep inside, hearing those sounds.

I knew she enjoyed this. Even though it was supposed to be a roleplay for me, I knew that she liked this too.

After a few more thrusts, I let out a small cry, holding onto her there, thrusting in as I spiled myself into her. I then felt her tense up, crying out loud as I pushed my fingers in, pumping and massaging her there, enjoying the sounds that she made. After a few more moments, she let out a small cry, enjoying it all as well.

We then finished up, both of us moving away, and after I caught my breath, I grabbed the handcuffs, getting them off her with the key that I had. She moved her hands, looking at me with a smile on her face.

"Shit that was good," she said.

"Sure was. I enjoyed every minute of it," I said.

And I meant that. It was the first time in a long time I really felt like I got this kind of enjoyment out of it. I looked at her, and she nodded.

"I wouldn't mind doing that again. I think it awoke something within me," she said.

"I hope something good," I teased.

She nodded.

"Very good honestly. And I'm glad that you could roleplay again. I knew that you wanted to stick around on the force, but they forced retirement on you," she said.

"Yeah, it sucks, but it's nice to be able to have this kind of control with someone. Anyways, I'll walk you out when you're ready?" I asked her.

She nodded.

"Of course. And you know when and where to call me when you need me for another session. I would love to explore more of this," she said to me.

I flushed, but then nodded.

"I sure would too. I figured that this is indeed something that you liked as well," I told her.

She nodded.

"Yeah, I really did," she replied.

We looked at one another, and then, I suddenly moved forward, giving her a kiss. Tyra didn't move, and instead, she accepted the kiss, letting her lips move with my own, enjoying the small, sensual touch of our lips together. Then, she pulled back, smiling.

"I wouldn't mind doing this more often if well…this is what I get out of it," she said.

"Hey, it could be. You never know," I told her.

And I meant that. It was strange to want something like that with someone, but I guess she opened up something within me.

She put on her clothes, and I paid her for the time. She was a call girl sure, but there was something else there, a deeper connection. After I paid her, I watched her go to the doorway, turning and looking me in the eyes, a smile on her face.

"Thanks," she said.

"For what?" I asked. I thought I was the one who paid her.

"For that. It really gave me…something thrilling that I loved and enjoyed. And I would do it again if you ever wanted to," she offered.

She did? I was surprised.

"I thought you just liked this for the cash," I told her, slightly taken aback by this.

"I do but…there is something exciting about the way that you treat me too. It shows me that there is that part of me, that side that likes it when I'm degraded. And I can trust you with it. I like what we have together, and I'm sure that it would be good for us," she told me.

"Yeah true," I said to her.

She then smiled, giving me one last kiss before running off. I stayed there, thinking about what had happened.

Things were interesting between Tyra and I to say the least, and I couldn't help but feel like there was something left unsaid to her. Maybe it was my imagination though, and an overreaction of course to whatever it was that she was hiding herself.

But all in all, I was just happy that I got to act out this fetish, this roleplay, and there was something thrilling about all of this. I loved it, and a part of me knew that no matter what, this would be the beginning of something more, something deeper, and something amazing for me.

I just had to hope that she would come back again, but something told me that she would, and I was more than ready to explore all of that, and everything in between that would come from this, and the fun this would begin too.

It was something that I couldn't wait for.

Her punishment

Daddy Domination, Foot Fetish

"Hey, Daddy…." I said out loud to my daddy dom, Martin.

Martin was an older man, someone who was clearly old enough to be my dad. But the two of us were in a deep and intrinsic daddy dom relationship.

He was my daddy, and I was his naughty little girl.

"I was naughty…." I said to him.

He looked at me, eying me up and down, the expression changing.

"How naughty were you?"

"I got myself off…without you around. And I broke the rule of not eating cookies before bed," I said, wiggling my butt around.

His expression changed to that of annoyance.

"Again, Princess? Didn't we have this conversation before?"

"So what? You know that it's hard to resist those cookies! And they're so good and--"

He looked at me, shaking his head.

"Addy, I thought that I told you if you disobeyed my orders once again…daddy would punish you. Is that what you want?" he asked me.

"Maybe that's what I wanted," I told him with my lip bitten. I mean, I wanted to see what he would do. He pursed his lips though, looking at me up and down.

"You are such a little shit," he said.

"Well, I just wanted a cookie. And you know how hard it is to stay sane when you want to get off, Daddy. I tried to wait but I couldn't…"

The truth was, I liked seeing him flustered when trying to deal with my shit. That was part of the fun of him being such a good daddy dom. He knew how to give out new punishments.

"Ugh, again with this…I swear, you don't make it easy for me, do you?"

"Why would I?"

"True. Well, get over here," he said.

I wondered if he was going to spank me, but then, he pushed me down onto the bed, grabbing my chin and looking at me up in my eyes.

"You're going to get the punishment of your life, and one that'll show you why you shouldn't disobey Daddy," he said to me, his voice dark as he said that.

I didn't know why, but I felt excited about that.

However, what I didn't know was the way his hands moved downward, getting right over the top of my feet, touching right then and there.

"Hey wait a minute—"

"No, Princess. This is your punishment. Daddy isn't happy that you disobeyed him. And this isn't the first time you did it either," he purred.

He wasn't wrong. I mean…sometimes I was a bit of a brat and liked to test my limits with how far I could go and take punishment. But not like this.

"Please, Daddy, I promise I'll be good and—"

"No, this time…you'll be getting quite the punishment. And maybe if you're a good girl and beg enough, you'll get daddy's cock," he said.

The sound of that was enough to make me moan to be honest. I wanted him, and I knew that me teasing him like this was quite fun. There was something thrilling about this, about the way that he already had the punishment laid out.

But my feet were a source of great irritation and pleasure to me. the truth was…daddy had a foot fetish. And sometimes he would use that as a punishment for me. Much to both my dismay and of course my enjoyment.

He would tease my feet, making me shiver and moan with delight, enjoying the way that I sounded, and he would continue to tease me, watching me respond to him, seeing both the pleasure and the distaste that came from this was always an enjoyable thing.

"Alright, you decided to disobey me. Now…I'm going to make sure you learn your lesson, Princess," he said.

"Oh, I bet you will," I said.

He then pulled off the bottom part of my stockings, leaving my feet bare. Shit, this is going to be even worse. I started to feel his hands move downward after pulling the stockings off, moving to the base of my feet and touching them. He examined my feet, making me gasp and shiver as I felt the touch there. His hands were a little bit colder, but I couldn't help but enjoy the way that this felt.

"Now, Princess, you're over here disobeying Daddy. You seem to like it when I punish you," he said.

His hands moved towards the middle of my feet. It wasn't even a massage or anything, but it made me gasp.

"Ahh," I said.

"Well? What do you have to say for yourself?" he said.

"Daddy…. the feeling…."

It was both incredibly pleasurable, but also sensitive. And yet, I loved everything about this. Daddy began to move his hands there, just barely touching the soles of my feet. But the little touch alone was enough to drive me fucking mad, making me shiver, cry out with delight, enjoying the pleasure that came off of this. It was so sensitive that I had no clue what else to do, other than of course to just let out a small cry, touching the tip of the bed, and feeling his hand slowly move there.

"I'm going to take care of your feet Princess since I know how much you love it when I do that," he purred into my ear.

Every little touch made me shiver, the very edge of his hand touching the tip of my foot, making me shiver and cry out.

"There you go. You trying to hold back those cute little moans of yours? How adorable," he said in my ear.

I was struggling to hold back. I wanted to moan and scream out loud, but I was trying not to show the pleasure that this was giving me.

I hated that my feet were so sensitive, that it turned me into a pile of goo like this. But as Martin did this, letting his fingers touch there, I started to move around.

"Hold still, or else I'll put the restraints on your feet," he said.

"Ahh, Daddy," I said to him. I liked the idea of being restrained, and at the mercy of his foot touches.

There was something so damn hot about that. His hands then moved towards the very tips of my feet, moving towards the toes, and that little area behind them that was very sensitive. He rubbed his hands there, and as he let his fingers graze against the very tip of the back of my foot, I cried out, holding the sheets and moaning in response. He smiled, watching me slowly come undone, and the control that came out of this.

"So, Princess, do you think you can handle this?" he asked me.

I wanted to prove that I could handle this. That's all I wanted, and I knew for a fact that he enjoyed seeing me slowly come undone like this. He let his hands roam and tickle against there, and as he did this, I let out a small cry, enjoying the touch of his hands, feeling it all just completely overtake me to the point where even I wasn't sure what to make of this anymore.

He then ran his fingers against the underside, pressing there, and when he did that, I let out a jolt, crying out loud in pleasure, and moaning in response to this. I reacted immediately, enjoying the touch. The sensitive nature of his hand against my foot, and what it created within me was something I both loved and hated.

It was strange to be at the mercy of this man, to enjoy every possible moment, every type of touch that came out of this, and I knew that he was enjoying the little tormented groans and moans that I made. He let his hands touch there, teasing against the edge of my foot, and as he did that, I let out a moan, tensing up, brushing my hips upward until finally, I let out a small cry, coming down from the high that I experienced, and then, moments later he pulled back, seeing that look there in my eyes.

"Well, Princess, looks like you enjoyed your little punishment," he said.

"No, I didn't, Daddy. You know how sensitive my feet are," I said with a pout. Of course, there was also something arousing about it.

I hated to admit that the feeling of my feet was such a turn-on, but then he smiled.

"Well, perhaps I can make this even harder on you too. In fact, Daddy does like how cute your feet are. I noticed your toenails were nicely painted recently. Did you do that for Daddy?" he asked.

I looked at him, flushing.

"Yes, Daddy., I figured that you would like it," I told him.

"Well, I sure do. I love the color," he said.

Hearing him praise me was like a drug to me. I let out a small gasp.

"Do you want to see more of me, Daddy? I also got myself ready for you, even though I know you have to punish me," I said.

"Well, we can see where we're at, and I'll see what kind of punishment I want to give to you," he said.

I moaned in response, turned on by the punishment that he had planned. Even though I had no clue what it was, a part of me figured it would be something pretty big, and something that he enjoyed too.

"What's the punishment then, Daddy?" I finally asked with a blush.

He pursed his lips, and then he spoke.

"Get on your hands and knees, Princess," he said.

My hands and knees? What did he plan to do with that? I wanted to ask him, but then I quickly got on all fours, my butt sticking out. He reached out, touching my backside and massaging it.

"Your butt is getting nice and big," he said to me.

"Thank you, Daddy," I said.

Then, he grabbed the panties I wore, taking them off. He still left the skirt on, but I felt exposed as his hand reached forward, touching the very tip of my butt. He let his hands move there, and I let out a small gasp of surprise, enjoying every single moment of his touch. He let his fingers graze against there, and even just the tiniest of touches was setting me off.

"Daddy, please," I said.

"Please, what, Princess? I have no clue what it is that you want," he said.

He was definitely feigning innocence here. I wiggled my butt around, and then, he started to smile.

"Well, my naughty girl definitely has been bad, but maybe I should make the punishment something a little bit…different," he said.

"How different, Daddy?" I asked him.

I heard the sound of a drawer open, and then, I felt a vibrator up against my ass. I shivered, moaning out loud as he started to slowly move it in.

I wasn't used to anal, but it was obvious that was the point of this punishment. He wanted to see me squirm, and what better way than well…this. I felt the toy begin to slowly shimmy its way into me, and then, I let out a small gasp of surprise, enjoying the feeling of this. I started to move my hips forward, enjoying the touch of this, but then he pushed it all the way in, turning it on.

The feeling of this sent shivers through my entire body, and it turned me on more than I cared to admit. I started to feel him push it up to the highest settings, making me gasp out with pleasure, but I also knew it would take a whole lot more than this to get me off.

"That's part of your punishment. Mostly because I know how much you utterly enjoy the feeling of your ass being filled," he said.

"I don't, Daddy. Please let me take this out," I asked him.

"No no. You're getting your punishment for being a very naughty girl. Now first, this," he said.

He moved his lips downward, and I expected him to eat me out until of course, I was close, and then he would stop. But he didn't do that.

No, he did something so much worse. He moved his lips downward until of course, he was right near the entrance of my pussy. I felt his tongue start to slowly snake out, licking there for a moment, but then trail down my legs. I whimpered in shock and surprise until he got to my feet.

He took the top part of my foot, touching it there. He then massaged the tip of it, making me whimper and moan with pleasure.

"There we go. Such a good girl," he said.

"Thank you…Daddy," I told him, unable to properly think straight because of this.

"But what if Daddy did this?"

What did he plan to—

Oh, this was it. A tongue snaked out, moving against the front part of my foot, and I let out a small moan, pushing myself forward, completely lost in the feeling of this. He teased the very tip of my foot, and the touch of it alone was enough to drive me completely insane. He then chuckled, letting his tongue move outwards until of course, he had it around my toes, licking and sucking on my feet there.

I knew daddy had a foot fetish, but I also feel like he was doing this on purpose because he wanted to see me squirm. And squirming was something that I very much did as soon as I felt the hands there, and tongue skirt on downwards.

Fuck I was already such a turned-on mess, and it didn't help that he got a kick out of this too.

He then moved his tongue away, the sliminess of my feet making me moan, but only then did I feel the feather there, draped against my toes.

I also felt something else there. I didn't know what it was until of course, he turned it on, and I felt the massager against my feet.

I let out a small cry, moaning and crying out in response to the actions at hand. Why did this feel so damn good? What was he trying to accomplish here? I don't even know, but I let out a low, guttural sound, holding onto the bed as he massaged my feet with the massager.

"Holy shit," I told him.

"What's the matter, Princess?"

"This is just…it's so damn strong. I don't know what else to tell you," I finally spat out.

I felt like I was experiencing a whole different world as I uttered the words. A world that I didn't even know much about, and yet, there was a thrill that came out of this, a thrill that I liked so much more than I cared to admit, and I knew that he liked it too.

He then moved the massager up my leg, moving towards my inner thigh, barely grazing the edge of this. I cried out, holding onto there, feeling the excitement and desire of my body making me enjoy it all right then and there.

I started to watch his hands move downward until of course, they got to my legs. I was already a panting, sweating mess.

"Alright, Princess, it looks like you did well with this part of your punishment. Perhaps Daddy would like to see your cute body now," he told me.

Of course he did. I started to move my body so that I sat there, looking at him.

"Take off your clothes, Princess. Daddy wants to see all of you," he said.

I flushed, feeling like his eyes were right on my own as I started to move my hands upward, undoing the top part of the lingerie that I wore. It was a string, and when I did that, it tumbled down, moving it out of my way. I did the back strap too, revealing my breasts, which were aching for his touch.

He looked at me, smiling as I sat there, flush crimson against him.

"That's not all I want to see removed sweetie," he said.

Fuck did he mean…my bottom half too? Probably, because he wanted to see me naked there. He simply watched me as I took off the skirt, pulling it off. I then took my panties off, revealing my naked body, which he simply admired.

"You look wonderful, Princess. Now don't forget, your punishment is to have that toy inside of you while Daddy teases you. And you aren't to orgasm until you beg for it, or I tell you to," he said to me.

I flushed, feeling a bit exposed by this, and this alone. Did he get a thrill from doing this? Probably, but I knew that there wasn't any way for me to stop this, and yet, in a strange way, I didn't want this to stop.

"Okay, Daddy. Please…take me. Explore me and make me feel good. I promise I won't cum until you say so," I said to him.

"Very good girl. I'll take great care of you," he said.

He let his fingers drape down until of course, he got to where my breasts were, touching the very tip of them slightly, watching me suddenly shiver and cry out with pleasure at the sensation of this. He simply moved his hands against my nipple, pressing against there, moving his hands slightly. The little touch against the nub was enough to drive me crazy, and then, moments later, I started to feel his fingers there, pinching against the very edge of my nipple, rolling it. As he did that, I let out a small cry, enjoying the feeling of this, the touch that came with it, and the excitement that this brought me.

"Daddy," I cried out, feeling like I was about to burst already. He simply chuckled, touching me slightly there, watching my eyes widen with surprise as he did this.

"Well, Princess, what do you think. Do you want something more?" he asked me.

"Yes," I cried out.

"Good…maybe I'll let you cum then," he said.

He moved his hands against my nipple, teasing and pinching it. I felt like I was about to burst right then and there, go crazy as he did this. But maybe I could hold back. I sure as shit hoped that I could.

He continued to dance his fingers on my nipple, making me bite my tongue and moan out loud. Moments later, he moved his hands downward, touching the very tip of my pussy, letting his hand move there. I cried out, feeling like I was a mess, and completely at the mercy of this man's touches and feelings. He continued this, holding me there as he looked into my eyes.

"Well, Princess? You're going to have to ask Daddy for it," he said.

He wanted me to beg. I knew that daddy liked seeing me in this state. I flushed, biting my lip and then speaking.

"Please…Daddy," I told him.

"Please what? I can't possibly help you if I don't know what you want," he said.

The rat bastard was trying to get me to lose control. I held my breath, and then, tried to withstand the ache, the pleasure, and the need.

"Please give it to me," I told him.

He looked me in the eyes, and then he smiled.

"Well, you'll need to do a little bit better than that."

"Please, Daddy! Fuck my pussy," I said, completely at a loss on how to hold back, and what to say. He looked me in the eyes, and then, moments later he smiled.

"Well, since you asked so nicely and with such a cute and needy sound, I guess I can give it to you," he said to me.

He was doing this to be a tease, and then, moments later, he moved toward my pussy, moving his fingers against the very tip of my clit. He rubbed there, little touches and strokes, and I cried out, completely enraptured by daddy's touches. I knew that he enjoyed the sounds, and I was completely lost in the feeling of this. Moments later, he pushed his fingers harder against my clit there, touching me harder. I let out a choked sound as he continued to explore me, pushing his fingers in. I was completely enamored in the feeling, enjoying his touches, the way his hands moved about, and the sensations there. He then began to pump within me, and he was just barely missing that one spot, causing me to tense up, cry out loud, and feel like I needed to beg for it.

"Please," I said.

"Please what, Princess? I can barely hear what you are saying," he said.

The bastard was trying to get me to slowly lose control. But I sighed, feeling completely amazed by how turned on and horny I was.

"Please…fuck me," I told him.

He looked at me, smiling.

"Well, if you put it that way, I'm sure that I can give you that. But first, I want you to have a taste of me, of Daddy's cock," he said.

I felt like salivating as he said those words. I wanted him so badly, and the ache was driving me crazy. I struggled with thinking straight, with everything that was going on, and for a long time, I simply just laid there, holding onto the restraints and looking at him. He then undid his pants, pulling them downwards, and that's when I saw his member, standing fully at attention, making me shiver and crave more.

It was a hunger that I couldn't merely explain, but then, when he pushed it into my mouth, letting me move my tongue against the tip, I was about to go completely mad. I slowly took him further and further into my mouth, feeling the rush of pleasure, and the excitement of this. I soon felt his cock move further down my throat, making me shiver and tense up, enjoying every single moment of this. I licked the underside, savoring the taste of his long cock, before he started to lightly touch the very tip of me, thrusting in and out, enjoying the touch of this, and I knew that he was enjoying this as much as I was. I continued to touch, to tease him, and as we did this, I knew that he liked this too. He continued to move his hips there, but then, moments later, he pulled back.

I gave him a look of mild annoyance. I thought he'd continue this, but I guess not. He soon looked at me, smiling.

"Alright there, Princess, I think you've had enough. And honestly, Daddy is at his limit too," he said.

I flushed, but then nodded, feeling his cock move slowly against me, teasing my folds. I bit my lip, letting out a small, breathy sound as he slowly pushed himself all the way in, and then, as he did that, he looked me in the eyes, the thrill of it all hitting us. He slowly moved his cock deep within me, and as he did that, I sat there, completely held in place by how good this was, and how just…amazing he was. Every single thrust, every single touch, it was all enough to drive me slowly but surely to the point of madness. I gripped the area, and as he continued to plunge himself into me, holding me there, I wanted more.

I wanted him to take my breath away.

I loved being choked. His hands were perfect against me, touching me like that, and as I was getting close, my body completely languid, I started to cry out.

"Daddy," I said to him.

"What is it, Princess?" he asked.

"Choke…me," I told him.

He gave me that catlike smile, holding his hands to my throat, cupping where he always made me feel good. It was then when, moments later, he started to thrust deep into me, holding me there. I let out a series of small sounds, and that's when I felt it.

The sudden, amazing force of my orgasm. It hit every fiber of my being, making me suddenly tense up, holding onto me, crying out as I felt the throes of this overtake me. Moments later, he continued his relentless thrusts, my body starting to feel the exhaustion. It was then when, after a few more thrusts, he pulled his hand away, plunging into me.

But as he did so, filling me with his seed, he gave me a long, passionate kiss. We stayed like this, kissing hard as he released. When he was finally done, he pulled back, seeing my body stay there, completely languid as I tried to figure out what to say to him. I wasn't going to lie, I felt good, but also…I wanted to know how he felt too.

When the high of the orgasm finally came down, we looked at one another. He undid the restraints, holding them there, and when I looked at him, I smiled.

"That was amazing, Daddy," I told him.

"You're good, Princess? Let me make sure your arms are okay," he said.

As he did so, he grabbed some lotion cream and rubbed it in the bruises that formed there. It wasn't the first time I accidentally had some injuries afterward, but he always took care of me. After he finished, he looked at me, seeing the spent nature of my body.

"So how do you feel?"

"Good. Tired as shit. That was…something all right," I told him. I didn't expect things to go like that. He looked at me, and then, he nodded.

"Yeah, you held out like a trooper there. I'm quite proud of you," he said.

"Thank you, Daddy," I told him.

He leaned in, giving me a long, passionate kiss as he pulled away.

"Well, you want to go over and take a shower? And don't worry, we don't have to have the dynamic," he told me.

I looked at him, feeling a bit of a flush ghost my face. I then took a deep breath, holding onto the bed there for a moment, smiling contentedly.

"Yeah, I'd like that," I told him.

He helped me up since I was fucked too silly to move, and I knew for a fact that I was completely spent, but also happy too. I was glad to have someone as amazing as this man, as cool as he was, and as we went over there, I struggled to move, but he helped me every step of the way.

And I couldn't thank him enough. I loved that about him. I loved that he was my daddy, and he would take care of me no matter what. I just wanted to spend the rest of my life with him, and I wanted him to take care of me, through thick and thin.

We took a shower together, both of us kissing one another. After we got out of the bedroom, we stopped the dynamic as much, and instead were two different people. I felt good though, and as he finished with this, he looked at me.

"So…you want to try that again?" he asked me.

I beamed, nodding.

"Yeah, I'd love to," I told him.

It was something I desired far more than I cared to admit. He looked at me, beaming.

"Well, I'm sure the two of us can plan something like that again. And I'm sure you did enjoy the punishment that you got too," he teased.

That's right. The feet. I flushed as I thought about it. I mean, I didn't find it to be the worst punishment he's given, that's for sure, and in a sense, I wouldn't mind that being a punishment again.

"Yeah, I wouldn't mind a punishment like that," I told him.

"Well, perhaps next time I'll go a little easier and give you a punishment that you can enjoy," he said.

I immediately felt excited just hearing those words. There was something super fun about this, and I knew that he liked this too. After a little bit, I nodded.

"Well, there is always next time, and I can't wait for the fun that we can share together…Daddy," I said.

He touched my head as it was under the shower, his wet hand meeting my wet hair.

"Of course, Princess. I'll always take care of you, no matter what," he said.

And when he uttered those words, I believed him. I truly, utterly did. There was something super honest about it, and I knew for a fact that he meant it when he said those words. I felt good, and I knew that he liked this too. For a long time, we stayed like this, enjoying one another, and I knew for a fact that this was the beginning of something more.

I was completely happy and smitten about this, and I knew that things were going to get better. He was so good to me, and I knew that I could always rely on daddy, no matter what it may be. There was something about this that made me excited, and I was more than ready for more, and ready to see just what may come about from here on out, and the fun that would begin.

He definitely had something else planned for me in the future, and I knew that he had a lot going on as well. But I also knew that he'd take care of me and that he'd be there for me, no matter what.

And that of course was something that I could rely on, that I could trust, and that I could accept no matter what.

The Forbidden Girl

Forbidden Romance, Bisexual Threesome

There she was.

Standing at the edge of the smoking area near the lab. It was Millie, and she was there with her boyfriend Jude. Two of the smartest people here in the area and two people who I thought were incredibly attractive.

And there I was, just a lowly intern.

Millie turned to me, taking one last drag and then looking over at me.

"Hey there Cammy. What's up?" she asked.

"Oh, nothing. Just taking a break. You two seem to be doing well, making names for yourselves aren't you?" I asked her.

"Yeah, we managed to submit our thesis over to the examiner, and they loved it. We'll be publishing that in the science journal next month," she said.

"Wow, I wish I was half as smart as you two," I told them.

Jude laughed.

"Well, you're working under us. I'm sure our tutelage and other characteristics will rub off on you. You're a bright and beautiful young woman Cammy," he said, giving me a wink.

I blushed, realizing that he called me such nice things. It made my heart skip a beat, the excitement of this driving me wild.

"Thank you," I told him.

"You're welcome," he said with a wink.

Millie and Jude went back inside, leaving me out here alone. I couldn't shake the feeling that I had, the desire for both of them. But I sure as shit knew it wouldn't become anything.

For starters, both Millie and Jude were together. They couldn't possibly want someone like me. I didn't think Millie was bisexual either. She never gave off the vibe, at least that's what I got from it. I also knew that Jude was kind of a flirt.

And not just that, they're two of the top researchers, meanwhile I'm just a lowly intern, begging to be found and seen as someone different from the rest of them.

There was no way the two of them would even take notice of me, even ironically. Which sucked, but oh fucking well.

I flushed thinking about this, unsure of what to say or even what to do at this point. There was clearly a whole lot that I wanted to just spit out and tell them, but I didn't dare bother them with it. It would make shit even worse you know.

Which was why I kept to myself, and I kept all of these feelings deep within me. that's the best way to do this, and the only way to have some sort of solace.

Over the next couple of months though, I started working more and more with Millie and Jude. Both of them included me like I was a part of their team without officially mentioning it. There was something thrilling about that, and something that I liked. But would it lead to anything more? Or was it just my imagination getting the best of me.

However, one day I was approached by Jude, who kept looking away as he tried to avoid eye contact with me.

"Something the matter there Jude?" I inquired.

"Oh, it's nothing," he said.

"You say that, but I see the nervousness in your eyes," I told him.

"Well, it's just…we wanted you to come work with us for this next experiment. We want you included on the research paper with us," he said.

Was he serious about this? I flushed, seeing the way his eyes looked down on me.

He meant it.

"Are you sure about that? I don't want to be a bother or anything," I said.

"You kidding me? you're far from a bother hun," he told me with a smile.

I appreciated hearing that because I felt like I was in the shadow of them. And his eyes were soft.

"Sure, I can help then," I told him.

He beamed, taking my hand and holding it.

"Then let's get started," he replied.

He brought me over to the room where Millie and he worked. They had their own private lab. I worked in here sometimes, but mostly just used this to report to them. But upon looking at this even more, I started to realize just how…nice this place was.

Their lab was easily one of the best, and I was a bit jealous that they had such a nice setup.

"Wow, this is cool," I told him.

"Thanks. Anyways, I'll have Millie brief you on what we're studying and what you can help with," he said.

His hand lingered for a split second on my shoulder before leaving. I felt a bit nervous, especially since I was alone with them.

Two of the hottest people that I knew and both of them were way the fuck out of my league. I was a little embarrassed to admit it, but I knew the way I felt was the truth.

Shortly after, Millie showed up, looking me up and down and beaming.

"There you are," she said.

"Hey, sorry about that," I told her.

"Oh, you're good. You should know by now that we usually don't start this shit till way later. Anyways, I guess I can brief you on what we're trying to accomplish here," she told me.

"Yeah, that would be nice," I told her.

"Well, here's the outline. If you have questions, ask me," she said.

I read it over, and then, moments later, we started to work.

But I noticed there was something left unsaid. It was clear that Millie and Jude both wanted to say something, whatever it may be. I flushed thinking about this, knowing that both of them had something on the back of their mind. I wanted to ask, but I was afraid that it may come off as a bit rude.

But I did wonder this. I was curious about how they well…felt about me. I noticed Millie's eyes gazing over my body and a small smile on her face.

"Something the matter?" I finally asked her.

"Oh, it's nothing. I'll ask you later," she told me.

I wondered what Millie wanted to say to me. I also noticed that Jude's eyes kept lingering against my body too.

Were they both hiding something that they wanted to say? Or was this just them acting a bit weird and all. I wanted to know, but I was afraid I'd be bothering them far too much.

We worked on the experiments well into the night, when I saw Millie take a deep breath, looking over at me.

"What's…the matter?" I asked her.

"Oh, it's nothing. Sorry, I'm a bit distracted by thoughts," she said to me.

What thoughts were distracting her so badly? But I wanted to ask. I felt a little nervous that I was prying into affairs that technically weren't a goddamn part of my business. But as we continued to work together, I felt the tension grow.

Maybe she was holding back certain feelings. But then, as we finished with the last of the experiments, she turned to me, smiling.

"We're done for the day. Thanks for everything, Cammy," she said.

"No, thank you, Millie. It's a thrill to work underneath you," I told her.

It seemed like it was a good thing, but maybe I was overthinking all of this. Millie looked away, taking a moment to process whatever was going through her head.

"Something the matter?"

"No, it's just…there was something I wanted to tell you, but I fear that it may be a little too embarrassing. I don't want to make you uncomfortable or anything," she said.

"You can tell me. I want to hear it," she said.

She then turned to me, looking me in the eyes, and then, she cupped my chin, pulling it so that she looked at me directly in the eyes. I looked at her, lust and desire obvious there, but there was also something else there. A little bit of concern.

"What is…this?" I asked her.

"Something I wanted to ask you for a while, Cammy. I think actions speak a little bit louder than words here though," she told me.

"What do you mean by actions and—"

As I said those words, she continued to kiss me. I suddenly felt completely immersed in the feeling of her lips against mine, and while this wasn't what I expected, I quickly and eagerly enjoyed it, kissing her passionately and deeply. She and I stayed like this for a long while, until finally, she moved back, smiling.

"I knew it," she purred.

"What do you mean?" I asked, unsure if that was a good thing or not.

"I knew you had a little crush on me. You kind of suck at hiding these things," she said.

"I…I do?" I asked her.

"Yeah, you do. And it's okay because I'm sure that Jude wouldn't mind either. He's been waiting for me to find a cute little friend to tease and have fun with, and I think you may be the one," she said.

She wanted me as a plaything? I thought she just thought I was attractive, not like this!

"Are you serious?" I asked her.

"Does it look like I'm fucking around here?" she said with a chuckle.

"No…."

"Well good. I'm glad that you see things my way. So, my dear, what do you think. Want to have a little bit of fun?" she asked.

Did she really want to fuck me this much? It surprised me to say the least, but I quickly nodded.

"I appreciate this, and I kind of…do want it. But what about Jude?" I asked her.

I didn't want to overstep any boundaries that she had with him. but then, she laughed.

"You kidding me? he's the one who put me up to this. Right honey?" she asked.

"Indeed," Jude said, his hands on my waist, his eyes looking into my own, grinding against me. I let out a small gasp, surprised by this.

Both of these people wanted me, these attractive as shit people who already had me as putty in their hands.

And yet, I couldn't stop thinking about this, and how good this was. I quickly nodded.

"Sure, but where?" I asked.

"Where do you think? Follow me," Jude said.

I did as he said, making our way over to the small little guest room attached to the lab. This was supposed to be a room that was used when you had to stay late. But I guess this worked here. Before I knew it, I was on the bed, and then, Millie's lips were on my own.

They were so soft and subtle, and I couldn't get enough of this. I quickly kissed her back. It was the first time I'd kissed a woman before, and honestly…I liked this. Meanwhile, Jude's hands moved against the sides of my body, touching me there. He skirted his hands upwards, until of course he got to my breasts, touching them slightly, making me shiver and cry out, turned on by this whole thing.

"Fuck," I said out loud.

"You good? Or are you just aroused by the mere touch?" he said.

"I'm…aroused," I told him.

"As you should be. You have a cute body there Cammy. Millie told me that she had a crush on you for a while, and I figured…why not have fun. We've always wanted to try a third, and see how it goes," he said.

"Indeed," Millie said, pulling away, smiling as she touched my chin. I started to flush, enjoying the touch of her hands.

"That would be nice," I told her.

"Good. Then that settles it," she said.

She moved her hands so that they were right up against the tips of my nipples from outside the shirt. I suddenly let out a small gasp, moaning in response as I put my hips upwards, enjoying the idea of both of these attractive people taking me like this.

It was like a dream come true, if I do say so myself.

And I honestly wanted this. Millie's hands moved towards my sides, while Jude's then moved upward, touching me from outside my bra. The little touch was more than enough, and I quickly let out a small gasp, enjoying the feeling of his hands. He started to move his hands under my bra, playing with my nipples as he turned his head towards mine, kissing me.

Jude was a good kisser too. No wonder both of these people were so good for one another. I was a bit jealous I couldn't have this for myself, but this was clearly the next best thing.

Then, Millie moved towards me, our lips and tongues moving and teasing one another. Jude did the same, our lips and tongues all fitting together in an interesting way. I couldn't get enough of it though, and I enjoyed everything that both of these attractive people brought to the table.

I ached for more, I craved their touch, and then, before I knew it, I felt his lips move back, and he bit down on my neck, licking and teasing there.

Then, it was just Millie and me. Her lips felt so perfect, and that, combined with the touch was something that I enjoyed a whole lot too. I soon noticed her lips move forward, the tongue massaging my own, and I ached for her.

"Fuck," I said.

"You like this?" she teased.

"Yes," I breathed.

"Then maybe we can have a little more fun then," Jude said, moving his hands downwards, grabbing the hem of my shirt.

I mean, I was already pretty far gone, and I wanted to feel more of this too. I started to nod.

"Please," I said, aching for more, craving the touch of their hands, and the pleasure.

Jude quickly did away with my shirt, and then moved toward my bra. He undid it, leaving me topless in the room with both of them. I saw Millie's eyes widen, and a catlike smile form on her face.

"You have such cute breasts," she said.

"Thank…you," I said.

I expected her to just touch them, but she soon captured one of the nipples against her mouth, sucking on the flesh there. I let out a cry, feeling her suck on the flesh. She moved her tongue against the edge, and I laid there, feeling the blissful sensation of this. She then let her tongue move around, teasing the area slightly, while her other hand pinched the nipple, causing me to let out a small moan of surprise, enjoying everything about this. It was like I was experiencing a whole different world, and I loved everything about it.

I craved more of her touch, desired the feeling completely, and then, I felt her hand pinch my other nipple, causing me to tense up.

Jude simply smiled, watching Millie's hands get grabby, touching every part of me.

"This is fun isn't it?" he said to Millie.

"Yes dear," she said.

She pulled back, looking at me, and then I moved down, grabbing at her shirt. I didn't want to be the only one like this. Millie then smiled.

"Of course you get a taste too," she said.

She pulled off the lab coat, and then undid her shirt. She then pulled off her bra, revealing her large, perky tits.

I reached out, touching them and watching her let out a small moan in response to the touches that I brought to her.

"She likes that," I heard Jude say.

"I'm sure," I said.

My hands got grabby, exploring every part of her. This was…different to say the least. I liked the idea of this, and Millie seemed to like it too.

Her breasts were so much bigger than mine that touching them felt so damn different. But she didn't seem to mind it either, and I liked feeling her up, and the sounds that she made. They were delicious, but also something that I could definitely get used to as well.

"Wow, you like them too," she said.

I put my lips against her nipple, pressing there, enjoying the sounds that came out of her. I started to pinch the other nipple, loving everything from this, and I saw for a moment the pleasure that was obvious on her face.

Jude seemed to like this too, but I could also tell that he wanted a little bit of the action as well.

I then moved back, laying down, hiking up my skirt to show my black panties. I rubbed them slightly, looking at Millie.

"If you want a taste…"

She grinned, spreading me apart, letting her lips move up the sides of my thighs, smiling at me.

"But of course. And you can give Jude a little bit of attention too," she said.

I nodded.

"Yes," I breathed out.

Her hands were right there against my panties, grabbing the waistband and holding it there. She looked me in the eyes, beaming, and then she slowly pulled them down. I looked at her, surprised by this, and she soon spread me apart, letting her fingers move against there.

"You're so cute, and I can see how sensitive you are already," she said.

Her little touches were more than enough for me, but then, I felt my own hands move upward, undoing the zipper and fly on Jude's pants, pulling them down to reveal his large, aching member. I looked at him, quickly pulling his cock closer to me.

It was big, much bigger than I expected. But there was something about this that turned me the hell on. I wanted this, and I knew that he did too. I let my tongue move out, teasing the very tip of his cock, hearing the sounds of approval directly from him. As I licked there, I slowly moved my lips against there, sucking and teasing the very edges of this, watching him cry out loud and then, I pushed about halfway down, sucking him off.

Meanwhile, I felt Millie's hands against me, slowly lick every part of me. She teased my clit, causing me to let out a small gasp of surprise, thrusting forward, enjoying the different feelings from this. He began to push it deeper down my throat, and she moved her tongue there, teasing the tip of my clit, sucking on it too. I let out a cry, muted by the cock that was there, but I didn't care, I liked it.

I loved feeling like I was their bitch. I noticed Millie spread me apart further, sliding a finger inside, and I let out a small gasp that was muffled once again. I pushed my lips further downward, and then, shortly afterward, I felt it hit the base of my throat. I gasped, enjoying the feeling of gagging, and he began to hold my head, fucking my mouth while his wife continued to eat me out, thrusting her fingers in and out of me. She pushed two fingers in, dipping deep inside, and then she pushed in harder, causing me to let out a small gasp, a needy sigh, and felt like I was losing every part of me.

I ached for more, the feeling of Jude inside of me, and for well…just a taste of Millie.

I was close already, and I felt the fingers press upward, teasing that one spot of mine. As she pushed there, I let out a small, garbled sound, enjoying it, and then, moments later, he pulled back, looking at me.

"You have such a good mouth, but I need to be inside of you," he said.

"You…you do?" I said.

"Yes," he said.

I felt Millie's tongue tease and continue, and while I loved the feeling, I knew that I needed to taste her too. Moments later, she pulled back, smiling.

"What was that honey?" she said.

"I need to be inside one of you now," he said.

"Well, why not me first, and then you can finish in her. Give her something to remember us by. You're on the pill, right?" Millie said, turning to me with the last line.

I flushed, but then nodded.

"Y-yeah, I am," I said.

"There we go, problem solved," Millie said.

But I already felt like I was at my limit. I ached for more, and I knew that she wanted to give me more. She then moved herself towards Jude, pushing him down on the bed. She then slid over him, pushing herself all the way down, looking at me with a look of lust, pure desire, and need.

"Fuck this is good," she said.

I looked at her, riding his cock, and I craved a touch. I wanted to feel her. I quickly scurried over, moving my lips towards the very edge of her pussy, licking the tip of her clit.

"Holy shit," Millie said, moving herself up and down. I began to tease the very tip of her clit, enjoying the sounds that came out of her as she continued to move herself up and down, enjoying the sensation of my lips and tongue. I began to move my lips a bit harder, sucking on her clit as she continued to ride.

Millie moved her body, and I reached up, pinching her nipples as I took a moment to feast on her. The sounds that she made, the movements of her body, all of this was driving me crazy, turning me the fuck on, and I loved every passing moment of this. I craved for more of this, and I needed to feel more of this too.

I continued to move my lips around, letting my tongue tease her. She let out a series of small gasps and moans, and I knew that she was close. But then, moments later she moved her hands to my shoulder, riding Jude until she let out a small cry.

I expected her to finish with a moan, but then she grabbed my face, pulling me closer, letting her lips move there. I quickly moved my own lips to hers as she pulled away, gasping as she was finished.

"Fuck that was good," she said.

"I can tell," I replied.

"Get on," she told me, motioning to Jude's cock. He was big, and Millie just took him like it was nothing. I was a tad bit jealous, but I didn't want to disappoint. I moved my body so that it was right over his cock, sliding down on it, looking at him with a smile as I felt him all the way in.

Fuck he was big. It took me a moment to get used to this, but then I moved a little bit. However, he grabbed my hips, pushing me so that I was on my knees. He then moved all the way in, causing me to let out a small cry of surprise and need as he plunged himself.

"Holy…shit," I said out loud. I was surprised by this. It was a different sensation, and it was one that I definitely enjoyed. I started to feel him thrust deep into me, making me tense up and moan in response. Everything about this just felt so damn good, and I craved the feeling of this, the touch that drove me insane, and the ache for so much more.

He started to thrust himself deep in there, plunging into me, making me cry out loud, aching for him as I started to feel as if I was about to lose it right then and there. I was definitely ready, and I knew that no matter what, everything was going to be amazing. He filled me up, holding onto my hips as he plunged in deep, but then, I saw Millie there, her pussy right there in my face, and I soon took a moment to explore her, touching the tip with my tongue, and then moving my tongue inside, exploring and enjoying her folds. She let out a small gasp, holding me there as I continued to tease her with my tongue, feeling her gasp and moan in response to everything that I did. This was heavenly to me, especially since it just…felt so right to me. it felt like it was what she wanted, and I knew that she was close again.

"Fuck Cammy you're amazing," she said, holding my head there. I pushed my tongue in, letting it sink into her, teasing that one spot, and as soon as I hit there, she tensed up, crying out loud, and then, she held onto me as she finished up.

Moments later, I felt something else push deep into me, holding me there as I let out a low, guttural sound. I felt a hand move to my clit, rubbing there as I felt the throes of pleasure hit me. it was then when I cried out, letting out a sound, and the feeling of release hit me.

As I felt this, his own cock pushed all the way in, filling me up with his seed fully and completely, enjoying the touch of this.

He then moved back, looking me in the eyes with a smile, enjoying the feeling of this.

"You good?" he asked me.

He pulled out, and I simply laid there, enjoying the feeling that this gave me. It was different to say the least, and I was completely enraptured by the touch that this gave me. it was like I experienced a little bit of heaven.

He pulled out, and I simply laid there on the bed, the cum inside, and the satisfaction that I felt. But then Millie moved between my legs, letting her tongue snake out, and she licked up the cum, teasing me too. I gripped the sheets, my eyes wide with surprise, and I quickly let out a small series of cries, enjoying the feeling of this. For a moment, I was in awe at this, and I enjoyed it. I stayed like this for a bit, and then, moments later, I came hard, feeling my whole body grow ragged with pleasure.

She licked it all up, satisfied as she pulled back, looking me in the eyes with a beaming smile.

"You good there?" she asked.

"Yeah, as good as I will ever be," I told her.

"Of course. I can see that you're quite happy," she said.

"Yeah, I am," I replied.

I didn't know what else to tell her, other than I was happy, and this experience was a whole new world to me. I didn't know Millie or Jude felt this way about me, and there was something exciting about this. I wondered what this may entail, and what will come about next.

"So, what does this mean?" I asked her.

"What do you mean?" Jude asked.

"Is this like…something official? Do you guys want to do this again? I've never…had anything like this before," I told her.

She looked at me, and then she shrugged.

"Depends., you want this?" she asked me.

"I mean…only if you guys want it," I told her.

"Well, I think it would be kind of fun. What do you think Jude?" she asked.

"I would love it," Jude replied.

I flushed.

"What made you guys…want me though? I didn't expect you guys to choose me or anything," I said to them.

"We just thought you were cute, and you're a big part of our team. I figured this would be a fun way to bond together, even though it's a little different from the usual," she told me.

She did have a point. This was different, and I kind of liked it.

"Well, I don't mind different, that's for sure," I told her.

"Alright, well I'm glad that you're fine with it. We should probably get dressed though. The last thing I want is one of the security guards to come over here and try to find us," Jude said.

"Do they normally do that?"

"Oh yeah. They've almost caught us having sex in here," Millie said with a chuckle.

I flushed. These two were fucking in the room here off hours. And maybe even during work hours too. I don't know, there was something kind of exciting about that.

"Well, I wouldn't mind doing this again, and staying with both of you on the team as well. I know that we're supposed to work together but…I wouldn't mind something else too," I told them.

"We can arrange that," Jude said.

"Of course. It would be fun for all of us," Millie said with a wink.

I looked at them, realizing that they enjoyed this. This was a fun little game for both of them, and I was just a part of it these days. And yet, I didn't mind that. It was something that made me feel good, and something that I enjoyed.

And yet, I wondered what would become of us next.

We got dressed, leaving the lab and giving one another little winks and smiles. We would have to pretend that we didn't do anything, and during the day, they were forbidden. They were a happy, married couple who weren't secretly degenerates that would fuck their lab partners, but I also kind of liked it like this.

It meant that they were kind of a dirty little secret for me, something that only I could know about, and something that I enjoyed. And while I wished I could just expose the truth, and come forward with my feelings, this was the best way to do it.

And not only that, but they also showed me a whole bunch of new things and awakened new feelings within me. If nothing else, I loved that they did that period, and I couldn't wait for whatever would come our way next, and whatever it was that they had planned not just for now, but for the upcoming future that we would share as well.

Lana's Secret

Bisexual Threesomes, Hot Wives

"Bye honey, I'll see you later," I said.

"Alright, Lana. Love you," my husband Charlie said to me.

I smiled, but then as he left my face lowered. I couldn't stop thinking about her.

Amelia.

I flushed thinking about Amelia, the woman who lived next door to me. I shivered with delight thinking about her.

The truth was, I had a big crush on Amelia. She was another lonely housewife, but her husband was gone. They did have an open relationship, where she could fuck whoever she wanted, but the truth was, I did have a crush on her but was afraid to tell my husband about it.

But would Charlie get it?

Maybe, I didn't know...

We planned to meet up for lunch today, and I was making sure that I looked my best. Amelia was gorgeous, and she didn't have kids, so it made things easier.

I did, but they were older.

So I had some free time. And of course, they could take care of themselves. I knew they'd probably be out with friends based on what they told me.

Which made things even better. I got ready, putting on the nicest dress possible, doing my hair up, and looking cute. I smiled, excited about this.

I was ready to see Amelia

I went over to her place, which was only one door down. When I got there, she opened the door, seeing me.

"Hey there hun."

"Hey! How have you been?" I asked her.

I saw her smile, moving her body a little bit towards me.

"Good. And you?"

"Pretty good. Excited to eat and catch up?" she said.

"Totally," I replied.

We went over to the living room, where the sandwiches were made. As we sat there, I could feel the tension growing. She wanted to say something, but I wasn't sure what exactly.

"Something the matter?" I asked her.

She looked at me, flushing crimson.

"So, there's…something I wanted to ask you," she said.

"What is it?"

She leaned in, whispering to me.

"Wait, you're serious?"

"Yeah…. I was thinking we could have a little bit of fun like that you know? It would be good for both of us," she said to me.

I flushed, and then I nodded.

"Yeah, I wouldn't mind that. In fact, I…I kinda wanted to ask about that," I told her.

She beamed.

"Yeah, I would love that too," she told me.

I was excited. We sat there, talking about it for a bit.

"You sure it's okay? Your husband won't be mad?"

"You kidding me? We have an open relationship for a reason hun. I want this, and I can make it a ton of fun for both of us. Because I know that you want it too," she told me with a purr.

I flushed, and then nodded.

"You got me," I said.

"Come on, you and I both know that this will be fun," she said.

"Yeah, I know," I replied.

I felt excited. We devised the plan. I texted my kid to make sure she wouldn't be home. Sure enough, she told me she was going to Maddie's house and wouldn't be home till the next day.

Perfect.

We got everything ready for when Charlie decided to come home. It was a bit nerve-wracking to say the least, but I also was more than ready to see what may happen next.

That's when we put the plan into action.

We started to hang out in the bedroom together, looking at the clock. Amelia was right there near me, looking me in the eyes.

"So…have you ever done anything with a woman before?" she asked.

I shook my head.

"No, but…I kind of want to… actually more than kind of," I said.

She reached out, touching my arm and looking me in the eyes.

"Well, I'm glad that…that you want to do this," she said to me.

I looked at her, seeing the way that her eyes focused on mine.

"Yeah, I'm a little nervous about this, but I'll try to do my best," I told her.

"Don't worry, just let me take the lead," she insisted.

I wanted to believe that this was something that I enjoyed. I felt a little bit nervous about this, and I knew that this was something that she wanted just as much.

She reached out, touching my hair and looking me in the eyes. She then moved forward, our lips mere inches away from each other. I looked at this, and then, moments later, she pressed her lips to my own. She kissed me, and for a long time, we stayed like this, enjoying the touch of one another and the feeling of this, and in truth…I kinda wanted more from her.

We stayed like this for a long time, simply moving our hands towards one another, and we made out slightly. There was a thrill that came from this.

Her lips were softer, much softer than a man's, and there was something I liked about that. She then deepened the kiss, our lips moving slightly towards one another, enjoying the pleasure of this. For a long time, she simply stayed like this with me, and we both enjoyed one another.

This was something that I wanted more than anything else, if you wanted the truth of it. I thought about having sex with Amelia beforehand. She was so damn attractive, and I'd been curious about experimentation. However, I didn't know how to…approach this until now.

But as we kissed, it awoke something within me, a new feeling that turned me the fuck on, and made me ache for more. We stayed like this, and for a long time, we simply enjoyed one another, and the feeling that this gave us.

That's what I enjoyed more than anything else. The feeling this provided, and the fun that it gave me a chance to experience.

We continued to make out for a bit, and Amelia soon moved her hands downward, touching the sides of my body, moving toward my breasts. Her hands moved there, cupping the orbs and making me shiver and tense up.

"Something the matter?" Amelia asked.

I flushed, shaking my head.

"No, it's just…this feels nice," I said.

She beamed.

"I know that it does. I take it you've never been touched by a woman before," she said.

"No, I…I haven't," I said.

I never had the balls to tell him about it, the secret that I had. I am bisexual, and I've always lusted after women, so it's hard for me to…to totally make this easy to explain. But I liked talking to Amelia about it. It made me realize that I wasn't alone and that there was someone else who liked me.

"Well don't worry, I'll be sure to show you a good time. I want to focus on you, and I'm sure that Charlie will definitely enjoy the fun that we have in store," she teased.

I hoped so too. But of course, my thoughts soon changed to that of lust as she moved her hands downward, right up against my lingerie. Was she going to take it off? A part of me hoped so, but I wasn't totally sure what her plans were for this.

She fiddled with the clasp of it, looking me in the eyes as if to ask me about it. I mean, it's not like I wanted her to stop or anything.

"Do you…want this?" she asked.

"Yes," I cried out.

I felt a sudden excitement start to flood through my body at the idea of her teasing, playing with me, touching me like this.

It brought a new sense of thrill to me, and as she moved her hands towards me, touching my curves, feeling me up, it awakened something within me.

A desire for her. A desire for so much more.

I knew Charlie would freak as soon as he got home, and I wondered what he would say. I didn't think it would be anything too bad though. He knew how I felt about…women, that's for sure, and I certainly was a bit curious about all of this, so I figured that this would be the beginning of something new, exciting, and fun as well.

As we kissed, she pushed me down on the bed, hovering over me. She touched the tip of my nipples through the top that I wore, and I let out a small gasp, holding onto her as she touched my body.

"Please," I said out loud.

"Please, what? I can't hear you there Lana," she said.

I let out a low moan, holding onto her as she did this. But of course, as soon as I uttered a sound, the door opened, and Charlie was there.

"Lana? What is this? He asked me.

I flushed, but then Amelia gave him a small smile.

"We wanted to wait for you to join us Charlie, but it seems we both…had other plans," she purred.

"But what…is this? What's going on?" he asked.

"I figured the three of us could have some fun together," I told her.

She looked at me, and for a moment, he sighed.

"Well…if you want this, I'm not going to say no to it, that's for sure," he pointed out.

"Of course, you won't say no. You want this too, don't you," she said.

"Yes," he said, his voice laced with pleasure. I knew that Charlie couldn't hold himself back either.

I smiled, and then moved towards him, giving him a long, passionate kiss.

"Don't worry, you know my husband and I are open," she said.

"Of course, and what about you Lana? Are you…okay with this?" he asked.

Of course I was. It was something that I felt deep within me, something that I enjoyed. It was like…like it was pulling me forward, and I wanted to experience more of this.

I felt a little bit shocked that this was something that I wanted though. And that it was actually happening. She leaned forward, giving me a small kiss on the lips.

"Don't worry hun. We'll take this nice and slow. Since I know that's what you like," she said.

"Yes," I said.

I wanted to feel both of them and to crave both as well. That's when I saw Charlie's eyes look into my own, pulling me there and kissing me with a passion that I hadn't experienced up till this point. Perhaps he enjoyed this as much as I did or something.

Or maybe, it was awakening something deep within him as well. As we kissed, my hands moved downward, and I felt her lips against my neck, touching me slightly with little touches. I let out a small whimper, enjoying the touch of both of them, but still lost in the feeling that this gave me, and the pleasure that I felt.

For a long time, I was completely in awe at how nice this felt, and how it made me feel…good in a sense. She then moved her hands down toward where the edge of my lingerie was. She teased the bra cup, looking up at me. Charlie pulled his lips away, his hands resting down at my waist, as I looked at Lana.

"Do you want me to continue?" she asked.

"Do you need to ask?" I told her.

She smiled, enjoying this.

"Well, I'm glad that the feeling is mutual then," she said.

"Ahh, it is," I told her.

It really was, and I liked the feeling of her hands against the very edge of my body, touching me there. She then moved towards the back of the little lingerie that I wore, unhooking the bra, pulling it off of me. I suddenly tensed up, feeling a bit surprised by everything, but also…it was nice to have this. I was just glad to experience the touch of this.

I felt Charlie's hands there too, touching and teasing my waist, while Amelia moved her lips to the tip of my nipple. She took the tip of it into her mouth, sucking on the flesh there, making me suddenly tense up, moan, and feel amazing in the process.

There was something about this whole thing that made my head spin. Her lips were like a drug, one that I couldn't get enough of, while I also noticed Charlie's hands were a lot rougher, and I liked that about them. I enjoyed the feeling of two different types of people, and of the way their hands and lips trailed against my body.

I noticed Charlie's hands move between my legs, touching my inner thighs, running his hand there until he got between my legs. As he touched me there, I let out a small gasp, surprised by how nice this felt, completely in awe at how much my body reacted to everything. It was so good, a pleasurable experience, and I certainly enjoyed this too.

For a long time, I felt like this was the beginning of a new life, a new world, and for me, I wanted to experience everything about it.

Then, I felt hands move towards my breasts, touching and cupping them. As she did that, she purred her words into my ear, making me shiver with delight.

"You have the cutest tits you know," she said.

"Really? Thanks," I said.

She giggled, letting her fingers drape against her body, and as she did this, I let out a small gasp, enjoying everything that came out of this. For a long time, I simply just laid there, enjoying the touch of her hands, and the feeling of her body.

She knew exactly how to turn me the fuck on, and I simply just enjoyed this, and I knew that she liked to hear me make delicious sounds. I felt Charlie's hands move closer and closer to the obvious heat between my legs, and it made me realize that he liked this too.

I didn't realize just how…good this felt, and as I stayed there, holding onto the bed, I felt her lips finally tease the tip of my nipples, kissing the edges, and then, her other hand moved to my other nipple, touching there slightly. When she did that, I gripped the sheets, letting out a small cry of pleasure as she continued to touch me there, the excitement, the tease, everything surrounding this making my body heavy with need.

It was rare to feel this good, but her lips were nice and soft, and they touched me perfectly, and for a brief moment, I simply closed my eyes, feeling my whole body move forward, reaching forward to touch her hair. She looked at me, smiling as she swiveled a tongue out, teasing the very tip of my nipple. As she did this, I held onto the edge of the bed, letting my moans fill the room, and the obvious enjoyment of such beginning to flow through me.

It was heavenly, it was so good, and there was something exciting about this that made me ache for her, and I knew that she liked this too. I then felt her start to move her hands against my other nipple, pinching and touching there. She smiled as I moved my hands up to her, feeling her lips deepen this, and her body start to move against my own.

"Fuck," I said.

"You're very fun to tease. I'm sure Charlie likes this. And maybe you can help him out a little bit too," she said.

I turned to Charlie, who had an obvious tent in his pants, and when he watched us, I saw the little lip-bite that he had.

"Of course. He just needs to give it to me," I told him.

"I will," Charlie said.

He moved towards the side of my body, undoing his pants, and I eagerly took out his cock. He was big and girthy, perfect for me, and I soon moved my lips to the very tip of this, enjoying the sensation that this gave to me. it was like he knew immediately what I wanted, pushing his dick right into my mouth and letting me hungrily take it there. I licked and teased the very tip of his cock, enjoying the delicious sounds that came out of this, but of course, as I did this, I noticed that Amelia's hands were moving downward, touching my taut stomach. I blushed as she got right over my panties, seeing the obvious heat that was there. She looked me in the eyes as if begging for me to agree to this.

"You ready?" she asked.

It would be the first time that I'd…do this with a woman. Sure, I've given head before, but I've never received this from the same gender. I simply nodded.

"Sure. Of course," I said, unsure of what to say, other than of course, the feeling of desire that seemed to just only drive me closer and closer to the edge. She simply nodded.

"Don't worry, we can take this nice and gentle," she said.

I watched as she spread me apart, looking me in the eyes. She grabbed each side of the waistband of my panties, sliding them off, looking me in the eyes as I nodded.

She then touched me there, feeling the obvious wetness that was there. She then beamed.

"Damn, turned on already? How hot," she said.

"Yeah," I said, suddenly unable to breathe. I took Charlie's cock in my mouth once more, letting my lips move against it, touching and pleasuring him. I wanted him, but I also wanted to see what Amelia would do.

What I didn't know, was that Amelia knew exactly where to go with her hands. the first thing that she did was run her fingers against the very edge of my pussy, the little touch enough to set me on fire. I watched her move her hands towards my clit, barely rubbing there, and for a long time, I simply just stayed there, completely lost in the touch. I felt the cock slide in and out of my mouth, and I was completely enraptured by the feeling of pleasure that came out of this. I started to move my hands towards his cock, taking the second half there, jerking it while I sucked and teased the other part of the tip with my lips. I felt good, and with every single touch, I could sense that there was something about this that turned me into something more, something needy, and I loved everything about it.

I eagerly sucked on his cock, but then I felt the finger rub up against the very tip of my clit, touching there. I let out a small, garbled moan, enjoying the feeling of this. I watched as he simply smiled, pushing it further down my throat. I felt a bit of a gag as he did this, but that didn't matter.

What did matter, was what Amelia was doing between my legs.

She let her fingers dance there, teasing every part of me. I suddenly felt her fingers slowly move downward, touching the very tip of my entrance, then moving against there again. She rubbed my clit a few times, repeating the motions, but then, as she did this, she moved her tongue outward, touching the very tip of my clit, licking and teasing the very edge of it, making me suddenly lose control. I held onto her, and then I let out a moan around his cock, feeling him let out a small groan of desire and approval as he heard me continue to get overtaken by everything that's going on here. I then watched as he moved his hands to the sides of my head, fucking my throat, but then, as he did that, it was like a signal to Amelia, and then, she moved her tongue there, letting it circle against my clit, causing me to let out a small series of moans and grunts.

I didn't expect this to feel that good, but here I was, completely reduced to nothing as I held onto her, whimpering with pleasure as I felt her move her lips around, and I looked at her, seeing how she was between my legs, buried there. I looked at her, seeing that she didn't want to stop. She then pushed her tongue in, letting it explore me, and it was then when she angled herself a bit, and her tongue touched a part of me that made me suddenly cry out, holding onto the very edge of the sheets, letting out a cry against Charlie's cock as I felt my orgasm right there.

But then, she pulled away, smiling towards me.

"I don't think you want to cum just yet," she said.

"No," I said, admitting that I was trying to hold back.

By this point, I needed something inside of me right now, whether it be him or her, and when I looked at Charlie, I saw the smile that he had.

"You ready?" he asked me.

"Born…ready," I told him.

Charlie gave me a nod of approval, pushing me down so that I was on my hands and knees, but instead of doing that, I shook my head.

"I think maybe…I should get on top," I told him.

"You sure about this?" he asked me.

"Yeah," I told him.

He looked at me, nodding in agreement, and then got on the bed. I quickly got on top, moving myself so that I was right over his cock. As I slid down on him, I felt the familiar sensation, but then, I looked over at her, surprised by the little smile of excitement that she gave me.

"You good?" she asked me.

"Yes, I am," I told her.

She beamed, and then took off her panties, sliding her wet, shaven pussy over my husband's face. She let out a small cry as he started to explore her with his tongue, touching, teasing, and playing with her folds.

Meanwhile, I began pushing my hips up, holding onto the bed for a moment. As I did this, I looked over, and she simply smiled.

"Fuck…Charlie is good," she said.

"He is. He's good at what he does," I said.

"Indeed. But I think I'm a little bit better," she told me.

I flushed and then smiled.

"That's something I'm not going to debate you on," I told her.

"Yeah," she replied.

She then moved herself away and started to ride him. I did the same. Both of us let out small moans of excitement and need, the pleasure obvious between our bodies. She looked me in the eyes, reaching out and touching my face. As she did so, she reached in, pressing her lips to my own. I kissed her passionately, feeling her hips move about, and there was something exciting about all of this.

I knew for a fact that she was enjoying this as much as I was, and soon, I noticed that Charlie's lips were teasing her. After a few more moments, she leaned in, giving me a passionate kiss, rubbing between my legs as she did. Moments later, I tensed up, holding onto her, letting out a small cry of surprise as I suddenly felt the urge to cum hard.

When I finally did, I laid back, feeling my whole body just relax right then and there. I looked at her, and then, she smiled.

"You good?" she said.

"Yeah but…what about you? You still need to cum. And so does Charlie?" I told her.

She looked at Charlie, who smiled.

"Want to take me for a test ride?" she asked.

"I thought you'd never ask," he replied.

She got down on her hands and knees, sticking her thick ass upward, and then, he grabbed it, pushing himself deep into her. She let out a small cry of surprise and pleasure, holding onto the very edge of the bed as she did this. She looked at me, giving me a small smile of excitement.

"There we go," she said.

"You good?" I asked her.

"Better than good babe," she said.

She then spread my legs once more, diving right in, letting her lips and tongue move and tease against me. As she did that, she let out a series of small cries against my pussy, letting her tongue loll over me. I noticed Charlie holding onto her hips, thrusting in deep, filling her up.

Honestly seeing them together was hot as fuck, and then, I felt her lips move towards my clit, licking and sucking on it, while two fingers moved into me, pleasuring me.

As she did that, I let out a small cry, holding onto her, and then, moments later, I could feel the throes of my orgasm start to wash over me once again. But she stopped it for a second, looking at me.

"I'm…close too," she said.

I could tell that Charlie was too. Then, after a few more thrusts, he reached down, touching between her legs, and then, she let out a small moan of surprise, and seconds later, Charlie groaned, spilling himself into her.

She pressed her fingers against that little spot once again, and then, as she did that, I started to let out a small gasp, enjoying the feeling. It was then when I came hard, feeling like I was suddenly lost in the feeling of this. Completely shocked by how good…it felt. It was amazing, totally different from what I expected, and then, moments later, I finished too.

We laid there, all of us looking at one another. There was clearly something more that we wanted to say, but then, I felt Amelia reach over, giving me a small kiss on the lips.

"You good?" she asked me.

"Amazing really," I told her.

"I'm glad. I knew that you'd enjoy this. Because I sure as shit did," she said.

I wasn't going to lie, I felt the same way too. But what did this mean for us? What now? I could sense that Charlie was curious too.

"Well…I had a good time with this, even though it was quite surprising to see you in that state there babe," he said.

"Yeah sorry, it was a plan that we had," I told him.

"Well, next time give me a bit of a heads up before you do that," he said.

"Aww but it was a surprise," I heard Amelia say.

"Well, we can hint at it a little bit better I guess," I told her with a small smile.

"Indeed. God that was fun. I haven't had a lay that good in a long time. You would think it'd be easy to find someone, but nope," she said.

"Sounds like it," I told her.

"Anyways, enough about me, so what do you guys say? want to do it again?" Amelia asked us.

I flushed, and in truth, I wanted to. But when I looked over at Charlie, I could see something else.

The flames of desire. He wanted this too.

"You sure about that?"

"Yes, I'm sure," she told me.

"Well, then I guess we can arrange something like that. I for one had a great time and well…it was nice doing this with you, Amelia," he said.

"Indeed. Anyways, I should probably get going. We can talk again later Lana," she said.

As she walked away, closing the door, I felt the awkward tension between Charlie and I, then Charlie sighed. "Next time you do this, can you at least let me know what's going on," he said.

"Sorry, it was a decision on a whim. But you seemed to enjoy this, right?" I told him.

"Yes of course. I enjoyed it," he told me.

I blushed, and then, moments later he leaned in, capturing my lips with his own. We made out for a bit, and I did enjoy this. Even though he was definitely my one and only, having a little bit of fun with Amelia was a good thing too.

"But next time warn a guy. Coming home to that was something to say the least," he teased.

"Sure was," I told him.

"But I'd be lying if I said I didn't enjoy this," he said to me.

I flushed, and there was something about the way that he looked at me that I enjoyed. I certainly had a wonderful time with him, and it showed me…something new about myself. There was clearly a desire there, something that excited me, and something that I was enjoying too.

For a long time, the two of us spent time just making out and having a good time together, both of us enjoying the touch of one another. While I did have fun with her, I was happy to be back with him, the guy that I loved and adored.

But I was also kind of glad that…my secret was finally revealed. That's what was so exciting about all of this. The fact that I was enjoying this, and the way that he seemed to like this, it was all simply magical, and very fun too. I certainly liked it, and I knew that he did as well.

But I did wonder what would happen next, or even what the future may hold. I also kind of wondered what Amelia thought about this, if she really wanted to do this again or not. I assumed so, but who knows. There is one thing that I knew for sure, and that was the fact that I knew that it was the beginning of an exciting arrangement. Her husband wouldn't be back for a little bit, so that would give us a lot of time to play around, to explore one another more, and to let me indulge in the secret fun that I wanted to have as well.

Forbidden & Explicit Sex Stories For Adults:

Taboo Erotica Collection- Gangbangs, BDSM, Rough Anal, Sex Games& Toys, First Time Lesbian, Femdom, Orgasmic Oral& 69, Tantra& More

Written By:

G.G. Goode

Goode Publications

~CHAPTER 1~

Rough Anal from The Mystery and No Face Man

Subway Sex – A lonely woman introverted and absorbed in her day-to-day life encounters a stranger from behind. He knows her kind. He knows she needs his dick, and he gives it to her. Slowly at first. From behind. She has no idea who he is. She has no control over what he does to her. All she knows is that it feels damned good. The whole time he pleasures her with his fingers she vows to herself that she'll stop before it goes too far. Before she knows it, he's penetrating her virgin ass and she is his, in more ways than one.

~HER~

Everyone around me was living in their own secluded lives. They had their minds in their own fucked up worlds. I knew this because no one in their right mind would ride this subway every day to a job that kept them barely alive in a city you could barely breathe in. New York was supposed to be the city that never sleeps. A city where dreams come true. Such bullshit. I used to think so five years ago when I had my suitcase in my hand, and I left my Kansas home to pursue my dreams.

Now I stand in a crowded subway with my hand clutching a metal pole as it careens me to my job. It was supposed to be temporary. It was only supposed to be a stepping stone. It was supposed to happen for me by now. Instead, I have gotten empty promises and nowhere paths. I felt lost, absorbed, invisible, a permanent part of New York, and I didn't know how to change it.

I gripped the cold metal pole as the train quickly stopped to take on more monotone faces. The car was getting tighter, the crowd around me pushing closer. Someone's elbow pressed into my side. Another body brushed against my back as they pushed past me to fight for the corner of a seat to claim. I used to look up when this happened. A small smile to pass along or an apology as I tried to move out of their way. Now, it's just part of my journey to and from work. As were the lights that constantly flickered threatening to leave us all in the dark on our evening ride.

I moved toward the wall to allow others access, my eyes glued to a woman's face standing on the outside platform. This wasn't her train. She knew this without moving her eyes from her phone. Hers looked much like this one but hers went to another part of the city. She'd know when it arrived. She'd move to board when it was time, her eyes never moving from her phone, absorbed in her own fucked up little world. She dressed much like I did, her skirt to her knees and her long coat dangling off her shoulders. She could be pretty if she'd just smile. She was a permanent part of New York too. I attempted a smile then aborted the mission. Why bother? No one would look. No one would smile back. No one gave a shit.

~HIM~

I was tired of the crowded subway and craved my spacious town car again. I suppose it was the part of me that felt I was better than everyone else, the narcissist in me. I tried working on bettering myself but all of the expensive therapists in the world couldn't help me. I was broken and my family did that to me. Filthy rich and always looking down on everyone, they taught me to live and love for money, not from the heart. My wallet grew, my heart did not. I married for looks and I fucked for dominance, and I didn't care who I hurt in the process. It made me a shell of a man. My supermodel wife left me when she caught me with her sister and her two best friends. A good prenup and a better lawyer left her penniless while I traveled to Bali. Yes, I felt guilty as hell, but not for hurting her. I felt guilty because I didn't feel bad. Does that make sense? I was fucked up but shoved it off by shoving my dick into another sex kitten who wanted to screw a rich man. No feelings, just sex, and greed. They all left when the prenup came up. This was when I knew it all had to change. And I knew what I had to do.

Looking across the empty faces I settled my eyes on her and I watched her. She was my goal. She was my way out of the mental room I locked myself into. I screamed to get out, but no one ever heard me. She'd hear me. She'd feel me. She'd change everything.

Each day I watched her I knew her a little deeper. Each day I learned her rituals, her schedule, her demeanor, and her mind. She became my focus. She needed me as much as I needed her. I just had to prove that to her, and I would. That evening. It was time to make her mine and show her how to break out of her mental room.

~HER~

The train moved slowly at first then as it picked up speed as the landscape rushed past and the lights flickered like a shorted-out strobe light. The scenery out the windows changed quickly, from graffiti walls to busy streets where the last light faded from the day. I leaned my shoulder against the wall and clutched my long coat to my chest, my bare legs a little cold from the December air. The lights went out just as the train went into another tunnel, the car going dark. No one moved. No one cared. It was an everyday occurrence. Cell phones lit up faces. A stranger pressed against my back. I couldn't move forward any further. I didn't think anyone could move anywhere until the train stopped to let some off. I ignored the body behind me until a hand slid up the back of my arm. I turned away slightly, and the hand disappeared. The lights flickered, attempting to illuminate the car again but failed. The hand returned, this time moving along the small of my back. I turned slightly again but the hand stayed. Letting my coat go, I pulled my hand up behind me to shoo the stranger away. His fingers wrapped around my wrist and held me there. My breath caught. I've had incidents before where men have tried to cop a cheap feel, but this was different. Controlling. Demanding. His body pressed into me pinning my hand between us.

"Shhhhh." The warmth of his breath surrounded my ear.

Chills covered my arms and fed up my back. Part of me prayed for the lights to come back on, but oddly, part of me felt a little heat from this heinous little fantasy. What would it hurt to allow a perfect stranger to touch me inappropriately? As long as it didn't go too far. I relaxed a little.

His grip tightened around my wrist, his other hand trailing around my waist between me and the wall. My coat was pulled open for access and I didn't move when his hand moved across my stomach.

I swallowed hard, a quiver spreading through me and taking control. It pushed a tingling sensation down between my legs.

He gripped my blouse and pulled it from my skirt, before slipping his hand underneath it. The warmth and the strangeness fueled my fire that began the moment he seized my wrist.

I reached back and grabbed his leg. It was firm, muscular, the material of his pants soft to the touch. The moment the lights flickered back on I jumped and pulled my hand away. He did not. I glanced nervously at the others around me, their blank faces still absorbed in their own thoughts. What was happening to me was invisible to them, but it consumed my entire being. This stranger slammed his existence into my life without an invite, without question, and without approval.

"Do not move, my pet." His whisper was close to my ear, and his claim to me excited me. "Let me." He directed me to face the wall and pulled my coat back around me before boxing me in.

My breath was shaky, my hands were cold, my pussy was wet. Excitement radiated through me. I'd allow him to go a little further. He was barely under my clothes. What was the harm?

"I see you," he continued. "You need this."

I was afraid to ask what *this* referred to, but I was certain he was going to show me. His hand found my bare stomach again, but he didn't stop there. He continued down past the belt on my skirt and tucked the material between his hand and my legs. He rubbed me there and I reached back for his leg again.

The cool air gained access to my legs as my skirt gathered in his hand. The hem raised up past my knees, past my thighs, past my soaked panties, and over my belt. He tucked it and pushed his fingers underneath the small elastic band of my underwear. I held my breath, my body trembling, my hands reassuring that my coat stayed down around me to shield me from the blank faces.

The moment he cupped my bare pussy, I inhaled deeply, forcibly, my head going back into his chest.

"Yes," he whispered. His fingers pushed into my lips and moved back and forth over my clit. If he continued doing that it'd be the fastest orgasm I'd ever had. But he knew this and stopped. I covered his hand with mine and tried directing him to continue, but he swiftly pulled my hand away with his free hand and bent it around my back between us.

"Don't do that again," he whispered.

He wanted complete control.

His fingers moved again. Arousal festered and threatened me. I moved my foot to the side, opening my legs for him. I needed to stop him soon. This was risky. Too risky. A little longer.

The subway train stopped and so did he, but his hand remained inside my panties. He held me there waiting as more than half of the people filed out the door and the train moved forward again. I glanced up at the sign. My stop was next, but his finger slipped inside me and his thumb rubbed my clit. I no longer cared who was around me, where I needed to be when the train stopped again, or how I was going to stop this stranger from finger fucking me.

"Listen to me carefully," he said quietly. "There are three more stops before this subway is retired for the evening. We will stay where we are until then."

My arousal heightened quickly but it was laced with panic and I tried turning toward him. He pinned me discreetly so that I couldn't.

"Your excitement for me comes because of the mystery. My excitement for you comes because I know you. I know what you need and I'm the man who can give it to you."

"I can't do this," I heard myself say.

"You can. I'll guide you." He pulled his hands away from me and I no longer felt him close to me. "If you truly do not want to continue, tell me now and I'll disappear forever."

I trembled harder. Did I want this to end so abruptly? I was just bitching in my mind about the humdrum life I was living. I was just telling myself I had wished for something exciting to happen for me. This wasn't quite what I had in mind, but it was here, rearing its sexual head and I had a choice to make.

The train stopped and the doors opened. I could hear myself breathing heavily. It was my stop. But I didn't move. My mind screamed for me to move, but my body froze where I stood. The doors closed and the train moved again.

"Good girl," he whispered. "You have pleased me." The warmth from his body radiated through me. His hand returned to my stomach. His tongue ran along the outside of my ear and his teeth nibbled the side before trailing down to my neck.

I closed my eyes when he cupped my pussy again, his fingers sliding inside me. My clit responded and added to the trembling I could not control.

My nipples ached for touch. I reached up and cupped them. My hardened nipples protruded through my bra and my blouse. They were hard against my palms and sensitive as I flicked them with my thumbs.

He pulled his hand from me, gripped my wrists, and pulled them to my side. "No. They are mine."

I forgot. He needs control. He pulled away, leaving me with my face against the wall, aching for his touch. I still sensed his body close to mine, but he withdrew from me. Why? Was he punishing me? I wanted his touch. I needed a release. Should I ask? Should I beg? I sucked my lower lip between my teeth and flicked it with the tip of my tongue. He was good and it made me crazy with arousal.

"I'm sorry," I whispered, slightly turning my head toward my shoulder I thought he was stood behind. The train stopped. The doors opened. He was still close but didn't say anything. He didn't touch me. He didn't move. I stared at the wall. The doors closed and the train moved one final time. Still nothing. I began to think I was imagining the warmth of his body and he had left me, but then he inhaled deeply. His hand slid around me once again and found my panties, then proceeded to delve deep into what was inside them. My arousal returned.

"The smell of your cunt intoxicates me," he growled, his lips brushing my ear. My arousal exploded.

He aggressively pushed his hand into my panties and his fingers into my pussy. They pushed deep inside me and almost completely withdrew before pushing back into me again. His other hand pressed against my back as leverage while he intrusively claimed every part of me. So many emotions were running rampant through me. I was scared to death, horny as hell, submissive to a stranger, and very aware that it was too late to stop this. I wanted to see him. I wanted to know who was dominating every fiber of my being. I wanted to know the man I was willing to give myself to without question.

But that was too late as well. The train stopped. The lights went out and we were alone. His fingers slowed. I could hear his breathing. It was ragged and labored. He let me go for the first time and I turned toward him. The only light came from a dim bulb on the outside tunnel wall and it was barely enough to see his silhouette.

"Who are you?" My mouth was dry. My body trembled uncontrollably, and I needed his hands on me but was afraid to tell him.

"Your savior." He wrapped his arm around my waist and pulled me into him, his mouth covering mine. He pushed his tongue past my lips and tasted me. I melted like butter in his arms until his hand pulled my blouse over my tits. He yanked my bra up and pushed me back until I bowed backward over his arm. He sucked my nipple into his mouth and bit down. Pain shot through me arrowing deep into my arousal and mixing them together deliciously. He held me there while his hand finger fucked me again. My arousal hit harder and an orgasm washed over me. I winced until his fingers stopped and he let me go.

I couldn't think. My brain was in a fog. He licked his fingers, taking my hand with his free hand and he led me to a seat in the corner. He unzipped his pants and pulled his cock free before sitting down in front of me. He directed me to my knees and slid his hand into my hair.

"Stroke it."

He was good at hitting my buttons. He had just pushed me to orgasm and I was feeling another one deep down inside me, merely by the words he said.

I reached out toward him, without hesitation, giddy with excitement that it was my turn to please him. My hand reached through the darkness and wrapped around it the moment my fingertips touched it. I stroked him and it felt so good. He was massive and thick, his veins bulging around it. I cupped his head and moved up and down the shaft. I licked my lips. I wanted to taste him. My eyes searched for his face, but it was futile. I couldn't see his face, only the shape of his head. What did he look like? I focused on his eyes but saw nothing but darkness. Moving my focus to the meat in my hand I wanted to please him. I wanted to make him happy. I wanted to submit to what he needed from me.

Stroking him felt empowering. I moved my hand along his heavy shaft pulling my hand with my arm in each direction. His head went back, and a moan escaped him. It was guttural and came from someplace deep in his throat. It fed my desire to please him. I sucked my bottom lip into my teeth, my body trembling with excitement. I leaned forward, my eyes glued to his exposed throat. My tongue ran across the tip of his dick and he immediately sprung his head forward.

"Yes," he growled. His fingers slid into the back of my hair and his grip tightened, my hair in his fist. "Suck me." He directed me forward and I easily complied. He was big but delicious. It filled my mouth easily. I wanted more. "Run your tongue up and down my shaft." His words were wavering, which meant I was doing a good job. I wanted to explore him further and I love that he told me what to do. He demanded my actions. And I complied, my tongue trying to move along his shaft as best as I could. He pressed my face down further and I knew I had more to engulf. But how? "Deeper," he grunted. When he pushed me further, I recognized the answer just before he demanded it. "Throat fuck it," he commanded. My throat was going to open whether I wanted it to or not. His head hit my gag reflex and I tried pulling away. His hand may as well have been a stone wall. I was there, not moving from my position, so I tried relaxing, squeezing my eyes closed. I had given blow jobs before but none of them were nearly this size. My ex-boyfriend was freaky, and we tried a lot of different things. It wasn't what I wanted, but I did it to try and please him. He had no response to what I did. I could have been doing everything right, or completely wrong. I had no way of knowing, so I left.

But this man, this stranger sitting before me knew just what to do and how to show me how I was doing. He directed me in ways I wished my ex would have done. Who would have known that I liked this so much? I opened my throat as he pushed me down further. I relaxed my muscles and caressed his thighs. Once it slid past the opening of my throat it moved easily and expanded my neck wide. He stopped and growled. He moved slowly back and forth and the friction of his dick moving along my esophagus made me want to swallow him. I wanted him in my throat, in my chest, in my stomach, in my pussy. I just wanted him to consume me. I bobbed my head up and down, slow at first then a little faster. My fingernails grazed along his balls and I felt them tighten against him. He let me go and I pulled myself off him, a deep breath of air forcing down into my lungs. I panted, I licked my lips, I tasted his pungent precum on my tongue and I wanted more. He laced my hair with his fingers again and pulled me down to his cock again. I eagerly opened my mouth and enjoyed the shape of it sliding against my tongue. Closing my lips around him I sucked him hard, bobbing my head up and down on his shaft.

"You are ready," he growled.

He stood up and pulled me to my feet, his mouth hungry for mine. He shared the taste of himself on my tongue. He moved his hands quickly to disrobe what he wanted bare. My skirt went up to my waist and my panties were pulled over to the side. He directed me to the seat where he had sat and turned me to face the window. I looked out but only saw a dimly lit tunnel wall with worn graffiti across it.

His hands went to my hips. I was dizzy with arousal. I felt his dick against my ass as he pushed the top of my back forward with his hand. He wanted me bent over in front of him, and I did. I grasped the sides of the seat and bent forward for him. My legs opened and I swallowed hard. This was it. I should have stopped. But I couldn't. I was his no matter the consequence.

He pulled the bottom of my blouse up and caressed my back, his dick still pressed against me. He wasn't in any hurry, but he was making me crazy. I wanted to beg him to fuck me. I wanted to push him inside me and ride him like a rollercoaster until I orgasmed. Then I wanted to do it again. I wanted him to demand things from me I had never done before. I was ready. I was more willing than I ever thought I'd be.

"You are so fucking sexy." His words were low, deep and they hit me like a boulder. I would have done anything he asked. But he didn't ask. He just did what he wanted with me. And at that moment, he wanted to fuck me. He was ready.

He lined himself up and I felt him push against my vagina. He opened me slowly and stopped with each inch. I wanted to push back. I tried to push back, but he held me steady and did the work he wanted to do. He caressed my hips and my ass cheeks. He pushed a little deeper into me. He stopped and caressed me some more. I allowed the sensation to seep into me and felt it flow through me like hot water over cold skin. His hands gripped my hip bones and he pushed slowly inside me, opening me wide, stretching me further, and filling my pussy with his entire dick. It hurt, but it was addicting. He stopped and held me there, his arms sliding around my waist. His weight was on my back and his mouth was close to my face. He licked the back of my ear as he slowly withdrew himself from me. His weight lifted off me and he pushed back inside. He moved slowly, too slowly. I was screaming inside for release. I was desperate for him to fuck me hard and make me cum. I was aching so bad for more of him and I didn't care how he delivered himself to me.

I wanted to scream his name, but I didn't know who he was. I didn't know what he looked like, and I didn't know if I'd ever see him again. I needed to make this count. I needed to make him need me again. I'd ride this same subway next to this same wall for the rest of my life if it meant being with him again.

I gripped the seat harder and tried pushing back into him. The only thing I could do was open my legs for him further. And I did. He reached up underneath me and cupped my tits. He held them tight and fucked me steady. My breathing came harder, faster, drying my mouth but soaking my pussy.

"Oh, God," I whispered. My entire body quivered under his control. What else could he possibly do to me to make this any better? I was in complete ecstasy. When he pulled himself out and stood behind me, I was certain I was about to find out. His hands were still on my ass cheeks, caressing them, moving in circles around them, his fingers sliding up and down my crack. I felt him staring at me there, even though we couldn't see anything except silhouettes and the outside walls. He ran his finger down and pushed it inside me, my breath catching as he slid it out and up my anus. I knew what was next. It was something I had only done once, and it hurt like hell. He was going to fuck my ass.

A new wave of fear spread through me. This man behind me was at least twice the size of my ex-boyfriend and I remember the pain well. When he stepped forward and I felt the head of his dick touch me there I jumped and moved forward a bit.

"I don't know if I...."

He stopped me by sliding his hand over my mouth. He pulled me upright and kissed my neck, his teeth grazing my skin.

"Don't speak. Don't say no. Don't," he whispered. His hand was still over my mouth as his other hand cupped my tit. He rolled my nipple between his fingers and electricity struck me down to my cunt. His hand moved slightly over my mouth so he could push two fingers in over my tongue. He slid them in and out as he played with my nipple, pinching it and twirling it until it was raw and sensitive. "Who do you belong to," he growled close to my ear. His words made me squirm with enthusiasm.

"You," I whispered.

"Yes. I know now where to find you and I will again. This isn't our first encounter, my pet. I will find you here again when I need to. When you need me to."

I nodded and lowered myself to the seat again. I could barely breathe, but each breath was heavy and deep. I could barely feel but every fiber of my being was electric and ready to explode. I could barely move but I was willing to move any way he wanted me to. I opened my legs and waited with anticipation.

"Good girl." His hands caressed my ass and moved along my pussy. He inserted his fingers again, finger fucking me slowly before pulling them out and sliding them across my anus. The moment his dick touched me there I flinched. But he stopped. He was good. He was slow. Sympathetic to my needs and my desires. The more pressure he gave the more heat I felt.

He pushed until my hole opened slightly, fighting its intrusion but exciting the hell out of everything beyond it. His hands moved in wide circles over my cheeks, slowly only to push himself a little deeper. I thought my brain would explode. The pain and the pleasure he fed me was so intense I honestly felt I was going crazy. I inhaled sharply and exhaled with a shaky breath. I gripped the seat so hard I thought it would break in my hands. I stiffened every muscle in my body until I felt they would cramp into position. He pushed deeper and stopped for a moment. He rocked back and forth, and something deep inside me welled up and began to surround me.

"No, no, no," he whispered, stopping his movement, but caressing with his hands. "Not yet, my pet. We have all night and I want this to last." He stroked my body as the pressure inside me slowly dissipated. I tried to swallow but my tongue was dry. I inhaled slowly and tried to focus but the darkness kept that from me as well.

When he began to move again, I concentrated on his body behind me. I imagined the way he moved, and what he saw, and the position of his back as he rocked back and forth. I felt that pressure deep inside again but worked on controlling it and the pace that it consumed me. He pushed deeper and I deliciously invited the pain in, mentally swirling it with the heated desire radiating from every part of me. I opened my legs further, as he slowly began fucking my asshole. His hands found my tits and he lightly caressed them as they swayed back and forth over his palms. He knew how to intensify my desires, he knew how to control what I wanted, he knew how to manipulate what I needed to mold it to his desires. He knew me deeper than I knew myself and he was exactly what I needed in my life. To control my inner desires, to be controlled by a dominant man that knew how to touch those desires.

I pushed back into him, my head moving back. My hair fell over my bareback and he scooped it up to hold me there. His fist tight around my hair, he pulled me back into him and fucked me harder.

"You're my whore, now," he growled. "Say it."

I let out a guttural groan from my tightened throat. It was all I could manage.

He yanked my head back a little harder and stopped fucking me. "Say it," he demanded.

"I'm…yours," I grunted.

"You're my whore." He began fucking me again as if it were my reward for complying with his demands.

"Yes." I tried nodding but it wasn't possible.

"You're going to be my whore whenever I choose you to be." His pace got a little faster.

"Yes." My voice trembled.

"I will fuck you when I see fit, but you will never know when that will be. I will fuck you where I want, but you'll never know when I'll be there."

I inhaled a shaky breath as the pressure built inside me. He fucked me faster, harder, his groin slamming into me with each thrust.

"This. Will. Be. Your. Wake up. Call." He grabbed my hips and slammed into me one more time before filling me up with everything he had. His yell echoed off the walls. His hands gripped me hard and my muscles tightened like a vice around his dick. I came so hard I stopped breathing and froze. My legs quaked underneath me. He withdrew his dick from my ass, and I collapsed into the seat, breathing hard, shivering from my head to my feet and naked except for my skirt still around my waist and my panties still off to the side. They were soaked.

He gathered me into his arms and scooped me up onto his lap. His hand caressed my hair until I calmed myself down and my breathing became somewhat normal again.

"Who are you," I whispered, looking up at him. Although my eyes had adjusted a little more in the darkened subway car, I still strained to see the whites of his eyes, unsuccessfully, however.

"I'm your savior, as I said before. You will no longer go through your days wondering why you're doing what you're doing, and why you feel stuck in a life you do not desire. The anticipation of seeing me or feeling me behind you again will change your entire existence."

"Just like that? You won't tell me who you are? I just gave myself to you."

"You did. You're a rare breed, my pet. You have given me as much as I have given you. As much as you are my whore, I am your savior. I am a new outlook on each day you wake up. I am an excitement you will look forward to each time you come onto this subway. Or perhaps in a café you frequent, or the fitting room at Macy's. How long have I been watching you?"

My heart skipped a beat. I had put myself into a bad situation, fucking a stranger, allowing him access to parts of me I wasn't even aware existed. And now that he has gotten in, I didn't think I was going to get him out again. He was right. He just changed my life. The anticipation of him lurking around each corner I rounded was going to keep my pussy wet and my stomach tightly knotted. How would I know when I passed him on the street? How would I know if he drove the next Uber I climbed into? How would I react if he was my next client at work and I had to work with him on a daily basis? How would I know? How would I keep my sanity?

"Stand up." He lifted me off him and I stood on my weak legs, still half-naked but worried this was the end of our time together. He knelt in front of me and ran his hands up my legs. My arousal returned. He caressed me between my legs, and I opened for him further. He tasted us on his fingers, his breath catching as he did.

His forehead rested against my stomach and held onto my hips. It was the first vulnerable moment I witnessed with him. It gave me strength and a need to take care of him. I stroked his hair and decided it was dark, perhaps black. And his eyes, they were blue, icy, deep. He hooked my underwear in his hand and repositioned them where they belonged before pulling my skirt back down into place. Rising to his feet, he towered over me at least a foot and assisted me with my blouse. He handed my bra back and I felt around and found my bag, pushing my bra inside it. Turning around, I let him slide my coat back onto my arms. He buttoned it and held on for a few moments more.

Not another word was spoken, but everything each of us needed surrounded us at that moment. He walked to the doors and pulled them apart, waiting for me, to assist me to the concrete platform just outside the car. I stepped out but kept my head down. There may have been enough light to see him, but at that moment I didn't want that. I merely waited for him to walk with me, but he did not.

"Until we meet again, my pet." He kissed my palm and walked the opposite way until he was out of sight from me.

Would I ever see him again? Would there be a next time? I was already aching for him. He was still very much around me, in my head, in my body. The evidence was there, and I didn't want to wash it away. My soaked underwear, uncomfortable against my swollen pussy was evidence. My ass sore from his cock. My mind no longer bored and defeated. He changed that just like he said he would.

The next morning, I went through my same routine but looked for him around every corner I rounded. I looked into every man's eyes, wondering if they were the ones I searched for that night in the subway car. Each man could have been him. Each man I walked by, each guy I caught glancing my way, any of them could have been him. What if I already knew him? A co-worker? My boss? The mail carrier? I was going crazy not knowing.

That night when I got back to my apartment, I dropped everything and lay on the couch. My body was on fire for his touch. I slid my hand into my pants and fingered myself, my mind drowned in thoughts of him. An orgasm hit me hard before I showered and went to bed. Maybe the next day would be different. Every day was much like that day. Every day became a new hope, full of anticipation on the what if. What if that day was the next time I encountered him? What if it was in the subway again? What if it was a café bathroom? What about a stock room at the local grocery store? He changed me. And I was grateful for that.

A week and a half went by with no signs of him. I was beginning to think it was a dream. He wasn't even real. Until the day he was. I stood next to the same wall, similar faces around me. Every nudge of an elbow heightened my senses. Every brush of a body aroused me. When his presence was behind me and I felt the warmth of his body again I began to tremble much like the first time. His body moved in close and his hand slid around my waist. My breath stuck in my throat like glue. I lowered my head and inhaled a shaky breath.

"Yes," he whispered. "We meet again, my pet."

We stood there for the entire ride, very close, his hand roaming my body under my coat as the crowd thinned from the car with every stop. When the train made its final destination, and the lights went out he turned me toward him. His mouth covered mine and his tongue claimed what it wanted. We were both hungry for each other, but he was urgent, non-sensitive, non-caring. I didn't mind. He was with me.

He sucked my chin into his mouth and traveled down my neck, biting at my skin and groping me with a hunger I hadn't witnessed before. He ripped my dress open from the front and yanked my bra up. He grabbed my arms and leaned down as if he needed to milk me. He sucked my tit into his mouth and devoured it. I stared down at him, eyes wide, trying to focus, trying to see any glimpse of him I could in the dim bulb from outside the subway car. He kneaded my tits with his hands as he licked and bit at my nipples before sliding his hand down my stomach and under my dress. He quickly found my panties and yanked them down urgently. I stepped out of them, breathless and trembling. Without warning he reached up between my legs and pushed his fingers inside me, finger fucking me fast and furiously. I wanted to tell him to slow down. I wanted to ask him why he was so desperate. I wanted to pleasure him like I did the first time, but he wasn't having it.

He pushed his fingers inside me over and over again until my pussy began to hurt. Where was his sexy dominance? Where was his need to control and take his time? I was confused and I didn't want to be there, but I didn't try to stop him. He stood up and I could hear him sucking on his fingers before he leaned into me and kissed me hard. I tasted what he did on his tongue and it surged through me. He spun me around and shoved my upper body forward. I flopped over, my hands barely catching the seat in front of me. I held the metal bar with one hand and the corner of the seat with my other. He didn't allow me to straighten up. He was there for one thing and that scared the hell out of me. I heard the jingle of his belt before he jerked my dress up over my hips. He stroked my pussy and ran it along my asshole before penetrating it.

Oh God! He was going straight for my ass!

I squeezed my eyes closed and braced for the pain. He pushed into me. All. The. Way. No hesitation, no taking his time. He pushed into me and held me there until I stretched and relaxed around his dick. Then he began to move. He grunted with every thrust into my ass and the pain didn't have enough pleasure to mix with.

I clenched my teeth tightly and held my breath, trying to put my mind someplace else until he was satisfied, but it took forever. Over an hour he fiercely fucked me without recourse. I reached down between my legs to help things along, expecting him to yank my hand away but he didn't. I sliced my fingers through the folds of my pussy and teased my swollen clit trying to get some satisfaction from this heinous act and eventually, arousal sparked. As he slammed into me repeatedly, I worked at my sensitive clit and expanded my arousal, eventually pushing back into him hoping for a better response. He never changed his rhythm or his demeanor, but I did cum. In the few moments before I did, I welcomed his intrusion and begged him to fuck my ass harder. Once I was finished, he continued for another fifteen minutes, at least. He was troubled by something and he needed release, not just from his body but from whatever was messing with his mind. I was his vessel, and I thought I was okay with that. My knees wanted to buckle, and my back wanted to break. How long could I withstand this treatment? I had to tell him to stop.

He gripped my hips harder, pushing into me deeper, grunting a little louder. This gave me the strength to hold out just a little longer. He blew his load, grunting from someplace deep inside him. It sliced through me like a knife, like I could feel what he was going through. His cock pulsated inside me while he worked to calm his body and regulate his breathing. He pulled out and I stood up, my legs weak from supporting him for so long. I attempted to touch him, but he turned away and pulled his pants up, his buckle clinking together.

"Are you…okay?" I asked softly.

He didn't respond. I pulled my bra down and attempted to fix my dress, but it was too damaged, so I buttoned my coat closed and stood before him watching his outline. He turned back to me and held my face in his hands for a moment.

"Some days will be exactly like this. It's what I needed."

He walked to the doors and pulled them open before disappearing around the corner. I fought back tears as I searched for my underwear and clenched my coat over my chest. I had no reason to cry. I was shaking, yes, but only because it was so abrupt and callous, yet I felt like I gave him exactly what he needed.

Days fed into weeks and my masturbation became more frequent. This man had left me in a state I couldn't control and every chance I had I was touching myself. I walked into a coffee shop to grab a cup to go, but more so to borrow their bathroom for some privacy. Walking into a stall, I locked myself inside and waited for two others to leave. Once it was quiet, I removed my bra from underneath my thin blouse and shoved it into my bag. Sliding my hand underneath my skirt I moved slowly fingering my clit and imagining his hands on my body and his cock in my ass. I made small circles around my hardened nipple feeling my arousal spread quickly. His aggressions were justified, and I felt I helped him cope with whatever demons he was dealing with. I didn't have to ask. I just needed to be. For him.

I closed my eyes and listened to my breathing as it got heavier. I looked down at my thumb as I mimicked what he did the first night we were together, and a folded piece of paper laid on the floor between my feet. I froze and listened intently. I was still alone, wasn't I?

I turned my head to read the upside-down writing and gasped at the words.

"Perhaps it's time to go beyond the subway. Regency on Broadway. Room 415. This evening."

A familiar tremble returned deep inside my stomach as I picked up the note and read it again. My other hand opened the stall door slowly as I peeked around the room. There was no one there.

"What the hell?" What was I feeling? Panic? Excitement? Fear? My mouth went dry.

I left the bathroom with the note clutched in my hand and a deep arousal in my belly. Standing before the barista I couldn't understand why the young man was grinning so much until I looked down. I never put my bra back on and the thought of finally meeting the mystery man had me so horny my nipples were telling the world.

"Uh," I raised my arm to cover them, but then lowered it again. I was tired of being invisible. It was freeing to know I was the reason for this kid's grin and potential erection behind the counter, even though it did take hard nips to make it happen. I smirked and straightened my posture before I ordered a chai latte with extra cream, three m's, and a smile.

The rest of my day I spent with pins and needles and my underwear soaked between my legs. I don't know how I made it through work, but I did, and the evening was upon me. I had fought with myself all day on whether I should go to this hotel room with this man. I didn't know him even though I have had his semen inside me. But he would have killed me by now if that was his thing. No. This was much more than that. He needed me as much as I needed him. It was fucked up, but it was my fuck up.

Maybe he wanted to take our relationship further. No matter how much I questioned it, I was not passing this opportunity up. I was finally going to see him, to know who this man was. Was I right to decide he had black hair and piercing blue eyes?

After I went home and showered for an hour, I carefully selected a simple black dress over a black lace bra and panty, something classy for him to see me in. The entire time I prepared myself for him I felt excitement. But my stomach felt sick once I stood in front of the door at the Regency Hotel. I opened it and walked inside as I tried to regulate my breathing. I was greeted with friendly smiles and beautiful décor as I walked through the lobby.

"Excuse me, miss?" The attendant at the desk smiled when I looked at her. "Can I help you?"

"I'm meeting someone." I didn't want to answer any questions. I didn't know who I was meeting, and at that moment I felt cheap, like a hooker meeting a client.

"Yes, miss. I was directed to give you this." The attendant held a key card toward me and smiled. "You'll be in room 415."

I scrunched my eyebrows down and hesitatingly took it from her. "That's right, but…how did you know I…." I looked around but saw nothing peculiar.

"It's okay, miss. You can go up. He has been expecting you."

I nodded slightly, still defensive, but I forced a smile and made my way up to room 415.

I shook my arms as I stared at the gold numbers on the door and breathed deep a few times before sliding the card across the lock. Opening the door slightly I peeked inside but he didn't appear to be there yet. The door closed behind me as I looked around the room. It would give me a little time to get used to being there. The room was beautiful, clean, with a bottle of wine waiting on the desk next to a white box and a note.

I walked to the desk and read the note.

Enjoy. Wine to relax with. A gift for you as well.

I opened the box, and it was a dress very similar to the one he ripped off me. *He does have a heart after all,* I smiled. In the middle of the dress was another small box with another note.

Wear this for me now and await my arrival.

I was giddy with excitement as I opened the box and pulled out a black silk blindfold.

"Shit." My insides turned to mush.

I opened the wine and filled the glass halfway, chugging half of it. I stared at the blindfold as the sweet taste spread across my tongue. It warmed my face quickly and lowered my inhibitions. I pulled the blindfold from the box and slid it through my fingers. It was soft, silky, teasing me, and demanding me to wear it. I didn't at first, but then I felt guilty. He wanted me to. I sat on the bed and placed it over my eyes, tying it loosely at the back. I nodded in approval. It wasn't so bad. Intriguing. Sexy. A smidge of light peeked from underneath it and if I tilted my head the right way, I could see a bit of my surroundings.

I sat there only a few minutes when I heard the door open quietly. My breath caught and I wanted to be sure it was him, but I didn't move my head. What did I call him? How would I be able to tell? I chuckled nervously to myself and listened intently. The door clicked closed and the moments grew longer. The silence was deafening. I jumped when I felt a hand on my face raising my head. It slid down to my chest and copped a feel, squeezing slightly before disappearing into the silence again. I turned my head to the side desperate for something, a sound, a word, something.

"Take off your bra and whatever else you have underneath."

I trembled at the familiar tone of his voice, making it a little harder for me to climb off the bed. I reached underneath my dress and removed my panties stepping out of them when I felt them fall down my legs. I pulled the straps of my bra out of my dress and fed my arms out of them, pulling it from underneath and discarding it at my feet. I could see them through the small opening at the bottom of my blindfold.

I didn't know what to do with my hands. I didn't know if I should get back on the bed or stay where I was. I didn't know if he was in front of me with his eyes on me or where he was. The blindfold over my eyes tightened quickly and I sucked in a little air, reaching up and barely touching it. The opening was gone, and I was in complete darkness again, just how he liked it.

"Drink," he said softly.

I felt the glass on my lower lip and opened my mouth until the sweetness filled my mouth. The moment I swallowed it, his mouth was on mine and his tongue was lapping up the taste. It threw me into overdrive without hesitation.

"Why are we here?" I asked, a quiver in my voice.

"You know the answer, my pet."

"I mean, I thought this was my chance to finally see you."

Silence filled the spaces around me. I reached up and slid my fingers along the mask. I wanted to pull it down. What would he do? Would he stop seeing me? The thought was horrifying.

His hands tightened around my wrists and they were lowered to my side. "Keep it," he whispered close to my ear. Chills. I nodded slightly. "Good girl."

He was close to me. His heat warmed me. I was lifted off the floor and the next thing I felt was the bed underneath me. I reached my arms out to either side. He had me in the middle, I didn't feel the mattress move with the weight of his body. I didn't hear the tone of his deep voice. I didn't smell his scent close to me. I moved my head to the side hearing only the silence around me once again.

"You look beautiful lying there in that dress."

My lower lip quivered. He was watching me. His voice came from the foot of the bed. "I want to see you." I shouldn't have requested again, but I did. My words dissipated into the room.

My legs were pushed open and I felt the air surround my pussy immediately. I felt his eyes there, his hands on my legs, the weight of him on the bottom of the bed. Hands slid slowly up my legs and brought the bottom of my dress with them as he moved to my hips. Arousal threatened my insides as a tickle cascaded over my mound. Warmth. Another tickle. More warmth. Was he breathing on it? I spread further.

"So fucking beautiful."

My lips were parted open and something slid inside me. His fingers? Two hands reached up and grabbed each of my arms holding me tight, and I gasped. He had his mouth on me, his tongue sliding inside my folds and flicking over my clit. I opened my legs as far as they could go, and my head went back in ecstasy. I moved my hips back and forth moaning at the sensation he pushed into me. His hands tightened around my arms as he tasted me and fucked me with his tongue bringing me to a delicious orgasm.

He moved on the bed, to the side of me but he was no longer touching me.

"You are an incredible woman. I'm very fortunate to have found you." His voice trailed away telling me he had his back to me. "What you have given me...."

"Are you breaking up with me?" I sat up quickly and reached my hand toward him.

"No," he chuckled. "Is this a relationship?"

"It's something, isn't it? You flood my brain daily. I dream about you every night."

"Hush, my pet. I'm not leaving you. I'm giving you an option."

"An option?"

"You have an image of me," he said, his deep tone surrounding me.

"Yes." I was a little too excited with my response but perhaps? Was he going to let me see him?

"Having the ability to create an image in your mind is why a book is better than the movie."

"I agree but, sometimes the reality of things is better than one could ever imagine."

"Sometimes. Other times not so much." He took my hand and sandwiched it between his. "What we have is beyond names and faces. You have given me so much without asking why. You have touched me deeper than anyone in my life. For this, I will leave it to you. You have one minute to decide. You can remove your mask and see me, or you can choose to keep it where it is. If you choose to keep it on, this will be our *relationship*. If you want to see me, things will change. They will never be as they are now."

I sat up and curled my legs toward me. Was he honestly giving me the option? I reached up and pinched the material with my fingers but stopped before I pulled it down. Was I ready to see him and shatter the image I had of him? It honestly didn't matter what he looked like. A drop-dead gorgeous narcissist or an average joe with sadistic tendencies. We both satisfied each other, and it no longer mattered what he looked like.

I leaned back and settled down onto the pillow, clasping my hands together across my stomach until the minute had passed.

His weight shifted on the bed until he was lying next to me, his arm draped over me, his head on my chest. I wrapped my arms around him and just held on.

"I like this," he said, his finger sliding along the swells of my breasts. "It makes me feel wholesome and cherished."

It was an odd thing for a dominant man to say next to a half-naked woman with a blindfold on, but I didn't question it. He had his reasons. I was just happy to satisfy him, no matter what he needed.

~CHAPTER 2~

Wife Gets Gangbanged During A House Break-In

A Gangbang is Needed – Sex with her husband has become a normal and quite typical half-hour. Same position, same thoughts, same fantasy. When their house is broken into during one of their sessions, three men creep through only expecting to rob them. They never expected to encounter the couple having sex. They watch until the husband notices them. He tries to protect his wife, but they have other plans. It's time to show this guy how to treat his wife properly.

~HER~

The position I slept in had cradled my body long enough. Keeping my eyes closed, I pushed myself over to my other side and curled up into Ronald, stealing his body heat and trying to wish myself back into my dream. I rarely remembered my dreams, but when I did, I hung onto them for as long as I could. They were almost always erotic and seductive, and I used them as my fantasies during our sexy time, as Ronald liked to call it.

I squeezed my eyes tighter and imagined myself back in the dream.

I couldn't see much with the blinding lights all around me, the heat from them producing sweat that trickled down the middle of my naked back. It was as if I was sitting on a stage and the hot lights were keeping the audience from my vision. Was I in a play? Was it something rehearsed or was it improv? There was no noise, no depth to the room I was in. I could have been alone, but somehow, I knew I wasn't.

A hand was placed on my shoulder. It moved, caressing me and massaging my neck. Two fingers under my chin lifted my head toward the blinding lights and all I could do was squint. A pair of lips on the side of my neck kissed me there, his tongue occasionally licking my skin. Another pair of hands coasted along the curves of my hips, up and down, slowly, seductively, exquisitely.

I didn't know these men who had conjured around me, but I loved the awakening I was receiving from their touch. I held onto a metal bar above my head a little tighter. Not knowing where they were going to touch me next was the biggest turn-on I had ever experienced, but it wasn't an experience, was it? It was only a dream. A gorgeous, luscious, opulent dream that I didn't want to end.

My legs were pushed open and a man crawled toward me, his head appearing between them. I could only see the back of his head, so I locked my eyes onto his luscious black curls, my mouth falling open. My heart pounded against the inside of my chest. Excitement trembled through me. The lights dimmed and my eyes adjusted to several beautiful men all naked and all horny for me. The man between my legs lifted his head slightly, and I locked my eyes on his face. He was dark and so sexy. His hands glided up my thighs, his dark chocolate hands contrasting against my pale skin. His tongue slithered out of his mouth and licked the inside of my thigh, achingly close to my sweet spot. I swallowed hard, my heavy breathing drying my mouth out. Hands slithered up and down my arms before moving to my chest. They picked my tits up and pressed them together before a blond-haired man blocked my view and lapped at my nipples. The tongue on my thigh that was dangerously close to my pussy, threatening to tease me there no longer threatened. The blond had moved just in time for me to witness the tip of the black man's tongue doing exactly what it threatened to do. It flicked my clit lightly, his dark eyes looking up at me and seizing my complete attention.

My pussy ached for satisfaction. It ached for a cock to fuck. It screamed out for a man to take me and dominate me.

His tongue flicked faster, harder, his hands moving back and forth across my thighs. He settled his lips around my pussy, and he began to hum. The deep tone of his voice sent volts of electricity through me before his tongue pushed into me. I grabbed the sides of the bench I sat on and gripped it hard.

A pair of hands slid down from my shoulders from someone standing behind me, the naked bulge of his cock pressing against my back. It moved up and down against me, slowly at first. As he picked up his speed, I knew he was getting off on me. I offered myself to him, but the man between my legs wouldn't share just yet. He continued licking me until arousal swarmed around me and threatened to make me cum.

I moved against the man behind me, his breathing more rugged than before. He was close. Another man stood idly by and stroked himself as he watched. I pressed back harder, looked down at the hands on my thighs, and left my body. I floated up into the air and looked down at four naked gods getting off on getting me off. I tried pushing myself back down to my body but the harder I tried the higher I floated. I could still see the tongue lapping at my pussy, and the cock sliding furiously up and down my back, his head falling back before he shot a load up my back. I floated higher, screaming for them to stop before I came. I wanted to feel it. I needed to feel it. I ached for it but could no longer have it.

"No!" I screamed. "Wait! Don't do it!" I desperately grabbed at the air around me and tried to swim back down to them. It was working, but I had to flail my arms hard and fast to get there. Sweat poured off me but I did manage to get close enough to settle back into my body.

The man between my legs was still watching my face and the moment I looked into his eyes a pair of hands grabbed my arms and pushed me away again.

"No!" I screamed.

"Victoria," a voice whispered.

The lights around me brightened again, blinding me, and everything stopped. I reached out into the bright light, begging for them to return. The lights died and I felt nothing but the coldness of the air around me.

"Victoria. Wake up."

My eyes flew open and I tried looking around the dark room. Where did the lights go? Where did my lovers go? "No," I mumbled. "Come back. I wasn't finished."

"Are you okay? Wake up."

"What? Where am I?"

"You're in bed. It's two in the morning. You must have been having quite a nightmare."

My heart sank. Nope. It wasn't a nightmare.

"You kept begging for someone to help you. Are you okay?"

"I'm fine." My tone was sleepy and slurred. "I don't remember it."

It was easier to lie than to tell him about it. He was never much for fantasy when it came to sex.

I snuggled into him hoping to get a little reward for the arousal that didn't go away when the dream faded. He merely kissed my shoulder and rolled the other way leaving me frustrated and horny. It wasn't our normal sexy time.

Ronald liked everything to be structured and in place, including time for sex. It got a little boring at times, but he was massive in all the right areas which made it good when we did fuck.

A soft snoring sound came from his side of the bed but no matter how hard I tried I couldn't get back to sleep. I imagined the hands on me again, the tongue inside me, the hard cock on my back, but nothing worked. I stared at the clock on the bedside table and the red numbers told me I still had three hours of lying there in my current state.

I rolled onto my stomach and pushed my hand underneath me, my fingers working into my panties. I positioned the tip of my finger between my lips so that when I moved it tingles would begin to form there and spread through me. Careful not to move the bed too much, I moved my finger back and forth imagining the dream I was dragged from. It wasn't long before a wave of pleasure wafted through me and the challenge was not to move until I was satiated. Well, as satiated as I could be. I sighed and enjoyed pulses that came from the muscles between my legs, allowing the numbing sensation of sleep to waft over me.

The alarm dragged me from my sleep and moments later Ronald's arm wrapped around me. It was his way of telling me he wanted sex.

The mornings he wanted a little were like this. He'd rub my stomach with his hands while he spooned me from behind. I'd glide my fingers along his arm until his cock pushed into my backside, then he'd roll me onto my back so he could climb on top, push my legs apart and *tease* me until he entered me and moved back and forth at his pace. His kisses got me more than his so-called teasing, but I took what I could get. He was very vanilla, but he was a damn good kisser. What he did with his tongue drove me crazy. I just wished he'd use his tongue in other places besides my mouth.

And it's not like I haven't tried different things or suggested changing it up. The way he'd look at me when I mentioned doing it in a public bathroom or even in the living room over the end of the sofa, you'd think I suggested something illegal like making him watch a bunch of big muscular men have their way with me. I smiled slightly at the thought, my dream flooding back to me. I closed my eyes and played it back in my head as Ronald continued moving back and forth inside me.

The contrast of that man's skin against mine, the feel of his tongue lapping at my pussy, the other men surrounding me all waiting their turn aroused me. I grabbed Ronald's ass and pulled him into me with each thrust, but it didn't change the pace or seem to turn him on any different than what I was used to. He pulled himself back and looked at me quizzically before smiling and burying his head back into the crook of my neck.

"Fuck me, Ronnie."

After a very nice orgasm, I stayed in bed for as long as I could before having to rush about to get ready for my day. I had a big meeting with some incredible artists for a new gallery show I have been working on for next month and I was feeling good about it. It was our semi-annual show, and a lot of the proceeds would help my gallery through several months until I booked the next one.

Ronald sat at the table and dove into his half of a grapefruit. "So, are you ready for your meeting today?"

"I think so." I guzzled half a glass of water and popped a handful of vitamins into my mouth washing them down with the last of it before grabbing a banana and heading back into the bedroom to select my attire.

"Are you nervous? I know the last meeting you had didn't go very well."

"No, thanks to the client."

"Clients always get what they want. You know that. It's just business, Victoria."

I don't know why he insisted on calling me by my proper name. Vicky was fine. Hell, I was even okay with Vic. Victoria made me sound like I was stuck up and bitchy. I didn't like that.

"I know," I said, throwing the banana peel away and devouring the fruit in only a few bites. "And they did, remember? That doesn't mean I have to like it." I turned the shower on and let the cold water run on my hand until it got warmer. Ronald walked in behind me and stripped down, stealing the shower before I could even protest.

"You're very good at your job. Don't let anyone tell you differently."

I pulled my top off and wiggled out of my panties before joining him. "Hand me your soap. I'll wash your back." I hoped it was enough.

"What are you doing?"

"Taking a shower with my husband." I kissed his nose and held my hand out. "Soap?"

"This shower is too small for the both of us. You know that."

"So, get closer," I smirked.

"Victoria. I have to get to the office. I have big deadlines."

I exhaled the air from my lungs and climbed back out. "You don't have to schedule *everything,* ya know."

"I'm a scheduler. You knew that when you married me," he said poking his head out and smiling. "Nice bum, by the way."

I smiled back until he disappeared behind the curtain. "You didn't even look at it," I mumbled leaving the bathroom with a pout. I sauntered into the bedroom and stopped in front of the full-length mirror on the wall. I looked at myself and analyzed my features. My breasts were pretty good in size. Thirty-four D was good, healthy. Right? My waist was still small, and I worked out a few times a week, so my stomach was flat. I turned and looked at my bum and ran my hand along my curves. It was still firm and tight. "Hmm." I turned back around and slid my hands up my stomach to my breasts, cupping them and pushing them together.

"What are you doing?" Ronald stood in the doorway with a towel around him.

"Am I attractive?" I stared at my face and cocked my head.

"What are you talking about? Of course, you are. I wouldn't be with an ugly woman." He went to his dresser and opened the second drawer.

"So, if I aged and wasn't so in shape, you'd leave me?" I wasn't sure where I was going with this. I wasn't insecure in the slightest.

"I don't define ugly like that. Where is this coming from?" Never skipping a step from his morning routine, he only glanced over at me a couple of times.

"I don't know. I guess I'm getting a little bored with our daily routine. Aren't you?"

"What would you like to do? We could take a small vacation, maybe fly to Italy for the weekend. Or, I can get the sailboat and we can go sailing to the Keys."

"Maybe." I sighed and left him in the room. It wasn't what I was referring to, and I knew he'd never get it. Before long, he was kissing me goodbye and walking out the door. "We will talk about it more this evening over dinner."

I tried staying busy as my stomach wreaked havoc on my nerves. I positioned and repositioned some of the artwork in the gallery, my eyes constantly looking up at the clock on the wall. When my new clients arrived the door chime sounded and I exhaled quickly. I plastered a smile on my face and went around the corner toward the door. My clients were all men and all very good-looking. I chuckled a little when my first thought was my dream from the night before. Imagining their hands on me sort of calmed my nerves as they introduced themselves. It was sort of similar to when you have stage fright, and you imagine the audience naked.

"It's good to meet you," I said, my smile more genuine than the one I started with. "We can sit here and begin our meeting." I motioned them toward a large round table in the corner of the gallery. "Would you like anything? Coffee? Tea? Water?"

I caught one of them descending their eyes down my body. I managed to look away before they noticed. "No. Thank you," he said sitting across from me.

"Aaron, right?" I asked, staring back at him.

"Yes."

Aaron had big blue eyes, icy and mesmerizing to look into. He was smooth with his words and charismatic with his actions. He didn't look much like an artist, but in my career, you didn't mention that. Whether you were good or not was in the eye of the beholder. Anyone could be an artist whether you looked like a calendar fireman or a jock fresh out of college, or if you look more like Stahlin. My eyes shifted to him. Stahlin was more the artistic type, his long black hair thrown back in a messy pony. You could tell by looking at him that he was gay with a hint of bisexuality. Watching him with the other three I would have put money on the fact they weren't just comrades by art. I had an inkling he was a little more friendly with a couple of them from time to time. He was sexy, deep, and mysterious.

Rufus was the straight-laced one. He was the manager of the bunch and had a computer in his hands more than a paintbrush or a coal pencil or lump of clay. Coordinator and scheduler, he knew his shit and how to try and manipulate things to go his way. I was ready to deal.

Then there was Malcolm. He was beautiful and a challenge for me. It was rather ironic that I was married to Ronald, the whitest and most straight-laced man I had ever met because African American men always did it for me. And this man in front of me was hopefully gay. His dark skin glowed and his black eyes pierced through me. I wanted nothing more than to jump on the front of him and ride him like a bull in a rodeo.

I cleared my throat and forced my focus on Rufus through most of the meeting, all the while noticing how wet I was getting between my legs. Why did I have to dream about a gang of men touching me just before I sat in the middle of a gang of men? It wasn't fair.

The moment I booked them and they left the gallery I went up the stairs to my office and closed my door. I leaned against it and closed my eyes, inhaling deeply. *Jesus Christ that was hard,* I thought. As if it had a mind of its own, my hand moved across my thigh and rubbed myself through my pants. It ignited something deep inside me.

The wall facing the gallery was all glass, so I tucked myself into the opposite corner almost out of sight and leaned back in my chair. Cupping my breasts with both hands I felt my nipples harden and it thrilled me to rub my thumbs over them. I closed my eyes and slid my hand down my stomach and into my pants. With one hand on my tit and the other rubbing my pussy, it didn't take long to develop a rhythm with my fingers as arousal bled through me. My dream replayed in my head but this time with the faces of Malcolm, Aaron, Stahlin, and Rufus.

Looking down between my legs, Malcolm looked up at me as he devoured me with his luscious mouth. His tongue darted inside me, pushing my lips open. I hummed as deep as I could, my fingers pushing into my cunt.

I picked up my foot and found a place for it on the corner of my desk as I fingered myself faster and worked myself into a heated frenzy that sent waves crashing over me. I clutched the arm of my chair until it subsided, enjoying pulses between my legs. When I opened my eyes, I caught a glimpse of someone in the gallery. I stood up and adjusted myself before turning toward the hopeful customer. But it wasn't a customer at all. Malcolm was standing in the middle of the gallery looking up at me. His portfolio was still on the table where we sat. I should have been mortified, but something inside me caught fire again at the idea that he watched me pleasure myself.

I didn't move. He slowly walked to the table, blindly scooped up his portfolio, and left, all the while keeping his eyes glued to mine.

"Oh my God," I shuddered as the door closed behind him.

~HIM~

I was frozen where I stood in the middle of the Gallery. I never dreamt in a million years I would look up and see her pleasuring herself and satisfying her carnal needs. I should have been the one up there taking care of that for her. My cock hardened when she looked at me and didn't move. She wasn't upset or embarrassed. I think she liked me watching her. I wondered if she wanted more. I kept my eyes on her as I located My Portfolio I had left behind. Should I go to her? Should I satisfy her the way she should be satisfied? She was an angel from heaven, and she needed to be saved.

He stuck with me, in my head the rest of the day and when I had gotten home Ronald was already there and already immersed in whatever it was he was doing on his computer.

"You're home early," I said, setting my bag on the table.

"Actually, you're home late." He nodded toward the clock before going back to his computer.

"Ah, so I am." I walked up behind him and slid my hands around his neck, kissing the side of his face. "How was your day?"

"Good," he mumbled, his fingers flying across his keyboard. "Productive. How was yours?" A passive tone settled into his words.

If I told him the truth would he even hear me? Or would I get a "That's good, honey"?

"It went well. The meeting was good. They are exquisitely talented. I booked them for the showing."

"That's good, honey."

I chuckled and started dinner.

After our evening routine, I had hoped he was up for a little sex. I could have used it after the day I had. Smiling, I tried setting the mood with a little nightie I found in the back of my closet. I hadn't worn it in a while. I walked into the bedroom where he sat on the end of the bed.

"I see someone is looking for a little sexy time tonight."

"After the day I've had, it would be a good stress reliever." I stopped in front of him and straddled him, his hands sliding up my legs.

"Well, I think I could manage a little loving myself." He patted my butt which told me to get into the normal position we made love in.

I tried kissing him with my legs still around him, moving my groin over his.

"Come on," he insisted. "Climb up into bed. I'll join you in just a few minutes."

I exhaled and did as he wanted. He disappeared into the bathroom and I heard water running, then the sound of a toothbrush in his mouth. When he climbed into bed his arm wrapped around me. He rubbed my stomach with his hands and spooned me from behind. I ran my fingers along his arm until his cock pushed into my backside. He rolled me onto my back and climbed on top, pushing my legs apart. When he pushed his dick inside me my pussy immediately tightened around him.

"Someone is worked up, isn't she?" He moved back and forth and planted little kisses on my mouth that deepened as we fucked. I wanted to devour him, or Malcolm, or someone, but too much was a turn-off for Ronald, so I suppressed my desire and let him do me as he did.

He moved back and forth with a rhythm and my arousal was building nicely. His face was buried in the crook of my neck which told me he was close, but then he stopped and picked up his head.

"What's wrong?" I asked, trying to pull him back to me.

"Shhh. I heard footsteps or something in the other room."

I looked out the bedroom door into the hallway and listened intently. "I don't hear anything," I whispered.

I pulled back out of the doorway just in time. She didn't see me. Giving it a couple of seconds, I listened for the repetitious movement of the bed again before peeking back into the room. She was so sexy laying there getting fucked, but it made me question why she was with him. He didn't treat her the way she needed to be treated. She was wasting her sexuality and I was going to show her the difference.

I watched her body as she moved back and forth underneath him, and my dick hardened in my jeans. My buddy tried to get my attention, but I waved him off. I think he was about as impatient as I was. Soft moaning came from the bedroom and I knew it wasn't gonna be long before we had to interrupt them. I grabbed myself and adjusted it to the side before leaning against the doorway waiting for her to see me watching them.

The moment her eyes locked onto mine, my cock lunged forward enough to tell me to get in there and take over. It excited me to see the fear in her eyes because I was going to change that to hunger. I was going to change that to lust. I was going to change her for me.

~HER~

Ronald planted his lips on mine for a few seconds as he started his rhythm again, then buried his face into my neck.

A noise much like he described came from the other room and I glanced toward the door again. This time I saw movement and a man with a black mask appeared just outside the doorway, his covered head peeking into the room. Panic rushed through me and I tapped Ronald on the arm. "Someone is watching us." I barely whispered and wondered if he even heard me as he picked up his rhythm. "Ronald," I whispered louder.

"One second," he grunted.

I pushed him off me and grabbed at the covers, my eyes wide and staring at three hooded men as they walked into the room.

"Ronald, is it?" one of the men said. "Oh, my man. Is that any way to treat such a lovely creature?"

"Who are you and what are you doing in my house? Get out, before I call the cops," he demanded.

"I don't think you'll be doing any of that." The same man spoke as they surrounded the bed.

My heart pounded against the inside of my chest and I could barely breathe as I clutched the blanket tight to my chest.

"What *are* we doing in his house?" the man asked the taller of the three.

"I thought we were just going to take a few things, but after seeing this, we can't just leave without fixing the situation."

"I agree." The two men high-fived each other.

"What… are you talking about?" Ronald climbed up onto his knees, not caring what he exposed. "Get out, now!"

"Oh, my dear Ronald. You are in no position to be barking orders, especially since we are here to help you."

The taller man, I'll call him Stretch, walked to Ronald's side of the bed and grabbed his arms from behind, while the spokesman of the trio helped detain him as he struggled to break free.

I tried to scream, but nothing would produce from my tightened throat. I was shaking in fear as I watched Stretch remove his belt. His eyes were glued to me, but he buckled it around Ronald's waist, bounding his arms to his side. "Now sit!" The spokesman demanded. "My colleagues and I are going to show you how you should be fucking your wife."

"What-what are you talking about?" Ronald's voice shook.

"I'm talking about an unhappy wife with all the right equipment and no way to express herself freely." His eyes glided down my body. "I'm going to give you a little sex education 101 my dear boy."

"You're going to rape my wife?"

"No. Not at all. In fact, I won't even touch her until she asks me to."

"We should get paid for this kind of teaching." The third one finally spoke up. I'll call him Three.

"I agree." Stretch went to the nightstand and picked Ronald's wallet up. Opening it, he pulled what money Ronald had and waved it in the air. "This doesn't look like it's enough to cover our services." He shoved it back into the wallet and went back and stood next to Ronald still sitting on the floor.

"Please. Just go," he pleaded. "Take whatever you want and get the hell out."

"Oh, we will." The spokesman smiled through his mask and approached the bed toward me.

I shook my head violently and pushed myself against the headboard. "I'll never…."

"Don't make a decision so quickly, my beauty." He stared at me and the panic that seized me subsided. There was something about his eyes, they calmed me. "You need this, don't you?" he said.

My body reacted with the same arousal I felt when I caught Malcolm watching me masturbate in the gallery. I couldn't deny it. I did need this.

"Think about it. Someone else's cock inside you, strange hands doing things to your body you have only fantasized about until now. It could all be yours."

I glanced at Ronald and loosened the grip on my blanket.

"Don't worry about your husband. He'll be on board before the night is through. I promise you."

I licked my lips as a euphoria swept over me. I lowered the blanket and glanced at Ronald again, a twinge of guilt sliding in before looking back at the man standing by the bed.

Stretch patted Ronald on the shoulder and glued his eyes on my tits. "Watch and learn, my man."

The spokesman unbuckled his belt and pulled it from his blue jeans. He doubled his cock in his hand and ran his fingers up and down on it. "Tell me, Vicky."

My name on his lips jolted me. "You know me?" Panic was in my voice.

"No. Your man here called out your name while he was making sweet, boring love to you."

I didn't recall him doing that, but it didn't make it a lie. Right? I looked up at the man moving toward me and swallowed hard.

"Tell me what you want." He licked his lips and I started to tremble. "Tell me to leave and you'll never see me again."

I glanced again at Ronald and shook my head slightly. "Touch me," I whispered.

"What was that?"

I inhaled deeply and repeated my words louder. "I want you to touch me."

"Let the games begin," he smirked.

He leaned over the bed and lassoed his belt around my back pulling it tight. I gasped at the cool leather against my bare skin. My arms stayed loose at my sides as he pulled me toward him, me obliging as I climbed to my knees and walked myself to the edge of the bed in front of him. His gloved hand ran across my tits and the smell of leather wafted into my senses as he snaked his arm around me. He pressed himself against my naked body, his jeans rough against my thighs. He lowered his hand to my ass and pulled me into him, his bulging cock straining against his jeans. He was big, as big as Ronald was, but he wasn't going to treat me like Ronald did, and that absolutely thrilled me.

My pussy ached for him to touch me there. And he did. His gloved hand moved around my thigh and pushed my legs apart before rubbing across my lips. He leaned down and devoured my mouth with his, his tongue pushing through my lips and filling my mouth. He inhaled deeply as his finger pushed inside my pussy. The leather was rough inside of me but excited me further. He fingered me with his leather glove and the roughness almost made me cum right on the spot.

He pulled out and pushed me back onto the bed, shaking his head and his finger in the air. "Not yet, my little slut."

His new name for me made me tremble with excitement as he pulled the glove off his hand with his teeth. His skin was dark and that thrilled me even more. I was going to get fucked in front of my husband by a black man.

He lowered his jeans and stroked his massive cock, smiling as he watched me tremble. "You want this bad, don't you?" He grabbed a handful of himself and shook it in front of me.

I nodded. It was all I could do.

He glanced up at Three and I looked over toward him. Stretch still stood next to Ronald as Three walked to the other side of the bed. He took my arms in his hands and pulled them over my head, his weight shifting forward. This was it. My fantasy was becoming a reality and everything I experienced inside that morning was nothing compared to what I was experiencing during the real thing.

"Open your legs for me and show me that pretty pussy."

"Oh, God!" Ronald spat. "Victoria! Don't do this!" He struggled to get up but Stretch kept him where he sat.

I directed my attention forward and positioned myself on my back for the man standing in front of me. I opened my legs, as Three held my arms down on the mattress. All they had to do was fondle me a little bit and I would have exploded.

The man stroking his cock climbed onto the bed over the top of me and devoured my mouth, his demanding tongue pushing in and making me dizzy. My breathing was hard and labored the moment he stopped exploring my mouth almost choking me with his tongue. He dragged it over my chin and down my neck, biting my skin as he lowered himself further. Before his mouth sucked my nipple in, Three took over kissing me and blocked my sight from watching what was happening to me. His tongue delved into my mouth a little more delicately. His hands slid up my arms as heavy wet smooches trailed down my stomach. My legs were forced apart and his mouth consumed my pussy lapping at my folds, something pushing inside me.

I was breathing so hard my mouth became dry. My entire body trembled uncontrollably. I had forgotten where I was until I caught a glimpse of Ronald tied helplessly to our oversized desk in the corner. Stretch had secured him with something and was walking to the bed, pulling his shirt off as he walked closer.

Oh, God! Three men at the same time!

"This looks fun," he said before climbing onto the bed beside me. "Mind if I join you?" His hand caressed my tits, and his mouth began trailing around my nipple. "Want to join in on the fun, Ronald?" He looked back at my struggling husband, red in the face and a cock so hard he couldn't hide it. "Not yet?" Stretch chuckled. "You let us know. I'm sure your wife would love it if you joined us."

The man was right. I would have, but at that moment I couldn't request much. I was dizzy with desire and my body ached with pleasure.

Three positioned himself on the right side of me as Stretch hovered over me on the right. My big black lover had his hands on my knees and was sliding them up and down my thighs, his beautiful cock pushing against my pussy. He leaned forward spreading my opening wide and agonizingly slowly he inched his way inside me. "You taking notes, Ronald?" he asked, not taking his eyes off what he was doing. "This is how you truly pleasure your wife. This is what she really wants." He pushed inside further and grunted. "Fuck! You're tight."

My pussy stretched around his cock and as he worked it back and forth, I felt the pressure build. Thumbs were rubbing over my nipples. A tongue filled my mouth. Hands were squeezing my breasts and fingers were rolling over my clit. Meanwhile, my mind was completely clouded, my body responded with every flick, bite, and lick and I couldn't hold back my orgasm any longer. I turned my head away from the mouth that devoured it and screamed as every muscle seized up and an orgasm hit me like a boulder. It held on and shook me for several moments before letting me go.

The massive black cock was still rocking in and out of me, the man between my legs grunting and gripping at my thighs. His grunts got louder and quicker, his thrusts went deeper and harder and when he pulled himself out, he flooded my stomach with his semen. Three had his cock in his hand and was stroking himself until it was apparently his turn. He took my hands and sat me up, motioning me to my knees. He directed me toward Ronald before lowering me onto my hands so I had to look up at him and he would see the whole show. I couldn't look at him, but I didn't want this to stop either. I rubbed my sensitive clit as Three slapped his hand on my asscheek over and over again. It began to sting but he'd rub it in between the slaps causing pleasure to seep into my pussy. I ached for him to be inside me.

"Tell me what you want," he said.

I trembled. I loved this. "I want you to fuck me."

"You can do better than that. Slut."

The term ripped through me. "I want to feel your cock inside me, pushing into me and claiming my pussy."

"Mmmm. Yes. Better." He slapped my asscheek. Pain searing over my skin. "Look up at your husband, slut."

The black man stood to the side, his jeans up but still undone. Stretch sat next to me, his hands cradling my tits over the mattress. His fingers fondled them slowly as he stroked himself. By this time, I was so aroused it wasn't going to take long to feel that next orgasm, something I had never done. Two orgasms in a night would be my first.

I looked up at Ronald, his face distorted but his dick hard as a rock. He was staring at my body and what they were doing to it. He liked this, too. Maybe he could be next. Four men fucking me in one night. I shivered in delight and pushed back into Three until the head of his dick opened me up. He slapped my ass again, grabbed my hips, and pushed himself into me with one thrust. I gasped hard. He filled me quickly and fucked me, my body jarring forward with each thrust. Stretch climbed off the bed and went to Ronald's side. He was whispering something in his ear and Ronald was nodding. He didn't seem so distraught and I wondered what he was telling him.

Stretch untied him and he approached me with his dick in his hand. Stretch grabbed a handful of my hair and positioned my head. I immediately knew what it was for and I squirmed with excitement at the thought.

"I had no idea," Ronald said, his eyes hungry. He stroked himself and stood before me. I opened my mouth for him as Three slowly fucked me from behind, his thumb stroking my other hole. Ronald stopped in front of me and I welcomed his cock with the tip of my tongue. As it eased into my mouth, I could feel the bulging veins along the sides, and I leaned forward to tighten my mouth over him. I sucked on it and twirled my tongue around his head trying to watch his face as I did. He was staring at the cock that was fucking me so good, his mouth falling open.

Three picked up his speed and slammed into me repeatedly, my nipples dragging along the blankets underneath me. Everything I was experiencing at one time all balled up inside me and a second orgasm exploded without warning. Ronald got aggressive and grabbed my hair, shoving his dick deeper into my mouth. It hit the back of my throat and pushed further until he was stroking my throat with it.

Three grunted a few times and pulled out before a wad of semen squirted up my back. Ronald pulled out of my mouth and I collapsed onto the bed.

"Don't tell me you're done," said Stretch. "What about us?" He slid his arm around Ronald's neck and smiled. He rolled me to my back and pulled me to the edge of the bed until my ass was on the edge. "Are you ready for more cock, baby?"

Amativeness tickled me again and the idea I was their sex toy titillated me. I shivered again and nodded. He waited for Ronald to straddle my chest and lean forward, pushing his cock back into my mouth before he entered me and started fucking me. He wasn't as big as the others, but I still had no problem feeling another orgasm deep down threatening to slam me again. I opened my legs, and he pushed my knees to my armpits around Ronald. He leaned forward, pushing my legs down further, and bobbed his ass up and down over me as his dick drilled in and out like I was an oil well.

I supposed with all of the previous excitement he was already so horny that it didn't take him long to shudder and cum inside me. Moments later Ronald did the same but in my mouth. I swallowed repeatedly holding my breath in between to avoid choking on it.

Stretch climbed off the bed and high-fived the spokesman as Ronald climbed over to me and kissed me passionately for the first time in a long time. "I want to fuck you," he whispered. "Wherever you want to go, whenever you want to do it."

I glanced around the room at the group of them, feeling so surreal and satisfied. "So, who gets the shower first?" I teased.

That night had rebirthed Ronald and our sex life has been on fire ever since. We never talked about what happened that night, but we also didn't admit that it was the reason we now try new things and new positions. My stress level has dropped considerably and when the day of the show came, I was more than ready.

After a long session of sex in the shower, Ronald and I had breakfast together and left the apartment at the same time. He squeezed my ass before climbing into his car and wished me luck on my show.

My gallery was beautiful and the pieces on display were sure to sell. When the artists arrived, I walked them through the itinerary and let them know that if they had any questions they could ask at any time. Several customers walked through the gallery during the course of the day and conversed with the artists. At the end of the day, I was exhausted but happy.

Aaron approached me with a smile. "What a successful day. How did we do?"

"We sold several pieces. I think we made over a hundred and fifty thousand."

"Very nice," he exclaimed with a nod. "Let's set up a meeting tomorrow evening?"

"Sounds perfect. I'll bring some wine and we can celebrate."

"Perfect." He smiled oddly at me before walking toward the front door.

"Congratulations," Malcolm said, approaching me.

"Thank you. To you as well. You have some beautiful pieces here."

"As do you." His eyes sunk into mine and it stirred something inside me. "I have just one question." The fact that he saw me masturbate was still fresh in my mind, but I wasn't going to make a deal out of it, especially after my new sexual awakening. This was my career, and we were professionals. I'd hoped he treated me with the same respect.

"What is your question?"

"How's your husband doing? Ronald? Is it?"

I froze and stared at him. I never introduced him to Ronald. I had never even brought up his name, or the fact that I was married. Ever since I lost my wedding ring a year ago, I was afraid to wear it. So that meant....

He walked away, pulling a pair of leather gloves from his pocket. He put them to his mouth and inhaled.

"Oh, one more thing?" he said, turning toward me. "Bring him to the meeting tomorrow night. I'd like to see him again."

~CHAPTER 3~

Fantasy BDSM Turned into Reality

Not Such a Stranger – She goes to a bar in NYC. He lives there somewhere. She doesn't know where. All she knows is his first name and several stories he used to tell her over the internet and telephone. She was addicted to him, but she had no idea who he was, until that night. She remembers the bar he mentioned frequently in his stories. And that night, she was about to become one of those stories. He knows her right away. He approaches her to thank her for being his muse, for being there to tell his stories to, for making him cum each time he spoke to her. He asks one final request. "I've imagined you so many times. I want to smell you on my fingers. Just one time." She allows it and he slides his hand up her skirt and into her panties. Removing his fingers, he intoxicates himself on her scent and begs for one more feel. She allows him and he keeps his fingers there until she's ready to cum herself. He demands that she move to the bathroom down the back hall. They end up in his apartment close by, with his playroom and many other exciting activities waiting for her.

I called the phone number again. And again, it rang busy. I couldn't understand it. How many times over the course of a year had I called this number? Rarely did he not answer, but never have we been disconnected for this long. Something was wrong, and I needed to know what that was. I needed to hear his voice. I needed to feel his words in my ears again. They'd seep into me like honey and devour my imagination, my mind, my sexual appetite.

I looked up his phone number in my emails from a year ago just to be sure I was dialing it right. I was beside myself. Did he change his phone number? Was he done with me? My mind raced back to the last conversation we had. He couldn't have been done with me. Our last forty-five-minute call was intense, highly erotic, and carnal. He often told me he could never go more than a few days without me. It had been over a week since I had spoken to him. Where was he?

I plopped down on my bed and reminisced about other conversations between us. I could never get personal with him and I could never ask to meet him. No 'I love you's' and no feelings could be talked about. It was strictly sex talk about experiences and dreams. But over the course of the year, I had put together bits and pieces of his life enough to know basically where he was. Not everything could be kept secret forever.

I slid my hands over my breasts thinking of him and a particular story he told me one evening when I was lying in my bed. It was late at night and I was almost asleep when my phone rang. It didn't matter when or where I was when I got his call. I found a way to answer, even if I couldn't say a word and had to listen only.

That night, he told me about a lover he had seduced in a museum around the corner from where he lived. It was a woman who knew what she wanted in life. She was strong, independent, and only needed a man for her sexual prowess, but when she met Robert her life changed.

He told me how he seduced her. He told me how she turned him down, and then he told me how he pursued her and won. By the time he got her into his bed she was so turned on by him that she became his play toy for months. Complete submission. I think she was married, but that didn't matter to Robert. What he wanted he got.

It made me wonder why he never pursued me. I was more than willing to do whatever he wanted. Yes, I was inexperienced, but I wanted him. One boyfriend and a few played-out fantasies were no match for the various women Robert has had. It wasn't because I wasn't attractive. I was always getting hit on. I was just picky. My fantasies far exceeded my lack of daring to try new things. When I met Robert that all changed, in my head anyway. After late nights of his stories, no man seemed worthy enough to try out.

I remember one afternoon when he was with her, he called my phone. I was sitting at the coffee shop working on my thesis when his name scrolled across my screen. I hit the talk button and held it to my ear. Before I could say hello, I heard him grunt and strain his voice. I closed my mouth and I listened. He was fucking her, and he was very vocal about it. He described what was going on and he told me what she was doing to him in detail. I was so turned on by it that I left my things at the table and went into the ladies' room. I pushed my hand into my pants and started pleasuring myself in the bathroom stall. When he told me, her mouth wrapped around his cock and she strained to take him all in, I imagined every detail of what she must have looked like. When he yelled out in ecstasy, I mentally saw his head fall back as he pumped his organ in deeper. "I'm going to cum, Mia." He'd call my name out, not hers and it jolted me. "Mia!" His orgasm was so loud and guttural that I orgasmed immediately after he did.

I couldn't be in love with him, but I couldn't stop thinking about him. What he gave me kept me insatiable, kept me wanting, my mind looking for the next fantasy he'd spoon-feed me. I didn't know him, but I knew I didn't want it to end. My girlfriend, Sasha, put me on to this dating site a year ago and that's where I met him but I never dreamt it would turn into anything like this. What we had between us was different than anything I could imagine. It wasn't platonic. It wasn't traditional. It was hot and steamy, and I wanted more.

"Do you know what I think you should do?" Sasha sipped her mocha cappuccino, her eyes glued to mine.

"I don't know what I can do. I've tried everything I know. I've called him a hundred times. I've tried texting him. I went back to that website. He's gone. Vanished. And he took my libido with him."

"Go to New York."

I looked up at her like she slapped my face. "What?"

"Go to New York."

"I can't go to New York. Are you insane?"

"Why not?"

"I… I have school."

"It's your last year of college. I know your schedule. You can juggle shit around and make this work. Just go and find him. You don't have to be gone for a long time."

"It's over five hundred miles away. How the hell will I get there?"

"It's called a plane? I'll cover for you at the restaurant."

"I can't…."

"You're making excuses, Mia. You have to go. Otherwise, you'll drive yourself crazy."

My stomach started to ache with the idea I just might do it. Sasha saw it in my face and smiled.

"But what if…."

"Don't," she interrupted. "Don't 'what-if' anything. Just go. If you don't, you'll never know, and you'll hate yourself forever."

I sighed, the ache in my stomach increasing. "I think I might puke."

"He's a New Yorker with a massive sex drive." She rolled her eyes. "Not some massively famous celebrity."

"How do we know that?" I waited for her to respond. "How do we know who he is? There's got to be some reason he has never webcammed with me or sent me a picture of him. Every time I ask him something about his life, he tells me another story and gets me all worked up again."

"I know. I'm so jealous."

"He knows what I look like. He knows everything about me. He could have had me killed by now if that was his thing, but since it's been over a year, I think I'm safe from that. He's probably married."

"Or has a girlfriend who doesn't put out how he likes."

"Maybe he's a she in disguise and he's afraid to tell me."

"Maybe he's ugly."

"It doesn't matter what he looks like."

"Obviously." She rolled her eyes. "I don't know what this guy has done to you, Mia. But you need to go."

"How would I even find him?"

"You know where he hangs out. He talked about MOMA and the subway. What's the name of that one bar he always mentions?"

"Ophelia's Lounge."

"Okay." She picked up her phone, her fingers flying over the keys. "Here." She turned the screen to me. "Write this down."

It was the address to Ophelia's Lounge in New York City.

"Go there and get drunk. Let him find you."

"And what if…."

"Mia. What did I tell you? No 'what-ifs'. Just go."

I nodded quickly and gathered my things together. I was going to do it. I was going to fly to New York to find a man I had never met. I couldn't allow myself to think beyond that. I'd talk myself out of going.

An hour after boarding the plane I wanted to turn back. I wanted to abort the mission and go back to my apartment. I wanted to forget about Robert and what he had done to my sexual appetite over the course of a year.

"Excuse me." A man's voice a few rows up from where I sat stopped the stewardess. It was familiar and it piqued my interest. "Do you have any wine? I would like white if you have it."

"I'm sorry Sir. We don't serve alcohol on this flight since it is only an hour flight. I apologize for any inconvenience. If you would like something else, I can get that for you."

"Just a bottle of water would be fine. Thank you."

"Of course."

I stared at the back of the man's head, my eyes wide. His voice. It couldn't be. Could it? I opened my phone, went to my voicemails, and listened to one of his messages. It was the one where he told me he needed me, but I wasn't there. It was the one he told me he was disappointed because he couldn't get a hold of me and he wanted to tell me a story. He told me he was rock hard and needed to hear my voice to cum for me. Since the day I met him, he has told me many stories, some fictitious, some true according to him. I didn't know what to expect when and if I got face-to-face with him, but Sasha was right. I needed to find out who he was and why he was so secretive. This man was more than just sex over the phone. He has gotten to me. He has gotten into my mind, into my consciousness, and into my mental state. I couldn't just walk away and forget everything about him.

I stared at the man a few rows up and listened to Robert's message again. What were the chances it was him? Maybe he flew to Ohio to find me and he was headed back to New York. Stranger things have happened, right?

I gripped the chair and pushed myself up to my feet. I needed to ask him something, anything, just to hear his voice. But when I moved into the aisle, a woman came from the bathroom the opposite way and kissed him on the cheek before squeezing by him. She sat in the seat next to him, her smile wide and her eyes twinkling. I plopped back down in my seat and watched them.

When the plane finally landed, and everybody climbed off I followed the couple as they walked through the terminals in the airport. They had met up with another couple who was welcoming them with open arms and small children clinging to their legs. I merely smiled at their happy reunion and walked away, satisfied that he wasn't Robert, but upset that he wasn't.

Pulling the notebook out of my bag I looked at the address I wrote down for Ophelia's Lounge and looked up a hotel close by. The Millennium Hilton just around the block was to be my home for the next few nights at least. It was a gorgeous hotel for the price. Not too expensive for Manhattan.

By that evening, I was settled into my room, freshly clean and dressed and I was sitting at the bar Robert had mentioned more than once in his stories and conversations. I ordered a drink and took a sip. I was in his world and honestly, it scared the hell out of me. It made me question why I was pursuing him. I was always worried about him coming after me. He knew enough about me to make it happen. Never did I ever, in a million years, think I'd be stalking him.

I was uneasy as I looked around at the faces. Everyone was with someone else, conversing, business, potential love interest. I sat alone at the end like I was waiting for someone. He wasn't expecting me. He had no idea I was here, but was he? My eyes went from one face to another. I could have been looking right at him but how would I know?

I saw elements he had described to me while we talked over the phone. There was the corner booth hidden partially behind a large pillar wall. He had seduced a young woman and made her orgasm right there. He had left that evening with her underwear in his pocket and her scent on his tongue. I carried my drink to that booth and slid into the seat. I ran my hand over the soft material that wrapped the seat and wondered where she sat when she came. Euphoria filled me and arousal hinted deep inside. He sat here next to her with his hand up her dress and when the bar closed, he tipped the bartender enough to keep his lover there afterward. He bent her over the back of the booth, her face pressed against the window and he fucked her. I ran my hand along the back of the booth and felt the heat spread through me. A couple walked by me and stared long enough to question what the hell I was doing, so I got up and went to another part of the bar.

Lower square stools lined a window that overlooked a beautiful skyline and each stool had white fur covering each one. My mouth fell slightly open as I walked to one of them and ran my hand across it. My mind went back to a conversation ... a story.

Robert had followed a woman out of the museum, and she led him here. She flirted with him terribly that day and he told her she wasn't going to get away with it. This was where she sat when he told her, or demanded rather, that she remove her bra and her underwear and hitch up her dress to sit bare-bottomed on the fur. He wanted them as a memento of their night together. He sat close to her and told her to touch herself. He wanted to watch her cum for him. He told me that he stole the fur and kept it for a souvenir to remember her by. The thought thrilled me, and I wanted one for myself. Maybe I would take one before I left back to Ohio as a souvenir of his story that stuck in my mind.

After a few more drinks and a full tour of the place with my eyes and my mind, I was convinced I wasn't going to see him that night. I sat back at the bar, finished my drink, and slid it forward. Before I got up another one was sitting in front of me. "Excuse me , I did not order this."

"Compliments of the gentleman at the table." He motioned toward a table and my heart picked up its pace. I pulled the drink closer and ran my finger up the side of the glass. Was it him? What would he look like? What would I say to him? I turned my head toward the table where an elderly gentleman sat with a smile on his face. My heart sank.

I raised my glass to him to thank him, praying that it was not the man I was looking for. He approached me and took the stool next to me.

"Good evening, young lady." The moment he spoke I smiled. It wasn't him. "I hope you don't mind my intrusion, but I just had to say hello. You look so much like my daughter before she moved away some years ago. I hope that's okay?"

"Oh, I don't mind at all."

He was a sweet old man, and he made my night not so terrible after all. He told me about the city and recommended a few places I should visit before I leave. I conversed with him over a couple more drinks before politely excusing myself for the night, thanking him again for being so nice.

The next day I walked around the city and imagined Robert close by. I visited the Museum of Modern Art. I walked in Central Park next to the water. Every man I passed I looked at twice, wondering if his name was Robert with a Jewish Jersey accent, wondering if his thoughts were full of the women he had seduced, wondering if he was looking for his next mission. Several of them I asked for directions to places I didn't plan on going, only to listen to their voices. His was distinct. Jewish. Dominating. Sexy. Smooth.

That evening I went back to Ophelia's and sat in the corner booth, then at the bar. I hoped that he would have visited and recognized me, but to no avail. I did the same the night after that and the night after that until I was about ready to give up.

"Excuse me." I got the bartender's attention as he walked by. "I'd like a glass of wine, please. And I have a question. I wondered if you could help me."

"I will try. What is it you want to know?"

"I'm supposed to meet someone here but I'm not sure what he looks like. Do you know a man named Robert that supposedly comes in here often?"

"I'm sorry, I don't. If he doesn't show and you'd like to leave a note for him I will be more than happy to give it to him. But most people usually let it go when they get stood up. Some even call them. Texting works, too."

His sarcasm was thick and blatant.

"Thanks."

"Any time."

I glanced around the room feeling defeated. I pulled my phone from my clutch and called Sasha.

"Tell me you have some news," she said before so much as a hello.

"I'm afraid I don't. I've been in Ophelia's every night since I got here and nothing. I even asked about him."

"And?"

"All I got was typical New York sarcasm. It's no use. I'm going to come back home tomorrow."

"I think you should hang out."

"These people here are beginning to think I'm either casing the joint or I'm pathetically lonely. I don't like drinking alone. You know that."

"Then hook up with one of those fine city boys. I hear New Yorkers know how to treat a woman right. Rough and hard."

"Sasha. I'm not hooking up with some random stranger."

"But you'll hold out for one you know has been around? You are an odd little bird."

"Thanks for the support."

"I love you, Mia. You know that. But, seriously, girl. You need some dick. Stay there and do some investigating work. You'll find him."

"And what if I don't?"

"Hopefully someone will pass by that feels sorry for you and he'll take care of you."

"You're a big help."

"I try."

"I will see you tomorrow."

"Suit yourself. Talk soon." She smooched twice into the phone before ending the call.

I gave a heavy sigh before finishing my drink and sliding the glass forward. The bartender had already filled another one and was headed toward me.

"No, thank you," I said, holding my hand up. "I'm going back to my hotel room."

"The gentleman behind you bought this one for you. You wouldn't want to disappoint, would you?"

I smiled, expecting to see the old man again, but when I turned around, it was someone different. He looked at me with an odd stare and a quirky smile upon his face, and he didn't say a word.

"Thank you, for the drink."

He nodded and cocked his head. "I've seen you in here a few times lately." His voice was low and controlled. "Where are you from?"

"What makes you think I'm from anywhere? There are eight million people living here."

"I overheard you on the phone. You're here visiting, aren't you?"

"Yes," I replied softly, concentrating on his tone. "And what about you?"

"I'm a native born and raised." There were hints of Robert's tone in the man's voice, but I couldn't confirm anything, nor did I dare. "May I?" He motioned toward the barstool next to me.

I didn't want him that close, but I wanted him there. He gave off the same energy Robert gave me. I felt myself nod.

Instead of sitting, he moved the stool over and rested his arms on the side of the bar as he sipped what I presumed to be bourbon or whiskey. His eyes stayed forward as if he were contemplating what to say to me.

I studied his features discreetly, his dark curls messed on top of his head, his pale skin against his icy blue eyes. He dressed superbly with a dark blue dress shirt underneath a black suit coat and black pants.

Armani, maybe. He was awkward, but his confidence gave him this sex appeal that was alluring and charming.

"What is your name?" I asked, my eyes glued to his lips.

"Why do you ask?"

"I'd like to properly thank you for my drink."

He grinned and turned around, leaning his back against the bar as he redirected his focus toward the back of the bar. "It is me who should be thanking you."

I crossed my legs as my skirt fell away a bit exposing my thigh. "How so?" I felt sexy, like I was fitting in. Even if this wasn't Robert, I liked the way it was going.

His finger dragged across my knee, his eyes watching as it did. "I'd like you to do something for me. A favor of sorts."

My instinct was to pull back, but I remembered what Sasha said. I needed more in my life. *Dick,* as she had put it. "What sort of favor?"

"Allow me access to you."

I chuckled smugly and drew in a breath. "Access?"

"Yes. Open your legs."

My breath hitched. It was him. Undeniably. I drew in a quivering breath and tried to maintain my composure. "What do you mean?" I knew exactly what he meant. I needed time to calculate what was happening. My entire New York City experience up until that moment was long and dragged out. It all piled up and suffocated me and I needed to dig my way out.

He turned his head toward me and his eyes penetrated mine. He lowered his face, demanding my attention. "I want to smell you on my fingers, taste you on my tongue."

My face flooded with heat. "Um. What?"

"Isn't that why you're here, Mia?"

I shuddered at the sound of my name on his lips.

"To experience what I gave you online? When you didn't hear from me for a while you desired me more, didn't you? You craved my words in your ears. You needed to feed your addiction of me."

"I don't think so," I forced a smirk, my face flooded with heat. "I'm not *addicted* to you, or any man."

"I think you're wrong. Why else would you have come? You can't get enough of me, can you?"

"Excuse me?"

Was I wrong all this time? This wasn't the confident, sexy man I talked with online. He was arrogant and cocky, and I was second-guessing myself for pursuing him.

"Why else would you be sitting here alone, in a dress like that, exposing yourself to any man with the description in your head?"

"This was a mistake. You're not who I thought you were. I'm sorry. I have to go." I climbed off the barstool and turned to go.

"You've been here every night this week looking for me."

I looked back at him, annoyed more than anything. "You knew I was here? Why didn't you…?"

"I wasn't sure it was you at first. But I watched you. When you soaked up the atmosphere in the corner over there," he said without looking or motioning toward the booth. "You wanted to feel what she felt, didn't you?"

My annoyance dissipated quickly. I couldn't stop staring at him.

"And the white covers on the seats in the back? Did you lift your dress to feel it on your naked skin? Did you masturbate and soil them?"

I swallowed hard. "Why didn't you…?"

"Because I like watching you, Mia." He picked up my drink and held it out to me.

I accepted it and took my seat again.

"This addiction doesn't stop at you. You have become a drug to me as well. Your reactions to my experiences. I find myself craving the next time I can hear your voice."

"Then why did you stop? It has been a week."

"Life happens. It's not always fun and games. I had some things I had to tend to."

"A wife?" Annoyance threatened me again.

"Nothing concerning to you, and nothing that would hurt someone else." He moved closer, this time turning his entire body toward me. "You need to trust me." His finger dragged along my leg again. "Allow me access, Mia." His words were barely audible but close to my ear, and the heat from his mouth sent a shiver down my side. "Just a touch," he whispered. "Right here."

His fingertips sliding up the inside of my thigh drew my hunger out. My heart hit steadily against my chest. My fingertips felt cold to the touch. My mouth went dry, but….

"I know you're wet, Mia." He inhaled a full breath, his nose gliding through my hair. "Let me. Touch you. Just a moment's touch will give me everything I need."

I nodded, my mouth slightly open, my breathing shallow, small. I was rigid, staring at the fingernail on my thumb attached to my hand that wrapped tightly around my drink on the bar.

"You aren't like the women in my life." The palm of his hand rested against my thigh and inched closer to my heat, my wet, my ache. "I fuck them, Mia. I always tell you the details. We share my experiences, and I like that. I like explaining my pursuit and my conquer. I like that you listen and you cum." He emphasized the last word as his hand brushed against my pussy. "My only regret is not being able to smell you, to taste you. I have craved this for so long."

My breath caught in my throat, my eyes looking around the room nervously.

"No one is watching. No one has a clue. It's just you and I here right now. In this moment. Give it to me, Mia."

I leaned forward in my seat and opened my legs, my hand clutching my drink a little harder. My eyes closed to enjoy the move of his hand up to the elastic on my panties. He pushed inside and slid his hand across until it covered my pussy completely. I could hear him take a deep breath and slowly exhale. His fingers moved slightly, then entered me, pushing inside. I glanced up at his face. His eyes were closed. His head was bent back slightly. His mouth barely opened. I imagined how this story would go over the phone as he told it to me on a late night. Very heated, very stimulating, much like now.

He withdrew his hand and lifted it to his face. He attempted another deep breath, but it caught. He held it in. He slid his finger into his mouth and sucked on it, his eyes still closed. Fire raced through me as I stared at him.

"My God, Mia." His hand rested on the small of my back. "You're so fucking intoxicating." His hand rested on my thigh again. He stood there not moving, his head down and his eyes still closed.

What was he doing? What was he thinking?

"May I? Once more?" He opened his eyes and watched my face.

I opened my legs slightly, glancing at the others around us still consumed by their own surroundings.

His hand rested against the inside of my thigh, inching closer. His fingers snaked underneath the elastic and crept inside until they were positioned against my heat once again. This time he stayed, his fingers slipping inside me. He moved them in and out agonizingly slowly.

"What are you doing?" I whispered, grabbing his wrist between my legs.

"I needed what you just gave to me. You were so incredible in giving it to me. Now, I'm giving what you need from me."

"No," I whispered. "Don't. Not here."

"Shall we go to the corner?" His grin was devious, his hand moved against me, his fingers spreading my desire further. "Let me," he barely said, his lips close to my ear.

I scooted to the end of my seat and took in a ragged breath, opening my legs a little further before he continued.

"Good girl."

He finger fucked me slowly and I concentrated on appearing as calm as I could. He rubbed his thumb through my lips.

"Ugh." I slammed my mouth closed and looked around. My legs closed around his hand. I was a little louder than I should have been. I faked clearing my throat and pretended to laugh at something he would have said if he wasn't finger fucking me in a bar in the middle of New York City with patrons around us. Robert chuckled, his hand still in place but not moving.

"Sorry." Heat flooded my face, and I downed the rest of my drink.

His fingers began to move only after I opened my legs for him.

"Would you like another drink?" The bartender had a smile on his face that one couldn't pry off with a crowbar. He did know Robert and the kind of man he was. But I couldn't walk away. I was in too deep, and I wanted him deep inside me.

"Please," was all I could muster without feeding his suspicions.

Robert's fingers moved inside me deliciously until the people around us faded away. I opened further. I rocked in my seat to the rhythm of his hand caressing back and forth, his fingers inside me then roaming down to my anus, then back up and inside me again. The more he played the hotter I got, not caring about those around me who started suspecting that something more than conversation was going on between us.

"Go into the ladies' room."

"Why?"

"Because I don't feel like getting thrown out of here. Sex in a public place, although thrilling beyond life itself, is illegal."

"Oh." I glanced at eyes on us.

"When you're the only one inside, lock the door and wait for me." He withdrew his hand and turned away from me, one hand on his drink and the other under his nose. He inhaled deeply, closed his eyes, and sipped his drink. "Go."

I was in foreign territory and the next decision I made could be one of the most dangerous decisions, or it could be one of the most thrilling of my life. I didn't bother adjusting my underwear. When I climbed off my seat my skirt fell back to where it should have been, and I walked away from him. Whether I stayed in the ladies' room and waited for him, or pretended to and disappeared from his life, the decision needed to be made in the next few moments.

Walking in, there was one other woman inside. I went into a stall and thoughts of masturbating in a stall to his voice on the phone flooded my mind. I listened as the woman finished her business and went to the sink. The water flowed as I leaned against the stall door, my mind was all over the place, my body was on fire, my pussy ached. The door opened and I was alone. My heart raced. I left the stall and quickly washed my hands, pressing them against my face.

I didn't know this guy well enough to sleep with him. I was fine with thoughts of it. I was good with self-pleasure. I wasn't good with ending up dead or with some STD. I was worried that he had disappeared. I sought him out and I found him. He was fine. He wasn't gone at all. Life gets in the way. I looked at my image in the mirror and nodded as my decision was made. I was going to sneak out of there and go back to Ohio.

Two knocks following a third knock sounded on the other side of the door. I froze and my vaginal muscles contracted sending a tremble through me.

I didn't move, but the door did. It opened slowly and Robert walked in. He didn't ask me what my decision was. He didn't look to see if we were alone. He didn't say a word. The moment he saw me next to the sink he rushed toward me, his hand sliding around the back of my neck and his other hand grabbing my side. He pushed me up against the wall and his body pinned me there, heat pushing into me from every angle. The palm of his hand cupped my chin and forced my head up, his tongue running along my collarbone before biting at the side of my neck. He wiggled his hand up underneath my blouse and glided his hand up until it was full of lace and breast. He yanked the lace out of his way and rolled his fingers over my nipple sending electricity through me. His knee forced its way between my legs and pushed them apart as his hand fed its way down between. His mouth captured mine and the taste of whiskey spread over my tongue. He moaned into his throat sending vibrations through me bringing my orgasm slightly closer to reality.

I dove my fingers into those curls as he devoured my mouth, moving his tongue over my chin and feasting his way down my neck. His hand gripped my blouse and shoved it upward until I was exposed to him. He pulled my other breast free and pushed them together before indulging on my nipples.

My stomach trembled. My legs were weak, and my breathing was labored as he moved further down past my stomach, his hands still on my chest. He lowered himself to his knees and looked up at me, dropping his hands to his lap before looking forward at my skirt. His hands connected with the outside of my thighs and they moved upward taking the material of my skirt with them. He covered his head leaving me with nothing to watch but my own image in the mirror beside me. The woman looking back at me wasn't me. I had never seen her before in my life, but I was jealous of her. I wanted to become her. She was exciting, bold, daring, and Robert's lover. Did I dare?

His hands slid up my hips and hooked into the sides of my underwear pulling them down my legs and they pulled my barriers down with them. His hands appeared on the outside of my skirt gripping the sides of my waist. I concentrated on the large ring on his finger as his tongue slid between my lips. The hardened tip swirled around my clit causing my thoughts to swirl around in my head. I was breathing heavily while he lapped at my folds and pushed me closer to the orgasm that threatened to grab hold of me.

I grabbed at something along the wall, something to hold on to as pressure built inside me. I picked my leg up, waiting for the explosion to hit when he stopped and let go, pushing my skirt back down before he stood up in front of me. He kissed me hard, but his hands were nowhere to be found.

I reached for his pants, but he held my arms to the wall above my head. "Please," I cooed. "Don't stop. I'm so close."

He pulled himself away from me and stood there as if he were looking for a reaction.

My eyes widened. "What…what are you doing?'

"Patience, my sweet girl. I have a surprise for you."

"No. I don't want a surprise. I want to…."

He pushed his hand over my mouth and leaned himself into me. "Shhh. Not yet."

I could feel his hardened cock pressing into me and I wanted to rub against it. He kept my hands against the wall knowing I'd satisfy myself.

"Robert," I pleaded.

He pulled me off the wall and slid himself behind me, his arms holding me to him. I bent my head to the side when his mouth kissed my neck. I reached back to his thigh and slid my hand to his sizable cock, rubbing him through his pants. Maybe I could get him hot enough to not want to stop. I jerked him off through his pants until the door opened. I tried pulling away, but he held me tight where I stood.

"Robert," I whispered.

"Shhh."

A large black man walked into the ladies' bathroom and stood in front of us, his eyes greedy. He licked his lips and I pushed back into Robert. Was this my surprise? I was just getting to know the physical Robert and he wanted to introduce another cock into my life? I wasn't okay with this, was I?

"This your girl?" the man said, eyeing me up and down.

"Yes." Robert's voice was soft, velvety. "My wife has always wanted someone to watch me fuck her."

A surge of air forced its way into my lungs as excitement, fear, panic, and hysteria raced through my veins.

The man grabbed his crotch and smiled. "I think I can oblige her wishes. She's fucking gorgeous. Quite a sex pot, huh?"

"Very exotic." Robert pulled my hair away from my neck and kissed me there. "Are you ready?" he asked close to my ear.

I could barely speak. I was about to do something only Robert could think up in his stories. I was about to become one of his stories and the eroticism of it all hit me like a boulder.

He leaned down enough to grab my skirt and lift it to my waist. My underwear was still on the floor at my feet. The air hit me between my legs as the man in front of me took me in. He shook his head and licked his lips, his hand sliding up and down the front of his pants. "Man, I don't know if I can just watch this. You got yourself a *hot* little pussy there."

"Yes, I do." Robert's tone turned carnal and somewhere between his desire to showcase me to a stranger and that stranger's eyes on my bare pussy, his pants came off. His hands ran across my thighs and in between my legs as his dick pushed in between my ass cheeks. He humped me, his wetness slick along my ass and on my thighs. He grabbed my hair in his fist and gently pulled my head back as he pushed into me threatening to penetrate me. "Tell him what you want, darling."

Panic mixed with my desire and I set my sight on the man in front of me. He was stroking his cock that protruded from his open pants. His mouth hung open and he stared at my body. I was center stage and was asked to perform.

Truth was, this wasn't what I wanted. It was too much, and it frightened me. I wasn't about to admit such a defeat, so I pushed away from Robert and walked toward the other man. "I want him, and I want you to watch him fuck me." I spun around and grinned at Robert waiting for his response.

His eyes flashed with anger. His plan had backfired. I'd be damned if I was to be just another quest. "What about what we talked about?" he asked through gritted teeth.

"Well, you know I always get what I want. Darling." I was pushing it. I could see that, and it made me nervous, but it also thrilled me.

Robert reached down and pulled his pants back up, securing them around him. He stayed silent while he did so. Our new friend didn't know what to do. He had put himself back together after Robert's reaction. Did I push things too far? It seemed we were done there, and all plans were off.

Not another word was said when he reached down and scooped my panties off the floor shoving them into his pocket. He walked by his friend and unlocked the door. I smiled. I won. He would have his way with me alone in that bathroom. Or so I had thought. He whipped the door open, lunged at me, and seized my wrist with his hand, yanking me out of the room.

"Don't say a word," he commanded as he walked me out of the bar. No one looked up.

Once we were on the street I stopped and struggled against his grip. "You can let me go now. Your little skit is over."

He continued to pull me along behind him.

"Where are we going? Where are you…?"

He stopped and whipped around, pulling me into him. His hand gripped the back of my neck as his mouth smashed against mine. He thrust his tongue into my mouth and kissed me hard, while his other hand reached underneath my skirt and immediately found my pussy still wet from his cock. He pushed two fingers inside me and slammed them in and out of me until I was panting heavily. I gripped his jacket with both hands and held on. If he continued, I was going to orgasm right there on the street at the mercy of his hands. But he didn't. He pushed me to the brink of orgasm then stopped and held me there.

"Don't test me, Mia. I know much more than you do. I can create the most incredible orgasm you'll ever experience, or I can punish you and torment you until I decide your fate. Do you understand?"

I was still panting, my head dizzy, but I nodded.

"Nothing I do is for anyone else except for me. Don't ever forget that."

I nodded again, nervous that he was going to hurt me. I needed to get away from him, but I let him lead me along.

We had walked a couple of blocks then down a narrow alleyway before it opened up to a large empty parking lot. He led me through the dimly lit lot and stopped in the center, large buildings all around us.

He pulled me closer and cupped my face, looking down at me. His face was softer, calm. His kiss was tender. It melted me. "Do you trust me?"

It was a loaded question. Did I? I knew what he could do, and it fed my addiction for him but was it enough to allow him full access to do what he wanted? That was what this question meant when he asked it.

I nodded, swallowed hard, and licked my lips. My fingers felt cold. *I don't! I want to leave! I was wrong for coming here.* "I do."

His hand slithered into the pocket of his jacket and he produced a beautiful black scarf. He wrapped each end around his hands and held it tight in front of my face. I knew what it was for. My body trembled with so many emotions at the thought of giving up all control to him.

He walked behind me and lowered it over my head. He slid it across my neck and the silky feel provoked my arousal. He placed it over my eyes and pulled it tight, tying it behind my head.

I lightly touched it, accepting the dark and homing into my other senses. His hand slid into mine and he tugged me forward. I extended my other hand outward and scuffled my feet forward as he led me along. "There are some stairs," he said quietly.

I tapped my foot forward and picked it up. I mentally counted as my foot raised up to each one. One, two, three, four, five, six, seven, eight, nine, ten, eleven. A buzzer, then the click of a door. The air became warmer as the door closed behind us. I followed, clutching onto his arm. We stopped. I heard my own breathing and nothing else until the ding of an elevator sounded. Doors opened and he led me forward. The drop of my stomach told me we were going up. I tried counting the floors, but it was impossible to tell how fast the elevator climbed.

When the doors opened again, Robert tugged me forward. A few hundred feet, a key in a lock and a door opened. The smell of roses and vanilla tickled my nose. It was pleasant, alluring. I inhaled and enjoyed the scent.

"Sit here." He was in front of me with his hands on my arms. I sat back, my hands finding the cushion of a chair or a sofa. "Leave your blindfold on."

I nodded and tried to relax. The air around me went quiet. No footsteps, no rustling around, no words. Nothing.

"Robert?" I listened intently. Nothing.

I didn't know how long I sat there alone in silence, but it was enough time to calm my arousal. I began questioning my decision to allow him to lead me to what I assumed was his apartment. If I left would he know? Would I know how to get out of there? I didn't want to go, but I didn't want to sit in silence and wait for whatever was going to happen, either. The wait was worse than the whip. I craved Robert's hands on me, his mouth savoring me, his cock penetrating me. I leaned back to wait and sleep crept in. When I awoke, I was lying out flat. A light blanket covered me. I jolted upright and wanted to tear the blindfold off.

"Hey, sleepyhead." Robert's voice came from somewhere in front of me.

I lightly touched the blindfold still intact. "I fell asleep?"

"You did."

"For how long?"

"Quite a while."

"Why didn't you wake me?"

"I want you rested. Calm. Ready."

I heard the clink of glass next to me.

"Open your mouth. Do you like strawberries?"

I nodded, opening my mouth as directed and a sweet berry entered my lips. I bit down at the succulent taste and allowed it to spread across my palate. He fed me the rest and then another before setting them aside.

"There will be more for you later. You'll have quite an appetite when we are done."

Sensation tickled between my legs. I jumped when his hands took mine and he pulled me to my feet.

"This way, my sweet."

He pulled me along and a door closed. I heard running water. The scarf loosened and was lifted away from my eyes. I blinked excessively as they adjusted to the light. Robert stood in front of me in a white dress shirt unbuttoned enough to expose part of his chest. His sleeves were loose around his arms and it hung loosely over his black dress pants. He was sexy as hell.

He leaned into a large shower with glass walls and adjusted the water. I looked around the spacious bathroom. It was luxurious and beautiful. A gift bag sat on the counter with a toothbrush sticking up out of it.

"There are garments on the shelf for you to wear after you shower. Toiletries in the small bag by the sink. Replace your blindfold when you are finished with everything. I will be back in when you are ready."

"How will you know when I'm ready?"

He didn't respond. He merely left the room and closed the door behind him. I looked around the large room, steam collecting up by the ceiling. There was no clock and somewhere along the way I had lost or misplaced my clutch and my cell phone. I had to trust that Robert had taken care of my things. Trust was all I had at the time, that and a deep craving for what was going to happen.

I emptied the gift bag and took inventory of its contents. A toothbrush, a razor, douche, perfume, lotion, and nail clippers. He liked a tidy woman.

I caught a glimpse of myself in the full wall mirror and I cringed. I looked rough, tired. This was all going to be needed.

I did everything I needed to with what he gave me, then went to the shower that had filled the large room with steam by that time. I watched through the heaviness and saw my reflection in the mirror as I pulled my blouse up over my head and dropped it at my feet. My arms slithered out of my bra straps and I unhooked it from the back, holding it at my side momentarily while I looked down at my breasts. I cupped them with my hands, pushing them softly together as my libido heightened.

Stepping out of my sandals I unbuttoned my skirt from the back and let it fall as well. And there I stood with not a stitch of clothing on. I examined myself in the mirror for a moment before stepping into the warm water cascading from a large square shower head suspended from the ceiling.

It felt good running down my body. I enjoyed the soap gliding across my skin, up my arms, across my stomach, and in between my legs. My fingers slid easily between my folds increasing my arousal. My hands caressed my tits, thumbs rubbing across my nipples.

Oh God, it felt good.

I closed my eyes and ran my hands down my ass cheeks, gliding my fingers over my pussy from the back, my thumb teasing my asshole. I opened my mouth slightly, arousal swirling around me. I worked my fingers across my holes and into my folds, pushing my fingers inside me as the water ran over me. I didn't know what Robert had in store for me, but I couldn't take it any longer. I needed release.

I huffed each breath out feeling my orgasm creep closer. My fingers worked the parts that I knew would give me what I craved and when it finally washed over me I shuddered, smiling at the sweet sensation.

The towel I found was big enough to cover my whole bed back home. I wrapped myself in it and walked to a shelf on the wall. The garments Robert had picked out for me were something out of a Victoria's Secret catalog. How he came to possess such things was a question I doubted I'd have an answer for, but it excited me to know he wanted to take care of me.

I picked them up and held them out in front of me. He had good taste, simple, sexy. I opened the towel and set it on the floor and fed my legs into the black lace panties. I held the satin mini dress up to my shoulders and it only reached the top of my thighs. I pulled it over my head and let it fall into place, the straps as thin as spaghetti. It was alluring and made me feel sensual. I ran my hands over the material and watched myself as I moved in it.

There was no hairdryer that I could find so I ran my fingers through my damp hair and let it hang loose over my shoulders. It cascaded down over my breasts almost to my navel. I was almost ready.

Taking in a deeper breath I set my eyes on the blindfold he had removed. This was it. The turning point. Did I really want this? I was excited to feel him where I had only ever imagined him to be. But I was also scared to death. Robert had the ability to do whatever he wanted with me, including hurting me or worse, death. Did I trust him enough to give him total control?

I picked it up and ran it through my fingers, a tingling sensation hitting me between my legs again. I raised it to my face, and watched the image in the mirror until it was taken from me by the scarf. I wrapped it around my head and tied it tight, plunging myself back into total darkness.

I leaned against the counter feeling vulnerable and timid. I was ready, but how would he know? Should I open the door? Yell out to him? Knock on the door? Was he waiting on the other side? The door opened and I stiffened, my hands clutching the side of the counter. There had to have been a camera someplace in that bathroom. Did he watch me the whole time? I worked on controlling my breathing and calming my nerves as he approached me. I felt the heat from his body close to me. A finger ran across my mouth, pushing inside and pulling me away from the counter.

"You look beautiful, Mia." His words melted me.

He took my hand and led me out of the room, my bare feet appreciating the cool tiled floor as it changed to soft carpeting. Rose and vanilla reminded me of its existence. I tried setting up the layout of his apartment in my head with every turn we took and the smells of each room. When he let my hand go, I stopped. Another door closed behind me and the faint smell of leather wafted around me.

My hair was pulled away from my neck and tugged back into a ponytail, his fingers trailing down the sides of my neck and down over my shoulders. They continued down my arms and intertwined with my fingers. He pressed himself against my back and kissed my neck, igniting my libido deep down inside. I bent my head to give him full access and enjoyed the sensation it gave me. A cool strap closed over my wrist and tightened around it. I brought it to my nose and inhaled the smell of leather. A similar strap tightened around my other wrist. I ran my fingers over them noticing a hook of some sort on each one. I had to have been in some sort of playroom, a red room, I think they call it.

My heartbeat increased and I found it harder to breathe than normal.

"Robert?"

His lips pressed against mine and his tongue pushed inside my mouth. He deepened his kiss and moaned from his throat, the vibrations washing over me. I raised my arms to wrap them around him, but he seized my wrists and held them between us. He led me further into the room and I heard something click into the hooks on the straps that bound my wrists.

"What was that?" I asked breathlessly.

My hands were being raised up into the air until my arms were straight above my head.

"So beautiful," he muttered. Hands covered my breasts, fingers trickled down my sides and raised the thin dress I wore until I was exposed to him. He pulled it over my head and somehow it disappeared. My panties were lowered down my legs, his hands picking each foot out of them. A strap was placed around each of my ankles and tightened firmly before my legs were cinched apart.

"Your breasts heave with each struggling ragged breath you take."

Something soft and cool raked across my chest.

"Your vulnerability is sexy." His voice broke. "Tantalizing. So fucking appetizing."

Warmth surrounded my nipple. He sucked on it hard, his tongue flicking the tip causing it to harden to a pebble.

He moaned.

I shivered.

He slid his hands up my naked sides and pressed my breasts together to indulge in both nipples.

I dropped my head back, the sensation of his actions flowing through me. Arousal began between my legs, an ache slowly spreading across my abdomen. His fingers moved down my stomach into my pubic hair and pushed into the folds of my pussy. I gasped as he moved them back and forth, his mouth still suckling my nipple. He only removed his hands for a moment but replaced them with something harder, something cold to the touch. It was large, wide but rounded. It moved back and forth across my clit, the coolness dissipating. I heard a click and the device vibrated. Arousal shot through me. I pushed my hips forward as best as I could in the position I was in. The vibration increased and my hips pushed forward further. I started humping the air like a dog in heat climbing one step closer to another orgasm. I wanted it bad.

"Yes," I whispered. A click and the vibration was gone. I panted in frustration. "Wait. No. I was so close. Please."

His body pressed against mine and his arms fed around my waist. He hugged me close, his lips nibbling on my ear. "I want you this way. Wanting. Needing. Craving. You weren't supposed to pleasure yourself in the shower, Mia."

"I knew you were watching me."

"I was. And I liked it." His voice was so close to my ear that it made me shiver when he spoke so softly but demandingly. "I would have punished you for what you did, Mia. But you were unaware of the rules. So, all I can do is push you to that cliff again. Bring you so close to exploding, then stealing it from you. I want you dangling on the edge so far that one soft blow of my mouth on your *cunt* will set you off."

I swallowed hard. His tongue trailed down my neck. He lowered himself to his knees and his hands gripped my hips. Without warning, his tongue pushed into my pussy and he lapped at my clit, the tip of his tongue teasing in just the right spot until I was panting and begging for release again. He let me go, stood back up, and kissed me with his tongue on mine forcing me to taste myself.

"It's just the beginning, my sweet." He let me go, his voice getting further away, then silence. Did he leave? Was he right in front of me, staring at my vulnerability?

My lip quivered. Something dragged down the center of my back and over my ass cheek. He made circles there before cracking it against my skin. I jumped and panted harder. It cracked again in the same spot pain searing through my cheek. The warmth of his hand rubbed me there, traveling down to my pussy and sliding a finger inside me. He moved it in and out slowly and my inner thighs were slick with my sex.

He removed his hand and slapped me with a flogger or some sort of leather whip, pain spreading across my cheek again. He rubbed it with his hand and slid down to my pussy again. This went on repeatedly several times until I welcomed the delicious mix of pain and pleasure. I was soaked between my legs and so aroused I could hardly breathe. My arms were lowered, and my legs were let go. He removed my blindfold, and I was introduced to the room for the first time. My instincts were right. It was his playroom. It was incredible. It was intimidating.

"Oh. My. Um." I walked around the room, the straps still bound to my wrists and ankles. A large X wrapped in leather was bolted to one of the black walls, several straps on each appendage. A black leather chair sat next to it with the same straps along the arms and the legs. The table along another wall reminded me of an OB-GYN appointment but matched the rest of the *furniture* bound in black leather. The wall behind me hung several vibrating devices, floggers, whips, and other scary things I had never seen in real life.

He watched me take it all in, a smile on his face and a bulge in his pants.

"Are you, um." I pointed at the wall of toys. "Are you going to use these on me?"

"I might. It depends on how I feel in the moment."

I sucked in a ragged breath and rubbed my arms, vulnerability seeping in.

"Come here." His tone was calm but still unnerving.

I walked toward him, my arms still crossed over my chest. He cupped my face and kissed me tenderly.

"I have been waiting for this day for a long time since I met you."

"You have?"

He nodded, his eyes drunk with desire. He turned me around and kissed the side of my neck as his hands roamed over my arms and down my sides. He gently pushed me forward until I was against the OB-GYN-like table. He pushed against my upper back and bent me over until I rested my chest on the cool leather. He spread my legs apart, his fingers playing and pushing me toward that cliff again. I heard his belt clink together as he removed it from his pants. He fed it around my neck and held it tight as he slapped my ass cheek. When he pressed his body against my ass, I felt his cock push between my legs. He was naked and hard.

I held my breath, waiting for the moment he penetrated me, but he didn't. He slid it back and forth against my pussy, his hand slapping my ass. He spread my cheeks apart and teased my asshole before slapping my ass again.

"Fuck," I grunted, frustrated and craving for release. I pushed back against him and he stepped away from me to watch me squirm. He moved around to the front of me, seizing my wrists. He pulled them forward and locked them into place on the table before sauntering around behind me again.

I tried looking back at him, but my compromising position wouldn't allow me much mobility. Where was he? I didn't hear a door open. I couldn't hear footsteps in the heavily carpeted room. I couldn't see him or feel him. He disappeared. His hands were gone. His mouth was gone. There was no more cock to push into me. I felt desperate. Then….

Click. Vibration. I inhaled deep and closed my eyes waiting for it to press into me. A whirlwind of emotions rushed back. The moments added together and dragged on. A whimper escaped my lips. The hesitation was killing me. When the hard plastic head finally touched me, I jumped as if it wasn't expected.

He slid it back and forth only a few times before I heard it hit the floor next to my foot. It still vibrated but nothing was done about it. Soon, it was forgotten as his hands grabbed my hips and his dick pushed against my hole.

I held my breath. He penetrated me inching in, rocking back and forth, the back feeding my craving on the brink of begging him for more, the forth pushing deeper just enough to release the crazy in my mind. The huffing and panting of my breathing didn't match the pattern. That's when I realized it was Robert's broken inhales that I was hearing. He was as mentally invested in this as I was.

That, in itself, gave me a level of satisfaction I had been waiting for since the moment I stepped foot in New York. I absorbed his hands as they caressed my ass cheeks. I savored the way he fucked me, moving with awareness, sensitivity, but dominating and controlling. It wasn't just in and out. It was pushing in all of his emotion, his passion, his desire for this moment and pulling out my need for his hands on my body, his cock inside me, his control over me, his experience to finally be written in my life instead of merely in my mind.

I was being shoved dangerously close to orgasm. I was hanging off that cliff and Robert was the only thing I had left to hang on to. But, in fact, he was hanging on to me; not letting me go, not letting me fall, but teasing, dropping me close to the point of no return only to yank me back up to dangle me there again.

I squeezed my eyes closed, my mouth dry from heavy breathing. I ached all over for release. Reality was disconnecting from my mind. I tried to keep a rhythm going, with my breathing, with my body, with everything even though I wanted to scream out to him. I was fearful that he'd stop again. I was there, ready to drop off that cliff, ready for sweet release.

But, even that was ill-fated. He knew. And he stopped, withdrew and disappeared from what I knew as the only existence at the moment. My release slowly slithered away. I cried out and fought the binds around my wrists. "Let me go," I grunted.

He appeared before me and did just that. The leather cuffs were unhooked from the table and I was free. He stepped back, only his white dress shirt on, unbuttoned and dangling off his broad shoulders. His cock protruded forward, his arms hung at his sides, his face wore a melancholy frustration. He was giving me the option to leave but silently begging me to stay. Leaning against the wall, he crossed his arms over his stomach and pursed his lips. He'd never beg me to stay. He'd never ask me if I wanted to.

I didn't give him the satisfaction of an answer when I stood up off the table and pulled my legs together. I ached from the position I had been in, but I ignored it. I trembled with the need for that orgasm he dangled me close to, but I fought to suppress it.

Walking around the table, I approached him. "You're giving me an option."

He nodded and drunkenly blinked.

"Why? It's not like you to give up like this. You pursue until you conquer. It's your ammo."

"You're different. I can't let you go. You're my queen I share my experiences with."

"Queen." The title empowered me. I was no longer one of his experiences. We were a team adventuring through his sexual experiences together. I stopped in front of him, inches from his face. Looking up at him, I was ready for the next step. "Let me show you what I was looking for, what I wanted, what I crave." I slid my hands across his chest and kissed close to his nipple, my tongue running across it.

He sighed heavily, his hands feeding into my hair. He straightened up off the wall, planting his feet and preparing himself for what he knew was coming.

I lowered myself down to my knees, my arms still stretching up to his chest. They caressed his body slowly moving down and around his hips to his buttocks. I rounded my tongue and cradled the head of his cock with it. I gazed upward to watch the hunger in his eyes grow, his mouth hanging open as he watched me work. Leaning forward I opened my mouth wider, my tongue protruding as far as it would allow. His head disappeared into my mouth as my tongue cradled it, pushing it up to the roof of my mouth. I closed my lips around it and sucked on the ridge flicking his hole with my tongue.

"Oh, fuck yeah." His head hit the wall and his hands pressed me closer.

I inched him in deeper relaxing to do what I set out to do. I moved my mouth around the hard piece of meat taking a big breath and opening my throat for what I had only done one other time in my life. Moving closer, his dick hit the back of my throat and cinched past my gag reflex. It threatened me, but I closed my eyes and meditated it away before moving my face closer to his pelvis. His cock pushed past it. I raised myself up to straighten the path inward and swayed my body back and forth, my mouth rocking on his cock. Each time I took him in it was another inch deeper until he filled my throat, and his veins scrubbed the tender tissue surrounding my esophagus. His pubic hairs tickled my cheeks as I held him there and shook my head before backing off to refill my oxygen levels. I continued this form of ecstasy until I began tasting the thickness of his cum. He was close. I rocked my mouth back and forth a few more times, his ragged breathing beginning to cut out. That was my cue.

I pulled him out of my mouth and stood up, wiping my lip with the back of my hand. It took him a minute, his head still back against the wall, his panting heavy and hard. When he finally looked at me, I smiled. "Tit for tat."

I turned to walk away and finish teaching him his lesson when he lunged at me, picking me up and angrily carrying me out of the room.

"What are you doing? Where are you taking me?"

He walked heavy-footed down a long hallway and into a bedroom where he threw me on a large bed. The room was dark, very clean but with not a hint of a sexual play toy. One would never have guessed it was a bachelor pad or jiggalo's bedroom.

He tore his shirt off his arms and jumped onto the bed over the top of me. "This is what you want. I can't play games with you any longer," he grunted.

He grabbed my knees and shoved my legs apart, pushed his hands underneath my head, and covered me with his body. There was no longer hesitation. There was no room for teasing or disappearing. This was it. He bit at my lower lip while he positioned himself between my legs. His tongue pushed past my lips and filled my mouth the moment he penetrated my pussy. He grabbed my shoulders and thrust deep into me until our pubic bones rested against each other and he stopped, his tongue dancing and exploring inside my mouth. He ignited me, a fire raging across every inch of my body and he rode me with a vengeance until my fire burned out of control. I was flung over that cliff and headlong into an orgasm that grabbed hold and rattled me like a rag doll. I cried out grabbing fistfuls of blanket in my hands.

He slammed into me, grunting like a dog in heat, his hands bearing down on my shoulders and his cock quaking inside me. He drained every drop he had inside me before collapsing over the top of me in exhaustion.

The next morning, I awoke in the same bed with the sun streaming through the windows. The room seemed different. Normal. My body ached. I looked around the room. I was alone. My clutch and my phone sat on the bed stand next to me with my clothes folded neatly on the chair.

I sat up, the blanket falling away from me. "Robert?" Was I truly alone? I climbed out of the bed and pulled his dress shirt that draped over the back of the chair on my body. Buttoning the front, I quietly ventured out of the room in search of him. The hallway fed into a large living room and a bay window that overlooked the entire city. A side door opened to a balcony and a man half-naked sipping a whiskey in a short glass.

I watched him through the window for a few minutes before opening the door and joining him. "Good morning," I cooed, wrapping my arms around him from the back.

"It is, yes. How did you sleep?"

"Like a baby. You seem preoccupied, or deep in thought. Care to share?"

"No." He turned around and embraced me planting little kisses along my forehead. "But I will say you have changed me."

"Have I? For the better I hope, if that's what you need."

"It is. And you did. I want more in life. Not just pussy when I feel it benefits me. I want a woman behind that pussy. When do you have to go back?"

"Soon. Will this change things with us?"

"Never. I'll always call you out of the blue to share me with you."

I smiled and rested my head against his chest. "Hmm. I like that."

"I'm not sure what I need, but it will always include you."

~ CHAPTER 4 ~

Married Bi-Curious Woman Finally Explores

I stared up at the ceiling lying flat on my back, the morning sun warm on my face. The little beach house was ours for the month and the gentle lapping of the waves just outside our open bedroom window soothed me.

Marcelo had just turned off the shower and I could hear him softly singing one of his songs he had written. He was happy, and that was important to me. I rolled to my side gathering the sheets around me as I watched the crack in the bathroom door, catching the occasional glimpse of my new husband's nakedness.

He was a beautiful man, muscular, dark Italian skin, and a full head of black hair. He came from old money, a big family, and a faith in God that he loved almost as much as he loved his mother. I had it all. I rolled to my other side and inhaled the salty air before pushing myself up to sit on the side of the bed. Burying my toes into the soft carpet I stood up and stretched, the sheets falling away from me.

The bedroom was light and airy in the daytime hours with lighting to soften and romanticize the area at night. It was the perfect rendezvous.

I shuffled across the room, pulled the balcony doors open, and walked out onto the deck. It was liberating to feel nothing but the cool morning air on my body as I enjoyed the ocean set out in front of me.

"Good morning, sexy baby." Marcelo's arms snaked around my waist and his warm body pressed against my back. I leaned my head to give him access to the side of my neck as his lips smooched against my skin. "You smell delicious this morning."

"Hmmm." I closed my eyes and smiled, feeling his hands roam up to my breasts. "Are you hungry?"

"For you, I am." His kisses pressed into my skin a little harder. "I cannot believe I get this every morning for the rest of my life."

"There is some fresh fruit from the market I left in the cabana."

"Bring in some strawberries. I'll run them along your pussy before I devour them, then devour you."

He cupped his hand under my chin and craned my head toward him, his tongue slipping through my lips and dancing around inside. He tasted minty, fresh, and he knew just how to touch me. His hands glided along my curves, reaching between my legs to cup my pussy for a moment. They wandered back up my stomach to my breasts to press them together then back down over my sides to my ass. Small arousal tickled me deep inside. He bent forward and scooped me up into his arms, his mouth on mine. His arms hooked around my legs and he lifted me off the deck and carried me down the three stairs to the beachy sand. I shivered when he lowered me onto the lounge chair facing the ocean. It could have been from his touch and the anticipation he was going to make love to me out in the open, but I was more inclined to think it was from the cool morning air.

Marcelo and I had only been together for a year before getting married. It wasn't a long time, but marriage seemed like the right thing to do. He was head-over-heels in love with me, he didn't want for anything and he treated me like a queen. His family adored me. I had everything I wanted, so why did I keep my true feelings buried so far down that even I didn't want to entertain them?

We were kissing heavily as he cradled me into the cushions of the lounge chair, keeping my legs open as he nestled himself over the top of me. His body was hard against mine and his mouth grew needy. His hands closed around my wrists and pulled them over my head pinning them to the top of the chair.

"My sexy wife," he growled, his teeth raking across my skin. "I want to buy this little beach house and live here forever with you. Make love on the beach every morning. Eat fruit and drink wine every evening. Long naked walks on the beach, swimming in the ocean. It would be incredible, don't you think?"

"Mmhmm." I kept my eyes closed as he planned one of many fantasy futures between heavy kisses.

I pulled my knees up and opened for him as I played a favorite porn scene in my head. Images of 'Kiara' going down on 'Jasmine' mixed with Marcelo's hands and lips all over me fueled my libido and pushed my arousal into overdrive.

I cooed while Marcelo slithered himself down past my navel and buried his knees into the sand, his mouth on my torso, lips smooching, tongue licking, teeth biting. I imagined long blonde hair caressing my breasts, fingernails softly scratching down to my sex. I arched my back and bent my head upward feeling fingers slide into me. It was exquisite the way they moved in and out, slowly, teasing me, drawing my arousal closer. His mouth covered me there, tongue gliding into the grooves, lips pinching lips, teeth biting what they wanted to bite. I winced at the pain, but it mixed deliciously with the pleasure pulsating within me.

Planting my feet on the edge of the chair by my ass, I thrust my hips up into the air. Marcelo moaned, bringing me out of my fantasy porn scene. His arms closed around my thighs and he held me there as he feasted, bringing me to the brink of orgasm. I pulled myself up off the chair into a full sit-up until I was sitting on his shoulders, my legs hooking around his head. He squatted in the sand, his mouth doing things to my pussy that spread a soft orgasm through me. This was always his first move during sex. He was proud that he could get me off so quickly, then he could fuck me for a long time after.

He let me down, and I dug my feet into the cool sand until he stood up and took my hand to lead me back toward the beach house. I followed him back up onto the balcony that hooked around the house to the hideaway jacuzzi the size of our master bed waiting for us back home.

He pulled the top off of it and ran his hand through the water giving me time to take him in. He was in amazing shape and I loved watching his muscles flex and move as he did. I always felt he deserved better than I could give him, but he insisted on me. He insisted on pouring all of his love and energy into my life, so I let him. It was better than living alone while I tried paying my way through art school and figuring out what I really wanted out of life. Honestly, I was as lost as one could be.

Marcelo climbed in and took my hand until I climbed the stairs, feeding my legs slowly into the heated water. It bubbled around us and tickled me until I was submerged. He sat across from me and watched me as he often did.

"I'm the luckiest man in the world, Gaia."

I forced a humble smile and shielded my eyes away from him the way I knew he liked. I did love him, just not the way he wanted me to. He always told me he'd change that.

I closed my eyes and tilted my head back to feel the sun on my face. This was nice. His hands cupped my face, and I opened my eyes to his lips brushing against mine. My mouth fell open and invited his tongue inside.

"Good morning!" A distant voice called up to us from the beach.

Marcelo grunted in frustration and pulled away a bit. His eyes set into mine, he smiled and shrugged. "We almost made it through our honeymoon without distraction."

I welcomed the rude interruption but waited for Marcelo to make the first move. He waved at two women walking toward us. I ducked out and climbed out of the tub from the other side, sneaking into the house to find coverage for us. I ran to the dresser and quickly slipped into a pair of shorts and a tank top while I looked around for something for him. His sweatpants were in a pile on the floor, so I grabbed them and walked back out in time to see them climbing the stairs. This entrapped Marcelo in the tub with not a stitch of clothing on. He shot a look at me that made me chuckle.

"Sorry for the intrusion, but my girlfriend and I had to take a walk on this glorious morning. We are renting the place just down the beach for the week." She leaned toward me and held her hand out. "I'm Jasmine."

Jasmine. I took her slender hand in mine and shook it briefly as I stole a look at her. Long dark brown hair piled high on her head and a simple strapless summer dress hugged her curves in all the right places. She had no makeup on, and her skin was flawless with a glow from the summer sun that appealed to me.

"This is Alex."

A little more on the manly side, but…strikingly beautiful. Her short blonde bob set off the features of her face, her piercing blue eyes standing out for the world to marvel at. She didn't seem much for dresses, but she sure could pull off old denim jean shorts and a white tank top.

I didn't know if it was the fact that they were a gay couple, or if it was the similar name, I was used to hearing moaning with orgasms from Kiara's mouth on her pussy, but something contracted the muscles around my vagina.

"It's good to meet you," I said softly, glancing at Alex. "I'm Gaia. This is Marcelo."

"Hiya," he called out behind me, still submerged waist-deep in the water. "How are you liking the island?"

"It's beautiful here." Jasmine leaned against the rail at the top of the stairs. "I don't think I ever want to leave."

I watched Alex. She didn't seem to want to be there like she was put out of her place. "We've been here about a month," I said, waiting for those blue eyes to look at me. She kept her head down as she twirled a gold ring around her thumb. "It is nice, but I'm starting to miss home."

"I can understand that. Paradise is paradise for a reason. I bet the locals don't feel the same about the place like we do."

The air between us grew a little thick as I struggled with conversation. Marcelo was usually the one to keep things flowing in awkward situations, but he was a little restrained at the moment.

"We don't want to keep you from anything, but we were talking and wanted to invite you to brunch later. We're pretty social people and there aren't many around. We'd love to get to know you."

"Tomorrow is our last day here, but I don't see why we couldn't." I turned toward Marcelo and smiled. "What do you think, honey?"

"I'm down for some good grub and conversation. Absolutely. It's a date."

Jasmine smiled at me, a little pink touching her cheeks. "I have to admit that we took a similar walk yesterday, earlier in the morning. We saw you here."

"We must have missed you."

"We didn't intrude because, well, you were sort of busy." She pointed toward the ocean where Marcelo and I swam during the sunrise before making love where the water crashed up onto the shore. It wasn't the most comfortable way of fucking, but it was good. The salt from the water had rubbed me in some of the wrong places and chapped my skin.

"You…saw us?" I asked, heat collecting uncomfortably between my legs.

"Don't be embarrassed. It was beautiful."

I wasn't embarrassed in the slightest. The thought turned me on. Alex turned me on. Flashes of what our new friends looked like in bed together formed in my mind. My favorite fantasy with these two. They were both slender and beautiful.

 I cleared my throat and looked at Alex. "You don't talk much, do you?"

"Not really. You learn more when you stay quiet." Her smirk was sexy. Her eyes smoldered when they locked with mine. It made me feel funny inside and I think she knew that.

"A little alcohol and she doesn't stop talking," Jasmine chuckled. "We will get out of your way. Let you get back to each other." She turned to go and hesitated when she looked at Marcelo. "We are the next beach house about a mile down the beach."

"Perfect. Give us a bit and we will join you."

"We will see you in, say, a couple of hours, then? Mimosas and steamed clams on us."

"We will bring a bottle of wine," Marcelo called out.

"See you then." Jasmine laced her fingers with Alex's, and they walked away.

I didn't move from the rail, watching them until they were several feet down the beach. "What do you think their story is?"

"I don't know." Marcelo sunk back into the tub. "They seem fun though. I love gay women. Men too. They know how to live life."

"And we don't? You could have been a little more social," I teased, realizing I still had his sweatpants over my arm. I flung them in his direction, and they landed in the water. He lunged at them but ended up losing them in the bubbles. I burst out laughing when he came up with them sopping wet in his hands.
"These would have been nice five minutes ago."
"Just like that?"
"Oh, yeah? You think that's funny?"
He scrambled up the side of the tub with them in his hands and set his sights on me. I squealed, knowing what his plan was. Running into the beach house, I thought it would have been my sanctuary, but he didn't care. He ran in after me, his dripping sweatpants still in his hand.
"No, no, no, no, no," I begged, my hands reaching out toward him. He had me in a corner, his pants balled up in one hand and ready for launch. "Listen. Let's talk about this."
"Oh, *now* you want to negotiate."
I straightened up and lifted my top to expose myself to distract him. He liked it. His cock rose slowly, and I played into his desires, rubbing myself for him. Just when he started lowering his weapon, I made a run for it past him toward the back door. He lunged at me and got a hold of my waist with his free arm, tackling me to the floor, both of us laughing at ourselves.
Small kisses turned into longer ones that ended up with tongue-to-tongue contact, deepening with urgency and intense breathing that was initially interrupted by our beautiful guests.
Marcelo wrapped his hands around my wrists and held them pinned to the floor above my head. He pushed my legs apart with his and allowed his weight to settle on me. I could feel the mass of his cock through my shorts, and it set my arousal free.
"God, I love you," he mumbled between kisses. He rolled off me enough to inch my shorts down my legs and hooked them with his toes to discard them into oblivion. He positioned himself back on top of me, laced his fingers with mine, held my arms high above my head, and pushed himself inside me.
I welcomed it, the massive fill of him stretching me. He moved forward and backward slowly at first, then picked up his pace. The soft carpet underneath me was a much better bed than the sand on the beach. I moved between him and the floor, my eyes catching the open door out onto the balcony. The thrill of our new friends coming back and catching us… again… lit me on fire. My breathing got heavier. I kept my eyes on the doorway and imagined them there, touching each other while their eyes were on us.
Reaching down, I grabbed Marcelo's ample ass and pulled him into me, wrapping my legs around him and thrusting my hips in a pattern with his movements. With the thoughts in my head and his massive cock inside me, it didn't take long to feel the excitement of my second orgasm threaten to spill over me.
"Oh, baby," he whispered, his nose nuzzling into my cheek. "Yes, baby."
He was close. He huffed each time he pushed into me. I rose my hips to meet those thrusts. When he grunted, I pressed my pelvis tight into the air pressing hard into him until the friction between us pushed me over the orgasmic ledge. I held onto his hands still in mine and enjoyed the ride back down to earth.
"That," he said, breathless as he rolled off me "was spectacular."
"Agreed." I ran my hand up his chest after rolling toward him. Small kisses along his nipple made him smile. I appreciated him. He was good to me.
"I'll race you to the shower," he said, not moving from where he lay.
"At this pace, I'll be done and at the neighbor's before you are on your knees."
"I'd get down on my knees for you."
"Come on, Casanova. Let's get moving." I slapped his shoulder and climbed to my feet.

~ ~ ~ ~ ~ ~ ~ ~

After a long hot shower, we dressed simple but beachy for our date with the neighbors. Marcelo selected a vintage wine he had purchased in town and we walked along the beach until we spotted the next beach house.
Alex was on the back deck pulling clams out of their steamer when she spotted us. She disappeared in through double sliding doors momentarily and reappeared with a smiling Jasmine right behind her.
"You made it!"

"We did. And we brought wine," he said proudly, holding it up for inspection. "Do you have a bottle opener?"

"If you go inside, you'll see the kitchen on the right. You should see one right there on the counter."

"Perfect." Marcelo leaned toward me and pecked a kiss on my cheek, then carried the bottle inside.

"It's so good to see you again," Jasmine smiled. "Please, make yourself at home." She motioned toward a small table with a bamboo umbrella shielding the sun. "We need glasses," she said, spinning on her heels.

"At least we didn't forget the wine," I chuckled. "I'm sorry."

"No worries. We always come prepared." Jasmine slipped back into the house leaving me alone with Alex. I sat with my back to the ocean, watching as she came down off the deck toward me with a drink in her hand. She tipped her glass back and took a sip, looking out toward the water when she sat across from me.

The air got awkward but not entirely bad. I didn't quite understand my attraction to her, but it tugged at me each time we were close. I had a small window of opportunity to break the ice, and I took it.

"How do you like it here?" It was a bad opening line, but it was an opening line.

She shrugged, her eyes shifting to me. "It's more her thing. I'm not much for the outdoors and beachy shit."

"It's nice, I think. Good for the soul. What are you drinking? Whiskey?"

"Sazerac. It's got bourbon in it." She held her glass out toward me.

I reached across the table and wrapped my hand around it, my fingers grazing her hand. I tipped it back and let the cold liquid spread across my tongue. "It's sweet, but still burns going down."

"Exactly." She smiled playfully. "Just how I like it."

Was she flirting with me? "So, what else do you like?"

Her gaze hardened. "You really want to know?"

My muscles contracted, bringing my awareness to my sexual appetite. "I do. I wouldn't have asked if I didn't."

I held her stare and fought to maintain my composure as she shifted toward me.

"I only found three." Jasmine popped out from inside holding three wine glasses and a mug, with Marcelo following close behind her with the open bottle of wine. Alex stood up abruptly, turned back around, and went back onto the deck to tend to the clams. This was going to be a long day.

After an incredible lunch and an empty wine bottle, Jasmine broke out the mimosas. "I think it's time to celebrate."

"We really should be getting back," I said, glancing at Alex.

"But we are having so much fun." Jasmine stuck her lower lip out.

"One more won't do any harm," Marcelo insisted, his hand sliding over my knee.

"I suppose not," I smiled, sliding my glass toward them. I didn't like the way I was feeling; a little on edge, a little flirty, a little daring that grew with each sip of my drink, and extremely aroused. I concentrated on anything but Alex while they chatted about life, giggled at Marcelo's terrible jokes, and Jasmine talked about their relationship.

"Yeah," Jasmine cooed. "We met at a wedding. Neither of us was looking for love but there it was." She took Alex's hand and gazed at her, while Alex suffered through the story. Her face was flushed and the smirk on her lips divulged how much it embarrassed her.

"Alex's parents were pushing her to dance with some guy she couldn't stand just to prove she wasn't gay, so she rebelled and grabbed my hand on her way to his table. She held me close, and we danced three dances in a row, slowly, whether the song intended for a slow dance or not. We've been together ever since. That was, what?" She asked her, cocking her head inquisitively. "Two years ago?"

"Something like that," Alex mumbled, glancing up at me.

"I think that's sweet," I said. "Sometimes I wished we had that sort of story." I tried sounding completely into Marcelo, but I didn't think I had everyone convinced. "We met at a music festival. Marcelo was there playing, and I loved his music. He found me when he was finished with his set and asked me out."

"And it has been heavenly ever since," he chimed in, kissing my cheek again. "Gaia is the best thing to happen to me. I've never been happier."

I forced a smile and finished my story, my drink, and stood up. "This was really great, but we do have to get back." I took Marcelo's hand and coaxed him up out of his seat.

"She's right," he said, following me away from the table. "It was super meeting you both. If you're ever in the New York area, look us up. We are in Manhattan. Marcelo and Gaia Romano. We'd love to show you the city."

"We may just have to do that." Alex fixed her eyes on me.

"Take care, and thank you, again." I pulled Marcelo along, turning away from Alex and Jasmine with a fast-beating heart.

We walked along the beach line, my sandals in my hand, silent for the first few minutes.

"Remind me again, why we had to go so soon?"

"We have a lot to do before we leave tomorrow, and I'm not feeling all that well. I think the wine sort of went to my head."

"Aw, baby." He hooked my arm into his and rubbed it sympathetically. "When we get back, I'll draw you a nice hot bath with lots of bubbles."

"I think I just need to lie down for a little while. A nap will do me good."

"Then a nap it will be. I'll go into town and get something for dinner."

Once I was nestled in bed, Marcelo did what he promised, leaving the house with a kiss on my forehead. I heard the motorcycle start up and speed away, my eyes wide open. I whipped the covers back and climbed out of bed feeling a little woozy from the wine and not sure what to do with myself. Grabbing a beach towel, I walked down to the ocean and spread the towel over the warm sand. Stripping my dress and other garments away, I set them to the side and sprawled out on the towel. The sun was warm on my skin. My eyes closed and I thought of Alex. She was so sexy the way she moved. I caressed my stomach with my fingertips and dipped them down into my pubic hair before grazing them over my mound. My mouth fell slightly open as my fingers slid into my folds causing arousal to stir. I slid my legs open and slowly circled my clit as the sun baked me. The ocean lapped at the edge of the sand as I imagined Alex's tongue lapping at my pussy. My breathing became ragged. My hips moved up and down. My finger circled faster. My arousal pushed me to the edge, and I came hard. My back arched up off the towel as I enjoyed waves of pleasure wash over me.

Getting up, I looked around me, not a soul in sight. I peered down the beach toward their beach house about a mile down, wondering if she had thought about me in the same way. I ran into the ocean splashing the cool water all over until I was in too deep to run anymore. I dove under and swam, savoring the feel of the water against my naked body.

~ ~ ~ ~ ~ ~ ~ ~ ~ ~

New York seemed busier than usual. It was probably the time we had spent away in a serenity that not even the birds knew how to rush by. I missed home, but I also missed the beauty of the beach. Once we got settled back into our apartment, I arranged for a cleaning company to stop by, caught up on emails, and began planning our next party.

Marcelo came out of the bedroom dressed in a nice dress shirt and his best pants.

"No," I pleaded. "You're going to work?"

"I have to."

"Actually, you don't."

He kissed the top of my head and grabbed a grapefruit on the way to the door. "I have a meeting with a record company. They are interested in my music. I can't pass this up."

"You didn't tell me."

"I did. You have been distracted."

I pursed my lips. He may have been right. "Sorry."

He opened the door and winked at me.

"Good luck," I called out as the door was closing behind him.

I let out a long sigh and looked around the apartment. I needed some action. Grabbing my purse, I hit Bryn's number and put her on speaker as I walked out the door.

"What are you doing?" I asked before she had the chance to say hello.

"Are you home?"

I nodded, "I am. Marcelo has a meeting with some record company, and I'm bored to death. Let's meet."

"You got it, girl. Coffee Project?"

"Something stronger."

"Let's meet at Bemelmans."

I bit my lower lip and smiled. "How about Stonewall?"

"Feeling daring, are we?"

"I just want to go someplace a little different."

"That is definitely different. You sure?"

"Yep."

"Okay, then. I'm on my way."

"Call Viv. I'll meet you there."

I hailed a taxi and within twenty minutes I was standing outside of the small bar. There were rows of gay pride flags hanging above it in protest of the happenings in New York a few weeks ago. It was something political, nothing of interest to me.

Walking inside, I felt a sense of freedom as if I were part of the community there and I was finally in a safe place. Bryn and Vivian weren't there yet so I bellied up to the bar and waited for the bartender.

"Hey," she said, her eyes lighting up when she looked at me. "You're a new face."

"Yeah, hi. I don't think I've ever been in here."

"Well, have a seat and enjoy. What can I get for you, sweetie?"

"I'll take a Sazerac?"

"One sweet bourbon for the pretty lady, coming up."

Looking around the darkened bar, I noticed a couple of women sitting at a table. They were holding hands over the table and seemed to be deep in conversation. The larger woman sporting tattoos up her arms and a large leather vest reached across and moved a strand of the skinny girl's hair out of her face. She tucked it behind her ear before returning her hand to the other three.

Another couple sitting on a window seat was doing everything but talking. One sat on the other's lap with her tongue so deep in her lover's mouth she was tickling her tonsils. One hand was up her shirt and the other one was fondling her ass cheek.

"Don't pay any attention to them," the bartender interrupted. "They are always in here doing that."

"Have they ever…?"

"Had sex here? No. I won't let it get that far. They live upstairs in one of the apartments up there and this is their excitement, I suppose."

"They seem happy."

"I guess. They have only been together a few months."

I took a sip of my drink feeling that familiar burn down to my stomach as I watched them. My face must have exposed how much I truly appreciated the mix of bourbon and slightly sweet liqueur.

"That good, huh?" the bartender chuckled.

"I'm… trying new things," I shrugged.

"So, what about you? You with anyone?"

If I told her I was straight, would she force me to leave? "I'm waiting for some friends. They are supposed to meet me here."

"Girlfriends?"

"Um, no. I don't have a girlfriend right now." I didn't lie.

"That's too bad," she smiled. "This one is on me." She tapped the top of the bar next to my drink.

I opened my mouth to say something, but thought better of it, deciding to enjoy the attention. It was why I was there after all, right?

The front door opened, and Bryn and Vivian walked in, Viv b-lining it directly toward me.

"Hey, guys," I smiled, hugging each one.

"Why did you choose *this* place?" Viv's eyes were wide, and she acted nervous.

"Why not? It's a little different, fun, could be exciting."

"People *died* out front a few weeks ago," she whispered.

"That's fake news," the bartender said, walking back to our side of the bar. "No one died. Promise." She dragged her finger over her heart in an x.

Vivian exhaled a big breath and mellowed out. She tended to be a little more dramatic more naive than she needed to be, but she had a sweet heart.

"What can I get for you?"

"Do you have White Claw?" Vivian asked curiously.

"I do. Lemon, watermelon, or black cherry?"

"Lemon, please?"

"I'll just take a glass of Merlot," chimed Bryn. "Let's grab a table."

After they got their drinks we sat at a table near the back, and I observed everyone around me. There weren't many there at the time, but as the day wore on it filled up with others.

Music played and the alcohol flowed nicely. I was getting used to the bourbon taste, but it was hitting me a little harder than I was used to, so I alternated a sip or two for water. Vivian danced with a woman she had met in the bathroom and seemingly couldn't detach from her. She pulled the woman to our table with excitement in her voice.

"You guys. You have to meet my new friend. Her name is Sasha. She is a talent scout from 42nd Studios and she is looking for some new girls." She leaned in, her eyes widening. "She said I was funny and there was something about me."

"It's good to meet you," I said, jetting my hand out toward the long slender woman. I shot Viv a 'be careful' look.

"Likewise. Your friend has a good chance at getting in with our agency. She has that certain something we are looking for right now. If she can act, she may just have what it takes."

"She's good," I confirmed. "Would you like to join us?"

"For a minute. I'm supposed to be meeting my girlfriend for dinner. She's late, as usual." She pulled a chair out and sat down, Vivian pushed a chair closer to her to sit as close as possible without being on the woman's lap. "Ah, there she is."

I heard the door behind me and watched as Sasha waved her hand in the air. She smiled, stood up, and slid her arm around the woman's waist.

"You're late," she said to the short-haired blonde woman.

"I'll make it up to you later." They locked lips and intimacy swirled around them.

I was entranced. She reminded me so much of Alex that my body instantly responded. Same haircut, same persona, same stance. It was uncanny.

"I'm sorry," Sasha pulled back a bit and smiled. "This is my girlfriend, Reese."

Vivian stood up, a slight pout on her lips. "I'm Vivian. This is Bryn and Gaia."

"Nice to meet you all," she said with a passive caution.

I couldn't stop staring at her. And I didn't until my phone buzzed. Marcelo texted me that he was home and had some amazing news, but he wanted to tell me in person. I hesitated to answer as I looked back up at Reese. Uncanny.

She leaned into Sasha and whispered something in her ear, seemingly a little on edge about being there. Sasha reached for her purse and I perked up. "Would you like to join us for a drink?" I spat. "I was just about to buy the next round."

"Just one," Sasha pleaded.

Reese nodded and sat down. The bartender noticed and came to our aid. We ordered, received, drank, and that round fed into others.

I picked up my phone and sent Marcelo a text.

Out with the girls. Sorry I didn't respond earlier. Will see you later tonight?

I set my phone back onto the table and gave Reese my attention as her girlfriend unraveled an epic story about one of Reese's embarrassing moments. It was obvious Reese wasn't pleased that she was being exposed in this way, but it didn't stop Sasha from telling it.

I wondered if all gay couples went through such torture. Jasmine couldn't wait to tell similar *epic* stories about Alex, even though it was evident she didn't want her to. And now, this.

I wanted to rescue her. The moment she looked at me I stood up. "Excuse me for a moment. Time to find the little girls' room." I left my things on the table and walked toward the bathroom.

"Hold up." Reese pushed her chair away from the table and joined me. "I'll come with."

We walked in silence to the back corner of the bar until we were in the bathroom.

"Your girlfriend seems nice."

"She's got to go." She leaned on the sink and looked at her face in the mirror. Her short blonde hair was spiked on the top. She wore a little lip gloss but nothing more. A tattoo sleeve wound down around her arm sporting skulls and a horrid-looking witch riding on her broom over the top of them all.

"You don't like her?"

"I do. But she's too much."

"How long have you been together?"

"A year."

"I guess it's better to find out now before commitment happens."

"I guess. What about you? Which one is yours?"

"I'm… um…. Neither of them. We are all just friends."

She nodded and stood straight. She watched me through the mirror.

"I'm married, actually," I continued. "Newlywed."

"A guy?"

"How'd you know?"

"Sixth sense. Thanks for the distraction."

"No worries. I'm sort of on one tonight, myself."

"Newlywed and you already need a distraction? Interesting."

"Not really. I guess I'm just used to doing things my way. But I can't be single forever. He's good to me. He's got a good family."

"That's important, I guess if that's what you want in life."

"You remind me of someone I met in Bali."

"Do I?"

"Her name is Alex. She and her girlfriend rented a beach house close to ours. The sad part was we all met the day before our honeymoon was over. Was probably for the best though."

She continued watching me in the mirror without saying a word.

"Sometimes I think I talk too much." I went into a stall to pee while her words played on my mind.

"I'll see you out there," she said, the door opening.

I didn't respond. "I'm an idiot."

Anyway, Marcelo deserved better. I wasn't going to hurt him.

When I went back and joined our table, Sasha was still talking about her story, giggling, and leaning into Reese as much as Reese hated that. I sat down and picked up my phone, opening a new text from Marcelo.

Where are you? Maybe I'll meet you out. Xxx

I slid my fingertips along the side of my phone before responding.

I'm leaving soon anyway. Will see you back at the apartment.

I finished my drink and stood up. "I have to get back."

"Aw, you should stay." Bryn pulled at my arm.

"Yeah, don't be a party pooper now." Vivian chimed in.

"Marcelo is home, and he has some big news. I can't keep him waiting."

Reese smirked and I despised her for wearing her thoughts like that.

"It was really good meeting you," Sasha smiled, holding her hand out toward me. "Maybe we can get together again, sometime. This was fun."

I shook her hand and glanced at Reese. "I'd like that. It was nice meeting you both." I stood up, directing my attention to Bryn and Vivian. "I'll see you both later?"

"Are you good?"

"Yes. No, stay. Have fun. Talk soon." I got out of there before I changed my mind and hailed a taxi on the street.

~ ~ ~ ~ ~ ~ ~ ~ ~

Marcelo was in bed watching television when I got in, his bare chest exposed from the blankets around his waist. "How was your evening?"

"Okay. We met up at Stonewall in West Village."

"That gay bar?"

"Mmhmm." I pulled my shirt off as I went into the bathroom.

"Why would you go there? It's a dive bar."

"Not at all. It was actually sort of fun. Something different."

"You always did like new things."

I turned on the water to the shower drowning out Marcelo's words. Stripping down the rest of the way, I went back into the bedroom to grab my nightshirt and Marcelo pounced playfully out of the bed toward me. He slithered up behind me and wrapped his arms around my waist. "So, did you get hit on by any pretty ladies? Do I have to beat a chick up?"

"No," I giggled, fighting him off. "I have to shower."

"Yes, you do. You smell like a whiskey barrel."

I went into the steam-filled bathroom and climbed into the shower where he joined me only moments later. Warm water ran over me raising goosebumps on my skin.

"You're so sexy," he whispered from behind me. His hand glided up my side while his other hand scooped up my soap and ran it across my stomach. With his mouth on my neck and his hands slipping across my skin my arousal awoke. He lathered the soap into his hands, set it down, and thoroughly cleansed me. I raised my hands to the wall above my head and closed my eyes to savor it.

His hands moved across my breasts and down my stomach. He pushed his hands between my legs and slipped them into my folds, working their magic to heighten my arousal. The water washed the soap away but did nothing for the exhilaration swirling around my insides. He grabbed my hips and turned me toward him, lowered to his knees, and lifted my leg to the side of the tub. I grabbed hold of the top of the shower door and held my breath. His tongue pushed inside me causing adrenaline to fly through my veins.

"Yes," I whispered. I closed my eyes, dropped my head back, and opened myself to him. Alex's face flashed in my head and I imagined it was her on her knees in front of me. Her tongue lapped at my pussy. Her hands were on my thighs pushing me apart to get deeper. When she looked up at me, it was Reese. I gripped the door harder, the tip of her hard tongue running over my clit repeatedly. My breathing was hard, ragged, heavy, and orgasm seized me. I shook, as he wrapped his arms around my waist and kept me there until it subsided.

He slammed the water off and climbed out, picking me up in his arms and carrying me to the bed. Our soaked bodies clung to the blanket as he pushed my legs open, settled his weight on top of me, and entered me. He fucked me hard and fast with no build-up to it.

My orgasm returned and threatened to take over again, working its way up, building slowly with pressure. He held my wrists to the bed, thrusting into me over and over again, grunting as he did it. I wrapped my legs around him only to feel him push them away. He pulled off me, grabbed my hips, and spun me around to my knees. I dropped down onto my hands with my ass toward him and lowered my head to the mattress. His hands caressed my ass cheeks as he pushed into me and fucked me from behind. His groin slapped my cheeks with each push into me, his movements getting more intense. He slammed into

50

me with a guttural groan from deep in his throat. His hands gripped my hips and he held me there. I could feel his cock pulsate inside me as he jerked several times.

I circled my clit a few more times with the tip of my finger until another orgasm filled me. He fell onto the bed with a smile on his face so wide it made me chuckle.

"Now we have to change the bed."

"I'll buy you a new one," he cooed.

I laid my head on his arm and grazed my fingertips across his chest. "So, what's your big news?"

"Remember that record company I met with today?"

I nodded.

"They are very interested. They want to sign me and start recording next week."

"That's great news."

"I have to fly down to Nashville for a few days and meet with some other people, but they love me."

"Nashville? What are you doing, going country?"

"I guess there is a market in the country genre for some of my music, but it's only a small part of it."

"A few days?"

"Four, tops. Do you want to come with?"

I hesitated, not because I needed to think about it. I didn't want to go. I was looking forward to some alone time, but I didn't want it to be too obvious. "I think I'll stay back. Do some planning for the party and maybe start a project of my own."

He kissed the top of my head, climbing off the bed and disappearing into the bathroom. "I need to leave in the morning. Is that okay?" The shower fired back up.

"Yes." The blanket had a large wet spot in the middle from where we were and I climbed off, pulling the blanket back. The sheets were still dry, so I went to the closet and fished another blanket out to make the bed. By the time I was finished, a clean Marcelo was walking in with a towel around his waist. He really was beautiful. He planted a kiss on my lips before losing the towel and climbing into bed. I took a quick shower myself before joining him.

The next morning, by the time I awoke, Marcelo was up, dressed, and ready for his trip. He walked in with half of a bagel in his mouth and a plane ticket in his hand. He took the bagel out with his other hand and leaned over me. "I didn't mean to wake you, but I do have to go. My flight leaves in two hours."

I nodded, pecked his cheek, and lay back down into the pillow. "Do you need anything before you go?"

"Only if you can fit inside one of my suitcases."

I smiled at how much he loved me. "When will you be back?"

"Hopefully by Thursday, but I'll let you know."

"Have a good flight. Let me know how things go."

"Will do. Kisses. Love you." He kissed his finger and blew it toward me before disappearing out of the room.

I heard his footsteps fade to the front door. The door closed and I was alone.

I walked around the apartment without a stitch of clothing on. It felt liberating. The smell of Marcelo's bagel still hinted in the air, so I grabbed one and pushed it down into the toaster. I went to the front window and pulled back the curtain to feel the sun on my skin. The people on the street were smaller than ants and the cars looked like little matchbox cars I used to play with as a child. I stayed there, leaning against the windowsill until my bagel popped up.

The rest of my morning was much like that. I talked with Vivian and found out her new connection with Sasha was a hit. She had an interview with them later in the day followed by drinks at Soho House with Sasha and a couple of others from the company. And yes, Reese was going to be there. I hinted about not having much to do since Marcelo was away and she invited me along.

I spent the rest of the day getting ready. It was more time than I had spent on my wardrobe and makeup since the day I met Marcelo. It also made me realize how badly I needed to update my closet. After finally settling on a short black sequin skirt and a white chiffon blouse that accentuated my black bra underneath, I found a pair of red three-inch heels matching my lipstick that set it off perfectly. I was probably overdressed but my excuse was an interview with an antique dealer to showcase some of my art.

The question never came up on why I had dressed so well for *just drinks.* By the time I had gotten to Soho House, Reese was leaning against the building outside. She looked a little pissed that I had taken so long.

"Hi," I said simply, stopping in front of her.

"It's about time." She dragged her eyes down my body and back up, connecting with my eyes.

"I didn't ask you to wait outside for me."

"I sort of got elected. Invite only here. If you're not a member you have to blow someone to get in. Just so happens…."

She didn't finish her sentence. Was she implying that she expected me to drop to my knees for her?

I would have.

She pulled the front door open and showed her card. "We are with the Rousche party."

"Go right into the Champagne room. Welcome."

I nodded at the maître d and followed Reese through the main dining room into a more private area. We walked in, but no one noticed we existed, so we leaned against the wall and waited for a moment to make ourselves known.

"This the first time you've been in here?" she asked.

"Yes. Honestly, I didn't even know about this place."

"Sasha has a lot of pull here. She likes to wine and dine most of her clients here. Makes her feel sophisticated, successful."

"I get it. Appearance is eighty percent of it."

"You'd fit right in," she said, eyeing me again.

"I don't usually dress like this." I thought about using the lie I had fabricated but I had a feeling she would have seen right through it.

"You look good."

My stomach knotted. "Thanks."

Reese tried to get Sasha's attention, but she was too busy with the others in her party. Vivian sat close to her and laughed at everything the woman said. That pretty much kept me out of the loop, too.

"Come on," Reese said, leaving the room. She seemed annoyed over anything else.

I followed her out and we found two stools at the end of the bar.

"They will never notice we are gone. What are you drinking?"

"Whatever you're having is fine." I watched her as she pulled a card from her pocket and set it in front of her. The bartender noticed and walked toward us. "Two maple whiskey lemonades please." The bartender nodded and walked away. Reese kept her eyes forward and twirled her thumbs around each other. "I don't know why she talked me into coming here today."

"She likes you near her. Maybe she feels more supported, even though she isn't paying attention to you. Just the idea that you're here…."

"We broke up this morning."

"Oh. I'm sorry."

She shook her head. "Like I told you last night, it has been a long time coming. I spent most of my day moving out of her place. She practically begged me to come with her tonight. Anyway, why are *you* here?" She turned toward me.

"Same thing. I came to support Vivian, even though she doesn't know I'm alive right now."

"You ever hook up with her?"

"Viv?" There was a little more shock in my voice than intended. "No. We are friends. That's all."

"Have you… ever? Hooked up with another girl?"

Her attention was dead on me, and her question struck me hard. How should I have interpreted that? Was she asking for future reference? Small talk? Did I detect sarcasm there? "That's a little personal, isn't it?"

"It is. And your avoidance in answering tells me a lot."

"And what is that? What does it tell you?"

"You're married, unhappily, but you feel obligated. You are interested in girls like me because we can treat you the way you want to be treated and pleasure you the way you crave to be pleasured, but you're scared to try."

Heat rose up into my face. "You have it all worked out in your head, I see."

"I don't think you've really been with a woman even though you may have dabbled in college. Your man comes along and treats you right and you make hasty decisions that tell you that you should be with him because it's the right thing to do. Now, you feel stuck." She leaned into me, her fingertips grazing my knee. "Am I close?"

Her touch tightened my muscles around my vagina and knotted my stomach tighter. "I have to go." I didn't move at first. Neither did she. When I finally climbed off the barstool she stayed. "Thank you for the drink."

She nodded and watched me until I turned away and walked out the door. I kept my composure until I was out the door and back on the street. I leaned against the next building, breathless and wanting. The night sky hinted around the city lights, but it was still early, and I did not want to go back home. I pulled my cell and called Bryn, but it went to her voicemail.

"Damn it." I hung up without leaving a message. Pushing off the building, I started down the street when a hand wrapped around my arm. I tried jerking away from whoever it was until I saw Reese there.

"I'm not playing games with you." She pushed me back up against the building.

I stared wide-eyed into her face. "What are you doing?"

"I want you, Gaia. And I know you want me, too. Why are we fighting this?"

She pinned her body up against me and pressed her lips into mine. My insides caught fire as she deepened the kiss. Her tongue played around with mine, a delicious hint of whiskey and lemon taunting my taste buds. Her hand ran up my chest and wrapped around my neck, holding me there as her other hand found my thigh. It inched to the inside and up underneath my skirt.

"You're so fucking wet," she whispered. "I knew you were hot for me."

She pulled my skirt up enough to cup my ass cheek pushing herself into me harder. She was sending bolts of sensation through me from every angle, and I didn't want any of it to stop. Her hand went between my legs and I let it, opening for her. My panties were pulled to the side and when she slid her fingers deeper, I wanted to lose it. I fed my hands up in between us, her breasts tight against her chest but still full in my hands. I wanted to touch them bare. I wanted my tongue on her nipples. I wanted to taste her. It was the only thing on my mind.

"Take me to your apartment." She pulled back, her eyes devouring me. I nodded, swallowing hard.

Everything I did from hailing a taxi, waiting for it, and climbing into the back was on the back burner of my mind. All I could think about was sex... with Reese... a woman. I was soaked.

She held my hand in the cab, her thumb pressing into the soft area between my fingers. She pulled my hand to her mouth and picked up my forefinger with her tongue. She inserted it slowly into her mouth, her tongue swirling around it and gently sucking it. I couldn't take my eyes off her mouth.

She slid her other hand up my thigh to my pussy and rubbed me through my panties, pulling her hand back and replacing my finger in her mouth with her own. She closed her eyes and tasted me. My breath caught. My pussy tightened. My heart raced. Was this really happening? I could hear my own breathing in my ears.

When we pulled up in front of my apartment, my legs felt too heavy to get out of the cab. Someplace in the back of my mind, I knew this was wrong, but I kept it shoved in the darkest place I could. If I didn't think about it, it was a problem I'd have to deal with later, right?

Reese climbed out of the cab after paying him. She took my hand and pulled me along until we were in front of my door. She fed her hands around my neck to the back and grabbed handfuls of my hair. She pulled me to her and kissed me the way I craved to be kissed, with her tongue, her teeth, her lips, and her soul. She fueled me.

I fumbled with the lock on the door, finally opening it. Hands on breasts, mouths on bare skin, hips pressing together. I couldn't get enough of her.

We stumbled and fell against the wall as she tried pulling my blouse off over my head. I unbuttoned the first few buttons and that gave her a better opportunity. She stripped me of it, yanked my bra down below my breasts, and bent down with her mouth. She sucked my nipple into her mouth and toyed with it until I could feel it in my pussy. I reached for her jacket and peeled it off her arms, grabbing at her pants. I felt clumsy, unsure of what to do, but crazily insane to get it.

She helped me out of my skirt then stood back and took a big breath. Her gaze shifted from one eye to another as she tried to read my thoughts. I was all naked except for my underwear and she had her pants undone looking hot as hell.

She held her hand out and waited for me to slide my hand in hers before she led me through my own living room to our bedroom. She sat on the edge of the bed. I sat next to her. Her hand ran up the inside of my thigh, slowly, delicately, softly. Her mouth was on my shoulder. Light kisses. Soft kisses. Her hand moved upward. She touched my pussy. My breath caught. I opened my legs. She slid her hand back and forth and I lay back. She joined me for a moment, then crawled down until her face hovered over my mound. I felt dizzy from breathing so hard. She tasted me a little, but it sent a sensation bigger than I had ever felt through me. She looked up at me and smiled, then tasted again. My chest heaved up and down with each breath I took. Her tongue pushed into me and her fingers were moving around in a way that brought my arousal to a very fast head then stopped and teased the hell out of me.

"Oh, God!" I shoved my fingers into her hair and pushed her into me, begging for release. She slammed my hands away and caressed my hips as her mouth sent me into oblivion. I thrust my hips up and down, sensations flooding me and drowning me in libidinous.

She sat up and watched my body writhe in ecstasy as it slowly dissipated. She stood up and lowered her pants, then her underwear. She wore a strap-on penis and caressed it with her hand.

"Does it turn you off?" she asked, staring into me.

I shook my head. "No."

I spread my legs and hungrily watched her crawl back up onto the bed over the top of me. Her face paralleled mine. Her lips kissed mine. Her tongue traced them. Her penis slid between my folds and inched inside me. Her hands buried themselves underneath my ass and she held on tight before she started fucking me.

I could barely hold on as my arousal swirled around me pushing my orgasm to a point where I couldn't think straight. I met her hips with each thrust into me feeling her lips on my neck as she pulled my orgasm out and held me there until it was done grabbing a hold of me.

She removed the strap-on and pushed her fingers inside herself, pumping her hand in and out aggressively. I stopped her, rolled her to her back, and moved my mouth down to unfamiliar territory. I touched her there, pulling her lips apart and exploring her. Her clit was large and swollen, glistening from her own juices. I licked her there and she jumped. I twirled my tongue around it, flicking over the top several times. She grabbed the blanket underneath her and tightened her fists, her back arching and her head going back into the pillow. I moved my tongue like a figure eight around the outside of her as I slid my finger into her. I hooked my finger and found her g-spot, stroking it until she yelled out and started gyrating her hips up and down. When she collapsed, I crawled back up to her and lay next to her side. I watched her in awe. She was incredible.

The bedroom door opened, and Marcelo stood in the doorway. My heart stopped. "Marcelo!"

There was no way to cover this up. Two women lying naked with each other, breathing heavily, their pussies glistening with their juices.

I jumped up and grabbed my robe, wrapping it around me. Reese snuck off to the bathroom leaving us alone.

He slowly walked up to me and I expected his hand across my face, but he did nothing at first. His hands fed up underneath my chin and around my neck, cradling my face in his hands.

I swallowed hard. "I'm sorry." My tongue stuck to the roof of my mouth.

"Don't be." His kiss was hard, fiery, passionate, and intense. His tongue urgently searched my mouth for traces of her.

I pulled away, completely confused.

"Gaia, this is what I've been waiting for. It's why I introduced you to Alex and Jasmine. I prayed that something would happen with them, but you were so damned worried about what I would think that you suppressed everything you desired to make me happy."

"You're kidding, right? You're okay with this?" I pushed away from him and almost felt angry. "Why didn't you say anything?"

"I did. Several times. But you'd shut me out, or you'd think I was just saying that to make you happy. I don't know, but I'm glad it finally happened. I knew if I stayed away long enough someone would tempt you enough."

Reese reappeared completely dressed and smiling.

"Did you know about this?" I pointed at her with an accusing finger.

"Not completely? But I was told enough to pursue you. I'm not disappointed. I hope you're not either."

All I could do was shake my head in disbelief. But one thing I did realize that night was how much I was in love with Marcelo. He always told me he knew I wasn't, but he'd change it. And he did.

~ CHAPTER 5 ~

Sex Games and Oral Orgasm - The Game

"How do you break down a complex mental process into something more understood? By dividing the process into smaller parts making them easier to modify and understand in part, thus creating a better understanding of the whole." I glanced at my door trying to ignore the giggles in the other room. Focusing back on my thesis, I continued reading. "Using two factors X and Y such that part Q is influenced by X but invariant with respect to Y, while part R is influenced by Y but invariant with respect to X. Given that these modules are functionally distinct…." I sighed as the giggling continued. Reaching toward my stereo, I flipped it on and turned it up enough to drown out my suitemates. "Continuing. If we are given pure measures such as FA and GR, each reflecting only part, we must prove that FA is influenced by X but not Y, while GR is influenced by Y but not X."

"You've got to be kidding me?" squealed a female voice from the other room. "That's so cute!"

I slammed my pencil down and growled at the door. Grabbing my water bottle, I opened my door and walked out with the excuse that I needed more water before continuing my thesis. I filled the bottle at the kitchen sink before poking my head into the living room.

Two half-dressed girls were bouncing around in their underwear on the couch cushions that were strewn across the floor.

"What are you guys doing?" I was irritated, but my tone did not portray that. In fact, it never did. I was always the easy-going one, but it didn't matter. "Claire. Stacy, come on. I'm trying to study."

Claire grabbed a small pillow and threw it in my direction. "Lauren, for God's sake. It's Friday. Take a pill, will ya?"

"And what would that accomplish? My thesis is due in less than a month. If I don't work steadily on it, I will not be finished in time."

Claire shot Stacy a look and I knew what it meant, but I didn't care. After this year was over, I would more than likely never see them again. Hell, I wouldn't be surprised if they never returned to campus. They were both borderline failing out of their classes. They were more concerned about the parties they attended and what they were wearing than passing their classes. I only needed the sleeping quarters. What they did with their time was none of my concern.

"Come here, Lauren." Stacy's face softened and she extended her hand to me. "Just for a minute."

I hesitated, but did as she asked, stepping over a cushion to join them on the empty couch. "What is it?"

"We have been roomies for a year and a half, and we both know how important your classes are to you. You're smart and you're going to be so successful in your neuro…psychiatry field."

"Neuropsychology," I corrected.

"Whatever." She waved her hand in the air. "The point is, you're *only* going to be successful in… that field."

"I don't understand what you mean."

"Lauren." Claire put her arm around me. "You have no social life. No fun. No sex. Nothing."

"I've had… sex before."

"That one time in your high school boyfriend's room doesn't count."

"It was more than once," I defended. "Besides, it's none of your business what I do. I need to…."

"Have fun. You need to have fun," Claire interrupted.

"No, I need to focus. My schedule is full, and I don't even know what I want to do with my life."

"We aren't trying to butt into your life, Lauren. We care about you. That's all."

"Yeah. We want to see you have some fun. Even if you don't go to a party and drink too much until you throw up. There are other things you can do besides shoving your face in your books all the time."

"Yes!" Claire jumped up. "You could go to the Collegiate Café and people watch, assess their brains, and figure them out."

"Find a hot guy and flirt obsessively with him until he's easily readable."

"Or, come out with us to a party and drink so much you puke."

I looked from Claire to Stacy and then back again. I smiled a big smile, then patted their knees with my hand. "I appreciate the gesture and the offers, but I think I'm okay. People watching is not really my thing, and as for the *hot guys* around here, I would rather watch paint dry. If there is any brawn, there is no brain."

"Who says he has to put a sentence together?" Stacy cocked her head. "Just flirt with him then fuck him. It's easy."

"You're easy," poked Claire.

"If you don't mind," I said, standing up. "I'm going to get back to my thesis. I don't intend on allowing *college life* to interfere with what's important in real life."

I walked back across the room but before I was able to get behind my bedroom door, Claire bit at me with her words.

"Work isn't everything, Lauren. You need to balance your life better or you're going to die old and alone."

"Whatever, Claire," I mumbled, taking a few more steps. I turned back toward her and crossed my arms. "For your information, I do not make this decision lightly. I have witnessed what *fun and recreation* can do to someone. I think I'm all set."

Claire erased her expression from her face and lowered her eyes to the floor. "I didn't mean...."

"I know you didn't. I'm sure you have all good intentions. But if you continue to go down the path you're trying to get me to go down...." Say it, Lauren. *You'll end up like my sister.*

I couldn't say it. Watching Kat destroy her life was the hardest thing I'd ever gone through. "Ugh, never mind." I pushed my door open and closed it quietly behind me. I bit back the tears and took a big breath. It took me a bit to get back into the breakdown of a complex mental process, but I shook all bad thoughts from my mind and sat down. Eventually, my determination persevered.

"If we are given pure measures such as FA and GR, each reflecting only part, we must prove that FA is influenced by X but not Y, while GR is influenced by Y but not X."

I glanced up at my door when the giggling began again. I had never met anyone who liked to flirt and play around more than Claire and Stacy. They loved to flirt with everyone they encountered, and when they weren't around others, they played around with each other.

Exhaling a big sigh, I closed my books, stacked them on top of each other, and shoved them into my bag. I pulled my sweater on and walked back into the living room expecting another lesson on life. But what I witnessed was more intimacy between them than wanting to inform me of how horrible my social life was.

I tried to be as quiet as I could to avoid conversation, but just before my hand reached the doorknob, Claire stopped me.

"Where are you going? Oh, wait. Let me guess. The library?"

"I have some research to do," I lied, still trying to be the easy-going one. No confrontation was my motto.

"Research." Her tone was dead but easily readable.

"I won't be late." I opened the door without looking back.

"We will be," Stacy giggled. "It's Friday night. I'm not staying in."

I closed the door behind me and sighed, leaning against it.

Claire's words muffled through the door. "At least she's going *somewhere.* It's better than being holed up in her room."

"Come here." Stacy's voice softened and I heard the smooching of passionate kisses.

I didn't know why, but I stayed there. I listened. I eavesdropped. I was intrigued. I knew why I stayed there. I cracked open the door and watched them. Claire's delicate fingertips ran across Stacy's breasts, through her top, and Stacy liked it. She dropped her head back, a moan escaping her lips. I gasped. She straightened her head and fed her hand into Claire's long black hair until their lips locked.

I stared, my lips parting slightly.

Stacy's tongue jetted out and teased Claire's lower lip then disappeared into Claire's mouth. Another moan wafted across the room to my ears. Who's was it? My mouth fell open, the tip of my tongue tracing my own lips. I reached up and cupped my breast as my attention got lost in their intimate scene.

Why was I so afraid of intimacy? Claire lowered her hand to Stacy's panties and wiggled them underneath the waistband. It disappeared behind the thin fabric and a moment later Stacy gasped, her head falling back.

"Yes," she cooed. "Oh, right there."

Footsteps echoing up the stairs around the corner interrupted my desire to watch and I straightened quickly, closing the door quietly. Forcing a smile just in time I nodded at the familiar girl who lived upstairs as she passed me in the hallway. Before I rounded the corner to the stairway, I glanced back at our front door, a tease of jealousy threatening me.

"Stupid," I mumbled, pushing the outside door open to the street.

The library was quiet, empty, haunting. I found a corner table and sat down for the next couple of hours where I absorbed myself into neurocognitive processes and experimental and clinical neuropsychology. Before I knew it, I was being asked to leave for closing which meant it was eleven.

If I knew my suitemates, they would have already left for some frat party or basement get-together by that time. I walked to the coffee shop and grabbed a coffee before getting back to the suite. There were still a couple of good hours in me before bed.

When I reached the suite, I heard noises inside.

"Oh, please no." I closed my eyes and hoped they had left the television on before going out. When I opened the door, Claire and Stacy were still on the couch, their faces lighting up the moment they saw me.

"Lauren! You're back." Claire jumped up and set her wine glass down before bounding toward me. Stacy followed suit.

I backed up to the door defensive to their actions. "What's going on? Why are you guys still here?"

"We have made some decisions. We need to talk to you."

"I figured you'd have gone to some party or something by now."

"Well, some things are more important than that." Claire took my hand and led me across to the couch. "Sit."

"I'm kind of tired."

"It's not a question, Lauren," she insisted.

Stacy popped in. "Yeah. It's an intervention."

"An… intervention," I repeated, my eyebrows raising.

Claire pulled me to the couch and sat down, pulling me down next to her. "Listen. We care a lot about you, and we are worried."

"About what?" I snarked.

"We get that your classes are important to you, and honestly, I'm jealous that you're so good at everything. Top grades, amazing academics, clubs, everything."

"Not to mention how beautiful you are." Stacy sat on the other side of me, her hand running down my long ponytail.

"You're the total package."

"So, then why the intervention?" As if I had to ask.

"You need a social life. You need friends. You don't seem to think so, but you do."

"I have friends," I bit back.

"You have associates or classmates familiar with the same stuff you're studying. They aren't friends. Jesus, you're closer to some of your professors than you are with students your own age."

"I don't see anything wrong with that."

"That's exactly what's wrong. You have that mentality."

I knew I weren't getting out of this conversation unless I pushed to the end. "So, what are you asking me to do?"

"One party. Come to one party with us. No books, no itineraries, just us."

I shook my head and opened my mouth to protest.

"Lauren," Claire said quickly. She scooted closer to me, her arm sliding around mine. "You're not going to turn out like your sister. You have too much control for that."

Her words hit me like a brick. An image of Kat lying on our bathroom floor flashed into my head. It was the last image I had of her.

"I can't do this." I stood up and shook the memory from my head, but they both pulled me back down.

"It's not going to be easy, but you need to do this." As Stacy leaned forward her eyes narrowed. I could almost feel her seeking some shred of vulnerability behind my attempted barricade. "You can't let bad memories destroy your life."

"How is my life being destroyed?" I defended. "I think I'm doing quite well."

Claire didn't seem to think so. "Why did you get into neuropsychology?" she asked. "The study of human behavior and why people do what they do?"

"What?" Her question threw me off.

"It's because you can't get any answers on why Kat died the way she did. Why she allowed all the bad into her life. You are the type of person who needs closure, and I get that. But wrapping your entire life around something because of bad memories is not the way to live a happy life."

"You seem to know all the answers," I said as tears welled up in my eyes. She was right, though.

"I know you aren't happy, genuinely. You soak yourself into the books hoping your answers will be there. But they won't be."

"Claire." I turned toward her to argue her point, but I had nothing. She was right.

"Just one party," said Stacy, plopping onto the floor in front of me. She rested her hands on my knees and looked up at me with innocent eyes.

"What do you say?" Claire chimed in.

"I really can't."

"Why?"

"I don't know."

"If you don't have a good time, we will never bug you again about trying to make friends. We will leave you alone and support you in whatever you feel you need to do."

"One party?"

"We will even let you pick what night you want to go out."

My anxiety level was already up at the thought of putting myself into a situation I didn't want to be in. But, if it got them off my back, I was willing to try.

"Fine," I said, wiping a tear from my cheek. "Next weekend should be fine. I'll plan for it."

"Yay! Saturday night then?"

"Yes." I nodded my head reluctantly, already trying to find a way to get out of it.

"You won't regret it. I promise."

"I already do."

The entire next week went by so slowly, agonizing my brain on the thought of going to some fraternity party with Claire and Stacy. I tried pouring myself into my classes, but my brain kept going back to the what-if-something-happens scenario. I had already made a plan to exit before it got too crazy. My own wine spritzers premixed and poured into a couple of water bottles didn't hold enough alcohol to get an ant drunk so I was good on that aspect too.

When Saturday afternoon arrived, Claire and Stacy couldn't wait to get their hands on me. I was pulled from my room and fussed over until I was wearing the perfect dress with the perfect shades of eyeshadow and lipstick, and my hair was styled to cascade down over my shoulders the way they wanted it to look.

"Perfect," Claire said with a smile.

I looked at my image and didn't recognize the woman looking back. The short black dress and heels were not something I would have chosen to wear. I did have to admit that I liked the make-up. It brought out my features nicely. I tried pulling the hem of the dress down.

"So sexy," Stacy chimed in. "You are going to knock 'em dead!"

"The only thing I'm knocking dead is this notion that you think I need to do this." I pointed at each of them. "Remember, you promised you'd leave me alone if I go."

Claire drew an invisible X over her chest and Stacy nodded excitedly before grabbing my arm and yanking me out of the room.

I only twisted my ankle three times on the way to whatever party they were dragging me to. "Where are we going, anyway?"

"You could say, it's a party in your honor."

"A... what? What did you guys do?"

"Come on." Stacy dragged me up the sidewalk and knocked on a large white door to a large red house with black shutters.

The sun was fading behind us as I tried to listen to any havoc being wreaked behind that door. As it opened, I followed them inside and was immediately offered a plastic cup of beer by a rather good-looking guy with a Sigma Alpha Mu t-shirt on. From my own research, I knew this fraternity was one of the better ones. They did a lot of community work and volunteered their time wherever they could.

"No, thank you. I'm not much on beer. BYOB," I smiled, holding one of my bottles up.

"Well, if you get thirsty the keg is right over there," he smiled, pointing into a corner. "Any one of the brothers or pledges will help you.

"Thank you. I appreciate that."

"I'll take it." Claire snatched the cup from him and took a big drink out of it. "Thanks, Todd." She winked at him before moving into the room further.

There wasn't nearly as many people as I had thought there'd be, but it was okay with me. I opened my drink and took a sip, feeling the tension ease up some.

Claire took my hand and led me inside further. "I guess there is a big party at Delta tonight, so there won't be a lot of people here."

"Bummer," I said, following her toward a group of people lounging on the furniture in the room.

"Everybody," she called out. "This is Lauren, my *other* suitemate. Lauren, this is everybody."

"You have another suitemate?" a male voice called out. "I thought it was just the two of you lovely ladies."

The guy was definitely a jock. His entire persona screamed quarterback, right down to the scantily clad female sitting on his right knee and the busty blonde on his other knee.

"Nope. We have a third and we finally dragged her away from her dungeon of a room to show her how the better half lives."

I glanced across the number of faces watching me and forced a smile, half wishing my drink had more alcohol than it did. I glanced at the front door, wondering how soon was too soon to excuse myself.

A strikingly beautiful woman stood up, her eyes locked with mine. She leaned across the coffee table they were sitting around and reached for my hand. "Lauren," she cooed. "You look a little out of place. Come. Sit by me."

I glanced at Claire and Stacy, I guess for approval, before taking her hand. Walking around the table, she moved over from where she initially sat and gave me space to *fit in*.

"I'm Sienna." She leaned toward me, sitting more on her hip closest to me. "Claire told me this was your first party and to treat you good."

"Did she?" I shot her a death glance.

"I love your dress."

I looked down at the basic black dress as her hand ran across my stomach and back again.

"Thanks," I mumbled, discomfort seeping in. For a lack of something better to do, I gripped my drink and took a mouthful.

"What are you drinking?" She was so close to me.

"Um, it's a wine spritzer. Something I made up."

"May I?"

No, you may not, I thought as I handed it to her. I watched her sip it and smile before handing it back to me. "Thanks. It's good."

Claire and Stacy mingled among the group, and the eyes of the others strayed as the newness of me wore off.

"Let's play a game." Sienna perked up.

"Since when do *you* want to play anything?" the jock blurted out.

"You're a guy, Jack. I don't play with guys."

He swung his arm around one of the girls to grab himself in the groin area and shake it. "Play with this tool. You'll never go back to pussy."

"In your dreams tough boy. I know what's good. You're not it."

I chuckled with a new respect for Sienna. I loved her confidence.

"So, I'm in."

I looked across the table at the voice, and I stared. He was beautiful. He didn't seem to fit the fraternity narrative at all. His hair was longer than the others, disheveled but sexy, which told me he wasn't a jock. Black rimmed glasses gave him a hint of intellect and the tone of his arms let me know he was into fitness. He smiled at me and I melted a little.

"That's Mason," Sienna said, leaning into me. "Definitely a good catch if you're into that sort of thing."

"You mean, dick?" Jack interrupted, laughing hysterically.

I leaned back, heat surfacing in my face. I glanced at Mason. Did he hear that too? He winked and smiled at me, and I melted a little more.

"In your dreams, jockstrap. Anyway," she continued, "this game is called Say It or Teach It."

"Never heard of it," said Jack as sarcastically as he could.

"Oh, you will," she grinned. I liked her a little more. "Someone asks you a question. You tell them a story of your experience on the subject. Then ask the same to someone else. If *that* person doesn't have a story, they are taught by someone in the group, giving *them* their first experience."

My stomach knotted and I glanced around at the others. This was not going to go well. I tried standing up without being noticed, but several eyes caught me. "I'm going to find the bathroom. I'll be right...."

Sienna grabbed my arm and pulled me back down. "Not yet," she whispered. "Trust me on this. You don't want to miss it. I'll go first." She cocked her head and looked right at Jack. "Lauren, since you're new here, I'll start with you."

I smiled an embarrassing smile and swallowed hard.

"Have you ever kissed a guy?"

"Yes!" I blurted, excited that I had a story to tell. "Billy Rothenstein. He was my boyfriend in high school. Not a very good kisser but he was really sweet."

The group cooed and chuckled.

"Okay, your turn." She leaned back and smirked.

I thought for a minute, and I was sure I knew what she wanted me to do. I tried choosing someone I thought had a similar experience. "Mason?" He looked artistic, down to earth, up for anything. How would I know? He was honestly the only one in the group I knew the name of, so I went with him. "Have you ever kissed a guy?"

"I have."

I wasn't sure why, but my heart felt like it skipped a beat when he confirmed it.

"A couple of times, actually. But the one I remember? Reynolds Chapman. He was a professor of mine. Taught me a lot." He stared directly at me and his grin captivated me. Tingles formed between my legs.

"What about you, Jack?" Mason asked, his grin spreading across his face.

"Fuck you, man! I ain't kissing no guy!"

"Then you're out." Sienna sat up straight. "Leave." She was curt and as serious as a heart attack.

"You guys are a bunch of fucknuts!" He pushed the two girls off his knees and stood up. "This is lame anyway. I'm outta here." He bounded out of the room, pushing through a group of people by the door, and disappeared outside.

"Wow," I said softly.

"Now that he's gone, shall we continue? Mason. It's still your turn."

"Sienna. I think I know the answer." He pursed his lips and leaned over the table. He nodded his head upward. "Ever kissed a guy?"

She slowly shook her head and leaned over the table, meeting him in the middle. He glanced at me just before they locked lips and a heated kiss was performed. A twinge of jealousy wiggled its way into me, but I pushed it away. I wasn't staying long anyway, and I certainly wasn't interested in any college guys.

"Mmm." She slid her thumb along her lower lip and smiled. "Very nice for a guy."

"Yeah, I am," he teased.

She looked around and rested her eyes on Claire. "Claire. Ever done a shot of tequila?"

"Just last week. A few too many to be honest. What about you, Lauren?"

"Oh, God, no. I don't touch the stuff." I made a face and shook my head.

"Well, tonight is your lucky night."

My eyes widened when I realized what I had just admitted to. "Oh, no. No thank you. I'm not much of a drinker."

"You're playing the game, aren't you?" Sienna leaned into me and put her hand on my thigh. I didn't know what it was about her, but I liked her touch.

I nodded quickly and pressed my lips together. One of the girls had gotten me that shot and held it in front of me. With all eyes on me, I took the small shot glass and inhaled deeply. Closing my eyes, I poured the contents into my mouth, trying to swallow it before my tastebuds had a chance to reject it. The taste of paint thinner filled my mouth just before the burn took over my esophagus and I did all I could do to hold my breath to avoid either coughing violently or throwing it back up.

The group cheered me on, and a few patted my back as if I had just won a gold medal or something. This game went on through the hour with a few more shots of tequila being offered to me as we played. I didn't care as much about getting out of there at that point.

"Claire, it's your turn to ask a question." Sienna smiled at me.

"Okay, Sienna. Have you ever been felt up by a woman?"

"Pfftttt." I waved my hand in the air. "I know this one." My words didn't want to form as easily as they did, but I gave it a valiant effort. I leaned toward Claire and whispered loudly. "I'm pretty sure she's a lesbian."

Claire burst out in laughter, covering her mouth, and turning away.

"I am. You're right, Lauren. In fact, my last lover felt me up on this very couch." That shut me up. "What about you?" She stared at me. "Ever been touched by a woman?"

My face felt numb. "Um, yeah." I looked away from her and scratched my head. "In school this one time, I um, went to this dance...."

"I think you're lying, Lauren." Sienna slid closer. "Are you lying?"

I nodded but I couldn't look at her.

"That thrills me," she said. "Do you know why?"

I glanced up at her.

"Because I get to be your first." She licked her bottom lip and gazed down at my mouth. She moved closer. The room around me faded away. Just before her lips touched mine, she looked at the others. Every eye was on us. "Not here." She grabbed my hand, pulled me to my feet and before I knew it, she was leading me up a staircase.

"Where are we going?" My head was a little fuzzy, but I kept up with her.

"Someplace a little more private. I want this to be good for you."

She pulled me into a random room at the top of the stairs and pushed me against the wall. I stared into her eyes and wondered if she was actually going to do this. Would I let her?

The warmth of her breath invaded my senses and she smelled like vanilla and mint. Her hands slid up my sides and cupped my breasts, and I remembered wanting to feel nervous and tense, but I didn't. I liked it. Her touch was soft, subtle, but demanding. Her lips brushed mine and the tip of her tongue teased my lower lip until it slipped into my mouth. She covered my mouth with hers and deepened the kiss, stealing my breath and feeding my body that nervous tension I had initially missed. I trembled uncontrollably as her hand slid down my stomach and between my legs. Her fingers massaged me there until I could feel my own wetness through my underwear.

"God, you're so soft," she mumbled through her kisses. "I want you, Lauren." Her mouth grew needy, her hands explored further, her body pressed into me tighter, and my mind wanted to explode.

A knock on the door interrupted our episode. "Are you at least taking pictures?"

I didn't recognize the voice, but it flipped a switch. I needed to get out of there. It was overwhelming.

I tried pulling away, but Sienna stopped me and cupped my face. "Listen. If you ever want to go down this path, let me know. I would love to see you again."

All I could do was nod before pulling the door open and fixing myself before joining the others downstairs. Sienna followed and gave the group a thumbs up.

"I'm gonna be dreaming about this one, y'all!"

They laughed and snickered, but I held my head up.

"It's your turn, Lauren."

I sat down and cleared my throat, looking around the small crowd. "Stacy, have you ever..." *what have I done in the past? Think Lauren.* "...flashed your boobs at a complete stranger?" I sat back with confidence remembering the concert my friends and I attended.

"I have not!" She smiled wide and instantaneously pulled her top up exposing her breasts for the entire room. She giggled and jumped around without a care in the world.

I shook my head. Why did that not surprise me?

"Have you ever had an oral orgasm... Lauren?"

Why is everyone targeting me? I stood back up and tried to invent an experience, but my mind wasn't working. I felt like an amateur and it was getting uncomfortable. "I have not, but I think I'm out. I had fun but I'm going to go."

"Aw, don't go. It's just a game."

"It's not... just a game. But that is neither here nor there. I'm going to... go."

"Wait." Mason jumped up and fumbled to get over to me. "Don't go." He stood in front of me and took my hands in his. "Stay. I like you. I'd like to know more."

"Knowing I'm naïve and immature compared to all of your sexually active friends isn't enough?"

"They are just being idiots. You don't have to play the game. But I would like you to stay."

I nodded, ecstatic that he wanted me there.

"Come here." He led me toward the back of the house and out the back door where a few stragglers hung out on the back deck. The night air was warm and the fact that Mason wanted to know me made me feel giddy. "You're new to this whole social thing, I get it. I was once there too."

"You were not."

"Well, no," he snickered. "But my little brother was. I helped him through it. There's nothing wrong with being innocent. There is something about you, Lauren. I want to help you." His fingers fed through mine and he pulled me closer. "I think you're so sweet." His kiss was so sweet. I didn't want it to end. "I'll get us some drinks and we'll talk, okay?"

I nodded and watched him disappear back into the house. Moments later he was handing me a glass of what he called the house punch. It was good, but strong, so I sipped it.

"Try this." He handed me a small white pill.

"I don't do drugs," I said, pushing it back to him.

"It's not… it's just… it'll take the edge off, make the party a little less suckish. Here, watch." He popped the same pill into his mouth and swallowed it down with a sip of his drink. "It's nothing. Just a little molly."

I watched his eyes. They were kind. Beautiful. I wanted so badly to believe him. I threw caution to the wind and took the pill from him. Without another thought, I placed it on the tip of my tongue and took a drink. He pulled my face to his and kissed me again.

"Are you really that inexperienced with sex?"

I shrugged. "I guess. I mean, I'm not a virgin or anything, but compared to everyone else, apparently I should have been born with a catholic veil on my head."

He chuckled. "You're funny. I like you."

"Thanks." I looked down and picked at the side of my cup.

"I'd love to be your first."

"What?" I stared up at him. "My first what?"

"Back there, your question was, have you ever had an oral orgasm."

"Um." I was speechless.

"I want to be your first."

My first instinct was to tell him no and leave quickly. Hell, if he'd have asked me the moment I got to the party I wouldn't have entertained him with an answer. I would have just left screaming, with arms flailing in the air.

But, in all honesty I was a newbie. There was a lot I didn't know. Where did it say I had to be in a relationship to experience life? The more I talked to him, the more I wanted to. I didn't have to say anything. He pulled me up to my feet and led me off the steps to the ground. We walked through a small, wooded area to a clearing by a small pond. It was calm, serene. He kissed me with more fervor, pooling me in the palms of his hands. I was slowly submitting to this gorgeous stranger and it intoxicated me.

He lowered me to the soft grass beneath us and hovered over me. The heat from his body seeped into me as his mouth explored mine. His tongue jutted out toward mine playfully as his hands worked my dress up to my waist. The occasional brush of his knee against mine. The drag of his fingertips across my bare thigh. The soft-touch he gave to my sex. It all heightened my arousal. Was this even me? Was I actually there underneath this beautiful man?

He pulled his lips from mine and hesitated, watching my eyes. His lips kissed my chin then lowered down until his next kiss was on my thigh. His fingers danced across my panties and he must have felt how wet I was from Sienna, and then from him.

I thought about the night that had already played out. So many firsts for me. A woman's kiss. Her hands on my body. And now…. I looked down at him as he pulled my underwear aside and swirled his tongue around my clitoris. My breath caught. Sensation poured into me. I swung my head upward and took in a deep breath as he pushed his tongue into my folds. His arms wrapped around my waist and he feasted. My head was spinning. My libido was raging. My body was on fire. I grabbed at the grass beneath me, my hips moving up and down along his face. When I didn't think it could get any better, he slid his finger inside me and slowly withdrew it, only to slide it back in again. Repeating this while his tongue drew a picture around my clit sent me into overdrive. With my mouth gaped open I pushed my fingers into his luscious hair, guiding him deeper, riding his mouth back and forth until an orgasm threatened me. I stopped and held my breath feeling it spread all throughout my insides.

A guttural moan groveled from deep inside my throat. My orgasm slammed into me and seized every muscle I had until it let go and left me breathing heavily on the ground. I dropped my hands from his head and relished in the moment. Complete satisfaction.

He stood over me, his eyes taking in the mess he had made me. He was delicious in the moonlight and I wanted to stay there and soak him in. He offered me his hand and reluctantly I took it. He helped me to my feet, and I adjusted my dress back down to a presentable state.

"Are you okay?" He pulled my face up to meet his.

"I'm more than okay. Who would have thought I would ever do something like this."

"You were incredible."

"I was?" I argued. "You did everything, are you kidding me? Did you go to school to learn that or something?"

He chuckled. "I enjoy giving women pleasure. That's all."

"Well, you're damned good at it. You must have had a lot of practice."

"I've… had my share."

"Have you been with a lot of women?"

"I won't lie," he said, nodding his head. "I've been with several people."

"People…. Meaning?"

"I'm bi-sexual. And I like my sex, a lot."

Arousal poked around again, confusing me. Shouldn't this be a red flag? Why was I this attracted to him, or the idea of what he could give me? Was I bi-sexual as well? I bit my cheek and smirked at the thought.

"I think I really needed this," I said, deep in thought about what I had done.

"Why do you say that?"

"For the first time, I haven't been pressed down about bad memories in my past."

"Do you want to talk about it?"

"No. Not really. I don't want to depress the night."

"Let me guess. I have turned you into a sex addict."

"Would that be a bad thing? "Anytime you want to do that?" I said, pointing back to where he lay me down. "You just let me know. Put me on speed dial, actually."

"Will do," he chuckled. "Honestly, if you like that, and you're up for some crazy shit, I've got some friends who'd jump at the chance to help you out."

A shiver ran through me. I inhaled deeply. "Friends?"

He stopped walking and turned toward me. "A couple of buddies of mine really like to fuck. They do threesomes all the time. No pressure though. I'll be right there if you want me to be."

"What if I said I might be interested?"

"I say I might be able to introduce you."

"Tonight?" There was the old me. Cold feet and ready to run back to my room.

"Only if you want. I know they would love to meet someone like you."

"What does that mean?"

"You're fresh, innocent."

My stomach was in a knot, but my pussy was tingling with excitement, and nowhere was there a bad thought of my past. I was feeling amazing and carefree, and I wanted more of what Mason gave me. "Let's go," I said, smiling wide.

He matched my smile, took my hand, and led me back into the house. He grabbed two drinks on our way into the living room and with a nod from him when he locked his eyes on two guys in the corner, they headed in our direction.

I leaned against the wall with my hands behind my back and tried to control my trembling.

"Hey, man." Mason slapped each of their hands as they approached us. "I want you to meet someone special."

Both of them looked me up and down.

"This is Lauren. She's new to the scene. Lauren, this is Randy and Charlie."

They were both tall and could have passed for brothers, each having sandy brown hair and brown eyes. I waved at them, my lips tight together.

"Lauren is possibly interested in trying a little soiree with us."

"Well, it is *very* nice to meet you." Randy leaned against the wall next to me, his arm over the top of my head.

"I, um…. I have never done anything like this before, but" I bit my lip and he swooped down and kissed me hard. He pushed his tongue into my mouth and dominated the area as his hand gripped my breast.

"That's all she needed to say," said Charlie. "I'll go upstairs and find a room. You have condoms?"

Randy pulled away and licked his lips hungrily. "Always."

"Listen, "Mason said. "Lauren is a sweetheart. Treat her as such. No rough stuff unless she asks for it." His grin was intoxicating.

"You're coming, right?" I pleaded with him.

"Well, I will be soon." He patted my behind and followed me up the stairs behind Randy. Charlie had already disappeared into a room.

I was so nervous; butterflies were fluttering around in my stomach. The moment I stepped into the room I heard the door close behind me. Randy and Charlie stood next to a small bed and they were looking at me as if they were waiting for me to start. I didn't know how. I didn't know what to do.

When I felt Mason's hands on my shoulders from behind, the butterflies went away. His mouth kissed the side of my neck and arousal stirred inside me. I closed my eyes to savor the feeling and when I opened them again Charlie and Randy were both bare-chested. Charlie was unbuckling his pants and Randy was rubbing himself through his jeans, looking at me like I was a piece of meat for his dinner. Another shiver delighted me.

Mason slid his hands down my sides and hooked his fingers under my dress, dragging it back up exposing me. As condoms were being passed out, my dress was being discarded to the side. This was it. I was about to become a slut, and the idea thrilled me. A sex toy for three college guys I barely knew. Somewhere between Mason's hands on my body and the other two disrobing, I lost my bra and underwear. I stood in the middle of them, their cocks protruding forward and their eyes hungry for me.

They closed in and I inhaled deeply, my breathing working a little harder. A mouth kissed my shoulder and worked down to my breast. It covered my nipple and his tongue swirled around the hardening nub causing a sensation to build deliciously. Another mouth bit at my neck while hands groped my ass and slid between my legs. Mason turned my head to kiss my mouth, his tongue teasing as he kept his eyes open to watch my reaction. I wrapped my hands around two cocks and started stroking them, remembering a porn show I watched with my ex-boyfriend one time. I tried mimicking what I saw, and it seemed to work. Moans came from their mouths as their kisses got rougher.

Teeth bit at my ear. "Suck my cock," Charlie whispered.

I got down on my knees in front of him and opened my mouth. The tip ran along my lip as I twirled my tongue around it. It felt natural, like I had done it a thousand times. He slid his hands behind my head and pulled me in, his cock sliding along my tongue until it filled my mouth. I sucked him, bobbing my head back and forth, my arousal surrounding me. I stroked Randy and Mason in each hand imagining what I looked like in their eyes. I worked Charlie harder, wanting to swallow him.

He pressed me in harder and his tip hit the back of my throat. His pubic hair crushed against my nose, but I held him there, my tongue stroking the side of him.

"Fuck," he whispered aloud, pulling out. He thrust his hips back and forth, fucking my mouth. He wasn't a big guy, but I loved the feel of him on my tongue. When he pulled out, Randy directed my head toward him. I hungrily obliged taking him into my mouth and sucking the tip. He was a little bigger, but I was easily able to fill my mouth with his mass. I stroked my lips back and forth along his shaft until he was panting, then I pulled away and looked up at Mason.

"May I?" I asked.

He still had his jeans on, unbuckled, and open in the front. He was so fucking sexy, I wanted him inside me. He stepped toward me and I inched his jeans down over his hips, leaving them mid-thigh. His dick sprung out of his pants and my eyes widened. He was twice the size of both Charlie and Randy and thick. I teased his tip with my tongue until his mouth gaped open. Twirling around him I tasted him on my tongue, and I wanted more. I adjusted my body in front of him and slowly took him into my mouth, filling it only midway up his shaft. He still had at least three inches to go.

"Can you fit me," he teased.

I stroked him with my mouth, preparing myself to try and please him. I pushed him to the back of my throat and tried controlling my gag reflex as he pressed against my tonsils. I pulled him out when I was unsuccessful and tried again. I sucked on him, easing him into my mouth inch by inch until the tip of his cock pushed against the back of my throat. I held my breath and opened my mouth as wide as I could. The feel of his mass stretching my throat as I pushed myself on him exhilarated me and I held him there.

"Oh, my God! Lauren! Yes." His head fell backward, and his hips moved back and forth slightly as he fucked my throat. I pulled back to get a breath and looked up at him. He was in heaven, his mouth gaped open, his eyes full of lust and his cock as hard as steel.

He picked me up off my knees and led me to the bed. He cupped my face and kissed me with fervor. He caressed my back, slid his hands down between my legs, and pushed his finger inside me.

Charlie and Randy came up on each side of me, their hands roaming my body, pinching my nipples, and slapping my ass. Mason slid his jeans off, pulled a condom from his pocket, and without taking his eyes off me, he rolled it on.

"Turn around, Lauren."

My name on his lips was so sexy. I turned around and knelt on the bed, my hands keeping me up off the mattress. Mason's hand ran across my pussy before he grabbed my hips and pressed his cock against me. He moved back and forth only slightly threatening to penetrate me until I was ready to beg him to fuck me.

He opened me and agonizingly inched his way inside me, stretching my pussy around his cock. I had only had sex with one other guy in my life and tonight I was going to fuck three of them. I buried my head into the mattress as the sensation of Mason's cock filling me pushed through every fiber of my being. He began slowly, his dick slick with my juices.

Charlie cupped his hand underneath my chin and lifted me back up to my hands. He sat in front of me, his legs wide. He directed my mouth onto his cock, and I sucked him all the way in. Randy stroked himself next to me while his other hand played with my breast. Each time Mason jarred me forward I pushed Charlie into my mouth as far as it would go, pulling my lips tight, and sliding them back off him until he grabbed my head and started fucking my mouth fast. He was moaning and I could taste him more and more. He shoved himself deep inside and cum filled my mouth. I swallowed him down, sucking his dick until it was clean, and he was limp.

I imagined what I looked like, a sex slut for pleasure, and it pushed me to a fast but very hard orgasm. I pushed back on Mason, my body shaking uncontrollably. He slammed into me several times, his hips slapping against my ass cheeks until he unloaded himself, grunting as he came. Randy took Mason's place once he moved out of the way and entered me easily. He slapped my ass and thrust into me a few times. I felt his thumb on my ass and the pressure was incredible. He teased me there while he rode me. They were somehow conversing amongst each other, because Mason chuckled, and high-fived Randy just before he pulled out and lined his dick up with my other hole.

My eyes widened. I looked up at Mason as Randy slowly pushed into my ass. I wanted to protest. I was scared to try, but I was also so excited and aroused it didn't matter at this point. I was ready for anything. I gripped the bed and tried to relax as much as I could. The further he pushed into me the more excited I got. My pussy was so wet, and I felt another orgasm swirling around me. I pushed back, rocking on his cock until I exploded, burying my head into the mattress.

Randy pulled out and I collapsed onto the bed, sated and exhausted. Mason sat next to me, his cock still semi-hard. He stroked my forehead while Randy and Charlie got dressed.

"That," said Charlie "was fucking insanely good. Thank you, Lauren for an incredible fuck."

"Anytime you're feeling like being a whore again, just give us a shout. We'll make you feel the part."

I nodded, smiling drunkenly at them. They left the room as they put their shirts back on leaving me and Mason alone on the bed. Moments later, my eyes grew heavy, and I fell asleep.

* * * * * *

I walked along the street my head still trying to wrap around what I did a few nights ago. I couldn't decipher my feelings. Was I embarrassed? Was I appalled? No. None of that. I wanted to do it again. The thought of calling Mason entered my mind a few hundred times since that night. Hooking up with him and his friends, I chuckled. Even saying it thrilled me. What was wrong with me? I had skipped my classes two days in a row and my phone was blowing up with texts and calls from my suitemates. Why didn't I care about any of that? My head was still in the clouds, still trying to figure my life out, still wondering where I went from where I stood.

They deserved something. I wasn't being fair. I pulled my phone and texted Claire.

I'm okay. Just trying to figure some shit out. I'll be home tonight.

The moment I sent it I shut my phone off and dropped it in my jacket pocket. I was still wearing Mason's shirt he had somehow put on me while I slept. I did a little shopping and bought some shorts and a toothbrush. That night I'd check out of the hotel I was staying in and go back to the suite.

It was time to get back to reality, even if I wasn't sure what that reality was.

I grabbed a wrap from a deli close by and found a bench in the park to sit at. Nibbling on the wrap, I watched a group of ducks paddling along in a pond.

"Hello." An older man cast a shadow on me, and I looked up at him. "May I?" He gestured toward the end of the bench.

"Please. Make yourself comfortable. I'm going to be going soon anyway."

"You seem troubled. I'm in the mood to listen if you want to unload."

"Unload. There's a perfect choice of a word. I think I'm good. But thank you."

He sat next to me and continued to watch me. His face was striking, bold, kind. "Are you sure? I have a good sense about people. I was walking by and couldn't help but notice you seemed to need someone to talk to."

Maybe it wasn't such a bad idea. He didn't know me. I could tell him everything. I learned that talking about bottled-up feelings helps get you to the end with a better conclusion. I was ready. I turned to him and took a big breath.

"Are you sure you want to hear my problems?"

"More than sure. I like helping people."

"I think I just turned a huge corner in my life, but I don't know where to go from here."

He crossed his legs and stroked his chin like a therapist would do. I thought it was amusing, but I *unloaded* everything to him.

"I've always been the one to pour myself into my studies, trying to keep away from the social scene and the drinking."

"Why is that?"

"My sister was in that scene, too much. It got a hold of her and she died… from an overdose. I found her on the bathroom floor that night and I haven't been able to get it out of my mind since then, until…." I took a big breath. "Until I went to a party with my friends."

"That changed you, how?"

"I met Sienna, and Mason, and Charlie, and…."

"They introduced you to something you were uncomfortable with, didn't they?"

"They did," I nodded. "Sex. There were a lot of firsts for me that night."

"Tell me."

"My first kiss from a woman. She touched me in places that aroused me more than I could imagine. Mason…." I couldn't say it, not to this man.

"Did he have sex with you?"

"To put it mildly. My first oral, my first with a man other than my ex-boyfriend, my first with three guys at one time. I became something I used to think was taboo. I was a whore, their sex toy, and even now as I talk about it, it thrills me."

"And you no longer allow the death of your sister to dominate your mind."

"Exactly. It was as if the sex was a gateway to my freedom. I don't know what it means, but I have this new outlook on my life, and frankly, it scares the hell out of me."

"Use it, Lauren. Use this new experience and mix it with your past pain."

"Excuse me? How did you know my name?"

"What?"

"You called me Lauren. I never told you my name."

He looked down as if he had gotten snagged in a lie. "Okay. You got me. I'm Steven Pernell, Professor Pernell."

"You're a professor at my college?"

"I'll be your professor during your senior year. I teach Neuropsychology and Human Factors."

"Oh, God." I shielded my eyes from him as my face heated.

"It's okay. I sought you out when you went missing from your classes."

"How do you even know me?"

"You'll be attending my classes. I like to know who my students are the moment they sign up."

"But, that doesn't explain…."

"Students talk. They've been talking about you."

Surprisingly, I was okay with it. I was surprisingly okay with a lot of things.

"Take the pain from your sister's death and use it to your advantage. Take your new sexual awakening and implement that into your life as well. There are a lot of different careers you can seek out after you graduate."

Like a light switch turning on, I knew what I needed to do. "Sex therapy. It's perfect. I can add some sex education classes to my schedule and teach what I love to do in my life." I was beaming with happiness. "Thank you so much, Professor. You don't know how much you helped me."

"I think you helped yourself by stepping out of your comfort zone. You just needed to be turned a little in the right direction. That's all I did."

I hugged him and wanted to scream to the world.

By the time I had gotten back to the suite, no one was there. It was around dinnertime, so the cafeterias were open. I took advantage of the quiet. I went into the living room and spread out on the couch where Claire and Stacy made out the night they intervened in my life. I slid my hand into my shorts and closed my eyes. Thoughts of Sienna's mouth on me sparked my arousal. I moved my fingers around my clit as I remembered what Mason and his friends did to me. I pushed two fingers inside my pussy and slowly moved them in and out until waves of pleasure threatened to dominate me. I worked them a little harder, a little faster, and ran my fingers over my nipple causing my orgasm to slam into me. I bucked my hips up and down moaning and enjoying waves of pleasure crash into me repeatedly. Feeling sated, I made my way to the bathroom, showered, slipped back into Mason's shirt, and sat down at my laptop to make changes to my schedule.

My phone beeped and I pulled it toward me. It was Mason. I smiled and opened his text.

Rumor is you've gone missing. Hope you're okay. I wouldn't want to think I had something to do with it. Would love to see you again. M.

The familiar arousal returned as I responded to him.

*No longer missing. Time to right what was wrong in my life. Celebrate with me this weekend. Bring friends. *winky face*.*

Taboo Explicit Short Sex Stories Collection:

Erotica For Adults- Threesomes, Cuckold, MILFs, Hard Anal, Bi-Curious, Femdom, Hot Wives, BDSM, Spanking, 69& Orgasmic Oral& More

Written By:
G.G. Goode

Goode Publications

Chapter 1

As I stood there, in the middle of my new apartment, I dumped the box on the ground and planted my hands on my hips. Well, there I was, ready to take on the world. Even if I had no idea what the world might have wanted from me right now.

I couldn't believe I had finally done it. Finally dumped Ron for good. When I had first met him, back at the tail end of college, I had known at once that he was everything that my family had ever wanted for me – rich, handsome, charming, all of the above. Oh, and he just so happened to be a raging asshole on top of all of that, too, but I didn't mention that part to them. Or to anyone.

But when we got engaged, I started to feel that creeping dread that I was doing the wrong thing. That sureness that I didn't want to be tied to this guy for the rest of my life. He had been my first real relationship – I wouldn't go as far as to call it love, because it had never felt that way to me, not a chance in hell. But I had lost my virginity to him, and I had soon learned that, even if you had never slept with anyone before, you could tell when it wasn't right.

And I knew it was never right with us. Never had been, never would be. After I'd graduated, and as the wedding day drew closer and closer like a meteor thundering towards my life, I kept on trying to find excuses to stay. I knew that my family loved him and loved what he could do for me – he was high society, the way that none of us had ever been before, and if I married him, we'd be front and center to get where we had always dreamed of being.

But that didn't mean that I was willing to go through with it. With any of it. And, finally, just two weeks ago, I broke the news to him that there was no way in hell I could ever marry his crusty ass.

Oh, it was a whole *thing.* My family was furious, his family were furious, he was furious. Even my friends were baffled as to why I had left him. I had always told them that things had been going great between us, even when it was a filthy lie. I just couldn't face up to the truth of what I was hiding, even when I knew that I should. But I was free – finally free, free of the man that I felt like I had been lumbered with these last few years. And I was going to live the life I'd always dreamed of.

And that started right here. With my own apartment. The very first place of my own that I'd ever had in my life. Nobody else to share it with, no other messes to clean up after – just me.

And nobody to keep an eye on who I was bringing in and out of here, either. I had lived with my parents till college, and they had been determined that I would stay away from boys for as long as it took me to get into a high-class college that suited them; I had pretty much been a social pariah, and I didn't blame anyone for treating me like one, either.

When I got to college, I had been so nervous about meeting boys that I had practically squirrelled myself away in my dorm room. Good for the grades, not so good for the ego. After that, I had started to go out with my friends. Or rather, they had coaxed me into leaving the house with them. And that's how I eventually came across him, Ron, for the very first time.

But that whole time, I was still human. I still found myself intrigued by sex, by everything that people got up to in the privacy of their own bedrooms and everything that they did outside of them, too. I knew that Ron was always going to be a lights-off-missionary kind of guy, and honestly, the thought of putting up with that for the rest of my life was enough to make my toes curl. And not in the good way.

And that was what I planned to put right with my new place. Go out there, into the world, and show it and everyone else that I, Jaida, was finally here and was finally ready to find out all the crazy stuff that I enjoyed when it came to sex and sexuality. Yes, I could hardly wait to find out how much I had going for me. And it started right here, with this apartment, with a place of my own that I could bring anyone at all back to that I wanted. I knew it was going to be a hell of a lot of fun. And I couldn't wait to see how far I could take everything.

"Those are the last of the boxes up," The mover, Jason, told me, as he leaned in the doorway. Maybe it was just the excitement of finally being here with him right now, but there was a fizz of a thrill in my belly as I turned to face him; his gray shirt had ridden up a couple of inches, showing off a strip of his strong abs beneath, and it took everything I had not to go sidling up to him and nuzzle myself against his strong chest.

"Yeah, thanks," I replied. I didn't have a lot to my name; Ron and I had lived together for two whole years, but most of the crap in our apartment had belonged to him. Almost as though I had always been looking for a way out and had finally just been handed it.

"You need help with anything else?" He asked me. His eyes lingered on me for a moment, and I felt a little heat rush up my neck. Was he thinking what I thought he was? And was I going to go along with it? Well, I had to start somewhere. And if this man really wanted to take it to that place...I sure as hell wasn't going to argue with him.

"Well, maybe," I replied, flipping my hair over one shoulder and taking a step towards him. I wasn't sure what it was about him, about the way he looked at me; maybe it was just because I knew I was finally free and could finally do anything and everything that I wanted to do. But I was attracted to him, attracted to him in a way that I couldn't imagine being attracted to anyone else right now.

And I was going to do something about it.

"Oh, yeah?" He remarked, cocking an eyebrow. I didn't even know his last name. I didn't need to. I took a step towards him. He must have been able to see in my eyes what was going through my head in that moment, and he stood his ground. It was strange to think that someone could want me, could really want me like this, but I needed to know that I was capable of taking what I wanted when it was right there in front of me. And that started right here, right now.

"Yeah, I need some help unpacking something in the bedroom," I replied, and I tilted my head towards the space that was going to be my room – I hadn't so much as put a mattress out there yet, but that didn't matter. All that mattered was that I got him far enough into the apartment that my new neighbors wouldn't be able to hear what we were getting up to. I didn't want them judging me before I'd had a chance to introduce myself.

"Sure thing," he replied, enthusiastically, and it was obvious that he was intrigued as to where this was going. How many times had he shot his shot, I wondered, and been left in the dust? Well, I was a single woman now, and I wanted to make the most of it.

I made sure to sway my hips pointedly from left to right as I moved, taking my time, feeling his eyes on my body as I went – it was a hot day in New York, and I was wearing a pair of shorts and a crop top, way more revealing than anything Ron would ever had let me put on.

Not that I was thinking about him right now. Not that I was going to think about him ever again. Once I was into the bedroom, I turned to face Jason again, and I noticed the way his eyes lingered on my body. I loved the way it felt to be the center of his attention like this, loved the way it felt to be the focus of everything for him right now. I tossed my hair over one shoulder and allowed him to draw close to me, my heart pounding so fast in my chest that I was sure he would be able to hear it from where he was standing.

"So," he murmured, his body mere inches from mine.

"So," I murmured right back, and I arched my back so that we were even nearer than before. My flesh was aching now, and I needed to feel him against me, needed to feel him touch me the way I had been craving all this time. I couldn't remember the last time my whole body felt as though it was on fire for anyone; I couldn't remember the last time I had craved, so desperately, the touch of another human being.

And, slowly, he raised his hand and let it rest on my hip, testing me, making sure that this was something I could take. I gasped, my lips parting, unable to hold in the desire any longer – and with that, he leaned forward, and pushed his tongue into my mouth for the first time.

I swear, my whole body sank against his like I was in a dead faint. I had never known the meaning of the word *swoon* before that moment, but the second he touched me, it became abundantly clear just what it meant and how it felt. His cock was already stirring to hardness beneath his jeans, and I pushed my hand up underneath his tee, feeling his strong muscles underneath his skin. His body was so new to me, so new and so exciting – so fucking hot, his hands moving to my ass to press me against him properly as his tongue roamed my mouth.

I had never been kissed like this before in my life, never been kissed like their whole life depended on it. His body was hard, strong, powerful, and he spun me around to push me against the door a moment later. His hands moved over me, across my waist, groping at my tits, down to my stomach and my thighs, as though he was determined to feel as much of me as was humanly possible before this was over.

He hitched me up off the ground, lifting me with ease, and slammed me back against the door; I wrapped my legs around him, unable to hold in a helpless little moan of want as I felt his rock-hard cock grinding against me through his jeans. I needed to feel him inside of me. Holy shit, I needed it so badly I couldn't think straight. I had to tell him, somehow, let him know that I wanted him, but I didn't know how to put it into words. I had never learned to talk something like this into being, but I was going to need to start soon if I was going to become the sex-vixen that I had always wanted to be.

I grabbed one of his hands, guided it to my shorts, and pushed it beneath the waistline; he took my guidance, moving his fingers beneath my flimsy cotton panties until they were against my pussy. His hand was rough, callused, but he could feel how wet I was, how much I wanted him and how badly I needed this.

"Condom?" He murmured into my ear. I reached into one of the boxes that I had dumped in here, and grabbed the brand-new packet that I had made a point of purchasing the moment I had gotten the lease on this place. I pulled one out and pushed it into his hand, and watched as he unzipped his pants and rolled the condom down over his cock. He was big, bigger than Ron, which meant that he was bigger than any other guy I had been with before. This made me more than a little nervous, but I calmed myself down. I could handle this. I could handle anything. I could take everything that the world threw at me. Especially when it was attached to a man as undeniably gorgeous as this one.

I wriggled out of my shorts a little, pushing them down my hips, and he ripped off my panties as though they were nothing more than a distraction in the way of what he wanted to get to. My legs spread, wrapped around him, finally I felt him pushing inside of me – and I let my head fall back against the door as the rush of pleasure coursed through me once and for all.

"Oh, fuck," I groaned, and he turned his head to kiss me again. This time, his tongue was hungrier than before, traversing my mouth like he was starving for me and wanted nothing more than to make sure that I knew it. He started to pound my pussy, going in hard and fast, driving himself into me in long strokes that made my whole body tremble. His lips traced down, over my chin, towards my neck, his teeth baring against my skin as though he wanted to take a bite out of me. I knew how he felt. My mind had all but switched off, the only thing that I was capable of wrapping my head around right now was the pressure of his cock spreading me open for the very first time.

He grabbed hold of my hips to keep me in place as he slammed into me. The sound of our flesh coming together, over and over again, filled the room around us, until I could do nothing but close my eyes and let the sensation flood through me. I could already feel my wetness slithering down the inside of my legs and I knew that it wouldn't be long until I reached my orgasm – I had always been easy to make come, even if my ex had never been able to work that out.

I wrapped my arms around him and buried my face into his shoulder, feeling his muscles moving as he filled me over and over again with his cock. My legs were trembling, the insides of my thighs twitching as he took me, and I groaned again, my breath catching in the back of my throat, as, finally, at last...

"Oh!" I cried out, letting the sound tear out of me before I could stop it – I knew that the people who lived in the apartments around me must have been able to hear everything that was going on in here right now, but I was finding it hard to care. All that mattered to me was the way my pussy was clenching around his length, the way he stilled inside of me as though the pleasure of it was too much for him to take. I was breathing hard, the pressure flooding out to each and every one of my nerve-endings until I couldn't think or see straight.

It didn't take long until I felt his cock twitch inside of me, the pleasure growing too much for him to take, and he came, hard, letting out something that sounded like a growl as he finished. I buried my face into his neck and breathed in his deliciously masculine scent, and wondered how the hell I had been able to go so long without giving myself over to someone like this before. It felt like my whole system was lighting up, my body responding to him in the way I had always known that it should, that it would, when I found the right person to make that happen.

"Fuck, you feel so good," he moaned, as he grinded himself inside me a couple more times before pulling out. He gently lowered me back down again, and I tried to plant my feet on the floor, but my legs were so shaky it seemed a miracle that I was able to stand upright. I leaned against the door behind me for support, and smiled at him, still catching my breath.

"Thanks," I replied, and he pulled me towards him and kissed me again. He liked me. He really, really liked me. He wanted me, and it had been a long time since I could remember being wanted by anyone at all, feeling that desire coursing through his body and into mine.

And I could already tell that this was going to be an addiction for me. I could already tell that this was everything that I had been waiting for this entire time. My whole system was responding to him the way that I had always dreamed that it would, and this was just the start – he was just the start.

And I was sure that I had plenty more to go before I got to the end of this journey that I was only just beginning. Plenty more men to be with. Plenty more pleasure to experience.

And frankly, I was more than ready to find out just how that would go.

Chapter 2

I hummed to myself as I arranged my knick-knacks on my newly constructed bookcase; okay, so it looked like it was about to collapse in on itself at any moment, but it was standing, and I would take it.

I was finally almost done with the set-up of this place, and damn, would I be glad when the whole thing was over. I had been working my ass off to make sure that it was all exactly as I wanted it; after I had waited so long to find a place all of my own, there was no way in hell that I was going to allow it to be anything other than totally and utterly perfect, that was for sure.

I had been tempted to hit up that moving guy again after he had left – he had given me his number, told me that I was more than welcome to call him up if I wanted to since he didn't live too far from here, but I had sworn that I wasn't going to get involved with anyone that soon. This was the single part of my life, and I was going to enjoy every damn moment of it. Not start calling up the first guy that I had sex with and asking him to keep coming over to see me.

I had a party planned for over the weekend, and I was looking forward to inviting around some of my old friends to check out my new place – since I had been the one to dump Ron, I had expected plenty of them to take his side with the break-up and stick around with him, but it seemed like, as with me, most of them couldn't wait to get rid of him. I didn't blame them; he was pretty boring at the best of times, and his work as an accountant had only limited the amount of stuff he had to talk about.

But for now, it was just me in here; I had taken the week off of work down at the café, and I was looking forward to resting up and taking some time to wrap my head around this new status that I was a part of now. The single life. Strange to think that I hadn't been here in nearly four years, since Ron and I had first met. Even before that, when I had technically been single, I hadn't exactly felt like it, because I had always been building myself up to so much as to leave my dorm room without someone by my side. This was the first time that I was going to be single and going to enjoy it. I wanted to look back on this part of my life with fondness, with all the memories that I'd need to get me through those cold nights when I was an old woman and had lost my mojo.

There was a knock on the door, and I abandoned the snow globe where it sat on the shelf and went to answer it, glad for the distraction. Honestly, this whole interior design thing wasn't really my bag. I pulled the door open, and, on the other side, found myself greeted by a couple a little older than me, who were wearing giant, matching smiles. The woman was carrying a basket, which she handed over to me at once, full of food and a few toiletries.

"Uh, hi!" I greeted them. She beamed at me.

"Welcome to the building!" She exclaimed happily. "We're always so glad to have new people in here. What's your name, honey?"

"I'm Jaida," I told her, extending my hand. "How about you?"

"I'm Courtney, and this is Paul," She explained, nodding to her husband. With his dark, messed-up hair, warm smile, and black glasses, he looked like the very cutest kind of nerd.

"It's really nice to meet you," I told them both. "And thank you for this, really. It's way more than I expected."

"Oh, that's just the kind of thing we do around here," she replied, waving her hand as though it was nothing to her at all. "So, is it just you in here? Or are you with your other half, too?"

"No, just me," I replied. "I don't have another half. At least, not anymore."

"Well, that sounds like a story worth hearing," Courtney remarked, tipping her head to the side curiously. Her long, auburn hair tumbled over her shoulder effortlessly, like she was in the middle of a shampoo commercial or something. With her near-glowing green eyes and flawless skin, she could have passed for way younger than she was, but there was something about the air of command around her that gave her away. As though she knew that she was the one in charge here, and wasn't afraid to say it.

"You should come around some time," she suggested. "Have dinner with us. I'm sure we'd like to hear all about it, right, Paul?"

"Right," He agreed. It was the first word he had spoken since she had opened the door, and something about it sent a shiver down my spine. Not that I was going to go wrecking my relationships with my new floor-mates by hitting on their husbands, of course.

"That sounds really nice," I replied, with a smile. It honestly did. I liked the idea of getting to know these people, making this place really feel like my home. I had to start over entirely, and that meant finding new friends as well, didn't it? I was looking forward to that part of it. Looking forward to everything that came with finding out the kind of person I truly was.

"Well, let's say Thursday night," she suggested. "How about it? If it works for you."

"Oh, yeah, sure," I replied. I had honestly thought that they were just being polite, but it was clear they meant it.

"Good," she replied. "We'll see you then, I suppose."

"I suppose you will," I agreed, and there was something about the way that she said that to me that made me wonder if she was flirting with me. And I liked it!

She nodded, and we said our goodbyes and I closed the door behind them. I could feel a little flush in my cheeks, and I wondered what the hell that was about.

But I found myself counting down the days till Thursday, wondering just what it was about them that had me thinking about everything that had happened. The way they had both looked at me, especially her. She seemed to want to sink her fingers into me, into my mind, and I didn't mind the notion of that one little bit.

I had never been attracted to any women. Well, I had never allowed myself to be attracted to them, that was for sure – growing up in my house, with my parents, the notion that I might have been attracted to anyone other than the most straight-laced boys that they approved of was totally, utterly and completely unacceptable.

But I would have been lying if I'd said that I hadn't noticed them a few times in my life. Not as much as I did with men, not even close, but enough that it made a difference. There had been girls in high school, friends that I had grown a little too close with, who I had become a little too interested in and who my parents had rushed to get me away from, as though they knew what was going through my head.

I had never so much as kissed a girl in my life before, though. Never so much as held hands with one. But I would have been lying if I'd said that it had never crossed my mind. And now, with all this freedom to my name, why shouldn't I find out what I had been missing?

I took my time getting ready for the date that I had with them – no, I couldn't call it a date, I was just being friendly with my new neighbors, that was it. But still, I used the toiletries in that little care package that they had brought for me, inhaled the deep, musky scent of the lotion as it sunk into my skin. It didn't seem quite right for just-friends. Almost as though it was meant for something else entirely.

I gathered myself and headed over to their place – she had popped a note under the door giving me the number of their apartment and making sure that I would arrive there when they were ready for me. I couldn't wait. I hovered outside for a moment before I knocked to announce my presence, but, before I could, the door sprang open, and I found myself face-to-face with Courtney.

"Oh, there you are!" she exclaimed. "I was just about to come looking for you."

She leaned towards me and planted kisses on each of my cheeks, the warm, amber-toned scent of her perfume filling my senses.

"Oh, I'm sorry," I told her. "Am I late?"

"Not at all, sweetheart," she replied, smiling at me warmly. "We were just so excited to have you here already. Come into the kitchen, Paul's just getting some wine for us..."

"Good to see you again," Paul greeted me. He was wearing a button-down shirt, with the sleeves rolled up, and I couldn't help but notice how strong his hands were beneath them. Not something that his demeanor would have filled me in on, but hey, I was more than happy to be surprised...

He handed me a glass of red wine, and I took a sip as I looked around the place for the first time; their apartment had to be twice the size of mine, easily, and it was gorgeously well-decorated and just beautifully put-together.

"I love your place," I told them, and Paul draped an arm around his wife's shoulders and smiled.

"Thank you," he replied. "Though I can't take any credit for it."

"Damn right you can't," Courtney shot back, and we all laughed. I was starting to relax; maybe now that a glass of wine was in my hand, I could let go of some of the tension that had been bugging me since I had stepped out of my apartment to come here. I wanted to make sure that they knew how much I appreciated their hospitality.

And just how far I was willing to go to ensure that.

"I designed this place myself," Courtney explained, as I took another sip of the wine, and Paul turned back to tend the stove where something deliciously fragrant was cooking.

"Would you like to see more of it?" She asked, and the way she phrased it, I knew she was talking about more than just the apartment. I nodded at once. Those eyes, pinned on mine, those lips, painted with a deep red – it would have been impossible to turn her down, even if I had wanted to. A desire throbbed inside of me, a desire that I had done my best to ignore for so long now that I had almost forgotten that it existed in the first place. But here it was, as insistent as ever, and I wanted to give in to the way that it made me feel.

She led me around the living room, where she pointed out some small, gorgeous sculptures, made from amber and granite – they looked as though they had been formed by the wash of a wave; soft, delicate and totally unique.

"We picked these up when we were in Italy," she explained, running her perfectly manicured fingers over the shapes. I couldn't take my eyes off her hands when she moved them, the way she caressed those sculptures like they could feel each and every touch that she made. I Wondered what it would have felt like to be in their place.

She guided me through to the bedroom, where a giant dark-wood bed was laid out with beautiful deep red covers; it was a far cry from the futon that I was currently sleeping on in my own house right now, but they didn't need to know that, right?

"I love your place," I murmured, as I cast my gaze around the room as a whole – I really meant what I was saying, too. There was something about the way it felt, the deep scent of incense that seemed to permeate every corner, that made my body light up with excitement.

Or maybe it was just because I was in the room alone with her right now. It was only the two of us here. And I couldn't help but wonder if her mind had gone to the same place that mine had right now.

"Thank you," She replied. I could hear it then, hear it in her voice – everything that I had been trying to pretend wasn't there, never had been. I wanted to turn to face her, but I didn't know what the hell I was going to say when I did.

So, when I felt her hands on my hips, it was almost something like relief. I knew that she was in the same place as I was right now – that her mind had strayed to the same delicious place as mine had. I turned to face her, slowly, taking my time, not sure what I was going to say when I finally met her gaze.

But there was nothing to say. Instead of words, she just sank her lips down to mine, and kissed me. She tasted like wine and wickedness and all kinds of fun. Her hands slid to my face, cupping my chin gently, her nails teasing against my skin and making my stomach churn with excitement. I couldn't believe I was doing this right now. I couldn't believe that I was actually going to go through with this.

She pulled me towards her, her touch more forward than I had expected, but I didn't mind. Her tongue parted my lips and she kissed me, slowly, sensually, like she was trying to taste every part of me. My hand, the one that wasn't still holding the glass of wine, was resting on her hip, and I couldn't believe how good it felt to touch her like this. How good it felt to have her body against mine. Her softness turned me on in ways that I never thought a woman could; I had believed, before this, that all I wanted was the hardness that men could give me, but she was proving me wrong in all the ways that she possibly could. And I wasn't going to argue with her. Not for an instant.

"Oh, didn't realize you were going to start without me."

A voice came from behind us, and I pulled back at once, turning to face Paul in the doorway; would he be mad that I had just been making out with his wife? My heart was pounding in my chest as I half-expected him to storm towards me and ask me what the fuck I thought I was doing right there in his house, but instead, a smile passed over his face that told me that he was enjoying every second of this. Courtney reached out her hand for her husband, and he moved towards us. My head was spinning – both of them? Both of them wanted me? I was still wrapping my head around anyone desiring me at all, but both of these gorgeous people wanted me and me alone...yeah, it was a lot for me to get through my head.

But as soon as he lowered his mouth down to my neck, his stubble brushing against my skin, as she kissed me once more, I knew that I had no problem at all with how all of this was going to turn out.

I had never had two people pay attention to me like this before. Let alone a couple as gorgeous as them – I could taste Courtney's lipstick, smudged over my mouth, as she began to kiss down my chin and over my throat, her hands coming to the buttons of my dress as she pulled my clothes right off of me. I hadn't bothered to wear a bra, given that my tits weren't that big, and when I felt her tongue twirl around my nipple, I knew that I had made the right decision.

Then, he was kissing me, pushing me back towards the bed – he was a little rougher than his wife, but I liked that. I liked the way that it made me feel. The contrast between them as he guided me back towards the covers made my whole body light up – I could already feel that flood of wetness between my legs, and I knew that it wouldn't be long till one of them gave me the relief that I needed so badly.

"You know, we've been talking about this since we first saw you move into the building," he murmured into my ear. The thought of it sent a hot shiver down my spine, that he traced with his hand, as she pulled my other nipple into her mouth. I looked down at her, at the lipstick smudged over my breasts, and wondered how the hell I was ever going to top this. I was barely a couple of weeks out of my old relationship, and I had already found something that made my whole heart feel as though it was going to explode. Did it get any better than this? And if it did...how?

"Show me," I breathed back to him. I didn't know how I wanted them to touch me, just knew that I had to feel it – had to feel them all over me, their hands hungry for every inch of my body. I couldn't remember the last time that my brain had been so fogged by desire, but I was more than willing to give in to it, to let it rush through me like this.

"With pleasure," he murmured back, and he guided his wife's head down, down between my legs, down until it was just an inch from my aching pussy. I felt her fingers brush down my hips, hooking around the edges of my panties as she eased them off me. She wasn't like that mover guy I had been with when I had first arrived, rough, hungry and forceful, she was careful, delicate, as though she was enjoying each and every moment of this and didn't want me to forget it.

I watched as he guided her head against my pussy for the first time, as her lacquered lips found my soaking-wet sex – I had no idea how I expected it to feel, but the shock of pleasure as it hit me was nearly more than I could take. Her mouth was warm and hungry for me, and this was clearly far from the first time that she had done something like this. Her touch was electric, every caress of her lips against my clit making my entire body rise from the bed like I was possessed by something that was not myself. I grasped the covers as he kissed me again, the feeling of his tongue against my lips matched with his wife's between my legs driving me crazy. I arched my back, pushed myself against her, knowing that I needed more, more, more – more than she could give, more than I could take. I moaned against his lips, his hands moving to my breasts, pinching my nipples where she had just been sucking on them. They both wanted me so much, and I had no idea how much more I would be able to handle without exploding and just tipping over the edge the way I longed to...

She sealed her lips around my clit and began to suck softly, swirling her tongue around my swollen nub mercilessly, until the orgasm had started to teeter right on the edge of the release I needed so badly. I gasped, my nerve endings burning with sensation as I waited for it – and waited – and waited.

When it hit me, I buckled back into the bed in a helpless heap, unable to control myself. My legs were trembling, my entire lower body burning with pleasure as she continued to lap at my almost painfully over sensitized nub. Of everything that I had expected from this night, this was at the very bottom of my guesses – and yet, it was everything that I had needed.

She moved back up on top of me, smiling, her lips glistening with my wetness as she brushed her tongue over my neck, my chin, and back into my mouth. She seemed to be enjoying every moment of this, especially the parts where I could barely think straight as the orgasm continued to rock through me.

"Oh, honey," she cooed playfully in my ear, like she could see the way that I was feeling right now. "And we were just getting started..."

And with that, she moved to straddle my face, as she moved her mouth back down to my pussy once more. Her pussy was soaking-wet, smelled sweet and musky, and I couldn't resist extending my tongue and lapping against it for the first time.

Oh, God, she tasted good. As she continued to kiss along the insides of my thighs, the outside of my lips, my clit still pulsing against her mouth, I tried to mimic the way that she moved against my pussy with my tongue. Her husband was behind her, pushing her down on me as she rode my face, as she continued to mercilessly eat me out, filling my mouth with the taste of her pussy and the sweetness of her scent. And I knew that she was right. We were just getting started.

Chapter 3

I woke on the morning of the party, feeling more excited for this than perhaps I had for anything that I could remember in recent memory.

I was pretty sure they called it *getting your mojo back.* That was what it felt like, at least – especially the encounter that I had shared with Courtney and Paul just a couple of nights before. I couldn't believe that it had really happened the way it had, but the three of us had spent the whole night together – pleasuring each other, touching each other, tasting each other, like we were starved of everything else.

And then they had even made me dinner afterwards. We had curled up in their bed and chatted and ate and hung out and – well, it had to be one of the best dates that I had ever been on, if not the very best that I'd ever had the joy of experiencing. They were gentle, caring, took their time, never pushed me to do anything that I wasn't entirely sure of, and I was so grateful for that. Grateful that I'd gotten a chance to experience my first time with a woman in a place that was so safe, so welcoming, so open to exploration.

And now that I had...well, I was pretty sure I could safely say that I was anything but straight now. I had always known it on some level, I supposed, but now, it was even clearer than ever before. Even the mere thought of Courtney with her face between my legs had been enough to drive me crazy, and I knew that it would be far from the last time that I went out of my way to visit my oh-so-welcoming neighbors.

Anyway, I had other things to think about today – a party. All of my friends were coming over to see my new place. And if I was going to convince everyone that my new life was as amazing as I had sworn it would be, that started here.

I climbed out of bed and did my last circuit to make sure that I had everything that I had needed for tonight. All the drinks, all the snacks, all the food, all of everything – the music ready to go, the playlists picked out and refined down to perfection for everyone to have something to enjoy.

There was one person I was looking forward to seeing particularly – and that was Ian. He had been a friend of mine back in my first year of college, and he'd recently moved back to the city after spending a few years living in another state. This just so happened to be the first event that he was going to be attending since his return, and I was seriously counting down the minutes till I got to see him again.

I had crushed *hard* on him when in my first year of college. And the little light stalking I had done on social media had served to remind me just what a cutie he was. Tall, dark, handsome, all of the above. Though I had been way too nervous to even think about doing anything with him when we had been at college together, I was feeling a whole lot more confident these days, and I planned to make sure that he knew it. I planned to make sure that he could see how much I had missed him...

He had always been a bit of a player back when I had first known him, but I'd be lying if I said that wasn't some of the appeal to seeing him again right now. I had never really gone for bad boys, always convinced that they would break my heart too badly, that they would know how to play the game in a way that I would never be able to wrap my head around. But since my liaisons in the last week or so, I was sure that I had stepped up in the world, at least a little from what I had been when we had last known one another.

He was the one I was most excited to encounter again. I wanted to show him how much I had changed. Maybe *really* show him, if he was willing to take it that far...

Anyway, I wasn't going to let myself get distracted with a boy. Not when I was going to make tonight my grand coming-out as a single woman, one who didn't need a man to keep her company, not a chance in hell.

So, I got myself ready for my first house party, took my time picking out the perfect outfit – jeans and a tee, the kind that looked as though I had just tossed them on for no particular reason, but that I knew looked hot as hell on my body. Honestly, as I got ready, pulled my bouncy brown hair back into a ponytail, I wondered if I would ever be able to see myself as anything other than hot no matter what I did. I figured, as I slicked on some dark lipstick, similar to the color that Courtney had been wearing a couple nights before, that it was all about your state of mind, not how you actually looked. I was the same as I had been before, but now, I was better. Stepped-up. Sexy as hell.

And ready to take on anything that the world threw at me.

My guests started to arrive a little past eight, and I would have been lying if I said I didn't notice and totally enjoy a few of the looks that the guys gave me – even the ones who were with their girlfriends cocked an eyebrow, glanced back at me, as though they were making sure that I was really who they thought I was.

"You look awesome!" Kaylee, my best friend, told me as she rolled through the door, holding a bottle of wine and wearing a huge grin. She gave me a kiss on the cheek and looked around my new place.

"So, this is it, huh?" She remarked. I nodded.

"This is it," I replied, waving my hand around. "The bachelorette pad."

"I love it," she gushed, giving me a hug and squeezing me tight. She had been the one who had totally stuck by me from the moment that I had admitted that I didn't want to keep things going with my ex any longer; I think she had been waiting for the day that I was going to come out of my shell and come clean about what I really wanted, and now that I had, she was totally here for it.

"So, you going to get me a glass for this wine, or what?" She asked me. But my eyes had already slid back towards the door, where someone had just come in – none other, actually, than Ian.

"Give me a second," I told her, and I strutted my way over to greet him. My heart was pounding double-time in my chest and I prayed that he couldn't see how nervous I was right now. I was going to give him every inch of the confident, cool, calm, collected woman that I knew I was going to have to be to win him over. I didn't know if I would ever be able to get him into bed, but hell, it would be fun trying, right?

"So good to see you again, Ian," I greeted him, and I leaned in to give him a kiss on the cheek – the kind that lingered a little longer than it had to, making sure that I brushed my lips against the very corner of his mouth as I did so. He still wore the same aftershave as he had all those years ago, a deep, piney cologne that filled my senses and made my toes curl with excitement.

"You too," he replied, and he cocked an eyebrow as he pulled back from me, looked me up and down. "You look...different than I remember."

"In a good way, I hope," I shot back. He grinned.

"Yes, in a good way," he assured me, with a smile and his eyes lingering on the generous inch of cleavage showing above my shirt. I liked the way it made me feel, to have him look at me like that – I knew that, back in the day, he likely wouldn't have even bothered to glance in my direction twice, but here, now, I was the only thing that he could pay attention to.

"I'm going to grab a drink," I told him. "You want anything?"

"A beer would be great," he replied. He seemed a little shell-shocked by my attitude – good, that was just how I liked it. I loved the way it made me feel, the control that coursed through me when he looked at me like that. As though he couldn't believe what he was gazing at right now.

As soon as I reached the small kitchen area, Kaylee pounced on me, her eyes wide, and her head cocked to the side with curiosity.

"Okay, what the hell was that?" She demanded.

"What was what?" I asked her, playing innocently, as I went to grab a beer from the fridge for him.

"You were totally flirting with Ian," she pointed out. I shrugged.

"So, what if I was?" I replied, grinning back at her. "This is meant to be a bachelorette pad, isn't it?"

"Wait, I didn't realize you were going to take it that far," she replied, shaking her head at me in shock. "You really...you're really doing all of that?"

"Looks like it," I replied, and she burst out laughing, shaking her head.

"Well, I never thought I'd see the day," she remarked, brushing her hair out of her face. "You're going to become a regular little sex kitten, aren't you?"

"That's the idea," I agreed, tossing my hair over one shoulder demonstratively. I couldn't wait to tell her about everything else that I had been up to since I had moved in here – if she thought this was crazy, wait until I caught her up on the rest of it.

"But if you'll excuse me, I have guests to take care of," I told her with a wink, and with that, I swept off to bring the beer back to Ian.

"So, this place is all yours, then?" He asked me, as I handed it to him.

"It sure is."

"Last I heard you were dating that Ron guy..."

"Oh, he's in the past now," I replied, waving my hand.

"I can imagine," he replied. "I knew it was wrong. I can't picture him with someone like...this."

I laughed. I knew that had to be a good thing. I could feel the way he was looking at me right now, as though he couldn't believe what he was seeing. That was what I wanted from him. That was what I wanted from everyone. That focus, that attention all on me and me alone. I was the one in charge here, I had always been the one in charge. They just needed to catch up with me and figure it out.

I made my way around the room, glad that so many people had showed up – the place wasn't huge, so with twenty or so people there, it felt as full as any throbbing club on a Saturday night. It was strange, I had never really been the popular chick, but tonight, I felt like it. People were coming up to talk to me, to say hi, to tell me how much they liked my place, and I knew that I would turn this into the ground-zero for all the fun that my friends could have. I wanted this to be the go-to place, where they turned when they knew they were ready to have a seriously good time.

And, as I kept everyone entertained, I could feel Ian's eyes on me. A couple of other girls tried chatting him up – I knew that I was far from the only one from back in the day who had felt that lingering attraction to him – but he brushed them off, kept coming back to me, trying to steal a moment of my time wherever he could get it. And I knew that I had him right where I wanted him.

He found me once things were in the groove, and I was taking a break in the kitchen, sipping on a glass of wine and just chilling out. I knew that I didn't need to go over there and beg for his attention – it was all focused on me, anyway. That's the only thing that mattered.

"You throw a good party," He remarked, as he leaned up against the wall beside me.

"I know," I replied, and he laughed. He had a nice laugh – it lit up his gray eyes, showed off the angular features of his handsome face. He had cropped his hair really short since the last time that I had seen him, and he was one of the few guys who had the kind of face that could pull that off.

"Cocky, huh?" He asked. "Not something I expected from you."

"There's a lot that you didn't expect from me," I replied. "People can change a whole lot, you know."

"Oh, I believe it," he replied. His eyes were fixed to mine, and there was something almost more unbearably hot about that than there was about the way they had traced down my body earlier. I kept my gaze steady for as long as I could, but eventually, I had to pull them away. I could feel a heat between us, a chemistry, and I knew that I wasn't going to be able to contain it for much longer. I longed for him. I could feel my body, in its tipsy wisdom, shifting towards him.

"You want me to show you?" I asked him. I could hardly believe what I was doing right now, but I wasn't going to stop. Not for anything. Not when he was looking at me like that, and not when I was able to give him everything that he wanted.

"Show me what?" He asked, leaning towards me, eyes glittering with excitement. And, peering over his shoulder, making sure that nobody was looking in our direction, I decided that it was only fair to show him.

And so, I reached my hand out, and slid it over his package.

His eyes widened as soon as I touched him. He hadn't been expecting that, had he? But if there was one thing that the last few days had taught me, it was that there was nothing wrong with making sure that everyone knew just what you wanted – and that everyone was on the same page about how to get it.

"Come to the bathroom, and I'll show you," I whispered to him, flicking my tongue out theatrically over my lips. God, the way he was looking at me right now, as though he could hardly believe that I was real – this was what I wanted, this was what I lived for. The power that coursed through me when I knew that someone wanted me. Especially someone like him, someone who, in a million years, I would never have thought could even look twice at a woman like me.

He didn't move for a moment, clearly too much in shock to wrap his head around what was going on. And so, I pulled my hand back from his swiftly-hardening cock, and sashayed away from him, towards the bathroom – I shot a look over my shoulder as I went, telling him to follow me if he thought that he could handle it.

And, sure enough, I had hardly made it through the door when he followed me in. I knew that everyone would guess what we were up to in here, but I found it hard to give a damn, not when one of my all-time hottest crushes seemed to finally see me for what I really was.

I grabbed him by the collar, pushed the lock over on the door, and pulled him towards me before I could talk myself out of it. As soon as our mouths met, I knew that I was doing the right thing, I knew that I couldn't deny this. I needed to get him out of my system, if I was ever going to be able to move on from my crush. And I was going to do it with style.

He grabbed my hips and pulled me towards him, kissing me hard, his teeth catching on my bottom lip and sending a shock of pain and pleasure through my entire system at once. I ran my hand down the front of his pants, squeezing over his cock just the same way that I had done when we had been back in the kitchen, but this time, I didn't have to worry about anyone else seeing it. He was swollen beneath his pants, and I could already tell that he was thick and hard and ready for me. I scratched my nails over his shoulder and down his back, and felt the way he pushed towards me every time I touched him.

And God, the power I felt in that moment – the power of being wanted by someone that I had never thought would look at me twice, it was impossible to deny. I wanted to show him just what he had been missing. And I wasn't going to be satisfied until I had done just that.

I dropped to my knees in front of him, unzipped his pants, and took his cock into my hand. He was as big as I had expected him to be – given that he'd had girls running around after him everywhere he went in college, I knew he had to be packing something impressive. My fingers didn't even meet around it, no matter how hard I tried, and I could see the oozing drop of pre-cum that told me he was ready for this just the same way that I was.

"Fuck," he groaned, as he watched me admire his cock right there on my knees in front of him. I pressed my thighs together, trying to contain the wash of want that took through me as I stroked him up and down a couple of times. I loved the way that he twitched when I touched him, as though he could hardly contain his desire in that instant. I wanted him desperate for me – by the time I took him into my mouth, I wanted him to feel like it was the first time anyone ever had.

I had never been into giving oral sex when I had been with my ex – what was his name again? I swear, it was getting harder and harder to remember these days – but maybe that was because he had acted like it was something he was entitled to. I had never much felt like doing it because the way he approached it, it was as though I didn't have much of a choice – and if I was to deny him what he wanted, then I was being a bitch and he would get into a sulk that wouldn't be improved by anything until I did what he wanted me to do.

But here? Now? Ian was looking down at me as though he couldn't believe that he was being gifted with something so sweet, and the way that made me feel set worlds between my last experience of doing this with this one.

Playfully, I extended my tongue, and lapped at the very tip of his cock – I could taste his pre-cum against my lips, and he groaned loudly, clearly not caring one little bit if anyone heard us.

"Fuck," he growled, and he reached down to wrap my hair around his hand. His grip was firm, but it was clear that he was still leaving me in control right now, ready for me to do anything and everything I wanted to him. I held back for a moment, not quite sure how far I was willing to take this right now. Maybe I would get to my feet and just walk out of here, leaving him with a hard-on wondering how long it was going to be before I came back and gave him what he wanted.

Who was I kidding? I had been waiting far too long for this to hold off now. I planted a wet, sloppy kiss on the head of his cock, and then moved forward to take him into my mouth.

The fullness of his cock as he penetrated my mouth for the first time caught me off-guard. Maybe because I hadn't expected to like it so much, the way that it felt between my lips, or maybe because I had never taken another man into my mouth before this moment. He flexed his hips to push in a little deeper, his entire body tensing as he groaned with pleasure again, and I reached up to grip hold of his thighs, squeezing my fingers into his flesh and reveling in the delicious sensation of him inside of me.

I was going to give him the best damn blowjob of his entire life. That much, I was certain of. I ran my hands down his bare thighs, letting my fingertips trace against his skin, and felt for the way he moved as I touched him. I responded to every motion that he made to me, all the ways that he shifted and bucked to push inside of me, as I softened my mouth around him, running my tongue up the underside of his erection, finding that seam that ran from his balls to his tip.

I pulled back for a moment, suckling on the very tip of his cock, looking up at him with what I hoped passed for innocence in my eyes. His gaze was already a little blurry around the edges, as though he could hardly believe that this was really happening. I knew how he felt. All the times I had dreamed of being with him, it had never looked like this, never looked as rough and as passionate as this did.

But I was a different woman than the one who had existed when I had first fantasized about him – I was a different woman now, and I was going to make sure he knew it. I twirled my tongue around his tip, around the thick mushroom of his head, and then dived forward again to take as much of him into my mouth as I could manage.

His erection hit the back of my throat, so big that I almost gagged on it in shock, but I managed to calm my muscles before I made a fool of myself, pulled myself together – and pushed forward further. I stared up at him as I took his cock deeper and deeper into my mouth, feeling it stretch and push inside of me, the way that it opened my throat to drive itself deep, deeper, deepest.

"Fuck, Jaida," he groaned, and he ran his hand over my head as though he was marveling at the sheer gloriousness of what I was doing for him right now. I pushed deeper, determined to take every inch of him, until my nose was pressed up against his pubic hair. And, even though I knew it was ridiculous, I couldn't help but feel a thrill of achievement when I realized that I had managed to fit his whole length inside of me, just the way I wanted to.

"You look so good like that," he growled, as he tightened his grip on the back of my head and pushed me down a little deeper. My lips were throbbing, spread wide around his cock, but I didn't care – I wanted to show him just what he had been missing this whole time.

The moment that he pulled back from me, I caught my breath, a string of saliva attaching my tongue to the head of his cock. I was downright proud of what I had just done – showed what was possible when I was actually into the sex act that I was performing, right? His eyes were shining down at me, as though he was seeing me for the very first time, and I rolled my tongue around his tip again, almost casually.

"Good?" I asked. I already knew the answer to that question.

"So fucking good," he growled. And with that, he thrust forward once more, and began to fuck my mouth properly for the first time in my entire life.

And fuck, it was hot as hell. To know that I had driven this man, this man who must have had a million women a million different ways over the course of his life, to such helpless arousal that he couldn't even come close to controlling himself – that was what I wanted, what I longed for. I needed him to look deep into my eyes and see that I was the woman that he had been waiting for all this time, that I was the girl that could pleasure him the way no other could. I wanted him to walk out of this party totally and utterly addicted to me, no room for anything or anyone else, and that was precisely what I intended to do.

I grabbed his thighs once more and pulled him deep inside of me, until I could feel his full length down my throat, and allowed him to use my mouth as his toy. I could feel the warm heat spreading between my legs, and I couldn't help but push my hand down to find it, caressing my pussy underneath my panties, the wetness already slick against my fingers.

And it was like that, in that pose, hand between my thighs, that I took him over the edge. As soon as he saw that I was getting myself off to this just as much as I was pleasuring him, any control that he might have been hanging on to just vanished at once, and he let out a deep, throaty groan and came hard, in the same moment that I did.

I didn't pull back from him, not for a moment, allowing the flood of his seed to fill my mouth, taking every drop of it that I could and swallowing its warmth down my throat without a second thought. And I knew, as I watched him catching his breath above me, as I watched him tip his head back and growl with delight, that I had given him something that he was never going to be able to forget. Of all the women that he had been with, of all the girls that he had experienced in his life, I would be the one that he kept on coming back to in his head.

Because he had never expected this from me. And that would endlessly mark it out as a moment to remember.

I rose to my feet, theatrically flicked my tongue over my lips, and smiled at him. My pussy was still throbbing from the orgasm that I had just given myself, and my legs were a little shaky as I went to wash my hands and smooth down my hair.

"That was unbelievable," he murmured, grabbing my hips and pulling me back against him, nuzzling against my neck for a moment. I glanced at the two of us in the mirror and couldn't help but smile at the sight of us together like that. I had never imagined that someone like him would be willing to look twice at someone like me, and here he was, clearly already lusting for more.

But I had a party to attend, and I wasn't about to let him distract me from it. I knew that he would have done just about anything to keep me there with him right now – but honestly, that just made it all the more fun to take a step back and give myself a break. I would leave him wanting more, and surely, it wouldn't take long before he came back to claim it.

"Anyway, I have guests to attend to," I told him, lightly brushing him off of me. He raised his eyebrows. I could tell that he would have done anything at all that I asked him to in order to keep me here with him, but it wasn't going to work. I wasn't going to let that happen. I wasn't the girl who just gave in to any boys who looked at her the right way – no, I was the woman who took what she wanted and got back to her real life. Because I wasn't hung up on any one person in particular, and I wasn't going to let myself get pulled back into that place in my mind again.

"See you back out there," I told him, flashing him a grin, enjoying the amazed look on his face as I did so – as though he could hardly believe that I was really turning down the chance to enjoy more with him. I supposed that not many women had, in his time, but he was going to have to get used to it if he wanted me.

Because I wasn't stuck on anyone right now. I wasn't pinned down to a single person. And I was going to do everything that I could to make sure that I got out into that real world – and showed it just how much it had been missing when I had been tied down.

Chapter 4

I ran my hand over my hair, patted it back into place, and eyed myself for a moment.

It was the first day that I would be back at work since I had...well, since I had changed everything about myself. And I was, frankly, looking forward to seeing if any of the people I had worked with for the last three years noticed anything different about me.

I wasn't sure if there was anything different to notice, not really. Not on the surface, at least. But they hadn't seen me in a week, and that week had probably been one of the most eventful of my entire life. I didn't want to let anything get in the way of how much I had enjoyed it – and, more than anything, I wanted it to come with the assurance that I was a different person now because of it.

Between my moving day, my dinner with Courtney and Paul, and the party over the weekend, I felt as though I had run the gamut of everything that I had expected to experience when it came to my new sex life. And honestly? It had been so much fun that I wasn't sure I had been totally ready for how much I was going to enjoy it. Spending time with these people, learning about their bodies, watching the way they reacted when I touched them – there was a thrill to that which I was sure I would never grow tired of, and I didn't want to let it slip through my fingers.

Not that I intended to allow that to happen – not for an instant. But I needed to turn around some of the focus to myself, I was sure of that, make sure that I didn't let my own wants and needs get forgotten in all of this. I needed to remember that I was at the top of my to-do list. And now that I was going back to work again, I was going to have to work double-time to make sure that my own wants didn't get forgotten.

I smoothed down my work shirt, and headed out the door to the café. I had been working there since I had left college; my degree had been in English Lit, and, as the old saying went, it turned out that there wasn't much in the way of work for people who only cared about words. Not that I minded – the coffee shop that I had worked at all this time was one of those little hipster-y places, filled with people who seemed to enjoy writing and talking about books and about all their many, many projects that they were definitely actually working on and not just coming down here to try and avoid looking in the eye.

My boss, Helen, was already opening up by the time I got there, and she waved at me as she saw me coming down the street.

"Hey!" She called to me brightly. I didn't know how she always seemed to be able to approach anything and everything with such a warm attitude, but it was a skill that I hoped I might be able to adapt for my own one day.

"Hi," I replied, offering her a smile. I was still a little tired – catching up on my rest from a very busy few days – and I knew that work was only going to strip me of more of my energy.

"How was the move?" She asked me, as she opened the shutters and led the way inside. I nodded.

"It was good," I replied, trying to keep the smirk out of my voice, but she must have heard it anyway.

"Something up?" She asked, and I shook my head at once. The last thing my boss needed to hear about was my many exploits with people I should have known better than to get involved with. Hardly very professional.

"Nothing," I replied, and I hustled my ass over to the coffee machine to switch it on. "Anyway, how have things been here?"

I let her talk away to me, and found myself relaxing into the familiar chatter of this place as the normal slew of customers came through the door. I greeted each and every one of them with a fervor that I had never had before, and I swear, a few of them noticed it. The men, especially.

If there was one thing that I was figuring out about men, it was that they seemed to respond to the barest hint of attention that you headed in their direction. Like they were just holding out for a woman to give them the merest nod, and they would do everything that they could to please her and make her happy. It was a powerful thing, and I intended to make the very most of it.

One of the regulars who had been coming in since I had started working there, Tommy, approached the counter with his usual cocky swagger. He would flirt with whoever was behind the counter, man or woman, but today, he was going to be met with someone who was actually willing to flirt back for a change.

"The usual?" I asked him, already firing up the coffee machine in preparation for his order. He nodded.

"Glad that I made such an impression," he shot back.

"Or maybe you just come here so often that you make it impossible to ignore you," I replied. He laughed. It lit up his whole face – slightly crooked smile, brown eyes, messy, curly dark hair. The kind of hipster dreamboat which many women must have fallen for in his time. Many men, too.

That part of him intrigued me, I had to admit it. I had never really known a man who had so much as held hands with another dude before, and the thought of actually getting to explore that with someone who knew what they were doing in that arena was...interesting, to say the least.

I made him his usual coffee, allowed him to hit me with the usual conversation that he did whenever he came in here. But instead of laughing off his flirtation, I engaged with it, throwing it right back at him in a way that I knew excited him. I could hear it in his voice, that tension, that fascination. He wanted me. God, had it always been this easy to get men to desire me? And I hadn't been making the most of it all this time? It seemed ridiculous now, now that I knew how simple it had been, and I wasn't going to let that slip through my fingers.

"You know, I don't think I've ever seen you outside of this place," he remarked to me.

"I try not to be seen out of here," I joked back. "Makes it easier to keep up the mystique."

"I'd like to find out what's behind it," he replied, leaning back against one of the tables behind him. Wait, was this really happening? Was it that easy?

"How do you mean?"

"How about I take you out sometime, and I show you?" He suggested. I grinned as I finished making his coffee, added the last dusting of cinnamon on top of it and then handed it across to him. Just as I had suspected – easy to get him right where I wanted him.

"Sure thing," I replied, and I pushed the coffee over the counter towards him. He handed me the cash to pay for it, and then pulled out his phone and gave it to me as well.

"Put your number in," he told me, sounding a little shocked that it had worked as easy as that. "I'll call you, okay?"

"Text me," I replied. "I'm going to be at work. I don't want to get distracted."

"Sure, sure," he agreed, and his eyes danced over mine for a moment. I could tell that a number of lewd thoughts were rushing through his head in that instant, and the thought of them, what they might have been, thrilled me.

"Speak to you soon," I told him, and I turned away from the counter again, hoping that he couldn't see the flush to my cheeks as I did so. I couldn't believe that I had been so bold, couldn't believe that I had done something so daring. Couldn't believe that this was really happening to me right now, that I was really living out all the gorgeously sexy fantasies that I'd barely even allowed myself to have when I had been with that boring-ass ex of mine.

Anyway, I tried to stay focused on work, but something about the interaction I'd just had made it impossible to keep my head on what I was meant to be doing right now.

I knew that this kind of power would change me. That I would shift inside myself, move to find a new version of the woman that I had been all this time. But I hadn't expected it to thrill me the way that it did.

As I moved around the coffee shop, smiling at the regulars, bantering with the rest of the staff, it was as though I was hiding a small, sultry secret inside of me. A secret that I just wanted to spill to the rest of the world already – a secret that I wanted to make sure everyone understood the meaning of.

But I had to contain it, at least for now, and that was driving me a little crazy. I could feel people looking at me, feel their eyes on me, and it was impossible to deny how much it turned me on.

To the point that I was having a hard time even thinking of anything else. How could I, when this was all that seemed to be playing on my mind right now? By the time my break came around, I had to shut myself in the bathroom to gather myself, trying to find a way to make sense of the flushing floods of desire that coursed through my brain every time I let myself linger on what had happened over the last week or so.

I bolted the door behind me, and leaned against it to catch my breath. God, I was horny right now. I couldn't remember the last time that I'd been dealing with this hormonal flush of want, at least not since I was a teenager, but it seemed as though my brain wasn't going to let me forget about it anytime soon. And maybe I – maybe I wanted that? Maybe I wanted to give in to my base urges right now?

But I was at work. Just outside of that door, there were my colleagues, my customers, my damn boss. If I got caught doing something like this in the bathroom, I would be in so much trouble...

And the thought of that was enough to tell me what I needed to do. I unbuckled my pants, pushed them down an inch or two, and shoved my hand down my panties so that I could find some relief.

"Oh," I groaned, my whole body tensing up as my fingers pressed against my clit. Just like they had done when I had been on the bathroom floor, sucking Ian's cock, a few days ago. The memory of that was blended with the lust that I'd felt coming off Tommy, full-force, and I could almost picture him in front of me now, his hard-on in his hand, begging me to suck him off.

My fingers started to move with more force against my pussy now, and I couldn't help but slide them down, guiding them against my slit. I pushed one inside of me, and gasped, imagining that it was Tommy's cock – imagining him in front of me, begging to fuck me, willing to do anything if it meant that he could pleasure me the way he knew I deserved.

I was breathing hard, my whole body tensed as I fucked myself with my fingers right there in the bathroom at work. I knew that, if anyone so much as knocked on the door, I would be exposed, found out. They would be able to take one look at my face and guess what I had been up to, and honestly, something about that thrilled me even more. Maybe I wanted to be caught, wanted to be exposed, wanted to be found out as the horny little slut that I seemed to have become...

And it was with those words in my mind that I came, hard, against my hand, my whole body shuddering as I found my release once and for all. I groaned, biting down on my lip to keep myself quiet, and hoping that the music they played in the café would be enough to disguise the sounds of my orgasmic pleasure happening right beside them.

I held my hand against my pussy for a moment longer, and then, finally, drew it back, going to wash up quickly before I made my way to the break room for something to eat.

Not that I was hungry. Not for food, anyway. No, there was only one thing on my mind right now, one thing that I wanted to feast on.

And I was waiting for his text as we speak.

Chapter 5

I bit my lip as I leaned on the bar, glancing around and wondering how long they were going to keep me waiting.

Tommy and I had planned out this date down to the last detail – honestly, I had been half-expecting him to just back out and tell me that all of this had been nothing but a joke at my expense. Not like he couldn't have found someone to take my place if he had wanted to, and truly, I kept on waiting for that penny to drop.

But it didn't. In fact, when he suggested this fancy bar downtown for us to meet at, it became even more clear how seriously he was taking this. He really wanted to impress me. And I wasn't sure why, but I was still surprised that any man gave enough of a damn about me to make that effort.

I had picked out a dress for the occasion, something flimsy and flirty that would fall off of me at a moment's notice when the time came for us to go to bed. Because Tommy had a hell of a reputation, with men, with women, with pretty much anything that was willing. And I was going to make up that side of it tonight. There was something else, though, something else that he had peppered into the conversation when we had been organizing this. And that was the other man he was bringing with him. An old college roommate of his, who was in town over that weekend and who wanted to see some of the city. The way he had talked about him, it was clear that it was more than just a friend of his, and I was curious to know why he thought he should bring him along to our first date.

But I would find out soon enough. And I was sure that I was going to like what came of this.

I glanced over my shoulder, and, at last, I spotted Tommy heading through the door. He was wearing jeans and a blazer, with a button-down, casual but cute, and he was looking over his shoulder when he got there, chatting to someone else.

And there he was – the other man. He was a little taller than Tommy, blond, classically handsome in that old-fashioned way, and I would have been lying if I said that there wasn't a part of me that tingles at the thought of getting to enjoy his attention for an evening.

I rose to my feet as they drew closer to me, and Tommy greeted me with a kiss on the cheek – way friendlier than he needed to be, but then, he knew what I wanted from this night, just the same way that he did.

"You look gorgeous," he told me, his gaze drifting up and down my outfit.

"Not so bad yourself," I replied, and I smiled at his friend. "And this must be...?"

"Johnathan," he introduced himself, extending a hand to me with total confidence. Given that he was basically crashing a date, I wondered how he could carry himself with such certainty.

Maybe because he knew that he wasn't crashing at all. Maybe because Tommy had gone out of his way to give him an invite.

"It's so good to meet you," I told him, as my hand rested in his warm grip for a moment. He was confident, that much was obvious, and he carried himself with a cool, calm sureness that made me feel safe at once.

"Drinks?" Tommy suggested, and I nodded.

"Sounds good," I agreed, and I turned back to the bar. Tommy and Johnathan were either side of me, I was pressed right in between them, and I would have been lying if I said that there wasn't a part of me that was thrilled at the thought of being seen out and about with two such gorgeous men.

Tommy insisted on paying for our drinks, and he was able to grab us a table in no time; the place was packed, but it seemed like he had a certain pull here. I wondered just what he had going for him. It was obvious that he oozed confidence, had been from the first day that I had met him, but the rest of the world seemed to respond to it just the way he wanted them to – that was a skill that didn't come quite as easy, I was sure of that.

The drinks were luscious and strong, and it didn't take long till any doubts that I might have been holding on to about this flooded from my mind, to be replaced with the bright, flirty energy that a couple of cocktails could give to a girl. The two guys bounced off each other with confidence, and it was clear that they had known each other a hell of a long time to be able to converse as easily as this. Maybe known each other intimately, too – I noticed the way that they spoke, the way they shifted towards each other on occasion, and it thrilled me to think of the two of them together. You know – *really* together.

"So, how did the two of you meet?" I asked them, leaning forward with interest. I didn't know what I expected to hear in answer to that question, but damn, I was curious. I had never really been around men who had any interest in other men before – in fact, I think my ex and most of the people that he kept around him would have rather cut their dicks off than spend a minute in the company of a dude who might have been attracted to them.

"College," Johnathan replied with a grin, shooting a glance over to Tommy as though recounting all the fun they'd had there. "We were on the same floor together in dorms, and it didn't take long for us to find each other."

"You make it sound like we were dating," Tommy teased him.

"Oh, yeah, it was never like that," Johnathan laughed. "More...casual."

"Like how?" I asked, shifting forward again, lowering my voice to make sure that nobody else could hear me. Honestly, I wanted this just between the two of us. I liked the thought of it just being here, being secret – even though we were in a bar full of people, I wanted to keep all of this to myself.

"Like, I had never been with a guy before," Tommy explained, and I could hear that edge to his voice that told me that this was a hot little memory for him to pull up. "And then I met John, and I – well, I figured out all the ways that I was different from the people that I had grown up with, put it like that."

"Damn, you make it sound like I dragged you out by your collar," Johnathan laughed. "You were the one all over me, remember?"

I could feel the chemistry between them now, and it thrilled me. The thought of them touching each other, the thought of their bodies together – the thought of me between them, with them, getting to experience all of it right alongside them. I had to cross my legs under the table, hoping that they couldn't see how absurdly turned-on I was just from this conversation.

It didn't take long till things took a turn for the – well, for the more interesting. Tommy suggested that we go back to his place for another drink, and I found myself nodding along at once, no idea how to say no, no urgency to do anything but agree, agree, agree.

I wanted to find out what else they had going on under there. If the chemistry that they shared translated to something that might just be able to involve me, if I played my cards right.

Tommy poured us both a drink once we had reached his fancy little apartment downtown, and Johnathan and I sat on the loveseat together. His arm was draped along the back of the couch, lazily lying there like he was trying to hint something that he didn't know how to say. I shifted an inch or two closer to him, wanting this, wanting more, wanting as much as I could manage. I needed to see where this could take me. I needed to find out where this could go.

"Fun night, huh?" He remarked, and I nodded. I felt as though I was going to dive towards him at any moment, lean my body against his and just let this happen. But I didn't want to jump the gun. I didn't want to get in the way of whatever it was that they had here. I knew that the three of us were working our way towards something, and I would be damned if I passed up the chance to see what it was.

I had already been with a man and a woman at the same time. And I wanted to find out what happened when I was with two men at once.

I bit my lip and nodded.

"Really fun," I agreed, and his hand traced over the top of my exposed shoulder. I shivered. I wanted nothing more than to see where he was going to take this next. His touch sent a shockwave through me, and his eyes pinned onto mine, clearly daring me to say something about this. Daring me to do something.

"Have you ever been with two men before?" He asked me. His words were so blunt that they caught me off-guard, but I sure as hell wasn't going to complain. Not when he was looking at me like that, not when the mere sound of those words was enough to make my entire body tense up.

I shook my head. I didn't know how to respond to that with words, not when I could have just let him show me the way.

"We've done this so many times before," he murmured, and his fingers traced over my neck, up to my chin, where he caught it in between his thumb and forefinger. My lips parted. I wanted to feel him kiss me, but the anticipation was almost as sweet as the actual feeling of him going and doing it.

"Have you?" I breathed. "I – I've never..."

But before I could get the words out, he leaned forward, and pressed his lips against mine.

As soon as our mouths met, I found all the questions falling away at once. I knew that none of them mattered, not really, as long as I was just here with him – here with this man who made me feel so alive, who made me feel like my whole body had been built for him. As I heard footsteps, Tommy entered the room once more, I didn't even pull back. If they really knew what they were doing, then this would be simple.

I felt the weight of him beside me, his hand on my leg as Johnathan continued to kiss me, and I swear it took everything I had not to give in to their advances on the spot right there – I could feel my body crying out for them, for the power that these two men could bring to me. I wanted to be with them. I wanted to feel their strength, I wanted that inimitable masculinity to surround me, more than anything in the world.

Tommy's hand came to my face, and he turned it to look at him – he smiled at me for a moment before he kissed me, and the feeling of his lips so soon after John's was so perfect it made my head spin. Johnathan's lips found my neck, soft kisses marking a line down my throat and across my shoulder, his hands pushing down the straps of my dress so that he could go further, further, until his lips had found my nipples.

Tommy pulled back for a moment, looked down, to see what his friend was doing to me. He grinned, and I could see the flush of want in his eyes, the desire that told me I was everything he had needed.

"Fuck, you look hot like that," he murmured, and he pushed his hand through John's hair and held him in place. I had no idea whether he was talking to him or me. I didn't care. All I cared about was feeling the touch of his lips again.

With Johnathan at my breast and Tommy at my lips, it didn't take long for me to settle into the feeling of being at the center of their attention. I wanted to be shared by them, had by them – I wanted to be taken. I knew that I was just another one of the girls that they'd brought into this little set-up that they had, but there was no way that I was going to argue with that when it felt so fucking good.

Tommy's hand moved to the hem of my dress, and he pulled it up, sliding his hand across my panties so gently that it made me gasp. He glanced down once more, and this time, took his hand to Johnathan's head and pushed it down between my legs.

"Here," he murmured to me. "I know what he's good for..."

Johnathan pulled off my panties as Tommy sank his lips to mine once again, and I groaned as I felt his lips caress my clit for the first time. I was already so wet that I was sure I would soak him, but hey, they would take that as a compliment, wouldn't they? My hips were grinding back against him, loving this, wanting this, needing it. Needing more.

Johnathan really was good at giving head – his tongue swept back and forth across my clit and then circled in around it until my legs were shaking. It reminded me a little of the night that I had spent with my neighbors, but I knew that it was going to take an entirely different path by the time it was done with. I slid my hand down to Tommy's crotch, feeling the hardness of his cock beneath his pants, and I swear it was almost as though I was being drawn by some ridiculous force to feel him inside of me.

"You want me to fuck you?" He asked me, his lips trailing oh-so-lightly over my ear as he spoke. I nodded. I didn't have any other way to put it into words.

"Think you can handle both of us?" He wondered aloud. I bit my lip. I had no idea what that was going to look like, but damn, I was intrigued to find out.

"I think I can try," I replied, and I looked down to see Johnathan peering up at me from between my legs – his lips were smeared with my glistening wetness, and the sight of him like that was almost enough to make me forget what they had just asked me.

But, as Tommy brought me to my feet and guided me to the bedroom, I knew what was to come. These two men – I was going to have both of them at once, and I couldn't think of anything in the world more exciting than that right now.

It was different to the way it had been when I had experienced my very first threesome – there was something harder about them, more passionate, and I was already finding myself well and truly addicted to it. As Tommy pushed me down to the bed, flipped me over so that I was on all fours and facing away from him, I couldn't help but moan at the feeling of his hands on my ass. He spread me open, as though admiring me, and then leaned forward to plant a warm, wet, sloppy kiss against my slit. I gasped.

"Couldn't let him have all the fun now, could I?" He murmured, and he landed a playful spank on my ass before I heard him unzip his pants and reach for a condom.

Before me, on the other side of the bed, Johnathan was standing, gazing down at me like I was the most beautiful thing in the entire world. I reached out to rub my hand over the bulge in his pants, and he cocked an eyebrow at me.

"You want me, too?" He asked, and I nodded. I didn't even need to speak. I felt as though the three of us were on some other level far removed from conversation right now. We just understood what we all wanted, and we were going to do anything that we could to make sure that we gave it to one another.

He unzipped, slowly, almost like he was doing a striptease, and pulled his cock from his pants. Behind me, I could feel Tommy lining himself up against my pussy for the first time, just as John guided his thick tip to my lips.

I opened my mouth, extended my tongue, and swirled it around him, trying to recall everything I had done to pleasure Ian back in my bathroom. I wanted to make sure that I kept up with them. I knew that I could have just given in to the feeling of being nothing more than a pair of holes for the two of them to fuck, but that would have rather defeated the point of coming here in the first place, wouldn't it? If I was going to do this, then I was going to do this properly, and I was going to make sure that I was a conquest that they'd never forget.

As though on a practiced pace, they both pushed into me for the first time – and God, the feeling of them taking me like that was everything that I needed right now. The fullness was almost a shock; I had never struggled with taking big dicks before, but having two of them at once was something else entirely, and I loved it. For a moment, my body sagged, unable to process the pleasure that they were both giving me and keeping up my part in this – but then, I arched my back, and pushed my hips down against Tommy to take as much of him as I possibly could. I was going to do this *right.* I was sure of it.

"Fuck," Johnathan groaned, and I flicked my eyes up to meet his as I took his cock into my mouth. There was a furrow in his brow, proof that I was doing everything he needed me to right now, and I wanted to make sure that I gave him everything that I could.

Behind me, Tommy had started to pick up the pace, driving himself into me hard and fast. The roughness of it was contradicted and contrasted with the sensuality of the way that Johnathan was letting me blow him. The mix of the two men, of the two styles that they took when it came to taking me, was everything that I needed right now. I was being pushed forward every time Tommy moved into me, taking Johnathan a little deeper every time that I did, as though the two of them were using me as some toy to pleasure each other, a translator to turn each other on.

I thought it would have bugged me, being treated like that. But honestly, the way that they were using me right now, it was like I was a tool meant to give nothing but pleasure, and I was crazy about the way that it made me feel. The power, the passion, the intensity of the way they were taking me was everything that I needed right now. I wanted more. Wanted more than I could take. I wanted to be filled right up to the brim and then pushed a little further beyond that – I wanted it to rush through me, the fullness that they were pushing through me right now.

Tommy's hands came to my hips and he pulled me back, hard, thrusting deep into me, right up to the hilt, so that I could feel his heavy balls slapping up against my pussy with each and every thrust. And God, I was already close – the mixture of having Johnathan go down on me and then to be filled by this delicious, fat cock was everything that I needed right now.

Johnathan's hand came to the back of my head, and I gazed up at him as he began to push himself deeper into my mouth. The feeling of it shocked me, the way that he slipped into me so deliciously I could hardly make sense of it. I found my throat opening, ready to take him, ready to take everything that he had for me.

"You're so good at that," he murmured, and he smoothed my hair back, nearly tenderly, if it hadn't been for the fact that his cock was thrust all the way down my throat. I moaned around his cock, and watched as the vibrations moved up through his body, consuming him. I knew that it wasn't going to be long until he came.

I knew it wasn't going to be long until I did, either. I wanted nothing more than to finish, feel that rough clench of my pussy around his cock as the relief coursed through my body, and I wasn't sure how much more I was going to be able to take. As Tommy filled me from behind, as Johnathan screwed me from the front, I could feel that warm, welcoming rush of pleasure starting to grow inside of me. As though something was boiling inside of me, something fiery with want, need, and desire.

Tommy reached his hand between my legs and began to roughly massage my clit as he fucked me, as though sensing how close I was to the edge at that moment. With my mouth full of Johnathan's cock, it wasn't like I could make much noise to react, but he must have been able to tell from the clenching between my thighs how good it was.

"You nearly there?" He asked me. His voice was playful, almost mocking, as though he was teasing me for being so unable to hold back, and it only sent another surge of want through my system. How could it not?

He shoved himself deep into me one last time and held himself there, letting my pussy massage the contours of his cock – and it was like that, filled with dick from two ends, that I finally felt myself reach my release.

The pleasure consumed me, burning through me like a flame down my spine – Johnathan pulled back for a moment, letting me catch my breath, and I couldn't help but let out this desperate, hungry whine as the orgasm tore through me. As he felt my pussy clenching around his cock, it seemed to give him everything that he needed to reach his own release, and just a few seconds later, I finally felt him finish inside of me.

And it seemed to be the sight of his friend – his lover – finishing in my pussy that took Johnathan over the edge, too. I opened my mouth, told him that I wanted him back, and he pushed himself inside of me just in time for me to feel him finish down my throat. I was becoming quite the expert at making men come with my tongue, wasn't I? I swallowed it down without a second thought, enjoying the sweet sensation of knowing that I had been enough to take them both over the edge.

And, as they drew back from me, I felt my knees buckle as I dived forward on to the bed. I didn't know what I had expected from this night – what I had hoped for, maybe, yes, but not what I actually thought was going to happen. But this? This was everything that I had needed it to be. And I knew that I was far from done with these two for the night. Far from done, yet.

Chapter 6

Kaylee sat down and sunk in the couch and looked around my apartment once more; she seemed shocked that I was here at all, let alone that I had managed the first full month of my time alone so well. "I just can't believe that you really got out from his shit," she remarked, as she took a sip of the wine that I had given her when she had arrived. I grinned at her, lifted my glass in her direction as I sank down onto the seat beside her.

"Trust me, I can't either," I agreed.

"How has it been?" She asked me. After the party, she had been clamoring to get me to herself for a while, and I knew that I had so much to catch her up on it was unreal. It was going to be a lot of fun, I knew that she would hardly be able to wrap her head around the fact that I had come as far as I had – sometimes, it seemed impossible even to me, that I could have unleashed this sex-kittenish version of myself after keeping her locked up for so long.

"It's been kind of crazy," I confessed, and she laughed and sipped on the red that I had brought for us to share tonight.

"Yeah, trust me, I was at that party," she reminds me. "I think I know how crazy you've gotten..."

"Was it really that obvious?" I asked, pulling a face and pretending for a moment like I was totally embarrassed by the fact that everyone knew what I had been getting into. But, when she tipped her head to the side and raised an eyebrow, I dropped it.

"He walked out of there looking like he'd just met God," she reminded me. "I think everyone knew what was going on."

"Wish I could say I regretted it," I fired back cockily, and she busted out laughing.

"Where did this come from?" She asked me, waving her hand in my general direction, gazing at me as though she couldn't believe what she was hearing. "I feel like this is a whole new side of you..."

"So do I," I agreed enthusiastically. "It's just...I feel like I've been trying to keep myself under wraps for so long now, and I don't have any time left to do that. I've got to be honest. I know what I want, and it's..."

"To suck dick?" She filled in for me bluntly.

"Something like that," I replied, flashing her a mysterious smile. For so long, I had just been everyone's good little friend, the girl who would never have gotten into anything that she shouldn't have. And now? Now, I had unleashed some new part of me, and I wanted nothing more than to make sure that everyone understood just what a bad bitch she was.

"Is it really just because you're single now?" She asked with interest. "I mean, I know that you were with him for so long, but I thought you guys had a... good sex life?"

"I thought so too," I replied. "Or at least, I managed to convince myself that we did. But I wanted more than he could ever give me. Really, I know that I deserve it. It's just...I've always wanted more than someone like him could give me, you know?"

"Like what?" She asked, shifting forward with interest. She might have been a wild child back in the day herself but that didn't mean that she wasn't curious to find out just what else might be out there – just what else she might have missed out on.

"Uh, where do you want me to start?" I asked, spreading my hands wide. She cocked her head at me.

"How much is there to hear?"

"A lot," I warned her.

"Then start at the beginning," she replied. My eyes flicked over to the bedroom door, where the moving guy had fucked me right on the day that I had moved in. I knew that she would never have believed me if I had told her, but hey, if she wanted to hear it, right...?

And so, I told her. I told her everything that I had been getting up to since I had come out here. And honestly, even hearing the words come out of my own mouth like that was something of a shock – I couldn't believe that I could say all of this and really mean it, it felt as though it had to be coming from someone else entirely. I knew that I had really been through all of that, but recounting it out loud like this – yeah, that was something new.

By the time that I was done, she had finished her glass of wine, and she was staring at me as though she had never met me before in my life.

"You really...all of it?" She asked. I nodded.

"I really... all of it," I replied, with a chuckle, enjoying how shocked she looked right now. I knew that I was the last person that she would ever have expected to come out with this sort of thing, and if there was one thing that I had found I truly loved about this new life, it was flaunting the expectations that people placed on me.

"I didn't...I guess I just didn't know that you had any of it in you," she remarked, and she lifted the empty glass to her lips again, like she had forgotten that she'd already drained it. I reached over and took it from her, and went to fill it up in the kitchen again.

I could feel her watching me, even as I got her another glass; there was something about the air in the room that felt thicker than normal. I knew that there was something on her mind, something that she wanted to say to me, but that she was too nervous to come out with it.

Which wasn't like her. If there was one thing that I knew about her, it was that she spoke her mind. As I came back to the couch, gave her the glass, I cocked an eyebrow at her.

"Something on your mind?"

"Yeah, honestly," she admitted, and she hesitated before she spoke again. "You...you were with a girl?"

"Yeah, I was," I replied. I still couldn't quite believe that I got to say that and mean it, but I did. It was an odd sensation, being the most experienced person in the room, even if the vast majority of those experiences had come in the last month.

"I've never done that before," she confessed. "But I was always...I mean, I was always curious to know how it would be..."

"Really?" I replied, tipping my head to the side with interest. She nodded.

"Yeah, it just always seemed like something...something I should try," she continued. Her voice seemed to have lifted into a slightly higher plane, as though she was trying to sound casual despite the seriousness of this inside her head.

"You know that you can if you want, right?" I pointed out to her. "I mean, there's nothing stopping you."

"Oh, I wouldn't know where to start," she admitted, a small pink flush tinging in her cheeks. "It would just be – no. I don't think it would be something I could do without seeming like the straightest straight girl ever, you know?"

"I guess," I replied. "But everyone has to start somewhere, don't they?"

"Sure, but where...where do I even begin with that?" She replied, as her eyes met mine again. And suddenly, it hit me what was going on here. She was hinting. Hinting to me that she wanted me to be the one to show her how all of this was done.

I would have been lying if I said I wasn't a little flattered to realize that she wanted that from me. Had I become, all at once, this arbiter of all things gay? I wouldn't have minded one little bit. At least, in this circumstance.

"Are you asking me to show you?" I murmured to her. I watched her breath catch, her entire body start for an instant, and I couldn't help but smile. I wanted this. I wanted to find out what was going to happen if I just shifted an inch towards her, just moved closer and closer. She didn't pull away from me. Her eyes were still stuck on mine, her lips slightly parted, as though there was something that she wanted to say to me but that she had no idea how to say it.

I knew how she felt, and I wanted to make sure that I gave her everything that I could to prove that this was real. My mind flooded back to the first time that I had been looked at in that way, by another woman, a woman who had seemed to want me, really desire me. The way it had flicked a switch inside my head, turned me into something else.

I reached out, traced a finger down her cheek. She closed her eyes. There was no going back no – no denying the fact that this was real, that this was happening, that we were doing this. I brushed my finger over her lips, and watched the way her tongue curled out to taste my skin, as though she was starving for me.

And I couldn't help but push my fingers forward, into the warmth of her mouth. She closed her eyes for a moment, and I leaned closer, marveling at the way that she reacted to me – enjoying the look of surprise on her face, the way she seemed to start when I was close to her. I skimmed my fingers down her waist, and found my hand on her pants, undoing them, pulling them away from her body. She arched her hips from the couch as she slid her tongue against my fingerprints, tasting me.

I drew my fingers from her mouth, and moved them down, leaving a line of her own saliva on her skin as I inched further and further down her body – marking a line down between her breasts, watching the way that her chest rose and fell like she was crying out for me to do more, to give her more. And I wanted to – God, I wanted to. I could already feel the pressure building between my own legs, the weight of it starting to draw my attention in a way that I couldn't deny.

As soon as my hand reached between her legs, I kissed her – properly this time, not the chaste peck that I had planted on her cheek when she had come through the door, all smiles and giggles and pretending we were nothing more than friends. I wondered if there had been some part of her that had been longing for this from the start. Maybe she had seen some other side of me at the party, and that it had drawn out a fascination in her that she had been nurturing ever since. Honestly, the mere idea of that was enough to send shivers of excitement through my system. I was obsessed with her, with the idea that she might have wanted me all along.

I brushed my fingers over her bush as I pushed my fingers into her panties, feeling her breath catch in the back of her throat for a split second in the moment before I found her clit. She moaned against my lips as soon as I did, and I felt that thrill of control, of power, of dominance. I was the one who knew what they were doing here, I was the one who made the rules and showed her just how to run things. It had been a while since I had felt like I had actually got some claim over any of this, since I had felt as though I was the one in charge.

Her tongue spoke against mine, as though all the words that we had said up until this point to one another had been nothing close to enough. I knew how she felt. The pressure of her body against mine had taken this somewhere else, somewhere new, somewhere that I had never even realized that it needed to be – when she touched me, pushed her hand through my hair, I knew that we had taken this to a level that we were never going to be able to bring it back from.

And I didn't mind one tiny little bit.

No, I wanted to find out where we could go next. As I massaged her clit with two fingers, our lips moving softly against one another's, I knew that I wasn't going to be satisfied until I'd made her come. I had never made another woman come before, not just with my touch, and I had to find out what it was like.

I slipped my fingers down a little further, to the wetness of her slit, and pulled that slickness back to her clit for lubrication; she lifted her hips and started to push back against me, letting me use her the way I wanted to. I knew that this was already spinning out of control. I knew that this was already going further than we had ever been ready for it to. And now – and now, there was nothing that I could do but give in to the way it felt to have her pushing back against me like this. Grinding on my hand like I was the only thing in the entire world that she wanted right now.

"Fuck," she gasped against my lips, and I kissed her again, harder this time, exploring her lips and her mouth with my own. In all the time that I had known her, I had never looked at her and craved something like this – but now that she was here, giving herself to me like this, handing her pleasure to me on a platter, I knew that there was no way that I could turn her down. The thrill of being in charge here, that was all that I had needed, and, as I kissed her deeply and played with her clit, I knew that I could have done this the whole night through if she had asked it of me.

I had no idea what I was expecting when she came – but it didn't take long till I felt the shockwaves of her body tensing, her entire system shaking against mine for a moment. I could taste the wine on her lips as I stilled my fingers against her clit, feeling her pussy spasming against my hand, and wondering if that was what I had been waiting for.

But, as she slumped back on to the couch to catch her breath, I couldn't help but grin. I knew that I had done it. I had taken her there. I watched as she stared at the ceiling, her chest rising and falling fast, her jaw trembling as though the shockwaves of all of this were pulsing through her still. I drew my fingers to my mouth, tasting her wetness upon them, and wondering why it was that the mere scent of her turned me on so much.

"How was it?" I asked her, as I rose to my feet, and went to grab myself another glass of wine again. She lifted her head so that she could look up at me, her gaze so distant and so lost to happiness that she seemed unable to control herself.

"It was..." she breathed, and I knew that she wasn't going to be able to come up with anything more impressive than that. I didn't care. I had just successfully made a woman come all by myself for the first time, and I was pretty damn proud of myself for pulling it off. Maybe I was starting to come out the other side of my sexual education – maybe I was starting to turn into the very person that I had always longed to be, the one in total and utter control of her sexuality and everything around it.

As I poured myself another glass and took a sip, mixing her sweet muskiness with the scent of the wine in my mouth, I grinned to myself. There was still so much for me to learn, and I wanted to find out exactly what this world still had to show me. Because I was sure that I would pass with flying colors.

Chapter 7

I pushed my door open, flopped down on the couch, and let out a long sigh. Ugh. It had already been one hell of a long week. And I felt like I was starting to lose my grip on the woman that I had been longing to become.

I had been at work every single shift from start to finish ever since one of our other baristas had quit. And normally, I wouldn't have minded putting in the time for them – after all, I had worked there for years, and it wasn't like my boss hadn't overlooked a few hungover shifts and the like – but that was the old me. That was the version of me that didn't have as much to claim to her name as she did now, and I didn't want to let that slip through my fingers.

It had been a week since I had seen Kaylee, since we'd fooled around on my couch, and normally, a week since my last sexual encounter would have been more than enough to keep me satisfied. But that had been then, this was now, and I was used to getting pretty much anything that I wanted as soon as I got the inkling that I'd have liked it. I was getting greedy. And I knew that I was going to have to take things to the next level if I was going to make sure that I kept things going the way that they needed to be.

I'd seen Tommy at work, a few days ago; I swear, it was just the sight of him that had sent me so crazy up in my own head, the memory of everything that I had gotten up to when I had been with him and Johnathan not that long ago. It had been a hell of a lot of fun, and I could tell from the way he flirted with me over the coffee that I made for him, that he wanted to do it all over again. And trust me, I would have been lying if I'd said that I wasn't a little curious to find out what else I could get into with the two of them – but I needed something new right now. Something I had never experienced before.

I knew that I wasn't going to have time to do much else but go home and get as much sleep as I could this weekend, and so, I had ordered myself something to take the edge off of my need – a collection of sex toys, paid-for by my last paycheck. I knew that I probably should have saved it for sensible things like takeout and wine, but honestly, I wanted to have a collection that I knew I could delve into whenever I needed to. I wanted to be able to rely on myself, no matter what – wanted to be sure that I always had something fun to come back to right here at home if I craved it.

And that's what I stayed focused on, over anything else. I got through all of my shifts that week sneakily checking on the shipping details for the toys that were headed in my direction, hoping that they would be there by the time I rounded off my run of shifts at the start of the weekend. I intended to lock that door, and indulge myself in all the ways that I could think of. It was self-care, wasn't it? Something like that...

And, sure enough, I spotted the package sitting next to my door when I went out to check on my mail. Yes! I grabbed it, shook it a couple of times to make sure that it was heavy enough to contain everything that I needed it to, and then dived back into my apartment to do what I needed to do.

I was going to make this an *event*. If I was going to do this, I was going to do it properly, and that meant starting slow, taking my time and really indulging myself in everything that I wanted to engage with. I ran myself a bath, dripped in a few drops of the expensive bath oil that someone had left for me after I had invited them round for the housewarming party, and sank beneath the water, closing my eyes and letting it soothe my sore muscles and tired spirit.

With the box next to the bath, I reached over without opening my eyes to pull out something new. My fingers closed around a long, slender dildo; I had picked out a few dildos of different sizes and shapes, wanting to find out what worked best for me, mainly so that I would be able to tell at a glance whose cock would feel the best before I fucked them. I figured that I was going to have to streamline all my sexual exploits if I was going to get the most out of them, and this seemed like an appropriate way to do it.

I pushed the toy beneath the water, admiring the slender contours of its pink, silicone length; it wasn't meant to look anything like an actual dick, I assumed, but that didn't matter. It was longer than anything I had actually had inside of me, and I wasn't sure that I would be able to take every inch of it, but hey – a girl could only try, couldn't she?

I took my time with it, sliding it over my clit a couple of times to get myself used to the slick feel of the toy against my skin – it was so new, so fresh, that I found my pussy responding to it almost at once, needing to find the relief that only something deep inside of me could give me.

Eventually, I let it slide down to my pussy, teasing it around the edges of my slit for a moment. I bit my lip, smiled. See? Who needed a man, when I had something like this to give me everything that I needed right now? Finally, I started to guide it inside of me, taking my time, sliding it slow and deep into my pussy, and feeling my slit spread to take every inch of it.

I watched, almost amazed, as it vanished inside of me. I knew that I had taken a lot down there in the last few weeks – a lot everywhere else, too, if I was being honest – but that didn't mean that I still didn't find myself wondering if I could really take it as far as this. My body tensed as I felt it plunge deeper into me, filling me, so deep that I was sure it wouldn't be long until it was lost inside me forever.

"Mmmm," I groaned theatrically. I knew that I didn't need to perform for anyone, but damn, there was something fun in making the noises, playing the game a little. I was sure that anyone who overheard me would have thought that I was crazy for playing it up like this, but as I tipped my head back, let my body slide down a little further under the steaming water, I groaned again. The fullness was delicious, enough to let the tension begin to leak from me, and soon, I found myself sliding it in and out of me deeper, harder, enjoying the grinding pressure that it sent between my legs, up throughout my entire body.

"Fuck," I gasped to myself. There was something freeing about knowing that I didn't have to worry about looking or sounding good, moving in a certain way that would prove that I was worth everything that the other person was giving me. I screwed up my face in pleasure, moved my other hand down so that I could play with my clit as I fucked myself. The oil in the water was clinging to my skin in the most delicious way imaginable, the touch of it so delicious that I could feel it prickling from the top of my scalp down to the tips of my toes.

I spread my legs further, hooked one ankle over the side of the bathtub, and pushed that toy in even deeper, harder. I didn't have to ask anyone to give it to me, I could just gift myself this delicious feeling, the treat of being fucked just the way that I wanted to be fucked.

And it didn't take long till all the tension that had been building between my thighs, deep in my belly, all week long started to consume me. I tipped my head back, almost submerged beneath the steaming hot water, and finally, finally, felt the orgasm shudder through my entire body at once.

I made a noise unlike anything I had heard come out of myself before. Because I wasn't moderating it to make sure that it didn't put anyone off – I was just doing what came naturally to me, letting the pleasure take control of me and choosing how I reacted in that moment. I felt my pussy clench around the toy, and I held it there, deep inside of me, my hand stilled over my clit, my whole body frozen in that moment of pleasure that made everything fade to black at the edges.

As I came back into my body again, it took me a moment to remember that I was actually still in the bath – the orgasm had been so intense that I couldn't think straight, and the feelings that were still pulsing through me made my head spin.

I pulled the toy from between my legs and dropped it over the edge of the tub, back into the box once more. Fuck, yes. That was all that I had needed. And even now, I didn't have to worry about getting anyone else off, have to worry about making sure I kept performing for somebody else who might have been watching or fucking me. This was just all about me, the indulgence that I could give to myself once and for all.

I lay back, let my hair float out around me in what must have looked like a halo to anyone else watching. Not that there was anyone else to watch right now. No, because this was all about me. Me, and me alone. And I wanted to make the very most of that time that I had to myself while I still could. Was there something to be said for someone else to keep you company – maybe even more than one person? Sure. But right now, I was all about indulging my own whims. And that was the way I was planning to keep it.

Chapter 8

I started up the laptop, bit my lip, and stared at the screen as I waited for it to come to life in front of me. I couldn't believe I was actually doing this. I couldn't believe I was actually going to see this through.

It had crossed my mind the night before, when I had been using that new little bullet vibrator that I had purchased to get myself off before I went to sleep. How much fun it would be to show this side of myself to someone else. Of course, I didn't want to do it in person – no, this weekend, I had decided, was about nothing more than the thrill of giving myself over to pleasure, the pleasure that I could deliver to myself, and nothing more than that.

But there were plenty of people out there who would have taken me exactly as I was. And I was determined to find out just how far they might have gone to show me just how much they enjoyed me.

I had woken up early that morning, and had found my mind already racing with a million questions, a million wonderings as to how I could make that happen. It didn't take long for me to track down forums where like-minded adults with the same penchant for sexuality seemed willing to share everything they've got up to, and I signed up at once and logged myself in. And, when I saw for myself what they've been getting into – I could hardly believe it.

Okay, so I knew that I had been pretty wild by any measurement system when it came to real life. But this? This was something else entirely, and I didn't know how to wrap my head around it. They were posting pictures, videos, stories, everything that they could, and seemingly focusing on their own exploits to fill out the details. I watched with fascination as a woman, her head just out of frame so that her identity was disguised, masturbated herself to orgasm, groaning loudly as she flopped back on the bed. The camera had managed to capture the pulsations of her pussy, and the sight of it was already starting to turn me on.

Not just because I wanted to be there with her, though that was a part of it. But because of the stream of texts up the side of her video – live-chat, people responding to her performance, telling her how sexy she was to them, how much they wished that they could be there with her, all of the things that they would have done to her if they had gotten even half of a chance to do so. I couldn't take my eyes off of that part, the things that they were telling her, and I knew at once that I had to find out what else I could do to get this kind of response.

I had never been the most tech-savvy person in the world, but I could get my laptop camera set up to shoot me – and make sure that I didn't show off my face in the process. I knew that the café I worked for was pretty liberal, but that didn't mean that I wanted images of myself mid-orgasm open-sourced for anyone who wanted them. I wasn't looking to become a porn star – well, not yet, anyway – and I just wanted to capture the attention of the perverts on this site along with me.

Once I had logged myself in, I spent a little while fussing over the set-up of the camera, making sure that it was exactly how I wanted it to be. I had positioned it next to the bed, playing it almost as a candid shot that I had been caught in the middle of. I wanted this to feel natural, even though I was going to be putting on the performance of a lifetime for whoever happened to be tuned in to the forum at that moment.

I climbed on to the bed, and looked at myself, reflected in the screen in front of me. I had to admit, I liked the way that my body looked right now – for a long time, I had been so busy beating myself up about the smallest details of the way that I looked that I had failed to notice that the whole picture really wasn't all that bad. I liked the way my body was, liked the way it moved. I swayed back and forth a little, admiring the curve of my hips, the way my waist slid in before it made space for my breasts. I ran my hand over my nipples, pinching them so that they were swollen and pink and clearly visible in the camera. I bit my lip, smiled. Okay, I didn't even need to turn that thing on right now, it seemed. I was more than willing to just get off on the way that I looked right now...

But I wanted to find out what would have happened if I took things to the next level. Just the next one. To find out what they would think of me. One of the things that I liked the most about this place was that they always seemed to find something sweet to say about the girls or the guys who put themselves out there. Nobody was treated like they were less-than, nobody was treated as though they weren't good enough. And God, I needed to know that much – I might have been embracing parts of myself I never would have before, but that didn't mean that my ego would have been able to take it if I had received some horrible feedback from someone who had been watching my feed.

I hovered my finger over the button that would allow me to broadcast live. This was my last chance to back out. As soon as I hit that thing, I wasn't going to be able to deny it any longer – I was going to have to deal with whatever those people thought of me, whether it turned out to be good or bad.

And I couldn't wait to find out what they were going to say.

I pressed the button, moved back on the bed, and made sure that I had the collection of toys in arm's reach. I was totally naked, save for a pair of panties, and I knew that whoever was going to log in and spot me was going to be in for a surprise.

I counted down the seconds – one, two, three – before someone popped in to watch my feed. My heart flipped in my chest, and I made double-sure that nobody could see my face.

"Hey," I greeted them. I didn't know whether they were a man, woman, something else entirely, but I didn't care. I just wanted to perform. I just wanted to show myself off to them and prove that I could give them anything and everything that they might have wanted. A message popped up into the chat, which I had enlarged to make sure that I could see it without moving from the bed.

You're gorgeous.

"Thank you," I giggled happily, and I twisted my body this way and that way a little, showing myself off for the enjoyment of whoever might have been seeing me in that moment. I wanted nothing more than to be admired, to be wanted, to be longed-for. Even if they couldn't touch me, they could still show me what they wanted, right?

"Can I show you something?" I asked flirtatiously. Another person who popped into the chat, told me *yes, yes, yes.* I reached into the box beside me and withdrew a small vibrator, spreading my legs and pushing myself up on my knees so that they would be able to see me properly. My heart was pounding, my adrenalin was pumping, and I couldn't believe that this was actually happening right now. Couldn't believe that I would actually be willing to go through with something so filthy.

But here I was. And there was no way that I was going to back out now.

I clicked the vibrator on in my hand, and pushed it down between my legs, underneath the panties that I was wearing. My lips parted theatrically as I felt it press against my clit, even though nobody else could see it. I gasped loudly, arching my back to push myself against the toy a little harder. A flurry of message notifications pinged up at once, and I took a long moment to toy with myself before I opened my eyes to see who they might have been from.

My eyes widened when I realized just how many people were watching my stream right now. At least twenty different users had sent me messages. And that wasn't even counting the ones who hadn't had a chance to yet – who were maybe too distracted by the show that I was putting on to think about it. I felt a surge of lust dance through my body as I realized just how much they wanted me, just how much they desired me. I couldn't remember the last time that I had felt this dizzy with desire, and I was glad that I had the vibrator pressed against my clit right now, because otherwise, I might not have been able to control myself.

"Fuck," I groaned, and I began to move my hand with more purpose beneath my panties, making sure that the people on the other end of this show could see how wet my underwear had already become just at the knowledge that they were watching. I squinted to read the messages as I played with myself. One of them was asking me to turn around and show them my ass, and I shifted on the spot, bent over, arched my back so that they could get a look at me.

"You like?" I flirted with them. I knew that I was risking showing my face right now, but I didn't care. All that I could focus on was the thrill of desire coursing through me right now, the power that I felt like I had over all of these men. My pussy was burning with want as I felt a million digital eyes on me, watching me, taking me in and admiring me at once.

I started to thrust my hips back against the vibrator – being on all fours like this, so exposed, was just the hottest thing to me. I couldn't resist reaching around behind myself to pull my panties aside, to show myself off to the people who were watching me. I wanted them to see all of me. I wanted them to take in every inch of my body, and the thrill of knowing that I didn't even have a clue who they were only made it more intense.

I heard the messages again, and I couldn't resist moving so that I could read them, making an effort to keep myself out of the frame; a dozen of them were asking me to show my face, so at least I knew that I hadn't managed to screw that one up. But the others were telling me how gorgeous I was, how sexy, asking me to bend this way and that way, asking me to show myself off and touch myself and get naked and – well, more than I would ever be able to do in just one of these little streams.

And besides, this was about me. I was gifting them with my presence, and I wasn't going to let anyone tell me how to do this. I planted one hand behind me, leaned back into it, and rolled the vibrator against my clit in circles. I was going to come soon, I could feel it, going to come harder than I had come in a long time. Maybe it was just the intensity of all the people watching me, knowing that there were so many out there getting off to the sight of me doing the same thing.

I thrust my hips against the vibrator, over and over again, losing myself to the way that it felt, to the feeling of the vibrations pulsing up and through my body. I felt as though every nerve-ending was alight with desire, and knowing that I was likely cresting towards the climax at the same time as the other people watching me just made it even better.

When I came, I didn't make a sound. I knew that they would all be able to tell from just looking at me what had happened. My whole body spasmed with pleasure, and I nearly crumpled into the bed in relief, only remembering at the very last second that I was making sure that they couldn't see my face. I pulled the vibrator out and tossed it aside, breathing hard, my tits shaking as I tried to come back down to Earth once more...

And it was only then, after I was sure that I was done, that I reached over and turned off the video. And finally let myself down in front of the laptop so that I could see what they had all been saying about me.

The thrill of seeing everything that they had said about me, my body, my pleasure, the way I moved, was almost enough to start a burning desire rising in me again. But I was so exhausted from the adrenalin that I could only lean against the bed and catch my breath. Enjoying the compliments still pouring in to me, the questions as to when I was going to be around to do that again.

But there was one message that stood out to me – one message that made me slow and stop in my tracks, a message that made me smile at once. A message that I knew there was no way in hell that I was going to be able to ignore.

A message from a man telling me that he wanted to meet me in person. And a specific list of all the things that he would do to me when he got the chance.

Chapter 9

I sat there, in the hotel bar, and stared down at the drink that I had poured for myself. I wanted nothing more than to down it to try and take the edge off everything that was going through my brain right now, but I knew that I wanted to be totally sober for when Tobe turned up.

I still couldn't believe I was doing this. Couldn't believe that I was actually thinking about hooking up with a man that I had never met before in my life. Of everything that I had done so far, on my long mission to uncover all the deepest desires in my sexuality, this was the craziest.

And maybe that's why it was the one I had been most excited about from the start.

Tobe and I had been talking for two weeks, on and off, ever since he had spotted the little live performance that I'd shared on that forum. I wasn't sure what it was about his message that had drawn me in – maybe just the fact that he had good grammar, compared to the rest of the people who had been horny-contacting me ever since – but I was fascinated by him at once. I had to find out if he could follow through on everything that he had said that he would do for me, and he was passing through my city at the end of the week on a work trip from somewhere else entirely. If I was going to find out if he could put his money where his mouth was, then it was going to be now, or never.

He had given me the name of the hotel that he was staying at, and we had agreed to share a couple of drinks at the bar before we did anything else. Much as I was tempted to just dive into everything that he could give me – to find out just how far he was really willing to take this – I knew that it was better for my own safety to play it cool. I had made sure to tell Kaylee where I was right now, even though she tried to convince me not to go at all. Honestly, I wouldn't have been surprised if she was a little jealous. She had been acting more than a little possessive of me since the night that we had fooled around together, and I was sure that she wanted a little more to come of what we had done there considering everything that I had given her.

Anyway, tonight, I wasn't about women. I was about men. Well, one man. One man who had promised that he would give me the fucking of my life. And I wanted to find out if he could follow through on it.

I had arrived a little earlier than we had agreed upon. I wanted to make sure that I had a feel for the place before he got there; he was coming from some big work meeting, he had told me, though I couldn't for the life of me remember what he actually did for a living. I still couldn't believe that I was even considering going with someone I didn't know at all; I knew that I had hooked up with Johnathan without really knowing much about him, but that was different. He came with a stamp of approval from someone that I actually knew, someone that I actually trusted. But Tobe? Tobe could have been anyone. And that was what I was most excited about.

I supposed it was the same as the way the anonymity of the people who had watched me thrilled me down to my core; I liked the thought of this, the thought of giving myself over to someone who knew nothing about me. They wouldn't come with any expectations, they would just take me as I was. And I wanted to know how that would play out.

And so, when I finally locked eyes with him walking into the bar, my heart skipped several beats. He had sent me a few pictures of himself, and truly, I had been ready for them to be a little more flattering than he actually turned out to be in real life. But, if anything, he was even cuter in person; dark hair, flecked with distinguished gray, blue eyes, a little light stubble that seemed intentional. Fancy suit, expensive tie. He greeted me with a kiss on the cheek, swooping down to plant a peck against my skin and nearly making me swoon in the process.

"It's lovely to finally meet you," He told me, and I could tell from the way his eyes seemed to melt into mine that he meant it. I nodded. I knew that I was meant to say something back in response, but I didn't know quite how to do it. I was just so dazzled by the fact that this guy was actually hot.

He sank down into the seat opposite me, not taking his eyes off of me for a moment. I stared back at him. I wanted to say something, but I wasn't sure what. We had been talking pure filth to each other, all the time that we had been chatting online, and I would have been lying if I'd said that it wasn't the only thing on my mind right about now. I wished that I could just reach into my head and pull out all the stuff that was rushing through it, all the things that I wanted to do to him.

He waved down a waiter and ordered a drink, and finally, I went about digging up what remained of my voice once more.

"I can't believe I'm really doing this," I confessed. He cocked his head to the side with interest.

"Why so?"

"I've never...I mean, I've never just met up with someone like this for..." I trailed off. I didn't know how to fill in the rest of that sentence. Even though I had sent him things that were far worse than anything running through my head in that moment, I wasn't sure that I would be able to say them out loud.

"Trust me, it's a lot more fun than it's given credit for," he replied, and he moved his hand to mine with confidence – his touch sent a shiver down my spine, the way he looked at me impossible to deny.

"You don't have to worry about what they might think of you, because chances are, you're never going to see them again," he explained. "You just have to worry about your pleasure. Asking for everything that you've always been too afraid to. Though I doubt there's much that you haven't asked for over the years..."

His eyes scanned down my body, to the generous hit of cleavage that I was showing off over the top of my dress, and I felt a flush hit my cheeks. Fuck, I wanted this man. He was right. There was an undeniable thrill to the thought of just – of just knowing that I could take anything that I wanted from him, and he would be gone by the time that dawn broke the next day. I crossed my legs, squeezed my thighs together, and hoped to God that he wouldn't be able to tell how unremittingly horny I was right now. I didn't want him to think that I was too easy or something...

But then, what was the point of pretending? If I wanted pleasure, then I was going to take it, and this man seemed more than willing to give it to me any single way that he could. I loved that. And I wanted to prove to him that I could keep up with him any way he wanted me to.

I leaned towards him, making sure that I pressed my tits together as I did so – I watched his eyes lower to my breasts, and I knew that he was having a hard time keeping his hands off of them right then and there.

"Let's go to your room," I murmured to him, and I tossed my hair over one shoulder, hoping that if I played the seductress, I would start to feel it, too.

I rose to my feet, and a moment later, he did the same to follow me. I didn't know where I was going, so when I felt his hand slide around my waist, I was relieved that I wasn't going to have to keep up this act any longer. I wanted nothing more than to just have him take me right then and right there, but I knew I had to play it a little more carefully than that.

He walked me up to his room, and to anyone who might have passed us by, we would have looked nothing more than a couple going back to our place after a romantic night on the town. Little did they know that we had never met before, that I didn't even know this man's last name – hell, I didn't even know if the first name that he had given me was accurate, and I was more than willing to make sure that he knew as little about me as I did about him. In fact, by the time I left this place, I wanted to make sure that the only thing that he was sure of about me was the fact that I was the best lay he'd ever had in his life. After all, he had found me, online, making myself come – the least I could do was see through that fantasy for him, wasn't it?

As soon as we reached the door, I grabbed for his shirt, and pulled him close to me. Our lips met, and I kissed him hard, marveling at how new this all was to me – marveling at how easy it had been to share myself with a man like this, without even having kissed him before. I had been texting him all about my deepest, darkest desires, and only now was I feeling his hands on my body for the first time.

He pushed the keycard into the lock without pulling back from me, and the two of us tumbled over the door together – his hands started to roam my body at once, his touch sending shockwaves of pleasure through me as he groped at my ass, my tits, my thighs, my stomach. He seemed to want to make sure that I was actually here, that I was truly real, after he had first encountered me in cyberspace like that. I didn't blame him. I knew that I wanted to be certain that he was really there, after the build-up our relationship had taken so far.

He kissed over my neck, my chin, pushing the straps of my dress down so that he could lower his mouth to my breasts. He was rougher than anyone else I had been with, baring his teeth against my nipples and making me cry out with a delicious mix of pain and pleasure. I couldn't get enough. I cradled his head right there for a moment, before he pushed me down onto the bed and climbed on top of me.

He ripped off my dress as though it was nothing more than a slight distraction between him and I; I knew that I had nothing to worry about in his desire for me. I had been a little concerned that things might not feel as fiery since we had only known each other online before this, but if anything, this was even more intense than I had predicted.

He kissed me again, pulled off my panties, and tossed them aside – his hands, now on my naked body, took control of me.

"You have no idea how long I've been waiting to have you like this," he growled into my ear, as I felt his cock begin to swell against my hip. "Ever since I saw you in that live-stream, I knew that I had to have you..."

The dominance in his voice made me ache for him in a way so intense it was almost painful, and my entire system was crying out for him, for as much as I could get from him. I pushed my hands through his hair and pulled him to my mouth again, remembering what he had said when we had met in the bar. That we could do anything that we wanted. We would never have to see each other again after this, and that meant that we could give in to those dark, crazy desires that we might have tried to hide from someone else.

"Spank my ass," I breathed in his ear. It was a test, really, just to see if he would do it. I didn't know how far he would be willing to take this, but the thought of this older man, taking control of me, showing me how he did things, made my pussy ache more than I could handle.

He flipped me over without a second thought, and smoothed his hand over my ass, like he was preparing a canvas for his masterpiece. And then, all at once, he brought his hand down upon me with a sharp slap that made me jump with surprise.

"Oh!" I squeaked. More at the surprise that it felt as good as it did than anything – I had expected myself to be a baby about the pain, but to my shock, it mellowed into something delicious as soon as he began to rub his hand over the impact site again.

"Good?" He asked. I could hear a near-smugness in his voice as he spoke to me, and I knew that he was enjoying making sure that I got off on the feeling of his hands on me. I nodded, glanced over my shoulder, to see him leaning down to plant a kiss on my ass. I remembered the first time that I had put on a little show back on that site, when I had pulled my panties aside to show everyone my pussy and my ass. Seemed like that had made a real impression on him, huh?

"Good," I replied, and he landed another slap on my other ass-cheek – I cried out, but this time, it was in nothing but total and utter pleasure. I was stunned at how good it felt, how good it was to submit to him like this – how easy I found it to let those feelings course through me. I closed my eyes, rested my head on the pillow, I almost felt as though I was getting a massage or something. But instead of rubbing out the knots in my muscles, he was spanking them out, instead. And I had every intention of making sure I enjoyed it as much as I would have if it had been a therapeutic massage.

He was gentle with me – I had seen videos where people went seriously hardcore with the spankings that they received, but he was careful, keeping it light and playful, while making sure that I knew who the one in charge was. It didn't take long till I could feel some wetness leaking down the inside of my thighs, and he noticed it too. Pushing his hand between my legs, he rubbed at my slit roughly, and I groaned. I wished that I had the words to tell him how good that felt, but I didn't.

"You're so wet, baby," he murmured, and he pulled his hand from between my legs and reached around to push it into my mouth. The taste of my muskiness on his fingers was everything that I needed it to be right now, and I sucked hard, rolling his fingers around my mouth, letting my tongue bathe him clean.

"You want me to fuck you?" He asked, pulling his fingers from my mouth and taking his time as he rubbed them over my slit once more – not pushing inside, just moving around me, letting me wait for him. I nodded.

"Say it," he ordered me. I clenched my teeth. There was a naturally defiant part of me that wanted to push back against him, but I knew that it wouldn't have gotten me anywhere. I wanted to feel his dick deep inside my pussy, and I wanted to feel it now.

"Fuck me," I hissed. And that was everything that he wanted to hear from me right now.

I heard the rip of a condom, the zip of his pants, and then, he grabbed my hips and pulled them back towards him. His tip pressed against my entrance and I groaned with an almost painful need. I wanted him to fuck me so hard I couldn't walk the next day. I wanted to feel his cock take me every way that I needed to be taken. I'd been stuck with nothing but the toys for a while now, and honestly, they weren't the same as having a real man, really wanting you, right there and ready to fuck.

He thrust inside of me in one motion, and my whole body trembled, slumping down into the bed so that only my hips were still pointed up to him. His hands were digging into my ass, spreading me wide as he slipped himself all the way inside of me, and I swear, it took everything that I had to keep from reaching around and pulling him into me even deeper.

I loved the way that it felt. Loved the feeling of his thickness inside of me. I couldn't even see his face, but I could feel the grip of his hands, I could feel him pulling me back into him hard, I could hear the sharp breaths that he was letting out right now, and I knew that this was everything that I needed. He wanted me, really wanted me, and knowing that he had wanted me from the moment that he had seen me performing in that stream was only getting me hotter.

He fucked me, thrust into me over and over again, until the only sound in the room was that of our flesh coming together and my helpless little moans of want. I managed to lift my head for a moment, turn to look over my shoulder. There was a darkness to his eyes that thrilled me and aroused me in the same moment – I knew that this was dangerous, but in the best way possible. That kind of measured risk that I always wanted to take, always craved more than I could put into words.

I turned back to grab the headboard and start pushing down against him properly. Fuck, yes – the fullness that coursed through me as he fucked me made my entire head spin, my brain narrowing down to just the thought of how good it felt to be with him, how much I wanted more.

I closed my eyes and tipped my head back, letting out a deep groan of pleasure that reverberated through my whole body, and pushed my hand between my legs to play with myself while he fucked me. I needed this. I needed more. I needed to know that I didn't have to worry about hiding my want or playing demure or anything like that. I just needed to take, take, take everything that I could get, and then, and only then, would I be satisfied.

He pressed his hips against mine and held himself there for a long moment, not pulling back as he kept his cock lodged all the way inside of me, grinding against me and making me squirm. The feeling of that fullness matched with the frantic motion of my fingers between my legs was taking me there, taking me to where I needed to go.

When I felt the orgasm crest, the climax took control of me, I let out a noise that I had never heard come from me in my entire life – the insides of my thighs were trembling with helpless pleasure, and I balled a handful of the covers in my fists to try and expel some of the tension that was riding and rising through my body. He held himself there, merciless, not pulling back, until he seemed satisfied that I had taken what I needed. And then, he began to pound into me again, harder than before, filling me deep, taking me, and then pushing himself over the edge in the moments right after I had done the same.

"Fuck," he growled, as he finished inside of me. I could feel his cock twitching, and I continued to move and grind against him, taking him deeper, taking as much of him as I could manage. I wanted him. I wanted this – I wanted more. I knew that he had just come, but that didn't mean that this had to be over, did it?

I flipped around, reached for him, and pulled him on top of me. I could feel the tension had left his strong body, and that thrilled me. I had reduced this man, boiled him down to his bare essentials, and I loved that. He might have been the one in control when all of this started, but I was the one in charge now, and there wasn't a hope in hell that I was going to let him forget it.

"I'm not done with you yet," I murmured to him, and I felt him grin against my neck as he moved to kiss me again. We had a whole lot left to discover about one another before this night was done. And I wanted to delve into the depths of everything that I'd been trying to hold back all this time.

Chapter 10

I swear, I walked with a swagger after that.

After the night I spent with Tobe – or whatever his name really might have been – in that hotel, it became clear to me that I had something that most people could only dream of. Confidence. Sureness. The certainty that my pussy was good enough to get pretty much any man to do pretty much anything that I wanted him to.

I had slipped out of his room first thing in the morning, before he'd had a chance to wake up. There was just something so naughty and so damn fun about the thought of sneaking away before he'd come to, knowing that the night we'd spent together had been nothing more than what I wanted it to be. He had dropped me a text to make sure that I'd gotten home okay, and I had assured him that I had. Oh, and sent him a picture of a couple of the red hand-marks on my ass from wear he had been spanking me, just for good measure.

I still couldn't believe that I had the nerve to do something like that these days. Back when I had been with my ex, I wouldn't have even dared to snap a picture of myself in my underwear, let alone naked. Let alone send it to someone that I barely knew. Let alone have had *sex* with that person that I barely knew. It was all so fresh to me, so thrilling to realize how much I got out of this kind of lifestyle. I had been sure that I was too uptight for this, but the more time that passed, the more certain I became that I had only scratched the surface of everything that I wanted to enjoy.

Honestly, the best part of my encounter with Tobe had been the power dynamic that we had exchanged – I had allowed him to take control the way he wanted to, and found some delicious relief in knowing that I didn't have to worry about what I was going to do next. I had dabbled in the idea of exchanging power like that, but this was the first time that I had actually gone ahead and done it.

There was more out there for me to explore in that world, I was sure of it. And now that I felt as though I had vanilla sex down – pretty much every version of it that I could imagine – I figured that it was only right I start expanding into what else the world had to offer. Even if I had no clue what that might have looked like.

If there was one person I trusted to help me into this particular side of sex, it was Tommy – and luckily, I still had his number. I dropped him a message, and he agreed to come out for a coffee with me to talk this stuff over. I was glad to have a ticket into the deviance that I knew must have been out there in this city, and truly, even happier that I got to pass the time with a cute guy like Tommy in the process.

"So, what is it exactly you're looking to get into?" He asked me. Now that we had sex off the table – or at least, our first time – I felt like I could actually talk to him like a real person, instead of dealing with the constant level of flirtation that he usually threw at me. I doubted that we would never end up in bed together again – in fact, I was already trying to push to the back of my mind the urge to ask when his friend Johnathan would be back in town once more – but for the time being, I just wanted to pick his brains a little.

"I just want to explore a little bit," I confessed. "I know that there's loads out there, and I'm not entirely sure what I'd be into. I think I just want to test something out, see how it goes, you know?"

"Interesting," he murmured, and he leaned back in his seat, not taking his eyes off of me. I cocked an eyebrow at him.

"Is it?"

"It is," he agreed, a filthy little smile flicking up his lips. "I didn't take you for...well, I guess we'll find out what you are, won't we?"

"Guess we will," I agreed. "So, what do I do? Where do I start? Is there, like, somewhere I can go to find out about this stuff...?"

"There are meets most months," he explained, and he pulled his phone from his pocket, pulled up a page for me, and handed it over. "For people into this stuff. Usually just to hang out, but sometimes they put on special exhibitions for people like you. People who are interested to see everything that they can get out of the scene."

"Oh, how long till another one of them?" I asked, feeling a little crestfallen. I had been so into the idea of seeing where I could go with this, and it seemed like it was going to be a while before I could come out and actually enjoy it.

"Well, I'm the one who runs them," Tommy replied, leaning back in his seat with a broad grin on his face. "So, I'm pretty sure I can make it happen sooner rather than later."

My eyes widened. I knew that he was big in this city's sex scene, but this? This was a shock. I didn't know that I had managed to hook up with someone who pulled the strings in such a major way. But hey – if I could use it, I was sure as hell going to. I felt like I had already proved to him without a shadow of a doubt everything that I was willing to get up to in pursuit of pleasure, so he knew that I was far from some fair-weather pervert...

And so, I left it to him to pull everything together – he seemed enthused by the idea of introducing me to this world, and I was glad that I had someone I knew already in the scene so that they would be able to show me how to make sure I didn't make a damn fool of myself the moment I stepped through that door. Within two weeks, he had sent me a formal invite to one of their performances – that's what he called them, his performances, like I was to be attending a live theatre event. I supposed, in some ways, I really was. After all, I knew that these were all performances, the same way that I performed for everyone that I'd slept with. The same way that I'd performed online in that livestream for everyone who had been watching me. There was something exciting about knowing that you didn't have to worry about a silly little thing like being yourself. You could just let go, have fun, and explore.

And that's just what I intended to do.

I think I changed my choice of outfit at least ten times before I was sure that I had something that would sell me the best. I had no clue exactly what I was looking for in this place – to dominate, to submit, both, something in between? I kept reminding myself, in the cab down to the hotel where this was to be taking place, that I didn't have to know going in. That I was showing up because I wanted to discover this part of myself.

Tommy was waiting for me by the time I arrived, dressed in a handsome formal suit – clearly the man behind all of this, and not afraid for everyone to know it. He offered me his arm and I took it, glad that I was to have some company tonight.

"You look lovely," he remarked. It was about the most PG-rated compliment that he had ever given me, as though he was making a point that this wasn't about the two of us – this was about me, me finding a chance to explore sides of myself that I had never touched on before.

"Are you nervous?" He asked. I nodded, as we made our way through the lobby. The receptionist locked eyes with me for a moment, and I wondered if she had any clue at all what was going on in their exhibition space. Did they have to hide it, make sure that nobody found out? Or did they want everyone to know?

"A little," I admitted. "I've never done anything like this before. It's...a lot."

"You're going to love it," he assured me, and we paused outside the large double doors that led into the main hall.

"You ready?" He asked, and I nodded, chewing my lip and hoping that he couldn't sense my toes curling with nerves inside my heels.

"Then let's do it," he replied, and he pushed open the door and let me inside.

And what I saw on the other side was enough to make my jaw drop.

I think the first thing that stunned me was the fact that there were so *many* people there. So many people who I wouldn't have looked at twice if I had passed them on the street – no, they seemed downright normal compared to what I'd expected. All of them seemed to be any natural person that I could have run into on any day out in the real world, but they were here, to enjoy this sensual night with me and the rest of the people we were going to share this with.

"Where do you want to start?" He asked me, leaning in a little closer to brush his lips oh-so-casually against my ear so that I could feel the overheated sensation of his breath against my skin. God, I still wanted him, still wanted him badly, but right now, I was distracted by everything else that was going on inside that room.

All around us, there were small stages, set up to show off the people performing on top of them – and what performances they were putting on, too. The one that drew my eye at once featured a man and a woman, her on her knees as she gazed up at him – he had a hand on her chin, tilting it up so that she had no choice but to look into his eyes. It seemed as though she wouldn't have wanted to be anywhere else right now, even if she had been able to. I didn't blame her. The focus in her gaze in that moment, the sureness of the way that she was staring at him, seemed like it was the only thing inside her right now.

"Can we go see what they're doing?" I asked him, and I nodded towards the two I had been staring at; he led me over there, and I followed behind him, hoping to God that I wasn't doing something silly or stupid. I knew that everyone here must have been able to tell that I was nothing more than an intruder in this land of theirs, but I needed to start somewhere, didn't I?

And so, start I did. A small crowd had circled around the stage that I was particularly interested in, and the way that the woman was staring at him was even more intense now that I was up-close and personal with all of it. I wanted nothing more than to feel what she was feeling at that moment – to feel the intensity of being wanted like that, of wanting in that way.

"Good girl," The man told her, and the sound of those words sent a long shiver down my spine. God, what was it about the way that he spoke to her that turned me on so much? It didn't make any sense to me, and yet, I couldn't deny how gorgeously sexy it was. His voice was cool, calm, confident and collected, and I adored the way that it sounded when he spoke to her.

"Thank you, sir," she breathed, and he ran his hand to the back of her head, his fingers wrapping around her hair so that he could pull her back sharply. Her eyes widened with excitement, and I could tell that she was savoring every moment of this. Every moment of what he could give to her.

"Open your mouth," he ordered, and she parted her lips at once – he pushed three fingers from his other hand into her mouth, and she sealed her lips around them and began to suck on them instantly. As though they were already well-practiced with this, with everything that it meant.

There was something almost painfully erotic about seeing that girl give herself to him like that. All she was doing was sucking and licking on his fingers, that was it, but it was more intense than if she had been down on her knees and blowing his cock in front of everyone in that moment. I knew that she must have been burning with want for him; even from the distance that I was standing, I could feel that coming off of her in waves.

I took another step forward, fascinated by what I was seeing. I didn't want to lose a single instant of this. I didn't know if I was ever going to get the chance to see something like this so close-up again, and I wanted to indulge myself with everything that came with it, all the ways that I could take it in. I was reminded of my hotel rendezvous a few days before, how hot it had been to be taken control of in that way, how good it had felt not to have to worry about anything other than just letting his want rush through me.

I didn't know if I would have been able to perform it like this for an audience, but I knew that I would have been pretty damn willing to try and find out. The thought of being watched as I gave myself over to someone like that, allowing a person to take full and utter control of me any way that they wanted to, was enough to send a hot, needy shiver down my spine.

He stirred his fingers in her mouth for a moment before he withdrew his hand once more, and I watched as she caught her breath, not taking her eyes off of him for a moment. I had to avert my gaze. I realized that I was breathing harder than I had been before, and I had to take a moment to control myself before I gave away in front of all of these people just how hot I found all of this.

"Would you like some privacy?" Tommy asked me, seeming to notice the change in my demeanor; I nodded, and, with an arm around my waist, he guided me to one of the rooms that ran along the side of the main hall, opening the door and gently moving me inside.

"Are you okay?" He asked me, softly, catching my face in his hand for a moment as he examined me carefully.

"I'm okay," I replied, hardly able to keep the smile off of my face. "I just...didn't expect to be so..."

I didn't know how to tell him what was going through my head, I didn't know how to express the want that had rushed upon me as soon as I had seen that woman in that way. I just wanted to be that girl, on her knees, consumed by the want that someone else had for her.

"It can be a lot to take in, the first time," he assured me, his voice careful, as though he was letting me come back down to Earth. I appreciated it. Honestly, I felt as though I was going to lose it if I didn't hold myself together as best I could right now. I could feel that deep, keening desire for something else inside of me, for something deeper and darker than I had ever experienced before.

"I really want to try something like that," I blurted out to him, and I managed to look up at him again – I had no idea what he was into, if this was even something that he would be able to handle, but I knew that I needed to feel it. Properly. Not just the control that the man I had been with in that hotel had taken from me, but something more intense than that.

He raised his eyebrows at me.

"Are you sure?" He asked, as he joined me on the small bench that ran around the outside of the room. I nodded. I felt like I was hypnotized, focused only on what I could find out next. I had already come so far in this journey of mine to uncover everything that I knew about myself; what was one more step? Just one more step forward to find out how it all unfolded?

"I know I am," I breathed, and I reached up to touch his face. "I want it to be you. I want you to show me..."

He rose to his feet once more. Something about the way he towered over me made my head spin. Even something as simple as that, as the mere difference in our height, was enough to make me feel cowed to him.

And I liked it.

"Wait here," he told me. "Don't move."

As if I was even thinking about it anyway. I stayed right where I was, not even twitching a muscle, as I waited for him to return. A few moments later, he did – and this time, he was carrying a small set of rope in his hand. Slim and red, I could already feel them biting into my skin before he had put them on me.

"Hold your hands up," he murmured, and I did as I was told at once. He slowly wrapped the rope around my wrists, the feeling of the fabric shocking and new as it caressed me softly. I didn't take my eyes off him. He was looking down at me as though he couldn't believe that this was really happening, that he was really going through with something like this.

"If you want to stop," he continued. "You say the word *red*. Okay? You got that?"

"I got that," I breathed. He tightened the rope around my wrists properly. I gasped at the feeling of it tying into my skin. Something about that restriction, about knowing that I couldn't pull myself loose, made me shiver with anticipation.

"How far do you want to go?" He asked me. I shook my head. I had no idea how I was meant to answer that question, no idea what I was meant to say.

"Just...show me where it starts," I replied. "Please. I want to feel what that woman was feeling back there..."

"I'll see what I can do," he murmured, and I could tell from the glint in his eyes that he was already excited at the thought of what he was going to bring to me next. My heart was slamming against my ribs and I was barely able to catch my breath as I waited for him to do whatever he was going to do next. Slowly, he peeled back my fingers, so that my palms were held upright to him in front of me.

I noticed a small whip that he had brought into the room with him – he had laid it on one of the seats surrounding the walls, and he now plucked it, held it in his hands for a moment. The leather glinted almost cruelly in the dark, and I had to bite my lip to keep from letting out a moan of excitement.

"Do you know what this is?" He asked me. I nodded.

"I do."

"And do you know what I want to do with it?"

"No, I don't."

"I want to hurt you," he replied, and he trailed the very tip of it over the upturned spread of my hands, sending a shiver all the way down my wrists, across my arms, over my shoulders, and down my back. In this state, it felt like every tiny little touch was enough to light me on fire.

"I am going to strike your palms," he explained, a dark want starting to cloud the edge of his voice. "And you're going to count out every single blow with me. You understand?"

"I understand," I breathed. He brought the whip back, and landed a short, sharp strike on my hands. The shock of it made me jolt, but at the same time – I liked it. I liked the way that it felt. I liked the way it felt when it caressed me like that, when I saw the soft pink mark turn up on my hands.

"How was it?" He asked me, reaching down to grip my face in his hand. I shook my head. I didn't know what I was meant to say, but I knew that I wanted more.

"Again," I breathed. And, without another word, he brought it down on me once more.

This time, I let out a cry – the shock of it was almost more than I could take, but I loved it, ached for it, and needed it. My entire system responded as he continued to hurt me, and I marveled at how magical it could feel right now. How wonderful it was to be hurt by this man, even though I knew that he wanted nothing more than to pleasure me.

He laid down five more blows on my hands, and I managed to contain myself, pressing my lips together so that I didn't make any hint of noise as he did so. Oh, he knew just what he was doing to me, just what he wanted from me – the sound of that leather biting into my skin was enough to send shockwaves through my whole system, and I had to clamp my legs together to keep myself from moaning with every touch.

He pulled the whip back once more, seeming to sense that I'd taken as much as I was going to be able to manage. His eyes were pinned to mine, looking for a reaction, and I was breathing hard, I couldn't hide it.

"How is it?" He asked. I tipped my head back, locked my eyes to his.

"So good," I groaned, and I pressed my thighs together again, trying to relieve some of the tension that had built there between my legs. I wanted nothing more than to get some relief, but I wasn't sure if I was allowed to ask for it or if I had to wait for him to gift it to me.

"Are you wet right now?" He asked. His voice had taken on a darker, deeper air now, something that made me nod along at once.

"So wet," I moaned, and he moved to put his hand between my legs, grazing his fingers against the outside of my panties. I gasped.

"Get up," he ordered, and he pulled me to my shaky feet and pushed me back down over the bench at the other side of the room, so that my dress heaved up around my hips and exposed me – he reached between my thighs and ripped off my panties, reaching around to stuff them into my mouth. The shock of feeling my own muskiness between my lips thrilled me, and I groaned against the soft fabric between my lips.

"I want to fuck you now," he told me, and he paused for a moment, giving me that instant that I might have needed to stop things before they went any further. But in truth, I didn't want them to stop. I didn't want to let this slip through my fingers. I wanted him to fuck me, hard and fast, I wanted him to make me come around his cock, and I wanted to feel myself finally get the relief that I needed so badly.

I heard the rip of a condom behind me, and, with my bound hands pushing me up off the bench, I arched my back to give him all the access that he needed to move inside of me. A few moments later, I felt the pressure of his cock at my entrance, and then, at last, his fullness sliding into me once more.

I groaned against the panties that were wadded into my mouth as he plunged into me for the first time. The restraints around my wrists and the fullness of his cock in my pussy was almost more than I could take – the throbbing pain still laid across my hands as the pleasure echoed all the way up and through my body mixed together, creating something seductive and sensual and impossibly sexy. I pushed myself back to meet him, needing more, needing all that he could give me. I wasn't sure that I would ever be able to have enough of this, this tantalizing mix of a man that I desired with such painful want and the control that I had to give him to let this happen.

"Fuck, yes," he growled, and he grabbed my hips and started to slam into me deeper than before. This wasn't the sensual sex that I'd shared with him and his man; this was something else entirely, something more intense than that. Something that seemed to wipe all logical thought from my mind and boil me down to the barest minimum of everything that I could wrap my head around.

"God, you look so good like that," he told me, and all I could do was let out another muffled moan to tell him just how good he felt, too. Anyone from that party outside could have walked in on us at any moment, and there would have been nothing I could do to hide how exposed I was right now. And for some reason, the thought of that fucking thrilled me. If he'd wanted to take me out there, show me off for everyone to see, let everyone in there take me in all bound and gagged and fucked like that, there would have been nothing I could do to stop it.

And it was that feeling of complete and utter helplessness that finally took me where I needed to go. I felt it, the same thing that I had been sure that woman had been feeling when she had been sucking on the fingers of her man the way she was– the certainty that all that mattered in the world was pleasing this person, giving yourself to them any way that you possibly could. I arched my back and pushed my hips back to meet him, hard, letting him drive himself into me over and over again, filling me roughly with his full length as the sound of our flesh coming together filled my ears.

I wanted to reach back and tell him to go even deeper, but he had bound me, gagged me, left me with nothing but the hope that he would be able to give me everything that I wanted right now. I could feel the breath overheating in my lungs, the corners of my vision starting to get blurry as I felt myself cresting – cresting – cresting – and then-

When the orgasm hit, I was glad that he had gagged me. Glad that he had quietened me down. Because the pleasure was so intense that I knew I would have screamed at the top of my lungs if he hadn't been there to shut me up. He drove himself deep, one last time, inside of me, and held himself there for a long moment, letting my pussy contract and clench around his length over and over again.

Finally, I felt his cock twitch inside of me, as I slumped forward on to the bench, trying to gather myself after the shock of that near-painful pleasure had started to subside. He pulled himself out of me, and my body slipped down to the floor, my pussy throbbing with relief as the last vestiges of that orgasm rushed through my system.

And I knew, in that moment, that this would be far from the last time that I ever came to a place like this – and far from the last time that I ever got to indulge myself in some power play like this kind.

Chapter 11

Waking up in my bed, all alone, with nothing but the tenderness of my pussy after the deep fucking that I had taken the night before – well, it was enough to make any girl feel glad that she had some time to herself to recover.

I still couldn't quite believe that I had really done all of that. Really gone to that party, really let myself get tied up and whipped, and been so helplessly wet from all of it that I had allowed the man who had done it to me to fuck me afterwards.

I snuggled into the sheets, letting out a happy little sigh. Hard to believe that I was still the person I was when I had moved into this place, right? Hard to believe that someone like me could have hidden this side of herself for so long. I felt like I was starting to come into myself in the way that I had always been meant to, started to embrace something deep and longing inside of me that had been waiting to come out for longer than I would have cared to admit.

But what else was there for me to explore? And what did I really want for myself if I had come to the end of the journey that I had been on that had led me here in the first place? I had no idea what this looked like when it was all over, whether it would ever truly be over, or if I would constantly be finding ways to evolve myself, my desire, the things that I wanted and the things that I never knew I needed.

I sighed as I lifted myself out of bed, went for a hot shower to wash the remnants of last night off of me. There were the barest hints of pink marks around my wrists from where he had bound me the night before, and I didn't mind one little bit. In fact, I wore it as a badge of honor, the way that I had been able to keep up with him and endure everything that he had put me through. I knew that I would soon be back for more, to find out what else I could take, and I loved the thought of pushing myself to another high – maybe even putting myself in the position of that woman who had been on her knees and taking everything her man had been giving her. Maybe there was something to be said for that, too.

The warm water of the shower rushed over my body, massaging out the kinks in my muscles as it went, and I smiled as it soothed me. Honestly, I wished that there was someone else with me in here right now, even though I know this alone time to recover was also feeling nice. I just felt like, the more sex that I had, the more that I craved it, the more that I found myself going deeper into my desires, the more they seemed to stir up. I had to laugh now, thinking about all the ways that I had tried to tell myself that I just didn't feel the same desire that other women did when I had been with my ex – looking back, I could tell that it had been nothing more than my own attempts to cover up the fact that it was *him* who was the problem, who had always been the problem.

I let my fingers trace down my body, till they came to a halt between my legs – the warm water over my skin had already gotten my clit throbbing with want, and I knew that I had to give in to it. I rubbed my fingers down either side of my clit, slowly, in a V-shape, feeling the pressure of the skin pulling taut around me for just the barest moment. I gasped, leaned my head back against the shower, and did my best to picture someone else's hand between my legs instead.

I could almost imagine it, and almost feel their fingers in place of my own – no, their fingers guiding mine, showing me just how I should touch myself. I moaned softly as I imagined this man slowly tracing his fingers over my clit, taking his time, making sure that he didn't rush himself. Making sure that he was going to make me wait.

He didn't have a face, but he had a body – a warm, strong body that I could feel all pressed up against mine, holding me close, touching me and telling me every way he knew how that he wanted me. I wished that I could feel the hardness of his cock against my ass, but for now, I would just have to stick with the thought of his fingers, teasing me, tracing me, caressing me. Making sure that I knew just how deeply I belonged to him, and just how uninterested he was in letting me escape from his touch.

Before I knew it, my back was arched, and I was thrusting against my hand harder than before. The pressure on my clit was intense, and I could already feel the orgasm starting to stir and build inside of me. God, I can't believe how bad I always want this now and how much I feel like I need it – I had to know what happened next, how it would feel to climax like this. The water was running down my body, between my breasts, down between my legs, as though it was tracing the shape of the pleasure that I was marking out on myself...

"Oh," I groaned, as it finally flooded through me. The relief of that orgasm made my knees tremble and my entire body shake for a moment. I had to hold my hand still to keep myself from tumbling to the ground on the spot. Reaching to grasp for the edge of the shower head, I held on for dear life, pulling it down between my legs so that the hot water could continue to massage my clit as I came, helplessly, the wetness meshing with the water so that I couldn't think about anything else in the world at all.

By the time that I had come back down to Earth, I realized that I actually needed to clean myself up and get myself off to work for the day. Sometimes, the pleasure became so much that I couldn't think about anything but how much I wanted to come, and come, and come again, until everything fell away, and the only thing left was the delicious and implacable joy that my body could bring me.

But a woman couldn't live on orgasms alone. Even as much as I might have wanted to. So, I did the responsible thing, got myself cleaned up for work, and headed out the door to make sure that I would be there on time. I promised myself that I wasn't going to let these new desires of mine run me too ragged. I flashed myself a smile as I got ready in the mirror for my day at work. I was sure that this was the very best way to start off any working week. And I intended to make sure that it was the best I'd ever had.

Chapter 12

"Hey, could you check that the till is all sorted?" Dinah called to me, as she headed back into the kitchen to make sure that everything was tidied away for the night.

"Yeah, sure," I promised her, and I hummed to myself as I headed round the desk to do as I was told. I was in a good mood today, probably thanks to the delicious orgasm I had given myself before I had left the house. Note to self – I needed to start doing that more often. If there was anything that would get me out of bed with a smile on my face, it was knowing that I could make myself come before I had to step out of the front door.

I could feel eyes on me as I cashed out the till, and I looked up to see Dinah, one of the girls that I had been on shift with that afternoon, watching me from where she stood. I smiled at her, furrowed my brow. "What is it?" I asked, trying to contain the little chuckle of surprise that I felt at being the center of her attention like this. Dinah had always been one of those girls who very much kept to herself, and she never did much talking to the rest of us unless it was for something about work.

"Nothing," she remarked. "It's just that there's...something different about you, I think."

"Different in a good way, or in a bad way?" I wondered. She chuckled.

"A good way, don't worry," she replied. "I wouldn't bring it up if it wasn't a good way."

"Hmm, glad to hear it," I replied, and I couldn't help but smile right back at her. She had a nice smile, warm and friendly, but usually it was aimed at the customers instead of the other people she worked with.

"Something changed recently?" She asked. She was trying to keep her voice casual, but I could tell that she was in anything but that kind of headspace right now. Was she curious about me? I was flattered - I couldn't remember the last time that she had shown any interest in any of us, not really, and the thought of that coming down to land on me made me happier than it should. If there was one thing that I had learned that I thrived on in these last few months, it was attention – especially attention from people who I didn't think really cared that much about me before they handed it over.

"I suppose it has," I replied with a shrug, trying to keep my voice casual. "I split with my fiancé recently. Maybe that's what you're noticing."

"Oh, sorry to hear it," she replied, the corners of her mouth turning down with concern. I shook my head and laughed.

"Oh, really, nothing to be sorry about," I assured her. "I'm much better off without him."

"I find that's true of most men," she replied bluntly, and I couldn't help but let out a surprised laugh.

"You had a hard time with them?" I asked, and she shook her head.

"Not with them," She countered. "Just...about them."

"What do you mean?" I wondered aloud. She had always been so secretive, and I knew that my curiosity was unlikely to be sated again if I missed the chance to do it now.

"My mom was always trying to set me up with boys she thought I would like," she explained, shaking her head.

"And it didn't work out?" I asked with interest. She chuckled and shook her head.

"No, because I was a lesbian and I knew it and she just wouldn't accept it about me," she replied. She sounded almost amused by it now, like she was glad that she could just laugh about something so horrible. I raised my eyebrows in surprise. For all the things that she had kept secret, this was about the very last thing that I had expected to come out of her mouth.

"Oh, shit, you're not one of them, are you?" She remarked, raising her eyebrows at me.

"One of who?"

"One of those people who's going to try and convert me, or something," she replied, warily. I shook my head at once.

"No, no, never," I promised her. "I'm just – I didn't know that about you, that's all."

"Oh, trust me, I didn't know it about myself for a long time either," she replied, with a sly smile. "Sorry. Didn't mean to dump it on you if you weren't ready to hear it."

"It's fine, really," I promised her. Honestly, now that she had said it out loud, there was a part of me that wanted to find out what else she had going on – a part of me that couldn't help but notice how cute she happened to be, with that cropped dark hair, those big green eyes, that slightly crooked nose that brought real character to her face.

"So trust me, I totally understand living in a world without men," She replied. "And how much better it can be for your sanity to keep them out of your head."

"Agreed," I laughed, as I finished cashing up the till. I noticed that the soles of my feet were starting to prickle, and I knew it had everything to do with this new revelation that I had just found out about her. I was drawn to her, intrigued in a way that I hadn't been before. It had been a while since I had last been with a woman, and honestly, though I had been picturing a man when I had been touching myself in the bathroom that morning, I wouldn't have minded one little bit if it had been Dinah in there with me.

"How are you finding being single?" She asked me. Her voice was carefully casual, but I was sure that she was trying to open up a few doors, figure out a few things that she clearly suspected about me. I could play along with that. I wanted to find out what she would do when she discovered that I was nowhere near as heterosexual as she had always thought I'd been.

"It's a lot of fun," I replied, tucking a strand of hair back behind my ear as she came to lean on the counter to talk to me. It was just the two of us in that place together, the shutters half-pulled down to make sure that nobody from the street outside would make the mistake of wandering in and thinking we were open, and there was something both peaceful and a little tense about being alone here with her.

"Oh, yeah?"

"Yeah, for sure," I replied, trying to ignore the urge to slide my hand across the counter and just lightly rest it on hers. It would be so fun to see what she would do – but we worked together, I didn't want to be the one to come out here and make things awkward. She was likely just making a little polite conversation before she returned to go back to business, get home for the night.

But there was something about the way that she was looking at me that made me wonder if there might have been something more to it.

"Getting to find out a lot about myself," I continued, pushing my hand through my hair again. God, I was flirting, wasn't I? There was no denying it. I could have sat here and played the fool, made like I didn't know what on earth she was talking about, but I was flirting with her and I was hoping that she was going to pick up on it sooner rather than later.

"Like what?" She asked, gazing up at me with those gorgeous green eyes, not breaking my gaze for a second.

"Like that I might not be..." I began, and then I trailed off, shook my head, laughed.

"No, no, I can't talk about that," I finished up playfully, and she raised her eyebrows.

"Well, now you have to tell me."

"Do I?"

"It's the rules."

"Well," I murmured, flicking my tongue out over my lips. I could see her gaze flicker down to meet it for just a split second, and I had to bite back a little giggle of amusement. Had it always been this much fun to flirt with people, and I had just been way too repressed to notice it?

"That I'm not as straight as I thought I was," I confessed, lowering my eyes for a moment, not sure how she would take this revelation. But when I looked up again, I found her smiling back at me, leaning a little closer over the counter.

"Oh, I already knew that," she murmured, and I raised my eyebrows in surprise.

"What do you mean?"

"You always gave me that vibe," she replied, with a shrug. "I've never been wrong about a girl yet, even when they're not out of the closet."

"I don't know if I'm out or in right now," I confessed, and she reached over to my side of the counter, pushed the stray strand of hair that had been bugging me away from my face, and then let her fingers trace down my skin for a moment. Her touch was practiced, and it was clear it was far from the first time that she had ever touched a woman like this.

"It doesn't matter," she murmured. "You're wherever you need to be."

"I think I need to be...with you," I admitted. I had thought that I was the one in total charge of this conversation and how it was going to unfold, but the more time that passed, the clearer it became that this had been her intention from the start, and I was just lucky to get caught up in it right now.

"Oh, yeah?" She prompted me softly. She wanted to hear everything that I had to say about this, and honestly, I wanted to tell her - I wanted to tell her everything that was on my mind right now, everything that had popped into it the moment that I had felt her fingers on my skin.

But why tell her, when I could just show her?

I leaned forward and planted my lips against hers for the first time. God, she tasted good – caramel, vanilla, something sweet and spiced and deep. I wanted nothing more than to just linger in that moment a little longer, feel the pressure of her lips against mine, let the thrill of it roll through me.

But before I could even catch my breath, she came around to my side of the counter to kiss me properly. Pressing her body against mine, she grasped my chin in her hand as she pushed her tongue into my mouth; dominant, controlling, passionate. I groaned and moved myself back against her, running my hand down her arm, feeling the strength of it as she held me right there in front of her. I was whatever she wanted me to be right now, whatever she needed of me, and she seemed to know that clearer than anything in the world.

The way she touched me reminded me of the night that I had spent at the kink party – she might have been a woman, but that didn't mean that she wouldn't take complete and total control where she wanted to. She shoved her thigh between my legs to spread them, gave me something to grind on while she continued to kiss me. At once, and as though on her command, I started to move against her, sliding my body against hers hungrily, needing more, wanting more, willing to do anything that I could to make sure that it happened.

"Hmm, see, I could tell you always liked girls," she murmured in my ear, her voice cocky with the clear enjoyment of the way that I was reacting to her right now. I wondered if this was something that she enjoyed, getting with women who were only just starting to explore the possibility of a lesbian journey in their own life. If she wanted to show me how things were done, then I was sure as hell going to let her...

She slipped her hand to the front of my pants as I pressed myself against her thigh, and slowly inched the zipper down until she could push her fingers into my panties properly. I was already swollen and wet, my pussy aching for a release like the one I had given myself in the shower this morning, and I was obsessed with how gentle she was, how careful – taking her sweet-ass time, making sure that she took in every gasp and every moan that I let out.

"You're so wet for me already," she teased me lightly, clearly enjoying the response that I had to her as she slowly massaged my clit with two fingers. I wanted to feel her inside me – no, I wanted her mouth on my pussy. No, I couldn't tell what I actually desired right now, only that I ached for more, as much as she could give me, as much as she was willing to share.

She hitched me up onto the counter behind me, pulled down my pants and my underwear, and shoved my legs apart roughly – sinking to her knees, she didn't take her eyes off of me as she went to sink her mouth against the inside of my thigh, making my legs vibrate with a desperate want as I watched her in action.

"Oh, you like that?" She asked, playing innocent, as she bared her teeth and bit down on my thigh once more, the sensitive skin practically lighting up at her experienced touch. How could this woman ever have had anything to do with a man, ever, in her whole life? It seemed ridiculous to even think about now – but, as she skimmed her lips towards my pussy at last, I wasn't thinking about much else in the world but how much I wanted them planted against me properly.

She grazed her mouth over my clit for the briefest moment, and I tipped my head back on the counter and let out a long groan. I knew that anyone walking the streets outside could probably hear me, and God only knew if the CCTV was still on in here and catching us in the act. Maybe I wanted it to be. Maybe I wanted to be seen like this with her, to be touched and pleasured for everyone to watch. I glanced up in the direction of one of the cameras that I couldn't remember if I had switched off yet, and wondered if there was someone on the other end of that line, watching me, taking me in, admiring the way I looked with having a woman between my legs who was willing to make me come.

She swirled her tongue around my clit before she drew it into her mouth properly, slowly rolling it between her lips like she was taking her time to savor every inch of me. And God, did it feel good – the pressure was already enough to make my legs tremble a little, and I had to bite my lip hard to keep from begging her for more. I knew that she would do this at her own pace and nobody else's, and as tempting as it was to just start grinding on her face to show her how much I was enjoying her attention, I knew that I had to be more careful than that. I knew that I had to let her show me how it was done.

"You taste perfect," she murmured, as she pulled back for a moment to admire my soaked pussy – her eyes flicked up to meet mine, and she smiled, the grin spreading over her face for a second before she dived back in to plant her mouth against my pussy once more.

This time, I couldn't hold myself back. I clamped my thighs around her head, squeezing her in place, not willing to let her go. I needed to come right now – I needed to feel myself finish here. I reached down, grasped her head, ran my fingers through her hair, and focused on the way that her soft mouth caressed me, curious to find out every way that I would react to every single little thing that was going on down there.

Her tongue lapped all the way from my slit to my clit and back down again, drenching me with a mixture of her saliva and my own juices; every now and then, she would pull back for a moment to catch her breath, and she would steal a look up at me to make sure that I was still desperate for her. And, once she was satisfied that I couldn't even come close to controlling myself, she would press herself back in, her tongue circling my clit once more as she worshipped every inch of my pussy with her lips and her tongue.

She teased it out of me for a hell of a long time, making me wait and making me suffer just a little before she gave me what I wanted more than anything in the world. As soon as she sensed the inside of my thighs starting to twitch, she seemed to give in to actually letting me come, lapping at my clit in slow, quick motions that made my body begin to spiral into that place of endless, impossible pleasure.

"Ohhh," I groaned, and I balled my hand to a fist in her hair, tightening my grip on her, not even caring if I was hurting her – all that mattered was getting where I needed to go right now, and nothing was going to stop me from going there. I was pushing back against her, my hips seeming to move almost of their own accord, my pussy starting to pulse and clench – I gritted my teeth, let my head fall back, held my breath, as I finally, finally felt it surge through me.

When I came, I swear that I left my body for a moment in time. Because there was no way that I could feel this good and still be the person that I had always thought I was before. Stars prickled behind my

eyes and I felt my legs starting to tremble, that helpless, hopeless giving-in to the way that it felt and the way that I wanted to keep feeling. I groaned, held her in place, hands meshed in her hair, as I thrust my hips back at her, over and over again until everything had fallen from my head except the need for more. By the time that I finally pushed her back from my pussy, there was a cocky-ass smile on her face, and I could tell that she was pleased with how she had made me come. She rose to her feet, kissed me once more, her tongue dancing around mine for a moment so that I could taste myself on her lips. I was still panting, my legs still shaking, and she seemed to be enjoying every single one of my reactions.
"We should close up together more often," she told me, and I giggled. I didn't know what to say. All I knew was that she was correct – and that I would be doing everything in my power to make sure that I got to spend as much time with her in the future as I possibly could.

Chapter 13

I hovered outside the theatre, looking at my watch, trying to seem as innocuous as possible. Which was pretty damn hard, given that I was lurking outside of a porno cinema, and waiting to slip inside once I had built up the courage to actually step through the door.

I couldn't believe that I was going through with this. The same question had been thrumming in my head over and over again, until I couldn't think about anything else – that I was really going through with it, that I was really doing it, that I was really, really, really about to slide into a place full of perverts as depraved as I was and give myself over to the helpless, hopeless want that we could all share together, once and for all.

It had been nearly a week since my hook-up with Dinah at the café, and I had been craving for something new to set my nerves on fire; this had popped up in my memory, some vague, distant picture of people going out to some cinema together where they would all watch the same porno movie and mess around with each other as they did so. An old-fashioned idea, one that I was sure I had gotten from a lifetime ago, but when I found out that there was an adults-only theater not far from my new place, I felt like I didn't have any other choice but to come down here and check it out.

I didn't even know the film that they were showing – just knew that if I got the nerve to go through that door, then I would be surrounded by people as horny as I was. People who were as desperate for the new thrills and spills of an erotic adventure like I had been these last few months. My people, in other words – and I wanted to find out what they had in store for me.

Finally, I managed to gather myself enough to walk to the desk, where a bored-looking young woman was handing out tickets. She barely looked at me through the slightly grimy glass, and I handed my money over to her at once. She slid a ticket back, and jerked her head inside the building. I didn't need telling twice. Before she could say another word, I went inside, and found myself in my very first porno theater.

It was actually cuter inside than I had expected it to be. In my mind, I had been ready to walk into a group of masturbating middle-aged men who were so horny they couldn't even hold it till they were inside the cinema. But instead, I saw a couple of guys, one close to my age, readying themselves to head in. I caught the eye of the younger one, flashed him a smile, and he eyed me for a moment before he turned his back to head inside the theater.

I followed him inside, the movie had already started to play, and my eyes were drawn to the heaving mounds of flesh on the screen, the way the actress moaned loudly as the porn star in front of us gave her a good dicking-down. God, I wish that could have been me – getting fucked so hard I couldn't see straight. Especially for an audience. Even better, right?

I looked around, to see maybe two dozen men filling out the rest of the theater around me. They were all sitting distantly apart from each other, but I could feel the atmosphere shift as soon as I walked into the room. I was the only woman there, and the thought of that thrilled me – the thought of being the only girl nasty and depraved enough to risk a place like this made my stomach twist in excitement.

I slipped down into a seat at the edge of the aisle. The smell of sex and want was heavy in the air, and it thrilled me to think of how much desire was pulsing around me right now. I glanced around at the other man down the row from me – he was rubbing his cock over his pants, clearly already hard at the sight of the screen in front of him, and when his eyes locked with mine, he paused for a moment, raised his eyebrows, as though he was asking me to come down there to join him.

Amongst the groaning and grunting and grinding on the screen in front of me, I knew that I couldn't say no. I didn't want to. I slipped a few seats down to join him, and he grasped my hand and drew it to his cock – he didn't bother waiting around, watching as my fingers rubbed at his impressive bulge. God, he was big – and hard already, too. I had brought condoms with me, just in case, and it was tempting...

I slipped his zipper down, and then slid my hand into his boxers, sliding my fingers over the top of his hard-on and watching as he tipped his head back and groaned with need. I bit my lip, stole a whiff of his smell, that deep, masculine scent that brought me to places that I couldn't escape any longer. I crossed my legs tight, letting the delicious warmth shiver up my system and control me.

"Fuck," he growled, as I took his cock out of his pants and started to stroke him properly. I knew that the other men in the cinema around us must have noticed what we were up to, and I wondered if they cared – if they were watching us more than they were watching the film in front of them, by now. I loved the thought of it, the thought of being a more erotic prospect than what was going on in the picture we were meant to be watching together.

His cock was so big, it was hard to fit my hand all the way around it – I slowly stroked up, up and down, using the few drops of pre-cum on his tip to moisten him so that I could jerk him off properly. He tipped his head back and leaned it on the chair behind him, closing his eyes while I pleasured him. I watched the tension in his face, realized that I didn't even know his name – and that I didn't care to find it out, either. All I wanted was to touch him, caress him, watch him lose himself to me and the way that I made him feel, and that was just what I intended to do.

I shifted towards him, sliding my other hand down his leg. I wanted to climb on top of him and feel his cock inside of me, but I didn't know if that would be breaking the etiquette in this place. Could I ask him? He opened his eyes again, looked at me, and I flicked my tongue over my bottom lip, telling him any way that I could that I wanted more, if he was willing to give it to me.

And, thank God, he was. He grabbed me by the hips and swung me up and on top of him, looking deep into my eyes with his blazing blue ones – the desire was so intense that I nearly swooned on the spot, but I managed to hold his gaze and look right back at him.

"I want you to fuck me," I moaned to him, theatrically. If he had come here for a show, then I was going to make sure that he got it – well, him, and everyone else who had come down here tonight, too.

I pushed a condom into his hand and watched as he quickly sheathed himself, and then pulled aside my panties so that I could ride him properly – I had only worn a skirt to this thing, not wanting anything to get in the way of the pleasure that I wanted to indulge in, and it didn't take long till I had pushed myself down on top of his hard cock.

He was even bigger than I had thought, the dark cloaking his hugeness, and I had to grip the backs of the velvet seats to grind down on him properly. His head was tipped back, his eyes starting to glaze, as though he could hardly believe that this was actually happening – as though he just wanted to lose himself to the pleasure that I was giving him. This was likely the last thing that he had expected, but that didn't mean that I wasn't going to show him just how much he deserved it.

I rocked my hips back and forward slowly, taking my time, getting used to the feeling of his enormous cock inside of me. My pussy was stretched to its very limits to take him in, but it felt perfect – just like the huge-dicked porn star on the screen in front of us, he was filling me the way I wanted to be filled. I tossed my hair over my shoulder, and I could feel more eyes on us – people watching us, checking to see what the live show was and if it had more to offer than the pre-recorded one they'd been watching up until this point.

I closed my eyes as I began to move up and down on top of him, until I sensed something in front of me – I opened them once more, and I couldn't help but smile when I saw the guy that had been there when I had walked in looking at me. Seemed like he just couldn't resist the thought of getting a little more out of me yet, huh?

I beckoned him forward, as the man below me began to thrust up and into my pussy. He was taking it hard, rough, showing me just how well he could fuck, and I wanted to take more. I was greedy for it. I reached out as the man behind us stood up, grabbed his jeans and pulled him forward – and I watched as his eyes widened with surprise as I unzipped his pants and began to stroke off his already-hard cock. "Suck it," he moaned to me, as he grasped the back of my head to push it towards his cock. I flicked my gaze up to meet his, playing innocent, even though I had another cock fucking my pussy at this very moment. I let him guide me towards his hard-on, and swirled my tongue around his tip before I took him in deep, all the way, letting him push up to the hilt into my mouth.

The man who was fucking me moaned loudly, and I knew that he must have been enjoying the show that I was putting on as much as the one who I was blowing happened to be right now. He slipped his cock all the way down my throat for a moment, and held it there, clearly testing how far I could take this before I'd have to pull back and catch a breath, but I didn't even flinch. I could feel my eyes starting to water, but I ignored it, showing him that I could take everything from him that he could give me.

By the time he slipped back from my mouth, I glanced around, and realized that a small crowd had gathered to watch us. The rest of the men who had been in the theater were surrounding us right now. Most of them were jerking off, the rest rubbing themselves over their pants, and the shock of seeing so many boys all gathered around me, all focused on everything that I was doing for them, was enough to make me push down on the cock below me even harder, and feast on the one in front of me with even more passion than I had before.

He slammed himself into my pussy, so hard it nearly hurt, but I didn't care. I just wanted all that he could give to me, all that all of them could give to me. I had never felt hotter than in that moment, surrounded by men who desired me and couldn't get enough of me, surrounded by lust that was all directed at me and me alone.

The younger man pushed himself into my mouth again, and I moved my head back and forth on his cock frantically, so much so that saliva started to drip down my chin and over my neck. I was a mess, but I loved it, loved everything about it. I hadn't come down here to play the good girl and make like I didn't want to give myself over to this, did I? I had come down here because I'd wanted to meet other people who were just like me, other people who were willing to let the sheer lust pulse through them and take control. That was what mattered.

The fullness was starting to wipe everything else out of my memory, just like it had done when I had been with two men for the first time. But this was different. This was less sensual, more purely physical – everyone who was here had come down to this place because they wanted to let loose and have some fun, and I was going to show them just how much fun they could have when I was around.

I could already feel the orgasm starting to brew inside of me, and I grabbed the hand of the man who was fucking me and pulled it to my clit. He started rubbing hard, nothing tender about it, as he filled me hard and fast and over and over. Soon, the man at my mouth was matching the very same pace, and I let myself get lost to it, the feeling of being taken by two cocks at once was enough to push me to where I needed to go...

When I came, a flood of wetness shot from my pussy and all over his cock, his pants, the seat around me. I clenched myself around him, massaging him mercilessly with my pussy, and he groaned and held me on top of him for a long moment as he finished as well. It didn't take long till the one who was fucking my mouth drew back just far enough to give me warning, and then shot a jet of sperm over my lips and tongue and into my mouth. I dived back on to his cock to make sure that I could suck up every last drop of it once and for all, not wanting to miss a thing.

The three of us practically crumpled into each other as we got lost to the pleasure that we were giving to each other – I was distantly aware of the calls of encouragement and approval from the men who were around us, and the sound of the fucking that was still going on on the screen in front of us, but I knew that none of it would come close to the show that I had managed to put on for them.

But God, there was something more that I needed, too. Those two men might have been spent, but I wanted something else – something more. I managed to lift myself off of the man that I had just come all over, my legs shaking, and looked to the men who were standing around me. All that I could see was a parade of cocks that needed my attention, cocks that I wanted to give my lust and my love to.

"Who's next?" I demanded, as I quickly unbuttoned the top of my dress to show off my tits – I couldn't remember a time in my life when I had felt more powerful than this, more wanted. Their eyes were all over me, taking me in with a hunger that I had never seen before in my life. I reached for the one closest to me, a man a little younger than I was, and brought his hand to one of my bare breasts – he grabbed and squeezed it like it was the first tit that he'd ever had his hands on in his life. I hoped it was. I felt like a fucking sex goddess, and I wanted these men to worship me as though they were never going to get a show as good as this one again.

He moved towards me, kissed me hard, his hands scrambling all over my body like he was trying to make sure that all of this was real. I grasped his head, pushed him back so I could look deep into his eyes.

"Fuck me," I told him, and I grabbed another condom from my pocket and shoved it into his hand. He spun me around, pushed me down so that my ass was hanging out over the edge of the aisle and my pussy was fully on display to him. Around me, I could still see those men watching me, needing me, their eyes all over me as they imagined what it would be like when they got their turn with me. Well, I had plenty of time for everyone here – as long as that movie was still playing, then I still had all the hours that I needed to give them everything that they had been longing for when they had first come to this place.

I felt his fingers toy with my messy pussy, the wetness that was still leaking down my thighs making his fingers silky-smooth. And then, to my surprise, I felt him...I felt him inch a little higher.

I gasped as I felt his finger test the ring of my ass. I had never been fucked there before in my life, but it wasn't because I had some great problem with it. It had just never crossed my mind to try it before, usually because I wanted my pussy fucked before anything else. But right now, my slit was a little sore from the pounding that it had taken from the man I had just ridden, and I wouldn't have minded a little relief for the time being...

His finger slipped just an inch inside of me, and I gasped. God, it felt...good. I was surprised to find how easy it was for me to allow him to touch me like that, how delicious it seemed for his finger to push deeper and deeper inside of me. Before I knew it, he had another one, spreading my ass open as he allowed me to push back on to his hand like the needy little slut that I was.

"You want me to fuck you in the ass?" He asked me, loud enough for everyone around us to hear. I knew that, if I wanted him to keep going, then I was going to have to admit in front of all of these people that I wanted nothing more than to get my asshole filled – the dirtiest and sluttiest of acts, right here in the middle of this public theater surrounded by men who I had never met before in my life and who I would never meet again, either.

"Yes," I groaned. I couldn't believe I was agreeing to this. I knew that, after this, I would have gone to some place that I would never be able to come back from – gone to some desirous, sex-drunken spot in my mind that I was going to have to stick out at from this moment on. I didn't have a choice. But, as I felt his fingers push inside my tight asshole, I knew that there was no way that I could turn him down, either.

Slowly, he pulled his fingers out of my ass, and slipped the condom over his erection. I glanced over my shoulder – I couldn't tell much about his size from where I was right now, but I knew that he couldn't be small as soon as I felt his head pressing against my virgin ass.

He popped past my entrance, and I had to inhale deeply to stop the pain from getting the better of me. But it only took a few seconds till I could let it rush through me, and I allowed the relief of his cock slowly moving into me to push everything else from my mind. I could feel the long breath out that he released as he moved all the way to the hilt inside of me, everyone around us practically holding their breath as though they were waiting to see if I could take a cock in my last virgin hole as well as I had already shown that I could in my others.

"Fuck, you're tight," he murmured, and he sank his hands into my ass to spread me a little wider open, making sure that I was totally available for him. I glanced over my shoulder and bit my lip, telling him every way that I knew how that I wanted more. Wanted deeper. If I was going to do anal for the first time, then I was going to make sure that I did it right. I wanted to be fucked. Really fucked. And he was the man to give it to me.

He pulled my hips back sharply, suddenly all the way inside of my ass in one fell swoop – my eyes bugged out for a moment and I let out a cry, but it was pleasure more than pain. He was using the wetness from my last orgasm as all the lubricant that he needed to get me where I needed to go, and it felt so delicious to have him slowly devirginizing my ass like this, in front of all these men.

I glanced to the screen, saw the woman let out a soft moan of delight, and mimicked the noise at once. I could see the men in the dark around me, lit only by the light coming from the screen, as they touched themselves – almost none of them were pretending to do anything other than jerk it right now, stroking themselves to the sight of me like this. I tried to take all of them in, but most of what I could see were just shapes, silhouettes. I didn't need to know who they were or see their faces. I just had to know that they wanted me, that they wanted me more than anything in the world, and that I was going to give that to them every way that they wanted it.

He took his time, sodomizing me, and soon, the feeling of his cock in my ass had started to grow seriously pleasurable. I couldn't help but slip my hand under my pussy and start to play with myself again – even though I just had the most incredible orgasm, I was already hungry for more.

"Yeah, play with yourself while you take my dick in your ass," The man behind me murmured, and he landed a sharp, playful slap on my behind. I moaned loudly, arched my back, and told him to go deeper. I wanted him to really fuck me, really get inside of me and use me the way he wanted to.

And soon, he did. It didn't take long till he was slamming deep inside my ass, his heavy balls slapping up against my pussy roughly as he moved into me over and over again. I rubbed my clit harder, tipping my head back, as he grasped my ass tightly, spreading it open so that he could have easy access to pound me out just like he wanted to.

"Oh, ohhh," I panted, and soon, the intensity of all of this had grown too much – if I had thought the orgasm I'd had the last time had been a lot, it hadn't come close to what I was experiencing now. My pussy was starting to clench, the feeling of his throbbing member inside my ass was building a pleasure that I had never felt before in my life.

When I came, it felt like an explosion, coursing out from between my legs and consuming me from top to bottom. I cried out, so loud that it drowned out the sound of the movie that was still playing in front of us, but I didn't care. All the times that I'd hooked up with people in risky places, knowing that I could have been caught at any instant, it had all come down to this – all built up to this moment, when I could do nothing but let myself get caught up in the thrill of being in public like this and being taken by men I didn't even know.

As soon as I came, the man who was fucking my ass finished, too, like he had just been holding out long enough to make sure that I got to where I needed to be before he took what he had to. He held himself deep inside of me, his cock throbbing deep in my asshole before he pulled out and let me crash down to the velvet seats in front of me.

I turned over, facing the men who were still left. I knew that they were all just waiting for permission, and honestly, I wanted nothing more than to give it to them.

"I need all of you," I moaned to them, loudly enough that they could hear me. And it didn't take long before I had a couple of volunteers step forward and show me just how much they wanted me.

There must have been a couple of dozen men in there in total, and each and every one of them wanted to show me just what a good fuck he was – and God only knew how happy I was to let them do that. I wanted to be used any way that these men saw fit. Some of them focused all on my pleasure – going down on me, sucking and licking at my nipples, massaging my feet – and others seemed more interested in what they could get out of it themselves. They were the ones who fucked me hard and fast, used me just as they wanted to, and God, the thrill of it was enough to set my body on fire.

My pussy was fucked plenty more – that seemed to be the one that most of them wanted to sample and there was no way that I was going to deny a single one of them the pleasure. A few more fucked my mouth, and I enjoyed every moment of tasting their cocks – the big ones, the small ones, the long ones, the short ones, the heavy balls pressing against my tongue so that I had no choice but to worship each and every one. The men changed, the smells and the tastes stayed the same. I just wanted more, more than I could take. I had already reached the very limits of what I knew that I could handle, and I wanted to see where else it could go after this.

And soon, they grew impatient. I didn't mind, not one little bit – no, in fact, as I felt one of them push my pussy down onto his sheathed cock, and another pressing at my asshole, I knew that I couldn't hold back any longer. I might have liked to think that I could contain myself, but I knew that I couldn't. I wanted to be used and I wanted to be fucked and I wanted them to have me.

The fullness of having two cocks in me at one time was almost more than I could wrap my head around, but I closed my eyes and let it move through me. The thin wall that separated my pussy and my ass was stretched tight, so tight that I could feel the men who were both fucking me right now moving inside of me at the same time. The sheer shock of it, the way that it felt, almost wiped my brain clean of any thoughts at all. How could anything be on my mind when I knew that they were taking me like this? When I knew that I could fit both of these men within me at the same time? How many more could I take, how much more could I handle? I knew that this should have been enough, but honestly, it felt as though I was just starting to understand everything that I could take.

By the time that I had worked my way through all the men in that theater, I was panting hard, soaked in sweat and my own juices, splayed on one of the heavy velvet seats as I caught my breath again. The men around me were spent, and I was proud to say that I had been the one to wring them all dry. I could take all of them, and I could take more on top of that – the girl performing on that big screen, she might have been good, but I knew that I was better.

And, as I smiled up at the dim lights above me, I felt a surge of confidence rush through my body. This was it. This was who I was meant to be – totally unstoppable, totally impossible to hold down. Something more than I had been before.

And something that nobody would be able to take away from me now that I had managed to find it.

Chapter 14

I eased myself slowly out of the bath, the warm water soothing my lower half a little after the rampant fucking I had taken just a few days before.

Honestly, I was still bathing in the delicious afterglow of everything that I had experienced while I had been in that theater. Honestly, in some ways, it still felt like it couldn't have been more than a fantasy that I was clinging on to – something that I had made up just to put a pin in the delightful sexual awakening that I had been through since I had come to this place and made a new life all of my own here. But I knew from the tenderness in my pussy and my ass that it had been as real as they came.

And that it wouldn't be the last time I would take a fucking like that, if I could help it.

But for now, I needed to rest up, make sure that I didn't get too ahead of myself thinking about what I could do now that I had started to uncover this new side of myself. I was sure that the kink club I had gone to would have plenty more for me to indulge in once I was feeling a little steadier on my feet again, but I was more than happy to relax and enjoy everything that I had taken in these last few months.

And it had all started here. On that very first day, that I had been with the man who had helped me bring my bags in and get unpacked in this new life of mine. Hard to believe that it had really been almost three months ago now – hard to believe that so much had happened that I never could have believed it would before. I had discovered that my sexuality was about as far from straight as I could imagine, shared threesomes, foursomes, more-somes – explored kinks, learned about the power dynamics that turned me on, and discovered how much I could enjoy my own company when it came down to it, too.

I had been so repressed before. I didn't even realize it until I had found a way to break free of everything that had been holding me back, but now, it was as clear as day. I was never going to go back to the person that I was, never going to bother dropping the pretense that I was anything other than the woman I had become. Any person who wanted to be part of my life, they were going to have to accept that I was a full-blown and totally proud slut – a girl who was willing to try anything once. And maybe just a couple more times after that, to make sure. You never know, right?

As I dried myself off with my towel, I heard a buzz at the door – I tucked it around me to cover myself up, and went to answer it.

"Hello?" I spoke into the intercom.

"Hi, sorry to bother you," A male voice came down the line. "I'm here from the moving company. We were clearing out one of our old vans, and we found a box of your stuff that we wanted to drop off. Can I come up?"

"Oh, of course," I replied at once, feeling a happy little flutter in my chest. I had no idea if the man on the other end of the line was the one who had managed to fuck me right the first day that I had moved in here, but damn, I was sincerely willing to try and find out. Would be rude not to, right?

"Thanks."

I buzzed him up, and there was a knock on the door a moment later – I fluffed my hair in the mirror, checking that I at least looked cute, and flashed myself a smile. I knew that it came off me in waves, the kind of woman that I was now, and nobody was going to be able to resist that from me.

I opened the door, put a smile on my face, and greeted the man on the other side — and sure enough, there he was. The very same one that had been there on that first day of my new life. I could hardly believe it, my lips parting with surprise, and I would bet from the way that he was looking at me, too, that he was about as surprised as they came.

"Oh, hey," I greeted him. I wondered if he remembered me. Surely, he didn't just go around fucking every woman that he did a move for, did he? Honestly, I didn't care. If he did, we would have been sluts alike. Maybe that was just one thing we had in common, but it was worth celebrating.

"You want to come in?" I asked him. He was holding a box of stuff in his hands, and I wasn't even sure that I recognized it was mine — it had been so long since I had stuffed all my stuff into boxes and gotten the hell out of my old place that I had forgotten everything that I had packed. I didn't care. As long as it had brought him back to my door, I would take anything that he gave me.

"Thanks for letting me in," he replied, and he slipped past me and into the apartment. God, he smelled good, I had almost forgotten how delicious it was to be around him. There was a reason that he had been the start of all of this for me, and I would always have that to thank him for, wouldn't I?

"And sorry for missing the box the first time around," He continued, as he planted it down on my coffee table.

"Oh, that's okay," I replied. He flicked his gaze back to me, his eyes travelling up and down my body. What he could see of it, hidden under this towel, at least.

"I was a little...distracted," he murmured. I knew what was going through his mind. And there was no way that, even with the tenderness from the gangbang that I'd been a part of, I was going to pass up the chance to do something about it.

"I think I remember that," I replied, playing innocent, even though I was anything but.

"Care to distract me again?" He asked, taking a step towards me. My lips parted into a smile. And I pushed the towel from my shoulders to let him know that he could have me any way he wanted right now.

As soon as the fabric hit the floor, his hands were on me. All over me. Starving for me, like he had been waiting for this since the last time he walked out. His hands sank into my ass, and this time, I made sure that I gave as good as I got, kissing him back, pushing my tongue into his mouth, running my fingers through his hair. I had forgotten how strong and sweet his body was pressed against mine, how deliciously tempting he was, how hard to deny.

I could already feel the hardness of his cock against my hip, and, even though I knew that I probably should have been giving my pussy a break from dick right now, one more wouldn't hurt, right? The way that my pussy was aching at the thought of it told me that she could still handle anything that any man threw at us — after everything that I had been through, everything that I had so deeply enjoyed, all the ways that I had learned that I could pleasure this body of mine, one more dick was going to be just fine. I guided him through to the bedroom and pulled him down on top of me; he kissed me softly, almost tender, or it would have been if it wasn't for the fact that I was hurriedly undoing his pants as he made out with me. How many men would I have in this bed by the time that I moved out of this place, I wondered — how many would pass through, get to fuck me, get to make me come, and then leave again? I had no clue. I didn't care. I wasn't sure that any number I could have come up with would have been enough...

I reached for a condom in the bedside cabinet and handed it to him once I had pushed his pants down far enough to expose his cock. He didn't need to be told twice. I doubted that he had come to this expecting to get another fuck from me, but he didn't know the woman that I had become since the last time that we had seen one another. I was new now. Different. Different than I had ever been, and I was sure different than I ever would be, the sweet feeling of being in this body, of really owning the way that I felt, the pleasure that I knew I was capable of, was something that I was never going to be able to get over. Not really. And I didn't want to, either. I wanted to stay in this sweet place, this place where I got to enjoy myself and my body and everything that came with living in it no matter what.

I looked down between my legs, pulled my knees back as he pushed into me, watching his cock slowly inch inside my pussy. I wondered if it felt different to him now, after all that I'd done, but judging by the reaction as soon as he thrust into me, it was still just as good as it had ever been – he groaned loudly, took hold of me hard. His hands sank into my body and I could tell that this was everything he had wanted it to be. Had he thought of me in the time that we had been apart? I was sure that he had. Sure that he had fantasized about being with me, about how it would feel to fuck me like this again.

How many fantasies had I filled out, since I had shared myself with so many different lovers over these last few months? I hoped that none of them would forget about me. I hoped that I would linger on in their memories, a part of our time together sticking out for them, no matter what.

The thought of it was enough to make me a little wild with want for this man. I grabbed him, reaching down to sink my fingers into his ass and drive him even deeper inside of me. I wanted to feel him fill me. I wanted to feel that cock of his plunge so deep inside of me it felt as though we would never be able to draw apart, ever again. I could already feel his breath in my ear, the heat of it boiling me from the inside out.

I was grinding myself against him, my clit pressed against his body, and I couldn't get enough of the delicious way that it felt to be with him right now. The sheer power of his cock as it moved into me. How many men had I fucked since the last time I'd seen him? I wished that I could whisper it into his ear, tell him how many guys I'd fucked since him – I bet he'd love it, love to hear the way I had allowed other men to fuck me the way I wanted to be fucked. How many?

"I've fucked so many guys since I last saw you" I breathed in his ear. I could feel his body tensing, but he didn't stop moving inside of me. Surprised, maybe, but not put off.

"How many?"

I didn't know, and yet, I still felt as though his cock was as good and as perfect as it had been the first time. Just went to show, it wasn't about the size or shape of the cock, but the man it was attached to. And what he could do with it...

2 More than I can count, 2 I murmured back, reaching down to grab his back and hold him in place. I looked into his eyes, wanting him to know that he was screwing a woman that he had no control over. That he would never own me – that I would always belong to the other men, the other women who wanted to fuck me.

"Was it good"? He asked. I traced my tongue over his jaw and smiled.

"So good", I moaned.

And that seemed to push him even further over the edge. As though he wanted to prove to me that he was more than some cuckold – that he was more than just another man to me. And this particular man knew just how to get me where I needed to go. I could already feel myself starting to clench, that familiar feeling deep in my stomach telling me that I was getting closer and closer to the edge – I needed this, needed to come, needed one more gift to take me where I had to go before I could relax for the day.

And, sure enough, it didn't take long, just a few more thrusts, before his cock twitched inside of me and he let out a deep growl of pleasure – and I felt my pussy contract around him, tightening to contain him. Once again, it was knowing that I had been enough for him that got me off. Knowing that I was hot enough, sexy enough, desirable enough. That's what I got off on.

We held each other as we came, our bodies wrapped up in each other, both of us focused in on our own pleasure and the way that it seemed to overlap with the other person's. I smoothed his hair gently, feeling almost tender towards this man, this man who had started it all, in the first place. This man who had taken me to places that I had never known I needed to go.

Slowly, he pulled out of me, and he kissed me again, softer this time, lips just skimming against mine. I smiled at him as he pulled back, gazing into his eyes, into the eyes of this man I hardly knew. I hardly needed to know him, either. All that I needed from him was the promise that we had found each other when we had needed each other most – that I had found him when I had been looking for someone to show me the kind of person that I could be.

No matter if we never saw each other again – he would always have a place in my heart. And, of course, in my bed, too.